DARK MATTER

Brett Adams

DARK MATTER

A Dweoming Well Book

Cover design by Nada Backovic
Cover images: Istockphoto, Hassan Pasha on Unsplash
and Sicnag @ wikimedia,

Brett Adams lives in Perth, Australia, with his wife and three children. He has a PhD in Computer Science, and develops mobile applications. He writes short stories and novels that invite scratching below the surface. You can contact Brett at dweomingwell@gmail.com

Also by Brett Adams

Blood & Ink

Strawman Made Steel

For Tara, who still isn't complaining

CONTENTS

"If the brain were so simple we could understand it, we would be so simple we couldn't."
LYALL WATSON

"One of the greatest mysteries in the cosmos is that it is mostly dark."
JOSEPH SILK

"Let there be light."
GOD

1.

RASPUTIN

A beautiful suicide.

It wasn't a phrase Rasputin had ever heard. He supposed it wasn't a deed attempted much either.

But tonight he would pull it off.

The idea had been simmering at the back of his mind for years, and now it had come to the boil. One minute he'd been eating sweet-and-sour pork in the foodhall of the cinema complex, his head a bucket catching every stray sound. The next he'd been treading the asphalt of the undercover car park, his body burning with the idea captured in those three simple words. He couldn't remember how one had turned into the other. It didn't matter anymore.

He would commit a beautiful suicide.

Everything necessary lay in his beat-up Datsun. The car would be his troubadour's wagon, holding both stage and props. In its backseat was a woollen blanket he'd bought from the Salvation Army for five dollars. In the car's centre console was a bottle of water, and in the glove compartment a small jar of opaque white plastic. The mail-order chemist's label wrapped round the jar said: Amitriptyline (150mg), take

1

orally once a day at bedtime. And on his driver's license was stamped in indelible ink the all-important instruction.

He would wind the driver's chair back to sixty degrees, spread the blanket over his body, take the top off the jar, and with the bottle of water begin washing down the dusty pink tablets.

After as few as ten tablets (so he'd read) his eyelids would grow heavy and close. His mind would sink into unconsciousness. His pulse and breathing would slow. Then stop altogether. He would not so much shuffle off this mortal coil as sublimate from it. His being would evanesce like dry ice.

Above all, he would do this without violence. The mere thought of slicing open the flesh of his wrist sent a thrill of panic through him. No, he would close his eyes and float away with the clouds.

He hoped he wouldn't dribble, or fit and spasm out from under the blanket. That would disturb the tableau. But he could bear that. How he looked wasn't the beautiful part.

He'd considered overdosing on Heroin, even tested it, but that ran the risk of throwing a red flag at organ appraisal. If you were sticking Heroin into your veins, what else was flowing in them? But Amitriptyline, an antidepressant, was the housewife's remedy. A nice, normal death. A work-a-day death that left all of your vital, and vitally needed, lumps of flesh in saleable condition.

Here was the beauty. Rasputin would cast his soul to the wind, but leave his body for who knows how many still-breathing folk.

And when it was parcelled out, what new sights would be seen through his corneas? What new aromas sucked into his lungs? What new toxins filtered by his kidneys? (A fleeting doubt: would Amitriptyline damage them beyond use?) He imagined a beneficiary of his largesse gazing at the Eiffel Tower, smelling the bouquet of a Château d'Yquem, and pissing it down one of those funny open-air urinals, a *pissoir*, found on the streets of Paris. And all of this courtesy of his hardware.

Perhaps portions of him would go all over the world, an inverse Frankenstein's monster. Today he was Rasputin T. Lowdermilk of 34b

Bell Court, Riverton, Perth, Western Australia. Tomorrow he would be many people. Legion. It was modern-day magic.

That was the plan. Until he stumbled on a fly in his ointment.

The fly stood about six feet tall. It wore dirty Converse sneakers, black jeans, and a hood top that had a price tag dangling from its hem. The fly was bent at the waist, side-on to Rasputin. Its right hand was gripped around a screwdriver, and with that it was jimmying a car door lock.

The fly was attempting to steal his car.

A combination of irritation and disbelief loaded insults onto the back of Rasputin's tongue.

He was thinking that experts say we use ten percent of our brains. Leaving aside the question of what goes on in the other ninety percent, he reckoned this guy would be hard pressed to make a whole number. For starters, his car—the car this guy was trying to *steal*—was a piece of crap. It was one bill from the wreckers. Second, the guy was standing in the only pool of light for a hundred feet. Third, any minute now the cinemas upstairs would vomit clots of moviegoers into the car park. And to top it all, here was Rasputin standing at the rear fender and *still* the guy was working the lock.

In the end it was the disbelief that won out. He tried to lighten the mood: "If you crack the lock, let me know the trick. It's been dicky since someone jimmied it with a screwdriver." Funny but true.

The guy froze for a heartbeat, then pivoted on the dirty sneakers. (Now Rasputin saw the headphone wires snaking out of his ears.) Grit crackled under his shoes into the silence. The screwdriver was still grasped in his right hand, but now he was holding it like a knife.

Rasputin's brain picked that moment to inform him he had blocked the only route of escape. His car and the next were hard up against the wall and made a blind canyon of concrete, glass and metal. He saw, too, that the man was a boy, no more than sixteen, and for some reason this terrified him most of all.

His eye fastened on the screwdriver. Its rusty shaft was pitted like the boy's acne-scarred face. In his mind's eye, Rasputin saw the steel puncture his skin and slide between his ribs. He imagined its lancing pain, and his body reacted by dumping adrenaline into his bloodstream. But instead of propelling him to action, the drug thrust his mind backwards in time, through his memory of the evening. All of a sudden the reason why he had chosen tonight to attempt a beautiful suicide was the most important thing in the world. He dug in his memory for how he had come to be facing down a kid with a screwdriver instead of sitting comfortably numb in Cinema 5. He had wanted one version of numb or the other. How had he ended up with violence?

His memory of the night coiled away in his head like ticker tape. He scrabbled back along it looking for *the moment.*

What he found was the foodhall, and sweet-and-sour-pork, and, blazing on the hall's ten-foot TV screen, a quiz show called *Temptation.*

That's right. He had been attempting Temptation's questions. Testing his wits against the contestants. It must have been a question that triggered tonight's long-planned, long-delayed final act. But which one?

He wound along the ticker looking for the question that had sent him out of the hall, through the rain, and into the underground car park on a mission.

The first thing he remembered was just a fragment of a question. Something about Moscow. The answer had been Napoleon, to which the show's host had added the redundant, "Bonaparte, yes." *(Must be nice to hold all the answers.)*

Nope. That wasn't the one.

Back in the car park, Rasputin saw the kid's gaze dip to the screwdriver and return to him. There was no mistaking what he'd been up to. His eyes kindled with an animal clarity.

Hurry up, dammit!

He scrabbled along the memory ticker tape for the next question. He had heard most of that one: "Who wrote: 'It is a truth universally acknowledged, that a single man in possession of a good fortune, must be in want of—'"

Bzzz.

A contestant had buzzed in. But Rasputin had been ready, and fired off his answer a split second earlier. "Red Saturn," he'd said.

"Jane Austen," the contestant had said.

He remembered how he had smiled a moment, thinking they had given identical answers, before the truth jolted him: Red Saturn wasn't the name of any author. Red Saturn wasn't even a name. He'd briefly wondered then if he had early-onset Alzheimer's. Or maybe it was astronomer's Tourette's, except he was no astronomer; his knowledge of the heavens didn't get beyond various things to say about Uranus.

Okay. That had been *odd*. But it wasn't his answer. He couldn't blame Jane Austen for flicking the suicide switch.

Down in the car park a flicker of motion caught his eye. The kid was moving—three feet away and closing.

And in that scintilla of time Rasputin realised his mistake.

It wasn't a question that had done it. It was something said by the *hostess*. One word that had blasted him like lightning from a clear sky. But what had she said? (*scrabble, scrabble*) He found the answer at last: "Warms the cockles of your heart."

Cockles.

That was the culprit. That one word had brought his mind to boil. Set his face to Eternity.

And, he discovered with a dip of the stomach, he had not the faintest clue why.

The flicker of motion swelled. A sense of urgency drowned his mind. He desperately wanted to know *why*, but knew it was the only answer he was going to get. He dragged himself back into the present, and the point of a rusty screwdriver aimed at his gut.

And found it moving fast.

On reflex he was already retreating when the boy lunged.

He saw the screwdriver flash in an arc. He traced its path high and wide of him and was surprised when a fist struck his face. His cheek lit with pain, and he caught only a blur of motion in his peripheral vision as the punch carried through, and the boy's chest shunted into him, knocking him backwards and sideways into his car.

Their bodies parted, and Rasputin took his share of momentum. He slid down his car's rear panelling and out into the throughway—straight into the path of an oncoming car. The boy disappeared, drowned in the darkness beyond the car's lights.

Behind the wheel of the gleaming Valiant '68, Eric Hewitt saw nothing. Nothing but the smug face of the teen at the movie ticket counter, and the image of the concession card Eric had left on his kitchen bench at home. He had fumed, run the sums, and decided there was time to drive home, get the card, drive back, scold the teen, and still catch the last trailers.

Rasputin, sprawled at knee height, saw straight into the Valiant's right headlight. His head collided with the car at the point where the headlight rim met the grille. The impact caused a cranial quake that created a new continental plate in the dome of his skull. Capillaries ruptured and spewed a mist of blood billowing over the surface of his brain.

The injury sparked off the natural response of the organism: COMA. The kill signal stormed through his nervous system, culling every non-essential activity.

But something else occurred while that storm raged. Deep in his brain, the most complex organ known to man—a few pounds holding more mystery than all the galaxy-whorled space of the Universe—a demiurge awoke.

Deep in the dark, quiet centre of Rasputin's brain, threads of electrical current waved and arced like fingers of a luminous hand. The hand lived between nanometres and microseconds. It reached from the city of lights that housed his memory and longings, and into a place that had been dark since birth, and blindly alighted on that dark matter. A finger, a tendril of flame caressed the dark place. The hand flinched back once as if stung, then dove forward and grasped flesh. The fingers swelled and became conduits of light. The barren place began to stir with life.

Before consciousness slipped away, he was struck by a random thought. Why his drowning mind chose this thought to leave him was a mystery. Perhaps it was like looking for meaning in the beating legs of a dying cockroach.

This was the revelation: Jane Austen was the author of Pride and Prejudice, true. *Red Saturn* was the imprint of his tatty old edition of Pride and Prejudice.

His answer had been right. His brain had simply judged the question wrong.

2.

CAIN

I was born Gottfried Schürmann. I was reborn Cain, one of the lucky few to walk again on History's miscarriage-strewn highway. I think you know my "brother."

Before I kill you, I want to tell you my story.

I say *lucky*, but luck is a phantom. If I had trusted to luck when I woke from my ordeal, I would have perished there in the dark, and made of my birth canal a burial chamber.

At first I had no name but *I*, and no sense except of *being*.

Then it was as though this *I* put on my flesh, put it on like one dons a winter coat that has hung forgotten in a closet through summer. My flesh became engorged with a will.

And with my flesh came other senses. But they told me only that I was blind, confused, in pain, and alone.

And still there was no name for this I.

Pain licked my body like fire. In that instant the compulsion to tear it off and fling it away was primal.

Which is the precise point at which so many have failed. Can you imagine how many have awoken to the same ordeal, their consciousnesses rising from the deep of slumber like pinpricks of florescence from the ocean floor, only to feel that first shock of pain, recoil from it, and sink back into oblivion?

No. I am here—I am *Cain*—because I am strong.

I really did think I was on fire. Then, as I forced my mind to order, my senses righted and I realised my mistake. How could there be fire where there was not a breath of air?

I felt a curious sense of inversion, and then knew the fire was not feeding on me but *within* me. My lungs were on the verge of collapse. I couldn't breathe.

I've known men who almost suffocated. One compatriot of mine told me how in Belgium he was caught on the upper floor of a townhouse when a shell punctured the ground floor. When the air filled with smoke, panic possessed him and reduced him to an animal. He beat against the windows and bayed for rescue. His eyes told me better than his tongue. They had a vulpine cast, and glared out at me from skin like melted wax.

Every man said the panic took over.

But not for me.

I had a problem: I could not breathe. The solution required a methodical process. I surveyed the map of facts to hand, like Kutuzov or Napoleon, and ordered dispositions for my relief.

I soon discovered the reason I could not breathe was a thick, elastic-feeling mass lodged in my throat. But when I tried to pull it free with my hands, they barely stirred.

Was I sick?

Perhaps I was smothered beneath my bedclothes? (I'm embarrassed to admit, but I called for my mother then.)

Stars began to appear behind my eyelids. I strained my arms, and found that what held me was rigid.

I strained harder and the stars burst into galaxies. The roar of blood in my ears was deafening.

Something gave.

9

My right arm came free. I tried to grasp the thing in my throat but was baulked by the same tough binding that had held my arm. A membrane sealed my mouth.

As I scrabbled for purchase, my left arm tore free and joined in.

Now the stars behind my eyelids began to fall. My lungs were hotter than a smith's forge, and my mind was beginning to fragment under the strain. One shard wondered if I might take a hammer to whatever was stuck in my throat and fashion a sword from it.

At last, wet and thick and heavy, it came free. It slithered from my throat with a sound, I imagine, not unlike the plunging of a root-clogged drain. I lay there gulping air like water till hunger began a fresh blaze.

Hunger. I remembered what that felt like. I knew what to do with it—feed it bread, cheese and sausage. I remembered their smell. I remembered the feel in my hands of a coarse loaf, to be torn open and shared with friends.

Friends. I had known some of those too.

Memories broke over me like an avalanche. Each memory fragment was a link in a chain that joined others. Soon I remembered Gottfried Schürmann.

I had finally recovered my name, I thought.

That was exciting. Like waking one morning thinking it is Monday only to find it is Saturday and a foot of powder has fallen in the night.

But as my memories continued to coalesce, I realised my mistake. Gottfried Schürmann was dead.

Well, I have no precedent for that rapture.

I tore the last of the tough, fibrous shroud from my face, and rose Cain.

I sat up and sneezed. I had been lying on a trestle table, and the air was laden with dust. I peered into a dim room; I had no memory of this place. A faint band of light leaking beneath a door revealed a clutter of objects that put me in mind of an attic, but there was no window.

When I planted my feet on the floor to rise, I realised how weak I was. And naked.

Later, as I hunted for clothing and tried to determine where in the world I was, I recalled something that dented my joy.

I refer to the visions spruiked to me, when I still bore the name Gottfried Schürmann, by our scientists and futurologists—the *Reich's*, the Americans, all of them. I don't mean the flashy, fast contraptions, and the monoliths; the Douglas DC-3s and Rockefeller Centers, and bombs guided by invisible beams. No, what angered me was their pontificating about technologies of the flesh: soldiers able to march for days in freezing cold without food (they said); reflexes fit for jet-propelled flight (they said); farms where organs could be harvested like corn; genetic therapies enabling a man to live two hundred years.

At all of these they had twice failed. Failed to achieve, and failed to dream. Even the novelists had failed.

I was outraged. They had lied, every one of them. Sinned the sin of omission.

I knew, on waking, they were culpably *short-sighted*.

Cain knew so much more was possible.

You're looking at it.

3.

A PSI TURN

Some comas last minutes.

Others never lift. For those, the soul sleeps, a dead letter, entombed in flesh that the years turn yellow, until somebody decides not to pay the electricity bill, and turns out the lights.

And then there is everything in between. On the 2nd of June, 2007, BBC News carried the story of Jan Grzebski, a Polish man who lapsed into a coma after being struck by a train. His bowels went on to process queued food rations and then waited. He woke nineteen years later to his wife's tearful, smiling face, and streets and shop shelves engorged by capitalism.

Rasputin's coma broke precisely six days after it began, to the second. His eyes snapped open. He saw the silhouette of a woman standing by a window.

He said: "My head hurts," and fell into a deep, dreamless, normal slumber.

He woke the next morning to see the sun spilling blinding light through the same window. His eyelids flickered against the blaze as he fought to keep them open. Through them he saw heavy drapes, bare walls, and, hanging over the end of his bed, a TV.

He was quietly confident this was not his bedroom.

"So it's true," said a voice from the other side of the bed. "The dead do rise."

Rasputin turned his gaze that way and hunted in the relative gloom for the voice's owner. He found a nurse, young with close-cropped blond hair.

She smiled and said, "How do you feel?" As she rounded the foot of the bed to draw the curtains, he sensed she was hiding excitement beneath a semblance of routine.

How do I feel?

Apart from a tightness at his right temple, his head felt starkly clear. Crisp, without even a ghost of static.

The nurse tugged the curtains together then came to the bedside. She checked a bag of fluid hanging from an IV stand, and then fixed him with unblinking eyes.

"Do you know who you are?" she said.

"The Queen of England," he replied. "Mind the corgis."

She smiled. "What's your name, Your Majesty?"

He sighed, said, "Rasputin T. Lowdermilk," and couldn't suppress a grimace. He had long since forgiven his parents his first name, and couldn't blame them for his last. The T was nice. Perhaps he should ask to be called Mr. T.

"And what year is it Rasputin T. Lowdermilk?"

"I don't know what year it is, but it must be the Last Day. For angels walk the earth."

He kept a straight face for a moment, before a snorting laugh opened his mouth. But in that instant pain lanced his temple, making him gasp. He tried to lift a hand to his temple but found it weighed down by the IV drip. He tentatively lifted the other to where he thought the pain was, but his fingers met only the coarse texture of bandage rather than skin.

"You'll have a nice scar there," she said, and guided his hand away from his head.

13

"Wonderful. Now it'll be Harry Potter references."

The nurse shook her head, surprise in her eyes. "You're in a good mood for a guy who nearly died."

"Don't tell me that," he said. "I thrive on ignorance." He tracked her with his gaze, wondering if she'd bought the bravado.

She retrieved a clipboard from the end of the bed and became engrossed in it. Either she was a slow reader, or whatever was written there was requiring some heavy decoding. Her tone, when she finally spoke, wanted to be conversational.

"You've been in a coma."

Coma. It sounded so soap opera.

"What do you remember?" she said.

His mind groped back over the coma's black void to dim shores. No, not dim. Light! The world had been suffused with light. For a moment he thought perhaps he had dreamed after all. Then he tasted sweet-and-sour pork. It was the spark, and total recall engulfed him like fire a dry bush.

"Someone tried to steal my car." He laughed in disbelief. "With a screwdriver. Pushed me in front of a car. I hit my ..." It was a revelation to him. He fell silent, staring at the nurse.

She stared back, the clipboard dangling from the end of her arm, apparently forgotten.

"Come to think of it," he said, "I'm not sure he meant for that. He bolted and—"

She sprang to life again, slotted the clipboard over the bed rail, and strode toward the door.

"Hey! Where are you going?" he said with a hint of hysteria. "How did I get here?"

"I'll page your surgeon," was all she said.

He eased back into his pillows, stared at the bar of dazzling light between the curtains, and tried to think of anything but the memory of the void that sat like a stone in his mind.

The pinprick of light bored into his eye.

"Good," said the surgeon, and clicked the penlight off.

Rasputin clamped his eyes shut and watched the afterimage turn green and fade.

"For a man who sustained a serious head injury a week ago, you are in excellent shape." The surgeon flashed a perfect set of white teeth amidst an expanse of five o'clock shadow. "The power of youth is unequalled."

Rasputin reckoned the power of feral automobile had given it a run for its money.

The surgeon stood up straight and ran an appraising eye over Rasputin. Behind him a group of what Rasputin assumed were interns was clustered and mimicked the surgeon's movements, unconsciously it seemed. They were the latest in a procession of rubberneckers that included, by his tally, seven different nurses, orderlies, flower ladies, and a newspaper man who had twice asked him if he wanted *The West*.

"Questions?" said the surgeon.

Questions were all he had. He just didn't want them answered by plebiscite. He remained silent and let his gaze flit across the faces. The surgeon either didn't catch the hint or didn't care.

At last Rasputin said, "Who are you?"

The surgeon's face betrayed mild shock. "Of course. I am Alexander Thorpe, holder of the Bletchley Chair in the Department of Neuroscience at the University of Western Australia. I practice here when I'm not there." He smiled as though this information had been a patent gift. "You're lucky I was here and not there."

Rasputin's train of thought finally connected the surgeon standing before him with the notion of surgery. His hand went involuntarily to the bandage covering his temple. Its coarse touch didn't surprise him this time.

"Why did I need a surgeon?"

Alexander Thorpe sat on the bed. He paused for a moment in obvious thought, and then swivelled his large shoulders to bring Rasputin beneath the beam of his deep grey eyes. Movement rippled through the congregation as though in response to an unseen signal.

"You presented here last Friday night with an obviously serious head injury." His hands squared off against each other as if he was telling the story about the one that got away. "Standard procedure is to score your response to a battery of diagnostics—"

"How'd I do?" Rasputin said, cutting him off. He was an exam junkie. It didn't matter that in this case he had been unconscious. He still wanted to know how he had performed.

"Very poorly," said Thorpe gravely.

Rasputin assumed he was embellishing the narrative, as clearly the ending was happy. He raised his eyebrows, waiting for more.

"I'll spare you the details. You only managed a five."

Rasputin leaned back into his pillows. A five? He had scored worse. His first physics test had been a novel thirty-three percent, and he had been conscious for that. "Not too shabby," he said philosophically.

"The range is fifteen to three," a helpful intern interjected. "Higher the better," he finished, and looked to his co-interns for confirmation.

Thorpe flicked an irritated glance at the amateur screenwriter flinging ink across his script.

"Prognosis for such a score is, ah, guarded," he said, leaving Rasputin to wonder which word he had almost reached for. "You had pressure building in your head and we operated to relieve that pressure and repair the damage done to your skull. You have stitches there," he indicated Rasputin's bound temple. "They'll come out in a few days."

Rasputin still felt there were empty spaces surrounding the surgeon's deliberate sentences.

"I'm clearly not a vegetable," he said, exasperation rising.

There was a crotchet-pause when his heart seemed to skip a beat, before Thorpe spoke again.

"No, to be honest you are making a good—*a remarkable*—recovery. Only time will tell if you sustained any lasting damage. An impact like yours." His million dollar hands mimicked his mind as he groped for the right words. "Can cause widespread, microscopic damage, undetectable by scans. It jiggles things up."

Jiggles?

"I got a bad boo boo on the noggin, huh?"

Thorpe's expression tightened.

Rasputin went on. "I could have brain damage, is that what you're saying?"

"To be precise: D.A.I," said that intern. Apparently he couldn't help himself. (Rasputin wondered if neuroscience students made a fraternal joke of pronouncing it *die*.)

When Thorpe spoke again his words came fast and in a tone Rasputin guessed he reserved for theatre.

"D.A.I: Diffuse Axonal Injury. Neurons are long cells. When impact shockwaves wash through cerebral matter, they are temporarily displaced, as with any fluid or elastic material. Some don't appreciate the ride. They are stretched to breaking point and pop, but unlike programmed cell death, they don't even clean up after themselves." Thorpe rose from the bed as he finished, his voice a jackhammer: "Enough break and you lose faculties. We call it neurological deficit. How much you have, if any, is hard to predict. If enough neurons die, you become a vegetable."

Rasputin processed the information, mollified and feeling sheepish. "Thank you."

A gap opened in the wall of interns allowing Thorpe passage to the doorway. He paused on its threshold.

"Time is all you have now. We'll see if it's your friend or not." He smiled with an odd intensity that left Rasputin wondering where his preference lay.

After the interns had drained from the room, swept along in Thorpe's slipstream, the room felt all of a sudden cavernous, and silent, barring the clunk of the second hand winding its way around the utilitarian clock hanging on the wall.

Rasputin dug his hand behind his back and under the pillows in search of the TV's cabled remote. Its volume control didn't zero, and the speaker built into the remote put out a perpetual liminal buzz, audible even buried beneath pillows. He dragged it by its cable into his lap, stabbed the *On* button and ramped the volume up. He stopped when the clock's tick had been drowned, and let his gaze wander to the window and the rippling foliage of trees it framed.

He turned his attention inward.

How did you take inventory of your brain? His thoughts swirled, but kept returning to that word: *vegetable*.

"Never did like that word," he said, just to hear the sound of his own voice.

The flow of nurses continued through the morning, but by lunch had begun to ebb. He guessed he was fast losing celebrity status.

Surely he was still more interesting than a half-dozen delayed bowel movements?

A man appeared at 1.33PM—the clock, it seemed, seeped into his subconscious despite attempts to put it out—and Rasputin knew at once the man was not of the hospital. He introduced himself as Detective Faraday, and asked Rasputin if it was true that he had been pushed in front of a moving car. Rasputin hedged, saying that 'pushed' was too strong a word, and tried to convey his sense of what had happened.

Faraday left ten minutes later, saying, "We'll nail this guy."

"I don't want to nail anyone."

"Yeah you do."

The afternoon dragged. Rasputin's memory of Thorpe's warning wore a rut in his mind until tiredness began, inch by inch, to bend it upon the dream loom. He was soon engulfed by a nightmare in which Thorpe was doing the dishes in his skull.

He was shaken from the dream by the telephone. Its noise caused the dream to flash with its inorganic blare, an outside source too strident, too discordant, for the loom to thread into its weave.

He fumbled for the receiver once with his mummified left hand before reaching with his right. He pressed the cool plastic to his ear, and before he had time to speak heard a voice gush forth.

"Monk? Is that you? Please tell me it's you." It was a female voice, breathless.

"Dee," he said, and knew it had been her silhouette he had seen the previous night.

"It *is* you! You're okay? It rang for so long I thought the nurse had got it wrong. But what a horrible thing to get wrong, and—did I wake you?" Her words tumbled over each other.

"It hasn't rung before," he said. "You're the first call. I thought it was an alarm." He heard her gulp a steadying breath.

"It was horrible, Monk," she said slowly, and he fancied he heard the rasp of her hair on the handset as she shook her head. He was mute. Tears budded in his eyes without warning, and it took all his strength to blink them back.

Dee said, "My boss is gone. I'm coming now," and hung up.

She appeared in the doorway twenty minutes later, flushed as though she had run. Her eyes peered through a curtain of hair that had come loose from a ponytail. The skin above her nose was pinched into a delicate V. Behind her, with a touch of colour in his cheeks, came the familiar clash of ropey limbs and buttoned-down dress that was Jordy.

Dee engulfed him in a hug, while Jordy rested a hand on his shoulder and said, "Monkey boy, you gave us a scare." The hug and the hand lingered.

When the scrum parted, Rasputin noticed two men standing with restrained politeness at the door. One of them was Detective Faraday. The other was introduced as Sergeant Hills, police artist with forensics.

"Call me Bert," he said, and proffered a hand, which Rasputin shook.

"Sorry, folks," said Faraday, "but we need a composite from Mr. Lowdermilk." His body language said that as far as he was concerned Dee and Jordy had already left.

Dee began to protest, but Jordy laid a hand on her arm, and said, "We'll grab a coffee and come back."

"This could take hours," said Faraday.

Rasputin noticed a frown ripple Bert's brow. "That's a lot of coffee," Rasputin said, to diffuse the tension he felt arcing in the air over his bed.

Bert interjected. "Let them stay. They might be of help," he said, but Rasputin doubted he meant it.

The visitors dragged chairs up to the bed and sat in a semi-circle around it, as though it were a pit and Rasputin a campfire. Bert sat to

Rasputin's right, near enough for Rasputin to smell the residue of his aftershave. The room no longer felt spacious, and the temperature had nudged above the ward's sultry default.

"So, Rasputin," Bert began, and smiled in a self-deprecating way that Rasputin found disarming,"—nice name, by the way. Not run of the mill."

"There have been days I would've given my left arm for something like Bert," Rasputin said, hoping it didn't sound rude.

"I understand. My middle name is Napoleon—"

Hearing the name caused Rasputin's mind to flare with a memory, a single slide slotted onto the viewing bracket of his mind's eye of a quiz show host smiling smugly. It shone vividly before Bert's voice whisked his attention back to the present.

"We're going to try to build a sketch of the fellow involved in your accident." He fumbled glasses from a leather pouch as he spoke, and had just seated them on his nose when he plucked them back off and interrupted himself. "But we're not after a portrait. Merely a likeness, an effect, an impression. Often that is all we need to get our man."

He replaced his glasses and eased back into the chair. "You have all we need up there," he said, looking at Rasputin's bandaged head, and tapped his temple. "Trauma can sear detail on the brain like charcoal on a hamburger. It's all in there. We just have to coax it out." He finished with another winning smile.

Rasputin was silent as he remembered that at no point had he said he had seen the kid's face. He suppressed a mischievous impulse to say as much, and instead peeled a fingernail from his left hand. He tossed it onto the bedside table, where it sat like a large piece of shaved coconut.

The behaviour was a bad habit learned in high school. His drama teacher had thought it clever to have a guest speaker on body language. Ever since Rasputin had used it on new acquaintances, like poking a stick at an ant hill.

Bert didn't even notice. He had slipped a laptop from his bag and was watching it wake from hibernation. Dee picked the fingernail up and flicked it at the bin, her habit since the same class. Jordy hid a smile behind his hand and visibly relaxed.

The laptop emitted a symphonic ping. Bert swivelled it to afford Rasputin a view of its screen. A layer of dust lay over it in a faint sheen, visible until an image blazed onto it. It was a photo of Bert wearing a pink paper hat, the kind found in Christmas bon-bons, and below his rosy-cheeked face, sitting in his lap, was a boy who had to be a grandson. The whir of the laptop's hard drive filled the silence, and icons began to spatter the photo. Bert clicked one lodged disconcertingly by his nose, and a banner appeared to pacify the onlookers while the program loaded. It read: EFACE(tm) v1.1.

"This is new stuff. I'm still getting used to it," Bert said, squinting. Faraday glanced up from his phone and smiled privately. "But the idea is to build an image of our man from bits of computerised face-Lego, then let the machine work its magic to smooth it all together." The hard drive whirred again and a palette of faceless, bald heads filled the screen.

"You're not going to draw?" said Rasputin, and felt a tug of disappointment. He had dabbled at sketching since childhood, and was eager to watch a forensic artist at work.

Bert shook his head.

Rasputin suppressed a sigh, and had just begun scanning the first row of heads when Bert switched the screen off.

"We'll get to that," said Bert. "First I want you to take me back to, say, lunchtime on the day of your accident. Can you do that?" he said, his voice holding a warm, avuncular tone.

Rasputin cast his mind back.

"Every detail you can recall," said Bert. He leaned back in his chair, and rested his hands on the rumpled cotton shirt covering his paunch. He appeared to have forgotten the computer.

"I had lunch on campus."

Bert interrupted. "—The University of WA?"

Rasputin sensed an alumni's fervour.

"Yes. I had a test that morning. Tests always make me hungry. This was on seventeenth century British empiricists. They make me famished."

Bert cut in again. "Studying philosophy?"

"Today," said Jordy, and avoided Rasputin's glance.

"I could've killed something stodgy like a Yorkshire pudding," Rasputin continued. "For all I know it *was* Yorkshire pudding. With a drink it came to $7.85. I ate in the café beneath the Reid library, overlooking the moat. I sat at the end nearest the study area, on a chair scabbed with three pieces of dried gum, and tried to figure out how there could be more teabags stuck to the ceiling than I could count and yet have never seen anyone drink tea, let alone hammer-toss them up there."

He paused. Bert was silent, eyelids drooping.

"Did I over-detail?"

Bert's eyes flicked open.

"No, no. But I feel confident moving on now. Let's talk about that night. What do you remember?"

Rasputin told him how he had caught a bus to the foodhall. He mentioned the sweet-and-sour pork, the quiz show, and even of hearing Napoleon.

Bert chuckled, but his eyes now had a questing cast.

Rasputin avoided any mention of Amitriptyline, and said only that in the carpark's gloom he had almost returned to watch a movie, some brainless piece of schlock that Jordy would have sublimed with the epithet *Hollywood Therapy*.

Rasputin paused mid-description, and said to Jordy: "Should've gone with your theory."

Jordy and Dee had both become still. He pressed his lips together. She stared at her lap.

"Jordy went that night," she said. "If you'd taken a minute longer at dinner, you might have bumped into each other."

And I wouldn't be sitting here with staples in my skull, talking to a forensic artist.

"The carpark," said Faraday.

Rasputin shook the thought off.

It was when he returned to his memory of that night that he was shocked by its crispness. Far from being vague or proportionless, like photos in cast-off newspaper, distended by water or smeared by grime, it had definition, *edges* that might cut. To recall the carpark was to be embodied within it, as though he walked in a film-set replica. He realised he had been describing the scene in present tense.

"How's the light down there?" said Bert.

"Dark mostly, but over by my car there is a pool of it."

A pulse of adrenaline was the first warning Rasputin was not alone on the set. Another actor appeared. "He's standing in it."

"Is he below you? At eye-level? Above?"

"A little below. I think I'm taller, but he's crouched."

"What is he wearing?"

"A grey hood top—stolen, I think—black denim pants, frayed over the right knee, and converse sneakers that might have once been white."

"Is the hood down?"

"Yes, but I can see his face." The boy had turned toward him.

"What age would you say he is?"

"Young. Sixteen? I've never been good at ages."

"Hair? What amount of hair does he have?"

"Black hair, maybe. He's been in the rain. It's slicked onto his forehead to just below his eyebrows."

"Do you have a good image of his face?"

"Yes."

"Excellent. I knew it was in there. Hold that face now."

What Bert seemed to want, that Rasputin should isolate his memory of the boy's face, and preserve it by dint of will, struck Rasputin as redundant. On the contrary, he knew that Bert could ask for any or all of that mental simulacrum, today or a thousand years hence, and Rasputin would have it.

Rasputin heard Bert sigh, and glanced over to see him coaxing the laptop back to life. The screen was again filled with rows of faceless heads.

"Still holding that face, which is the best match?" said Bert.

Rasputin trawled along the line-up, first row, second, last.

"None of them."

"Which is closest? Give me your first guess, then we'll hone and home."

Rasputin stabbed a finger at a faceless head that looked no worse than any other. Bert clicked on it and another batch of heads appeared, all more or less patterned on the one he had chosen.

"And now?"

Rasputin picked again, with equal ambivalence.

The hour wore on and the pattern became entrenched. They progressed from heads to eyes, noses and lips, and even skin. With each iteration the computer appeared to draw a tighter rein around the features of subsequent candidates.

At 3.43PM Bert wiped a sheen of sweat from his brow and clicked a button. Faraday failed to stifle a yawn. Nothing happened for the time it took him to stretch as far as his starched shirt would allow. Then alone, framed within the laptop's screen, appeared a face. It was not a human face yet—it appeared hewn from orange stone. Then its angles disappeared, blurred into softer lines, and over its surface various shades pulsed and wriggled as though it were a worm-eaten apple in time-lapse. Stubble dotted the skin, lifting the face to photo-realistic detail, and finally it became still.

The face had become a person. A boy in his late teens. He stared with dead eyes at Rasputin.

Bert paused, breath held, then said, "Is this our man? The one who pushed you in front of the car?"

Rasputin stared back at the face.

"It can be an emotional time," said Faraday, without lifting his gaze from his phone.

Rasputin said at last, "Looks nothing like him."

Jordy laughed. Faraday excused himself to use the toilet. Bert deflated beneath his crinkling brow.

Rasputin tilted his head and squinted. "It's okay," he said, in a salvage attempt.

It rekindled a spark in Bert's eye, and he said, "What would you rate it out of ten?"

"A four—" he began, but saw the spark die again. "Make that a five," he amended. "His chin wasn't like that, and—" He cast about with his right hand clutching at the air, groping for a way to communicate the missing five.

His gaze happened upon a pen left by a nurse on the bedside table. He picked it up along with a clean serviette leftover from lunch. He put the serviette on the trolley table over his midriff and began to sketch the boy's face.

He merely meant to give Bert an idea, a nudge in the right direction. Anything to get the wreck back on the rails. But when he brought the pen into contact with the serviette's shallow weave and conjured the boy's face to see its contours, a strange thing happened.

For an instant a single eye, the boy's left, flared in the vault of his mind. It cast everything else into darkness. The intensity of its gaze pierced him with an almost physical pain.

He began to draw it.

After the initial shock, his flare-blindness died, allowing all of the boy's face and what surrounded it to seep back into view. But Rasputin's inner eye remained riveted to that eye.

As he left the first strokes of black on the serviette, he began to catalogue the eye's features, iris, pupil, white, veins. But no sooner had he brought them to mind as precursor to sketching them, than the ties between word and thing, abstract and concrete, evanesced, faded and disappeared. Lost too was his perception of where he was and who he was with. Even the ticking of the clock vanished from his consciousness, although this realisation came later.

He was aware only of face and pen, and the flesh that connected them, aware of it as never before, at a creaturely, instinctual level. He felt the bundles of nerve-lines, infinitesimally small, that fed circuits of motor cells driving the brute pack of muscle that encased his shoulder, driving it in concert with bicep and triceps, and finer muscles that worked tendons like puppet strings to grasp the pen and nuance its stroke.

Stroke by stroke, ink left the nib, stained the paper, and began to mirror an eye.

As he began to sketch the other eye, he examined the one he had drawn. Its detail surprised him: the thickness of the lower lid, shot with clusters of highlight that ran along its length till it met the marbled iris; the inner corner of the eye, an inlet whose waters were girt by twin strands of lid that terminated in the dark bowl at the wall of the nose; and the haphazard tangle of eyelashes sprouting from the top lid, clumped in irregular sheaves.

He wondered, as the second eye emerged from his pen, how it was that two objects so different could ever be called a pair.

As he drew the nose, beginning with the negative space made by the cheek and puffy underside of the eye, he realised with a start that his mental self—the one standing within the carpark—was touching the boy's face. Rasputin's finger was tracing the contour of the boy's nose, feeling its shape, conjuring its substance, so that he could express it in two dimensions.

His was the only movement in the otherwise frozen scene. His hand spidered over the face, his touch that of the sculptor testing his art—wondering if he had caught the likeness, fearing to mar the stone further.

He drew straddled between two worlds—the mental and the real—until he had coaxed the portrait into the hospital room's seventy-watt light. The face emerged, beginning in the centre of the serviette and growing outward, as if it had been submerged in water then brought to the surface by its own buoyancy.

When he at last lifted the pen from the serviette, he did not scuff or shade to amend a stroke or obliterate an error, as in the past. There was nothing to remove and nothing to add.

He grasped the serviette in both hands and appraised it in the whole. Seen through a slight squint, it could have been a black and white photograph. It was immaculate.

Only then did he hear the ticking of the clock again. It was the only sound he could hear.

Everyone was staring at him.

He tossed the serviette into Bert's lap with a flippancy only skin deep. It folded in flight, and Bert's mottled brown fingers did not move to open it.

Rasputin broke the silence. "Why don't we run with that."

Faraday was the first to pop. "Why didn't you bloody well say—" Hysteria bubbled through his professional mien. He crossed his arms and sat back so quickly the cushion on his chair hissed.

Rasputin was caught without an answer. He spluttered, "I can't remember the last time I drew—"

Dee cut over him. "You've *never* drawn like that."

He met her gaze but couldn't read it. Or perhaps he could. It was something he had never seen in her green eyes: awe.

Jordy knitted his brows and his gaze made laps between the serviette still folded in Bert's lap and Rasputin.

Bert's eyes remained on the folded portrait. He rubbed his nose with a finger.

From somewhere within Rasputin a surge of fury welled up. Its heat prickled his skin as though he had stepped from shadow into full sun.

"I don't know where the hell that came from. But it saved us another hour staring at a bloody screen. You should all be happy. I'm tired. My head hurts. And—"

He caught the sharp tone in his voice like the whiff of something dead. With effort he reined in his anger. "Maybe I needed today to do that, a prod."

He changed tack, petitioned Bert. "Isn't that how it goes? In spurts? Years of practice with nothing to show, then bang: you crack it." Bert lifted his gaze as though it weighed a ton to meet Rasputin's. His smile was a shadow of its winning best.

"Monk," Jordy said, and paused, gathering all attention in the room. "You're left-handed."

Rasputin took a moment to comprehend. He lifted his right hand, turned the palm up, and splayed his fingers. The tips of his thumb, index and middle finger were smudged with ink.

When José Raúl Capablanca of Cuba, world chess champion of the 1920s, was asked how he decided his next move—how deep he delved in the labyrinth of possible moves—he responded: "I see only one move ahead, but it is always the correct one."

Capablanca perceived the game in stark contrast to the novice, for whom the chess board stages a seemingly random clutter of pieces, of barely understood capability and worth. Capablanca could name that bishop surrounded by a gaggle of pawns—*a fianchettoed bishop in the castled kingside*. His mind was the product of year upon year of study, reflection and refinement, where each insight folded into the previous until all were submerged by their own weight into his subconscious.

In all likelihood Capablanca wasn't being arrogant to say he simply chose the correct move. Intuition might well have been the only object perceptible to his mind, the residual tang of long-forgotten fruit.

For Rasputin, the sublimation of his rudimentary drawing skill had taken but a single day. The speed of transition afforded him a kind of double-vision, with which he saw the old way and the new way, the old clumsy perception that created rude sketches and the new that transcoded memory or vision directly to paper.

But that double-vision produced an unnerving sense of disjointedness, so he forced himself to forget the old. Now he saw, he drew. Hadn't it always been that simple?

When Dee visited the next day, the room was already littered with a dozen portraits. Even the newspaper man had been immortalised, as much as something committed to serviette can be said to be immortal.

It was mid-morning when she poked her head around the curtain that hid the bed from curious passers-by. Rasputin was watching kids' television that appeared disconcertingly like an acid trip. Her arrival supplied the impetus he needed to switch it off.

She hugged him, a rib-creaker. It had all of her in it today. Part of his mind mused over why she hadn't become a nurse—she had always been such a physical person—while another part tried to read her mood.

She sat and began unpacking supplies from a shopping bag. She didn't stop chatting as she pulled item after item from the bag and distributed them about the room: magazines, a toothbrush (substitute for the 'hospital's tile cleaner'), his age-cured thongs, and enough chocolate to make a hippy diabetic.

"Want a portrait?" he said.

He lobbed the question like a stone into the flow of her words, grinning at her back as she put a photo on the windowsill. It was of the three of them, poorly exposed, taken at dusk on a sandbar in the river. She paused mid-reminiscence, the water curled around the stone, it sank, and she continued as before.

He guessed she was still disturbed by the sketch. It irked him, felt like a slur on his character. Since yesterday he had marshalled what were, to his mind, more convincing explanations. But they stuck in his throat. There was something else amiss with Dee. Her mood was like a chord with a note he could not put a finger on: she was unsettled; happy to be talking with him about mundanities; and ... what?

She emptied the bag at last and dropped into an armchair, silent, and content it seemed for her eyes to roam the room.

"You could have come earlier," he said, casting a glance at the dead eye of the TV poised above the end of his bed. "Nearly got my second head injury watching that crap."

She crooked an eyebrow. "Kids' TV is standard for trauma patients," she said. "It's back to square one for you junior." She smiled as she said it, and it almost came off. But there it was again. Her gaze would not stay with him. It drifted out the window.

"There's a boy chasing ducks down there," she said. "There are enough ducks that if they gang up, he's dead meat." She looked at Rasputin finally, pupils dilating to suck in the light. "Sorry. I did mean to come earlier."

"Knock it off."

"Patricia's dead," she said.

Her words evoked an image of a funeral party gathered about a Volkswagen-sized coffin.

She went on, "I turned the key this morning and all I got was a whir and a rattle. Called the RAC, but the guy said it was the death rattle. Or repairs upwards of a thousand bucks, which is the same as saying it's the death rattle."

He stared at the sheets for a moment. "It's odd, but I'm going to miss that purple monstrosity."

She nodded. "So I called a taxi."

"A taxi? I really was kidding."

"I know."

He was first to speak again. "Speaking of death, the physiotherapist visited me this morning." He swivelled his legs over the edge of the bed and sat up. "No, not for my brain," he said in response to her blank stare. "Apparently the brain is connected, indirectly, to all sorts of things. Who'd've guessed."

He eased himself over the lip of the bed the way he had slid into a heated pool just two weeks prior. But the air in the room did not buoy him as the chlorine-saturated water had. Instead it seemed to thrust down upon his shoulders, threatening to buckle him at the knees. He stood up straight and waited for the fireworks behind his eyelids to die.

"What are you doing?" she said, alarmed.

"My catheter's out (sure you needed to know that) and I don't fancy sitting in a pool of my own urine this morning. Tomorrow perhaps, but not on a Sunday."

He took a step with his right leg toward the bathroom, and as he began to shift his left in the long familiar counterpart motion, it dragged, biting on the sticky linoleum. It slowed him, sucked at his balance. An alien sense of mutiny slid up his leg, and his shoulders twisted to compensate.

Finally, grudgingly, the leg prodded forward.

Dee moaned. He didn't need to look at her to know she had covered her mouth.

"It's okay," he said, reaching the bathroom at last. He paused to catch his breath. "It's just fallout. The surgeon said there would be some. It'll work itself out." He didn't tell her Thorpe hadn't said the last part.

They talked until lunch, and by then it almost felt normal. An orderly laid lunch out and asked Rasputin where in his skinny frame he was planning on stuffing it, all the while looking at the portrait he had sketched of her at breakfast.

When Rasputin began to dig in the dishes, Dee stood, hugged him over the lunch tray, and wedged a piece of paper among the plates.

"I finally got hold of your parents," she said, and left.

He retrieved the note and unfolded it. It was an A4 sheet. Crisp peaks and valleys remained where the paper had been folded, dividing it into eight segments. Printed on it was a small amount of text, and from its layout and font he saw immediately that it was an email.

He scanned its message:

"Our Dearest Rasputin.

Deanne told us you have been in a very serious accident, but have come through it! What a rich vein of insights must now be open to you. We're envious. :)

Her email caught us on the brink of exploring Prague! We had intended on travelling direct to Moscow, but had a little accident of our own. We were in Verona—home of Romeo and Juliet, you know— and did not make it to the airport on time. Italians drive as if they are walking in a mall!

Stay well. We will trade stories.

Love, Beatrice and Mark."

Rasputin sat staring at the letter as the echo of his mother's voice died in his ears. He closed his hand in a fist over the paper, destroying its symmetry, and flung it at the gap left by the open toilet door.

He took his head in his hands and, for the second time since coming out of the coma, broke open and spilled tears.

Two weeks later he sat in the hospital foyer waiting for the courtesy car that would take him home. He wore blue jeans and a faded green t-shirt instead of the pale blue hospital pyjamas he had been wearing when he had woken from the coma. His chin and cheeks were unevenly shaded with dark stubble. He hadn't looked at himself much lately. The purple seam of his surgical scar could just be seen beneath his cap. Its starkly defined suture marks had what Jordy termed a Frankensteinish feel. Otherwise he was the image of the young man who had entered the foodhall a month earlier with a hunger for Chinese food. But only while he sat still.

His fingers drummed on the lounge's vinyl to the rhythm of a song he had heard belched from a mobile phone that morning. He had heard only a sliver of the song, four seconds of ring tone, but it had been enough to get the earworm wriggling. He had hummed it around a mouthful of toothpaste, tapped it with his knuckles on a toilet's porcelain, and even pressed his thumb to his fingers in time with its rhythm while he rode a lift in silence with a nervous couple taking their newborn home.

Perhaps that was why mobile phones were banned in the hospital, *worms*.

The other reason for the worm's persistence, aside from its sheer groove, was what entered in when his mind fell silent. Thorpe had visited that morning for his discharge check-up, mercifully alone. He had given Rasputin the all clear, barring only the possibility of a time bomb in his head. He had saved that revelation for the finale. He charged Rasputin, with that odd intensity, to be vigilant for signs of deterioration. He talked of biochemical cascades and listed symptoms: blurry vision, loss of concentration, muscle quivers, seizures, irritability, depression, mood swings. Rasputin was glad Jordy had not been there to hear. He would have said Rasputin's brain trauma was congenital.

When Rasputin realised he was laughing at his own joke, he furtively scanned the foyer. It was empty save for a lady shuffling toward the lifts with the aid of a Zimmer frame.

He looked at the walking stick resting across his lap. It had become his twenty minutes earlier. He had arrived in the lobby and laboured toward the lounge using a hired elbow crutch. A receptionist had tracked his progress then followed him to the couch. She had borne the stick and asked if he was Mr. Lowdermilk. The stick (black, plumed with a pink bow, and riven by a scintillating blue lightning bolt) had been left for him, a gift.

He knew straight away it was Jordy's doing, and briefly considered denying knowledge of this Lowdermilk fellow. But a thought occurred to him: with bones needing breaking, a hefty stick would be useful. He took it.

When the courtesy car eventually came, neither the ring tone nor Thorpe's voice was on the air at Radio Rasputin. Without being aware of the transition, he had begun savouring the memory of a lazy breakfast on the patio and Jordy's banter.

4.

CAIN

I called the enterprise of our scientists and surgeons—their 'progress'—short-sighted.

Another phrase springs to mind. In English it goes something like: one cannot polish a turd.

You think me too harsh?

Consider this. When artillery blew a soldier's flesh off, the surgeons' response was to attempt the reverse. But if you had seen their sorry monsters you would have wept. Photos of these creatures were published in medical journals and I was hard pressed to say which was *before* and which *after.* Better to die a warrior's death than skulk forever in fear of your own reflection.

What was needed was a rethink from the ground up. A return to the font. A revolution. You need only look at me for proof, although I'm not the first.

Not that my appearance offered much proof of anything when I stumbled from my tomb. You might well have taken me for a gross caricature of a man. But I soon brought form to the chaos.

My tomb was in fact a museum. The Metropolitan Museum of New York, nestled on the East side of Central Park. While asleep I had been *curated*. Or, I should say, archived, along with insignificant curios and items awaiting the scrutiny of their particular expert. Alas, there had been no expert for me. Or rather, none that would come forward.

It was night. I was confused. When at last I could move silently, I explored. Eventually I escaped via a back way into the park itself, and soon came upon a trysting couple. Their accents were American. That was the first clue that the *Reich's* New Order had failed, but by then it was not their dull vision of a Greater Germany I hungered for.

I waited in the dark, out of sight of the couple, the smell of damp leaf litter in my nostrils, its slickness underfoot. I watched and listened, willing myself to understanding. I was behind enemy lines, and following that revelation came the fruit of my training. I prioritised. I first needed food and shelter. Then I would need information.

I surveilled the couple, thinking perhaps from them to gain all three. I remembered the mantra of the soldier behind enemy lines: delay is death.

I took the man first. His throat muscles were strong. The woman's reaction was unexpected. She did not scream, and she did not stare at my nakedness. She simply looked at my face, mouth agape, then fainted.

I got no information from them but took what I could, the man's clothes, his wallet, a watch the likes of nothing I had ever seen (it sent a shiver through me). I rummaged in the woman's bag and found little of use. There was a mirror I took, and thankfully looked into before I entered the streets.

In the mirror's circle I saw my face, and it repulsed me. Its skin was like melted plastic, and clinging to it here and there were threads like coconut husk. My cast-off flesh.

I dragged the man and woman into the cover of darkness, for prudence and to hide from my reflection. I dressed like a blind man, and only then sent my fingers searching over my face. I found the stray fibres and tore them off with that small pain of scabs. Then I closed my eyes and went searching in the halls of my memory for my face.

I found it, and some intuition prodded me to concentrate on it, to want it, to want it very much.

It is hard to describe the sensation I then felt. It was as if my mind was a wheel that suddenly *gained purchase* and *bit* on the image of my face, which was latent just below the surface, like a statue sunk beneath murky water. As I concentrated on my own visage, the flesh of my face began to tingle like an arm numbed by pressure. I dared not touch it, so, motionless, endured the pain. Half an hour later I stole into the light to see my reflection. I was heartened to see those oh-so-familiar features.

I wandered across parkland and through coppices, over a hard place that turned out to be a life-size chessboard, and past benches on which people slept.

Someone followed me for at most a minute. Whether it was a man or woman, I don't know, but I'm sure whoever it was saw strength in my gait, which my long-dormant frame was gathering, and thought better of approaching me. My confidence grew with every stride.

I emerged on the southwest side of the park's rectangle, West 59th street. Stretching out in front of me was the backbone of Manhattan Island, a teeming palimpsest of life, a stacked, cubic cityscape that obliterated the horizon.

With difficulty I kept a rein on myself. Yes, the streets were thronged in an altogether familiar way, man on foot, man conveyed, and above them, man housed. But what clothes they wore! What machines moved them! What Olympian monuments housed them! (My admiration for hard technology experienced a little renaissance.) Stunned, I realised I was staring at the throne of an empire.

I merged with foot traffic, an emperor in waiting, and, careful not to stare like a tourist, threaded my way into the city.

I found a hotel in a place called Hell's Kitchen, and paid in advance with dollars. The room was not quiet. It was small and smelt of cigarette ash. But it was mine, my own space. I lay on the bed (you probably think it funny I would lie down after having lain so long) and fell straight to sleep. I was spent from the adrenaline coursing in my veins. It had vivified me, but in the process swept away my meagre stores of energy. Those stores took some rebuilding.

I slept much in the following week. I became increasingly sensitive to the idiotic rumbling of a bass instrument played by the tone-deaf occupant of an adjacent room. It was when I broke into his room to confiscate the guitar while he was out that I discovered the purpose of the box-shaped object sitting in the corner of my room. He had left his playing. I hurried back to my room and activated my own.

Television, *das Fernseher*, moving pictures, many channels, twenty-four hours a day, every day. What a godsend.

With television I could condense months of intelligence gathering into days. I activated it, ordered food, and absorbed. I watched until I dreamed in channels, and my dreams had advertisements.

I've since heard television called the idiot box, the masses' new opiate. Such is human contempt for the familiar. On the contrary, I learned the importance of white teeth, and that the corollary of nihilism is youth worship. I learned that man had walked on the moon (though I mistook this for fiction at first). Crucially, I learned of the global communication network called the Internet. This was fascinating, because I once met its inventor, a man, at that time, of broken spirit. There lies a curious irony, but I will come to that.

When I could watch no more I began to train. I sat on the toilet in my room's cramped en suite, and observed myself in the mirror. I had a magazine—Cosmopolitan?—and flipped through its pages until I found a model. I began with men. I lay the magazine open on my knees and concentrated on the man's face. I remember vividly the first I tried: forty-something, lantern-jawed, bearing a nose that was pinched inward below the brows. His eyes were brown, the skin at their corners angled, suggestive of an Asian admixture in his ancestry. I would do it for you now if our situation were different.

I concentrated on that face as I had on the memory of my own, days before in the dark and damp of Central Park. My skin tingled, as before. I glanced in the mirror once, and stared with the fascination one has when smitten by a disease, marvelling at flesh's reaction—the pustules and hives and alien colours. It seemed that, before changing, it was necessary to pare my features back to neutral, further than neutral, to something resembling a tailor's manikin. My face looked all-over bee-stung, but the impression was not so much of swelling as of the expunging of detail.

I renewed my concentration upon his face. Pain stabbed me so hard and unexpectedly I passed out. I came to sprawled over the toilet. I had cut my head on the toilet roll holder and bled on the paint. (The cut had healed while I was unconscious.)

Apparently moulding bone, tendon, and muscle required resolve.

I tried again, gently, tentatively. I approached that face inwardly as one approaches someone with whom one desires to speak at a dinner party, unsure of what the reception will be, circling, drawing nearer as if by chance.

By God it hurt. But I tolerated the pain. I remained conscious.

You would probably be fascinated by the physiology underlying *the change*. It fascinates me, how it is I am a man-sized embryo of unlimited potential manifestation, a six-foot stem cell. Sadly I am unable to operate upon myself to uncover the biological mechanisms, and other subjects are, predictably, rare. Therefore I can only speculate, by mapping how the pain shifts location and intensity during the change.

As the agony crescendos early, I gather the process begins at the deepest level: bone. It is eroded, mined by enzymatic machines, sluiced along reticulate capillaries to protein-marked sites, where it is re-deposited, re-fashioned. Working outward, next come the tendons, which are thinned or thickened, digested or seeded with large-body cells—an introduced species. By the same method, muscles are augmented or atrophied. Then sub-cutaneous fat is shifted, its mass shucked and injected elsewhere. Strangely this has the most effect on the final form. Eye colour is tweaked by modulating melanin levels. The old hair is truncated, ejected, and hair cell protein factories are accelerated by orders of magnitude to the desired colour and coarseness. And for the final touch, the voice. My imagination supplied me a baritone for my first change, and my body matched it with the finest of actions upon the muscle and cartilaginous mass of the Adam's Apple—fittingly the final deception.

When at last I felt the tremors of that first change abate, I looked into the mirror and saw the face of the magazine model staring back. He smiled at me. I was sweat-drenched and shivering from the change-flux of fluids in my veins. But, *mein Gott*, the euphoria!

Immediately upon completing the transformation, I learned another lesson. It should have occurred to me beforehand. The sheer magnitude of the change's call upon my metabolic pathways knocked me out. It was a lightning strike on an unprepared grid. I would need to improve my endurance.

Days later, when I felt up to another transformation, I used it to solve a problem. Obtaining a new identity was next on my list of priorities, and more cash. So I took both from my friend, the bass player.

I waited until the plumbing told me he was showering (an infrequent event) and broke into his room again. I took with me the A-string I had cut from his guitar, and now wound its ends around my hands. When I pushed open the door to the bathroom it took a full second for his face to register shock. His hands were halfway to his head and lathered with soap. It wasn't until I'd wrapped the string around his neck that he tensed. Perhaps he was drugged?

The garrote choked off a scream and split the skin beneath his jaw. Blood fountained and turned pink in the suds. It was a good thing we were in the shower.

I decided that next time I'd try the thicker E-string (though, it occurs to me, throttling someone with a G-string would be amusing).

I towelled off and studied his form. The morph took less than five minutes, but I don't claim it would have fooled his mother.

I'm not sure at what point in re-starting my life I became aware of how long I had slept. I do remember buying a newspaper and noting the date: March 20, 2008.

I had been asleep for over sixty years.

5.

UPTRAINS

If reincarnation were to be believed, then in all the earth's vast tracts there are few places free of the danger of stepping on an ancestor.

Ants are on par with humans by aggregate weight, and outnumber us by six orders of magnitude. They build, husband, cultivate, nurse, teach, learn, govern and fight. All with a brain weighing less than a milligram.

Rasputin paused to admire an ant pathfinding on the bricks beneath his folded legs. He watched it career through the wood shavings he had dropped, noting how it repeatedly halted with a flurry of antennae. He tried to imagine himself into its body, to feel the shock of force as it changed direction. It was exhausting.

He closed his eyes and stretched. His hands were starting to cramp.

He heard the flywire door rattle open, and the scuff of thongs. Someone cast a shadow across Rasputin as they moved through the light from the patio's only globe.

"Thought I'd find you here," said Jordy.

"Why were you looking?"

Jordy ignored the question, and said, "I can't believe you're carving the stick. I should have got you a monogrammed towel."

Rasputin lifted the black walking cane to his squinting eye and blew chaff from its grooves. "Bet you've never whittled," he said, and couldn't help laughing. "You should. It's so visceral. Once you dig the blade in, the wood is changed forever."

"Sounds violent."

Jordy lay on the bricks, hanging his legs over the patio edge. The sun had long gone and the air was cooling. A handful of stars struggled to shine through haze. The silence was broken only by moths beating out staccato notes on the light globe.

Rasputin picked up the knife again and began enlarging a groove in the wood.

"What's it going to say?" Jordy said. "Looks like a dog's been at it."

"Tyrfing," said Rasputin.

"*Gesundheit.*"

"It's a name."

"I would've gone for Barbara. You can count on Barbaras."

"I don't want it baking me scones."

Jordy sniffed. "People told me not to flat with an Arts student."

"Good advice." As Rasputin ran the knife down a groove, it skipped out and nicked his finger. He watched the blood bead. It was not a bad cut. "Do you want to hear the story?"

"Do I have a choice?"

"Tyrfing is a sword, from a very old poem called the Waking of Angantyr."

He recited:

"That would I have which I had yesterday;
heed what I had:
men's hamperer, word's hinderer,
and speeder of speech.
Aright read now this riddle, Heidrek!"

"Deep," said Jordy. "What does it mean?"

"It means get me a beer."

Rasputin put the knife down, noting how the blood on his finger had already lost its gloss. He lifted the cane and prodded its foot at the brick, making half-past seven with his arm. He gritted his teeth and hauled himself upwards, pushing with his free hand. He stalled mid-rise and Jordy rescued him.

"Keep treating Barbara like that and she'll dump you," Jordy said, slinging the flywire door back on its rails, and entered the flat.

Rasputin followed. He slumped onto the couch and muted the TV, feeling as though he had swum twenty laps. He told himself he was unfit, but he wasn't buying it.

Jordy returned with two stubbies. He gave one to Rasputin and dropped into an armchair, twisting the top from his mid-fall. Rasputin raised the beer to eye-level and examined the stubby holder. It was a plastic replica of Ned Kelley's helmet. He lifted the hem of his t-shirt and twisted the top off the bottle. The seal broke with a sharp hiss and a mist boiled in the bottle's mouth. He took a swig. It was bitingly cold.

Movement drew his attention to the TV, where hundreds of babies were floating in a cerulean sky trying to sell him something.

Jordy was watching too. "I'm in the wrong business. Imagine if clients came to me and accepted 'flying babies' as a solution."

"A few more beers and I'd buy from the babies."

Rasputin's thoughts returned to the stick laying at his side. "Tyrfing had a thirst, and was cursed to quench it no matter the company."

"A happy poem."

"Once, the sword was drawn in the presence of brothers."

Jordy mulled this over. "I'm still pitching for Barbara." He had finished half of his bottle, and sunk lower into the chair, all angles.

Rasputin felt compelled to explain himself. He tried to remember the details of a murder committed with Tyrfing. A name rose from his memory, *Hervor*. Simultaneously, the horizon of his mind rolled, vibrating, as though someone had degaussed his head. He looked at his beer suspiciously. He had barely dented it.

"A shield-maiden named Hervor had Tyrfing in her possession," he began, and found a string of words riding her hem. "Hervor secretly gave her son the sword Tyrfing. While Angantyr and Heidrek walked, Heidrek wanted to have a look at the sword. Since he had unsheathed it, the curse the Dwarves had put on the sword made Heidrek kill his brother Angantyr."

"Where do you get this stuff?"

"Wikipedia," Rasputin said, lowered his gaze and sucked on his beer. "Last edit January 7 at 13:21. A million contributors can't be wrong."

"A million monkeys, more like," said Jordy, then fell silent. Rasputin could hear his beer fizzing against the glass.

"You're a mutant," Jordy said finally. He stood and left the room. It hadn't sounded like the end of a conversation.

Presently, a voice floated down the hallway. It was John Cleese's of Monty Python fame, and it said: "'Ello, I wish to register a complaint," the first line of The Parrot Sketch; Jordy had logged into his computer. Key-presses and mouse-clicks punctuated the silence, followed by Jordy's murmuring. A moment later his head poked around the hallway door.

"Tell me that bit about the brothers again."

Rasputin did.

Jordy disappeared again. When he reappeared seconds later, he said, "I thought so. It's word for word from the web page."

Rasputin was dumbstruck. "Sue me. I'll footnote it next time."

"Word for word, from a document you read—what?—nine months ago, on the other side of a broken skull." He stopped abruptly. His shoulders sagged. "Wait. You didn't just cut and paste it somewhere? Again and again, got saturated with it?"

Rasputin shook his head, still wondering where relaxed, beer-drinking Jordy had gone.

Jordy began to pace. The room was small, and Rasputin wondered if this was what Japanese boot scooting looked like.

"I swear you did the same thing a week ago, on the phone to Dee, the *whole* takeaway menu."

Rasputin shrugged. "So I have a good—"

"Empiricism."

"—memory—What?"

"British Empiricism. You visited that wiki page too. It's in your browser cache. What is it?"

Rasputin flushed. He was supposed to be studying philosophy at university level. He had only checked the wiki for a birth date.

"Why do you want to know?" Rasputin said. "Not your cup of tea, is it. You can't program a Briton."

"Humour me."

"Fine. In philosophy generally, empiricism is a theory of knowledge emphasising the role of experience, especially sensory perception, in the formation of ideas—"

Jordy cut in again. "Word for word."

Rasputin couldn't remember ever seeing him this animated before.

Jordy turned to the bookshelf nestled in a corner of the lounge room. He scanned it, then jabbed a finger at the lowest shelf. He turned his gaze on Rasputin, and said, "Churchill's History of World War II. You read it last year, right?"

He had. How could he forget? He suspected the dirty, jacketless tomes, which smelt of mildew, had given him carpal tunnel syndrome.

"One doesn't read Churchill. One chews him."

"Whatever. You kept quoting bits of its preface to me. Do you remember it?"

"The whole preface?"

Jordy nodded.

Fine. Another test. He might as well ace it.

But he wanted something more than the answer, because Jordy was right to be reeling. The feat of memory Rasputin had performed had been accompanied by a prescient sense of certainty. He had not needed to wait for confirmation to know he was right, word for word. Fear crept into his mind. Had he stumbled across a trace of Thorpe's time bomb? Who knew what feats a mind might perform if conscious of its own fabric fraying?

So as he framed the request—the preface to Churchill's history of World War II—he bent his concentration to observe, to introspect, to espy his sleight-of-mind. To catch his thought in flight.

The effect of this scrutiny surpassed all expectation.

He grasped the split-second in which his mind went after memory—a process so fleeting it barely leaves a trace on the conscious mind—and fashioned a world from it.

He entered that world.

He could not say whether his attention sank within his mind, or if his imagination reached out to swallow him, extruding into the real world like an Octopus's stomach. He hoped, at any rate, not to be bathed in the mental equivalent of digestive juices.

Colour whorled about him before the vision resolved into a place. He was standing in a hall. Its walls were wood-panelled, like those that connect rooms in museums and old libraries. The smell of formaldehyde and mouldering paper mingled in the air. As he watched, a door burst open and a clerkish-looking man appeared. The clerk wore a starched shirt and suspenders, and pre-occupation wrinkled his brow. He scurried away without a glance at Rasputin, fixed upon his errand: to find the preface.

On instinct, Rasputin, the Rasputin within, sped after him and pressed close to his shoulder. For a moment he was faintly aware of the TV's flicker and Jordy's sagging arm, before he focused his attention on the nimble-footed clerk.

He was intoxicated by the familiar sense of being embodied within his mind. It was so crisp, vivid, rich. His imagination spared no detail as it manifest the process of sifting his memory in search of something consumed in the past and put aside. The clerk's footsteps ricocheted from the walls, and his breath huffed. The smell of dust and archival fluid grew heavy in the musty air.

The clerk searched backward in time, in halls pocked by nooks lit by green-shaded lamps, Rasputin clamped to his side. Other halls branched off at regular intervals. The clerk's balding head tracked their advance, and he turned down some without hesitation.

Rasputin looked beneath this illusion to the reality. Time was orderly and linear. Days, weeks, months, years, all packed together in known ways. And such was the route his little clerk navigated. Straight halls, sharp corners, no-nonsense doors.

But no sooner had he made this observation than the environment changed.

He noticed the clerk's steps slow, and suddenly they wheeled downwards on the steps of a spiral staircase. They were plunged into gloom. He felt the smooth wooden steps give way to irregular rock, and knew a moment of the sickly sensation of misjudging a step. Then light bloomed again and drove the darkness back.

By the light of a flaming torch, Rasputin stole a glance at the errand carrier and suppressed a shudder. Gone was the officious little clerk. Rasputin had no name for what padded next to him now. It had arms, or rather, limbs. With one it held aloft the torch, with others it moved. But it wasn't picky about which did what. A cluster of its limbs came and went amid a shagpile of fur, now rising to grasp, now falling to stride. Nothing Rasputin could see in the wavering light resembled a face, but a wet, snuffling sound evidenced a nose.

After a moment's hesitation, he thrust his hand into the creature's coarse hair and clung on.

The sphere of light bobbled to the stairwell's base, and revealed rough-hewn tunnels departing in every direction. Their dark mouths gaped to the left, right, and centre, and covered the roof and floor. From somewhere came the sound of water dripping, and other, furtive noises.

Without warning, the creature shuffled to the lip of a tunnel mouth and tumbled over its edge. Its hair slipped through Rasputin's grasp and he plunged in weightless free-fall.

The shock made his heart hammer, and his hands flailed after the creature.

For a moment his mind raced to understand the implications of ending in a bloody heap in the bowels of his own memory.

Then his hand snagged a tuft of hair. He hung on until his forearm burned.

Again the horizon swung, and he found himself walking upright along the tunnel, leaving the one they had exited a dark hole in the floor behind.

Soon the creature clambered up a wall to another tunnel mouth. He let it haul him up, and on reaching the tunnel's lip, felt gravity self-correct again, washing away the drag of the old and leaving him feeling buoyant.

Gradually he began to see method in the madness. His imagination was mapping a new journey through his memory. Whereas before with the clerk he had regressed in the rectilinear halls of time, he now foraged in the twisting labyrinth of *things*, the remembrance of which was a tangled web of connotation and cue. The clerk had brought him to the storehouse of his mind occupied by memories of a time in the previous year. The creature by his side now sought a path to a particular object, the preface to a book entitled The Second World War, by a man named Winston Churchill. Finding remembrance of it was not straightforward. The task required a bloodhound. He had the smell of it, that mildewy, almost salty smell of old paper, and on the strength of that lead they hunted.

The first quarry the creature unearthed was the memory of a bag Rasputin owned. It lay crumpled in the dark by a tunnel wall. A year before, the bag had carried books bought at a library sale, among them Churchill's history. He remembered its weight knocking against his hip as he had walked to a bus stop. It had been peak hour, and the bus had been full. He had stood, clinging to a rail for dear life while the driver flung the bus around corners.

Soon the creature halted again, and Rasputin saw, snagged on a rock jutting into the tunnel, a handkerchief. He smiled, remembering how on the bus he had wondered if he should risk retrieving it from his pocket, and whether the world was ready for it. A day of heavy use, thanks to a cold, had left it sodden.

The creature strained forward, and was soon slavering over a bright orange packet. Rasputin tasted cough lollies. He remembered sucking one in bed while he read Churchill. He had torn the lid off the lolly box for a bookmark.

With that realisation, they entered a room. The smell of mildew was strongest here. He looked, and saw something lying on the floor in the flickering light, amid a tangle of straw.

He had found the book.

"Good boy," he said, and bent to retrieve it.

But when he opened it, its covers flopped apart to reveal a bare spine. It was empty. His elation died.

Was that all he remembered of it, the cover? Nothing of its content?

He scanned the grotto again. Torchlight lit all but its corners, where darkness gathered. He stooped to peer at the floor, at what he had taken to be wisps of straw. He plucked a piece from the ground and, holding it near the light, discovered it was not straw but a sliver of paper. Along its length ran a fragment of text, a handful of words blotted in places by ink:

"—repair ****** the errors of former years and thus govern, ******* with the needs and glory of man, the awful unfolding science of the future."

A smile split his face. This was from the preface, the very sentence he had told Jordy struck him, that the Allies having endured blitz and battle had reached the brink of an abyss even more terrifying: the nuclear age.

But where was the rest of it?

He turned to look at the creature. Its limbs had stilled. Though it held the torch aloft, its posture was apologetic. It looked to Rasputin how a bloodhound might look had it missed the fox but caught the frog.

He held the strip of paper closer to the flame to see if by its light he might discern the missing words. A muted glow struggled through the yellow paper, but only made the blots darker by comparison, gaps in the sentence his memory would not yield.

He became aware of Jordy in his peripheral vision, out there in the real world. He seemed in stasis, standing by the bookshelf from where he had sent Rasputin into the bowels of his memory.

With a stab of anger he thrust the paper into the torch flame. It ignited and flared, coruscating like an arc welder.

A blaze ran down the creature's arm, consuming its fur, and engulfing it in a white bonfire. Rasputin smelled burning hair, but the creature was silent. As the bonfire shrank and grew more intense, he was forced to shield his eyes. Through slitted fingers he saw the errand carrier collapse into a brilliant orb floating by his side.

For the first time, Rasputin wanted out of his brain.

But now a greater transformation began. The brilliance of the orb washed the walls. Its light smote the stone like furnace fire. The stone began to sweat, and soon cataracts of molten lava poured upwards and down, fleeing the horizon, dissolving imperfections, obliterating edges.

No sooner had he realised the once-square room had become a sphere, than the fluid slowed. It grew sluggish and congealed, and as it cooled, its colour slid from red, to orange, yellow and white, dimming as it went. The sphere was becoming translucent.

It was then Rasputin felt the first real tremor of fear. Beyond those walls, something moved. His imagination was no longer in command.

The surface became clear as glass, and finally the errand-orb flung its light beyond the sphere. The light sprang into an endless dark, and for Rasputin, it was as though he witnessed the birth of the universe flaming into life.

But it was not an empty universe.

Out beyond the sphere, the sky was flocked by objects beyond counting, which were tugged by unseen currents.

He tried to fix his eye on something, anything, floating in the void, and was shocked to discover his own face.

It shimmered on an ovoid blob drifting just beyond the sphere's surface. The blob had a sheen like opal-lustre, and over this film played images of him, seated and laughing, holding a black cane topped by a pink bow. It was his last day in hospital, which meant ...

The blob is a memory.

With wonder he cast his gaze further into the deep and saw more remembered things afloat. Some contorted like wax in a lava lamp, full-bodied sense bundles. Others drifted, mere shards of preserved vision. Everywhere clots of the stuff tangled in a profusion of colour, submarine detritus in ocean-refracted sunlight.

It dawned on him where this journey had brought him.

In his quest for Churchill's book, he had first travelled the corridors of time, and then hunted in the maze of serendipity, only to find its vestiges. But here all was laid bare. His mind's eye was a telescope trained on the heavens of his being, able to probe the farthest galaxy. Travel was no longer necessary. He had only to bring the thing desired into focus in its great lens.

At last he turned to the orb at his side.

"The book?" he said.

It pulsed.

Rasputin gritted his teeth and commanded: "The Second World War. I read it last year. I want the preface. All of it."

A thin, red arc crackled across the orb's surface. For an instant it seemed a vast, luminescent marble.

It smiled at me.

Then everything moved.

The great eye gyrated, sifting the skies for one object. When seconds later it was trained upon a pinpoint glint, it flung its focus out, and drew on that lone ray of light as upon a tether.

And so it came, a single memory, a bundle of five-fold sense, compressed but complete. It came near, shy but curious, in a first contact of sorts.

It was motionless a moment, and then its surface peeled back like opening petals to reveal a book.

Without lifting a hand, he opened the cover and leafed to the beginning of the preface. Words stood stark on the page. None were obscured by ink. Even a small, brown speckle, a stain left by someone during the book's life in the library, was preserved in the memory.

He smiled and began to read.

The smile remained while he read every word, reveling in the sense of power it brought him. It was the same feeling that had intoxicated him, so briefly, when sketching alone the night after his interview. But now he had bottled the lightning.

As he read, his consciousness drifted back into the lounge of his flat. The words, he found, were on his lips. Jordy stood at the bookshelf holding the real book in his hands, glancing at it now and then without moving his head, a wicked grin affixed.

But just before the transition back into the real world was complete and his sense of the dazzling errand carrier waned altogether, he saw colour flicker across its surface. He felt its attention turn from him, from his centre of consciousness, to the constellations of his memory.

He had the strangest sense it was *curious*.

The thought terrified him. Fear tugged at the last words to fall from his lips.

"... the awful unfolding science of the future."

Jordy was a statue for the time it took Rasputin's heart to squeeze a few hundred mils of blood through its chambers.

"Word," he said suddenly, and snapped the cover of the book closed. "For," he said, and bent to slide it into the hole it had left on the shelf. "Word," he finished, and stood up straight.

Rasputin sighed.

"I know," he conceded.

"Don't tell me that's normal," said Jordy.

"No, not normal." He remembered the wall-come-to-life, and what had emerged from its dying fire. "Quite abnormal."

"But you don't look excited."

He wanted to be, but his last glimpse of the errand carrier, and the proprietary gaze it had cast over his memory, left him feeling bone-cold.

"One last test," said Jordy, and disappeared into the kitchen.

Test?

Rasputin decided Jordy was being suspiciously goal-directed.

Jordy returned holding a glossy magazine. It was an edition of *Food Ideas*, in which every page featured the kind of lushly prepared and lit delicacies that earned it the term food porn. Dee had a subscription to the magazine, and left old copies on their fridge in the hopes of lifting the culinary standard. Rasputin liked the photos, hated cooking.

Jordy searched the magazine, stopped at a page, and said, "Mongolian lamb."

Rasputin took a moment to decide it wasn't an insult.

It was a good test. His eyes would have barely scanned the recipe. He recalled it without looking within. "500 grams of lamb," he began, and rattled off the rest verbatim.

"It was either that or a tampon ad," said Jordy.

"Now I'm hungry. And why are you so excited?"

Jordy sat and fished over his chair's arm for the TV remote. "Your memory might have improved, but you're still thick."

He strafed the free-to-air channels, and evidently found what he was looking for. "Like it was meant to be," he said, and unmuted the sound.

Jordy had stopped at channel Nine. It was broadcasting the same quiz show Rasputin had watched in the foodhall the night of his accident, Temptation. Jordy's behaviour finally made sense. One-dimensional sense.

"Tempted?" he said.

Rasputin took a swallow of his now-warm beer before answering. "This is the most animated I've seen you since I came out of hospital. And the reason?" He jerked his head at the TV. "You've got dollar-bill vision?"

Jordy didn't have a comeback. That was odd. He returned to the kitchen. When he reappeared, he was carrying an envelope.

Shit. Not another one.

"What's that?" said Rasputin. "Thanks from Eric Hewitt's panel beater? Or did I win lotto?"

"The opposite," said Jordy, and dropped the envelope into his lap.

Printed on it was an icon of a snake-entwined staff. It was from the medical clinic. It had been opened and inside he found an invoice for his surgery. He skipped over the blurb and found the dollar figure. It had three zeros, and more than one figure in front.

"Sorry," said Jordy. "It came yesterday and I thought I'd be able to pay it. I called the clinic to say there must be some mistake, but the receptionist just crapped on about gap cover, and hung-up when I mentioned the ombudsman. I know student assistance isn't exactly the mother lode. But that ..." He shrugged.

Is game over for study. Rasputin pictured himself telemarketing pet shampoos.

Jordy changed tack. "Your leg will mend. When it does, you can pay it out of your night fill."

How am I going to tell him?

Rasputin's gaze weighed a ton. "I already owe money. Night fill was barely paying the interest."

"What money?"

"You and Dee were in Sydney."

"What money, Monk?"

"The money I borrowed to buy"—his tongue refused to form *Heroin*— "painkillers."

"For your leg?" said Jordy.

"You're not listening. This was over a month ago, before the accident."

"What then?"

"Does it matter?"

Jordy's expression collapsed as understanding dawned. In a voice unfamiliar, he said, "Is there any left?"

"A little. I was almost done with it," Rasputin said, and attempted to lighten the mood. "No great revelations were forthcoming."

"Where?"

"Under the bottom drawer of my desk, in the cavity." He almost added: the cache of guilty things.

Jordy strode into the hall. Rasputin heard the rasping sound of a drawer being wrenched free. When he returned, he went straight to the front door without sparing Rasputin a glance.

"Where are you going?"

"To get rid of this shit properly. Past the S-bend isn't far enough for some junkies." He slammed the door, but not before Rasputin heard him mutter, "Selfish bastard."

Rasputin stared at the invoice. It had stuck to his sweaty fingers. His gaze drifted to the crisp green icon on the letter head, the snake-and-staff.

"I never did get the snake and staff," he said. "But of course. The snake bites you, and if you survive, they beat you to death with the stick."

He lowered the letter to look at the TV. Temptation was still on. He remembered with a pang how animated Jordy had been only minutes earlier.

A booth lit as a contestant buzzed in, and said, "The locomotive engine."

The host nodded, already prepping another question card, and said, "Correct. George Stephenson invented the first steam locomotive engine for rail."

I *knew that*.

The camera cut back to the contestants, and behind them sat the jackpot. It stood at a quarter of a million dollars.

That had three zeros and some numbers before it.

The next three days came and went as if the conversation had not happened. The only inkling something was afoot was Jordy's unsinkable geniality. He was like that when fixing things, but the current flock of warm fuzzies were on amphetamines.

Nor could Rasputin stop Temptation percolating through his mind. In the light of day, without the leaven of beer, the idea was preposterous. Who had even met someone who had been on the show? They weren't real people. The show was probably concocted in a computer using the showbiz equivalent of EFACE.

So why couldn't he let it rest?

He lifted a spoon to his mouth and sucked soggy cornflakes from it. It was barely eight o'clock and he had already been daydreaming.

Jordy sat opposite, balancing a cup brimming with coffee in one hand, holding a sheaf of paper in the other.

"Hey, Einstein," said Jordy. "Can I call you Einstein?"

"No."

"Pack your bags. We're going to Disneyland."

"What, *the* Disneyland?" said Rasputin in monotone.

"No. I lied, Poindexter—can I can call you that?"

"No."

"Disneyland was my little joke. We're going to Melbourne."

"What's in Melbourne, Bill (as in Gates)—can I call you that?"

"Sure."

Amiable prat.

Jordy continued. "Temptation auditions."

Rasputin sat silent and still, spoon poised before his lips. No reason to hurry. The cornflakes weren't getting any soggier. In fact, there was every chance they would begin to crisp up again.

Jordy slipped a sheet from the sheaf of paper.

"Two tickets to Melbourne on tonight's red-eye. Mum has been using her credit card like a whetstone. She has frequent flyer points to spare."

He was serious. Rasputin placed the spoon back in his bowl and nudged it away. His mouth had gone dry, which was funny. He had always assumed that was a literary invention.

It was still dry when that night he tipped awkwardly into a window seat of Qantas Flight 785 from Perth to Melbourne. He had never flown before, and Jordy had insisted on him taking the window.

Ethereal elevator music wafted about the cabin. Outside, angry red and yellow lights held back the night sky and illuminated airport staff buzzing in and out of sight beneath the plane's belly. They disturbed him, in the way he imagined Caesarean delivery crews disturbed a prospective mother. A cargo hatch closed and sent a shudder through the plane.

Amateur surgeon. Great.

Rasputin and Jordy had been the last to board. Rasputin had refused to board at the call for children and disabled. Dee and Jordy had had a moment together. Then she had hugged him and told Jordy to look after him. She had glanced at his cane when she said it, though Rasputin thought she had tried not to.

A hostess came past with newspapers and magazines. Jordy took *The Australian*. Rasputin leaned over him, but before he could ask for a paper, Jordy waved her on.

"You're on a reading plan," he said, and from his bag produced an encyclopaedia.

"What are you, my agent?"

He smiled evilly. "Agent, coach, scrutator, whatever. Just read."

Rasputin grimaced. Jordy leaned over, and said, "You do realise this could be your ticket to the big city. Why stop with the bills. Temptation is just a beginning." He winked. "The road goes ever on."

At his words, an image flashed through Rasputin's mind of Bilbo Baggins setting forth under a star-scintillated sky.

"But why an encyclopaedia? Why can't I read that?" He indicated the paper covering Jordy's lap. "It's current. They ask current."

"It's rubbish."

"So why are you reading it?"

"Good IT section. Plus, if I get cold, broadsheets make passable rugs."

The plane took to the sky with a roar of defiance. Rasputin felt pressed into his seat, and couldn't help smiling. Disneyland had been right after all.

Jordy clasped headphones over his ears.

Over the thrum of the plane's labouring engines, Rasputin said, "You look like Stevie Wonder."

Jordy lifted an ear-cup and said, "What? These are noise cancelling."

"I said, you look like Stevie Wonder, when he was hip."

Jordy put the paper down, leaned back into the chair, closed his eyes and said, "And I'm going to sleep like I got hit by a Valiant."

"Except you're not black," Rasputin went on.

Jordy's breathing slowed.

"And you can't sing."

Jordy's mouth fell open. Rasputin couldn't believe it. Asleep in under two minutes. A new record.

He turned his attention to the encyclopaedia lying in his lap. It was a Funk and Wagnall's circa the 70s. They were a dollar a pop in charity shops. He turned back the cover and began to read.

"Did you know the Aardvark—" he shouted, and then remembered Jordy was asleep.

The plane dropped toward Tullamarine airport in the pre-dawn gloom. Rasputin's face was plastered to the window. His hands gripped his chair. He had watched since the hum of the engines had changed pitch, and his ears had popped. The runway appeared below, stretched out to receive the plane, and then raced like a river in tumult, daring it to find safe purchase.

At the baggage carousel Rasputin and Jordy joined the throng waiting for it to come to life. Most waited silently, pensive or half-awake. The smell of percolating coffee drifted from a niche café squatting at the end of a row of hire car counters. It lured a few stragglers. The snap of its cash register was jarring in the quiet.

The carousel lurched to life. Miraculously their bags emerged first. Jordy hauled them into the brisk air outside, and they caught the first taxi in the rank.

As they crossed the Bolte Bridge at ten clicks above the limit, Rasputin got his first view of Melbourne city. The CBD was a mass of spires anchored in darkness and twinkling with multi-hued light. The first rays of sunlight were glancing off the eastward facets making the city a cluster of crystal. Rasputin cupped the city in his hand and, for a moment, possessed it.

Their hotel was a grey block tucked away in a sun-starved lane in the CBD. Jordy slumped onto one of the single beds. Rasputin used the toilet.

"Barely enough room to swing a cat in here," he said, pivoting on the spot to avoid sitting in the sink. His cane rapped the porcelain, evoking a dull clang.

"Always room to swing a cat," Jordy replied sourly, and was soon asleep again.

Rasputin moved about the room, picking over its contents. It gave an initial sense of warmth, but he soon penetrated the illusion. The room was dead like the needle-strewn carpet of a pine forest. In a drawer by the bed he found a Gideon's bible, and leafed through a few pages before returning it. On a mantel above a row of coat hooks sat a small, die-cast sailing ship, proxy for ornaments on warm hearths the world over. He picked it up and enjoyed its heft. He toyed with the idea of boiling the kettle, but knew it would wake Jordy. Besides, he wasn't thirsty. He had plenty of caffeine buzzing in his veins, which put sleep out of the question. The auditions would start at five that night.

He retrieved paper and a pen from his bag, and then slipped through the door to the balcony. Outside the air was cold.

The balcony was a concrete perch that held a small table and chair. The view it afforded was of more grey blocks and, at the end of the lane, a building façade running at right angles, aflame with the rising sun.

He sat, arranged the paper on the table, and readied his pen. He prepared himself to recall a memory. Panic darted foxlike through him. Then he forced his consciousness downwards, *within*, his will a hand plunging his own head beneath the waves. Swallowed by his mind's eye, he stood again at the centre, and in every direction the galaxies of his memory blazed.

He sought a very old memory, one of the oldest. He found it quickly, amid the kaleidoscope, a distant supernova.

He pulled it near, the eye's focus extending telescopically into the distance to retrieve it. The memory was like a rose, wrinkles of interlocking manifolds, an organic, five-fold bundle of sense.

He pried it open.

Laughter and screams wafted from it like perfume. Something terrible had happened. But he already knew that.

He was three years old, his self-consciousness dawning. Though his eyes and ears had worked as they did now, they were warped by the feebleness of a toddler's understanding. Images, sounds, and smells dashed against him disjointedly, and would not cohere. He concentrated, tried to impose order on these unparsed senses. He felt the wind bite on the sweat of his face.

He hunted for a face. A girl's face. Her face. He dug for it like a dog at a buried bone.

The first thing he saw was a flock of white birds, and he felt the echo of his toddler's excitement. They had been novel. He could name them now, seagulls. The recognition unlocked another image, of vast, frothing blue water. The ocean. That had been novel too. He felt more than saw the presence of two people. Mother and Father. They were near and far like the sky. He heard a giggle, saw a girl run past with bouncing hair. She turned and he beheld her face, vivid and clear.

Her arms were extended, hands cupped together. From them came the gleam of white shell. Cockle shells.

Cockles.

The word was like the closing of a circuit breaker. It was an itch his fingers had hunted for a long time finally scratched. Another memory mingled with this for a moment—*warms the cockles of your heart*—and was gone.

Then the earth moved. An image, hitherto hidden in the rose's heart, smote him. He saw the girl crumpled beneath a car wheel, one leg bent unnaturally. His adult mind knew she was dead.

Dizziness swept over him. He realised he had stopped breathing. He released the memory, let it collapse upon itself and drift away. He opened his mouth and gulped air.

The view from the concrete perch reasserted itself. The daylight had grown stronger. The city's hubbub was rising from the streets.

He had not found what he sought, but he remembered her face. He began to sketch it.

When Jordy woke an hour later, he found Rasputin on the balcony, staring into space. Beneath his arm, secured against the wind, was a portrait of a girl, cloven in two by the sun's angling rays.

It was past two before Jordy and Rasputin emerged from their hotel. As they navigated the CBD's maze toward the audition, Rasputin was struck by the contrast Melbourne made to Perth. Here lush grass sprouted beneath ornamental trees and untended verge. In dry Perth, even in spring, grass grew with restraint in foreknowledge of summer's hammer. Melbourne felt older, too. It spoke with the rumble and spark of trams, and wore clothes fraying at the seams.

Near the railway, Rasputin fingered posters plastered so thick on a billboard they hung in curls like dog-eared paperbacks. Graffiti covered them in an urban poetry of expletives and tags. One oddly unobscured phrase caught Rasputin's eye. It was scrawled in paint like prop blood, and said, "There is a hope." Or perhaps it said 'home'.

They crossed the Yarra River at Flinders Street Station and found a café on the Southbank strip to unload their feet and eat Turkish bread. Rasputin watched cruise ferries chug to and fro on the brown water of the upside-down river while he tried to force the bread down his dry throat. He gave in and laid two-thirds of the sandwich down. He hung his head over the back of his chair, closed his eyes, and sighed. The lowering sun filtered through his eyelids a deep red, and warmed his face. For a moment he forgot about the audition.

Chunks of Turkish bread were still inching down Rasputin's throat when he entered the waiting room. It was an anteroom crammed into the guts of the Crown complex, which lay along the river, and rose up in stacks of identical casino floors, and restaurants, bars, and shops. The mood of the crowd was that of a proctologist's waiting room.

The doors opened at 5pm sharp. Jordy said, "Good luck," thumped Rasputin on the shoulder and left.

The audition, which had reared up in Rasputin's imagination as a many-headed, clawed thing with bad-breath, was, in the event, a written test. He received a blank piece of paper and pen, and allowed himself a smile.

A twenty-something girl, dressed in a neat, black executive suit-top and skirt, with channel-9 badge affixed, instructed them in an overly loud voice.

"Fifty questions. A few seconds to answer each. Any questions?"

"Fifty, apparently," he quipped to himself, then readied his pen.

"Question One." She glanced at her folder, and launched the first challenge: "Who was Australia's first Prime Minister?"

He panicked.

It was his driving test all over again and he couldn't find the steering wheel. In his mind, second hands raced on the faces of a million clocks, while part of him worked the question backwards to pry it for hidden meaning.

Then clarity.

It was a simple question. A primary schooler's question.

Only a second had passed.

He wrote the answer at the top of his sheet, Edmund Barton.

The studio exec spoke again. "Name the architect of New York's Guggenheim museum."

Sucker punch.

He knew without looking up that a smile had fallen from most faces in the room. He could hear them drop. But he was still smiling.

He braced himself, and dived. He went *within*. Like the prodded anemone, he triggered a controlled implosion. He opened the Eye, and willed himself to its centre. He became Rasputin condensed, splinter of himself, ghost in the machine, psychonaut, homunculus.

And a side serve of crazy.

He spoke into the vastness. "Who was the architect of the Guggenheim?"

The eye gyrated on its axis. It sucked at a constellation, pulling stars from an earlier epoch so close he would have burned to a cinder had they been real.

A blue giant dominated the cluster, and its name was *Ayn Rand*. It had birthed a star, a red dwarf that burned angrily. And Rand had birthed a book, *The Fountainhead*. He remembered reading it two years earlier, prompted by a lecturer proselytising Rand's philosophy. The book's text bubbled over the surface of the globular memory like pepper in tomato soup. It was all there. He could read it now, but he only wanted the answer to the question.

He peered at the memory, searching for the answer.

Two objects swung in ellipses around the book-star, like planets gripped in its gravity well. One was the book's angular protagonist, architect *Howard Roark*. Roark was one half of a binary system, a coupling of planets. The other was a real person, *Frank Lloyd Wright*, the architect of the Guggenheim. Rand had denied that Wright was her inspiration for Roark (claims and counter-claims floated like space detritus about the planets). But it didn't matter. Rasputin had found the name he needed.

He rose from within, breached the surface, and scrawled it on the sheet: Frank Lloyd Wright.

But there was no time for self-congratulation. The studio exec fired off the next question. "What is the chemical symbol for gold?" He wrote *Ag* on reflex, then paused. He frowned at the couplet of letters. He glanced at the man next to him, who was stretching his neck as though dodging bullets in slow motion, and when he focused again on his answer, it irritated him.

There was nothing for it. Again he exerted his will, and wrapped the eye around him like a cocoon.

He requested without words: Gold. The sphere tilted and spun. It slowed when a far constellation drew level with his gaze, and drank the distance in a single giddying gulp.

As the memory unfurled, he saw, for the first time, faint, writhing tendrils of a glittering substance. They were attached to the memory and curled off into the void surrounding it.

He focussed his attention on the content of the memory, and recognised his Year Seven classroom. A blackboard was visible from the view afforded by a three-quarter chair. Chalked onto it in a ballooning script were rows of chemical element names and corresponding symbols. He scanned along a row and struck gold, *Au*.

Idiot.

He had to correct the answer. But this time, instead of surfacing, he attempted to write from within. At first his hands moved sluggishly, over-correcting, as though they were sheathed in radiation-proof gloves and his pen was a fissile rod. The *Au* came out like *Hv*, but he trusted it would do.

The next question was already coming, but he was determined to stay in the eye. There would be no more trusting to reflex.

The studio exec's voice filtered inward sounding like TV heard through a closed door, and he found he had to shuffle his concentration from foot to foot, between his mental world and the real. As time wore on he managed it with increasing deftness. The eye spun and gyrated with his requests like a contested ball, but gradually a rhythm emerged; from outside the question, from within its echo, then spin, and suck, and pluck, an answer from the heavens.

He was master of every sight he had ever laid eyes on, every sound he had ever laid ears on, every perception drawn from his other senses and construed as memory. All of it hung somewhere in that night sky, and an inner, invisible logic guided the ship of his consciousness inerrantly through its vast distances.

He echoed Question 29—"What road lent its name and image to a Beatles album?"—and in answer a pod of memory-stuff burst open. In it he was seated on a familiar scraggy armchair. Jordy lay in a couch, a bag-of-bones. A TV flickered with scenes from a documentary about the making of the Lord of the Rings movies. In it the director was leading a procession over the famous zebra crossing outside Abbey Road Studios, where the movies' soundtracks were mixed.

And there was the answer to Question 29.

He wrote: *Abbey Road.*

But he held the memory a moment longer. This time his eye was primed. He caught the shimmer of elastic curlicues snaking away from the memory into the darkness. They caressed objects within the memory like things that see by touch. They licked, seeming to like the taste of some places better than others, and where they touched left faint auras. One fell upon the movies' composer as he talked about leitmotifs. It coiled up from his head like moonlit smoke.

But the stuff had substance. Its haziness, he saw, came from the way it forked as it fell, in ever fainter, thinner tendrils. They went on forking chaotically in fractal webs at the limit of his vision. He marveled. He fancied the memory—every memory?—was not simply anchored, but *enmeshed* in an arterial film of light.

He wanted to touch it.

But the studio exec's voice came buzzing through again. Now she wanted to know the second book of the Bible.

He stepped back mere hours to his hotel room and the memory of the Bible he had leafed through. The contents page had been visible for scant seconds, but there it was, vivid, clear—clearer than real life, hyper-real. The answer was *Exodus*.

Serendipity struck at Question 34: "Who directed the recent Lord of the Rings movies?"

He almost wrote "Peter Jackson" from conviction, but hesitated. Due process in the court of Rasputin demanded verification.

He called for the memory of Boxing Day 2001, when he had sat in a sudden hush as a dark cinema became flushed with light. Emblazoned on the screen was the movie's title in heavy, gilded lettering. He sat in the eye, an audience of one. He felt again a sense of anticipation powerful as narcotic, as a fey elven voice prickled his skin. The movie's timeline was warped by the memory's organism, played out of order. The screen flickered, a name appeared in the same heavy gold lettering, Peter Jackson. He had been right.

But he didn't write it. Dense threads of silver were anchored to the name, rippling like the roots of a sentient tree. He was absorbed by them, cat-curious. He knew the filaments snaking away into the gloom terminated in many memories. One was anchored to the face of the man who owned that name in a memory he had already consulted.

Fear tickled his neck. But it was too faint to heed.

On instinct he reached out and grasped the gold lettering hanging in the black frame, itself framed by the inconstant envelope of the memory. His touch crystallised the name, as if he had struck freezing cold into the fluid memory. The name became cool, cast metal, rough to the touch. He yanked it with both hands. It resisted a moment, and then with a wet, inaudible rupture, came free. Its weight fell on his grip, and he staggered before shifting to counter balance it. He laid it on its edge and squatted for a better view. It had the feel of a long-lost attic treasure.

He was dimly aware of the girl's voice speaking the next question. He had to hurry.

He glanced over the name and saw it had left a deep black void in the memory of that night. The silhouetted heads of the cinema-memory beat spastically out of time, as if in ripping the name free he had decapitated a cockroach. Into the violated place, silver tendrils groped and waved blindly.

Silver thread had come free too, sticky and clinging, like gizzard. A thick rope of it writhed inches from his face. Over the name's metal, tiny tongues forked and forked again, falling like lightning, always in contact yet flitting over its surface to find best purchase. Their play emitted a fizz that strobed to and fro across the threshold of hearing.

She was still speaking, but time had slowed and become tacky. The man next to him was tugging an earlobe, and it took forever for his thumb and forefinger to draw down and pull free.

Balancing the heavy metal with one hand, Rasputin examined the tangle of threads reaching back umbilical-like into the memory. He chose the thickest, the one terminating on the letter *A*, and grasped it.

At first there was nothing.

Then a droplet.

The raw sensation of a single remembered *A* touched his mind. The A had an aftertaste of *hospital*, and he knew it had come from the memory of a road sign.

The droplet became a trickle.

More ghosts of memory came down the silver cord to sift over his mind like a light shower. Curlicues, and tri-strokes, and puffs of breath that said "æ". They fell from memories of books and signs and report cards, and speeches and songs and shrieks.

The shower grew heavier as impressions drained from a widening catchment. They began to wash over him and mingle, and swamp his ability to separate and perceive them.

He felt the cord swell in his hand and noticed it shone brighter than when he had first touched it.

He was on the verge of dropping it when it juddered and wrenched his arm. It was as if somewhere upstream a lock had opened and hammered the pressure in it. It blazed to a white-hot intensity.

Something new was coming down the line.

With horror he realised the downpour had only been the vanguard, the first froth blasting through the opened gate. Behind it was an inconceivably large cataract of sense uncurling, beginning to force its ponderous body through the cord. He felt it coming, a subterranean rumbling.

The cord would drain him whole. And fill him again. It would pour the Universe into him. It would buckle the beams of his mind.

He tried to wrench his hand free of the cord but it clung to him elastically. With a shriek he saw it begin to fork fractally and clamber over his hand and up his arm.

It clung long enough for the true flow to touch him.

Behind the first impression *A*, a chain reaction ignited. *Alpha*, then *first, single, alone, is*—they tumbled over each other and each bloomed in a fresh payload of sense (Beta, Gamma, Delta / Second / Third— Fourth— Pair— TripleMarried- DivorcedAndOnesilencedamintrical- idegopsycheremit@er#@Iii_I ...) Every bush, a garden, and every garden a forest.

Then the feelers snapped back like overstretched glue. The connection collapsed. The flow died.

Silence. Sense. He lay sprawled in the eye. He saw the name (Peter Jackson) sitting benignly again in its place, of one piece with the memory of that night in the cinema, snug in its tissue of silver veins, and floating amid others.

He understood. The venous tissue formed associations, relating each memory to every other with some relevance, some affinity. An infinity of affinities, even within his memory alone.

And 'tissue' was right. It was alive.

Only then did he realise why it was silent. In the real world, he had fallen from his chair. He lay prone, and was staring at a thigh draped in a red silk skirt.

He clambered into his chair, feeling his cheeks flush under the combined gaze of every eye in the room.

The studio exec was unfazed. Perhaps men routinely fell off chairs in her presence. She repeated the question.

But as Rasputin's embarrassment died he found he was trembling. Other questions jostled at the back of his mind. *What if I hadn't let go? What would it mean to be swallowed, assimilated by my own memory? Infinite regress? Permanent coma?*

By Question 42 he could read signs of resignation all over the room. Some slouched, others sat bolt upright. One lady gazed out a window that didn't exist. A man he had noted earlier wearing fluorescent pink board shorts seemed to have mistaken his pen for a pipe cleaner, and subsequently his nostrils for pipes. As the question was spoken a few perked up, "Which actress won the 2007 gold and silver Logies?"

By now Rasputin was grown so adept at plying his new mental apparatus that he reached for the answer with the merest flex of will. The act required the subtlest shifting of weight of attention from out to in. More was his surprise then when he came up empty-handed.

With a flicker of irritation, he dove deeper.

Memories drifted in the night of his mind as the eye yawed gently.

He spoke the question again. It paused. The deeps stood still. Then the eye rolled sharply one way, halted, and returned at double the speed. Rasputin bit back bile. The eye slowed, then floated, aimless.

He repeated the question through clenched teeth.

The eye pitched forward, sending the constellations careening overhead. He steeled his will, drove it harder, only to have it spin more wildly still, zigging and zagging as if in REM sleep until the sky became a chaotic tracery of light.

At last, nauseous, he relented. The globe resumed a gentle drift.

Are you telling me I didn't catch one TV commercial, one magazine cover, one shred of hairdresser gossip about the 2007 Logie Winner? That nowhere in the entire catalogue of trivia tucked away in my head is that one useless fact?

He knew he had aced the audition, but his pride was stung. He answered the remaining eight questions without fuss, but 42 sat on the paper, blank and obvious, taunting him.

Of course, he had known there would be *holes*, in theory. He was no All-Seeing Oracle, was he? But the experience left him disturbed. What was the sum total of his experiences compared to the unknown? A speck. His fears suddenly inverted. It was the *unknown* that would swallow him whole, and round that speck to naught.

The voice of the studio exec broke over him. She sounded relaxed. (Rasputin wondered if she was auditioning for the role of auditioner.) "Some of you at least are eager for the answers. Swap your sheet with someone to mark."

Rasputin perked up. He looked at the 49 answers arrayed on his sheet, thinking there had never been a cat better bagged. He handed it to Mr. Bullet-time, who reciprocated without making eye contact.

The answers came quick-fire, and Bullet-time's eyebrows rose a little higher with each until they threatened a tryst with his receding hairline.

The answer to 42, Kate Ritchie, struck the bonnet of Rasputin's pride and took a little paint. It might have stung less if he thought it would ever be of use. He began to cross Bullet-time's answer by habit when he read it: Kate Ritchy. He glanced at the man, who returned something that wanted to be a smile.

When the marking was done, those with the lowest scores left until only the 30+ club remained, twenty-three people in all.

Rasputin soon found himself sitting in a cubicle with a studio representative. She had glossy black hair, and TV teeth that glistened below the camera she was pointing at him. She snapped a photo, and checked the result in the camera's screen. From her expression the subject might have been a septic toe, or so he thought.

"So, Mr. Lowdermilk," she said, "I need some personal information from you. When you get on the show—"

"How soon is that?"

"Could be weeks, could be months," she began, but then evidently catching his mood, "But more likely weeks. We're short of meat (no offence) hence the rushed audition."

"Sorry to nag," he said, "but ..." *But what?*

"Wouldn't have picked you for a serious player Rasputin. Most people we get are neighbourhood Trivial Pursuit champs looking for their five minutes of fame."

"Must be easier ways to get on TV," he said. "There was a guy back there who got 7cm of pen up his nose."

"I'll pitch it to the station: Extreme stationery."

She thumbed the form in front of her. "Family?"

Rasputin sighed.

She raised an eyebrow.

She waited, then wrote "Issues" big enough for him to read upside down from the other side of the desk.

"Occupation?"

"Can I say it depends on how I go on the show?"

"You *can*, but seeing as how you're yet to give a straight answer, I can't see that going so well." She left it blank.

"I also need an anecdote. Can be anything, a story, a unique talent (but nothing pen-related). The host will introduce you with it."

He pondered. He could say he had had cranial surgery following a life-threatening collision, or that his memory was the love child of the Library of Congress and a Guinness-record-holding ball of yarn that had been bitten by a radioactive spider. The first was morbid for dinner-time TV. The second was flat-out disturbed.

"When I was young I shook the Queen's hand."

"Gotta love Liz," she said, and scribbled on the form.

Why did I lie? It pricked him, and he wished then to undo it. But what did they say about lies? They found you out? By the heaping up of lie upon lie, the mortal memory breaks under the strain and reveals the deception.

Yeah, mortal *memory.*

She finished writing and opened her mouth to speak, when a man appeared at the cubicle's entrance.

"Mr. Lowdermilk?"

"The one and only," he said, and swivelled his chair to face the newcomer.

"I'm sorry, sir," the man said, "but there are no more slots available. There's no point in you staying."

"Come again?"

"The auditions are closed. Our quota is full."

Rasputin shot a look at the girl, who had just closed her mouth. He spoke to the man, unable to keep the anger from his tone. "What do you mean full? I got 49. Doesn't 49 make your quota?"

The man was silent a moment before a storm head developed over his brow, breaking his professional composure.

"Yes, the other scores ranged between 0 and 37. Yours is—"

"The highest."

"Passing credulity."

Rasputin's volume shrank in disbelief. "What?"

"We don't know how, Mr. Lowdermilk, but we believe you cheated."

Rasputin strode past a row of cubicles, oblivious to the conversations bubbling from them, and summoned a lift. When it arrived, he entered, and punched the button for the floor above, the street level. The doors hesitated a moment, then began to close. They were scant inches apart, when a hand shot into their path. They jolted to a halt, and opened to reveal the girl who had interviewed him. She appeared out of breath.

"Here," she said, thrusting a slip of paper at him. "For what it's worth, you don't look like a cheat." Then she was gone.

He unfolded the slip. Apparently 'it' was worth $300. He held a coupon for credit in the Crown Complex, enough for a fancy room or fancier meal. It was the kind of courtesy you gave a successful, out-of-town auditionee. Not a cheat.

He *was* hungry. All that thinking had burnt up a lot of energy.

He licked his lips. He was thirsty, too, for a drink that would drown the voice of the studio man still looping in his head—*cheated, cheated, cheat…*

He ran his gaze over the lift buttons again, then stabbed a finger at one promising a bar and casino floor. The cabin jerked once and then lifted him toward the heavens.

He was passing the tenth floor when he remembered he had arranged to meet Jordy in the foyer below. But his tongue was already tasting the promised drink.

Within ten minutes he had made good the promise. He was seated at a bar, draining his first Guinness. The barman had rung up his credit, and told him it was good for anything in the complex.

The second Guinness looked smaller than the first. He cradled it in a hand numb from the chilled glass, feeling as if he had snuggled a blanket over his legs. From his vantage point atop the stool, the casino floor seemed somehow both dark and bright. Tables littered the floor like giant counters, some empty, some thick with patrons, and at the far wall a bank of slot machines glittered. Smoking was not allowed, but a layer of haze obscured the ceiling's faux starscape, which pulsed from blue to green to white and back again. He let the alcohol knock the edges off the room, and waited for it to knock the edges off his anger.

Rasputin guessed it must be working, when he realised someone had been trying without success to talk to him. Rasputin swivelled on his stool and found the bartender looking at him. The man was fortyish, with sideburns sharp enough to cut.

"Come again?" Rasputin said, feeling like an idiot.

"What's the deal with the voucher?" the bartender said. "I normally get them from fat guys in suits."

Ah. He had asked the question.

By now Rasputin's anger was cushioned by a layer of Guinness-fuzz. It was a de-clawed cat, wrapped in a towel. He recounted the audition and interview, while attempting to read the man's body language—not enthralled, exactly, but curious. The story was novel to a guy who had heard a lot of grief, and grief was a bartender's staple, wasn't it? So long as it was someone else's.

"So did you?" the bartender said.

"Did I what?"

"Cheat."

"Get me another. And no, I did not cheat."

The bartender began drawing the brew. It lapped against the side of the tilted glass, then rose like liquid velvet.

"So what are you?" the bartender said. "Med student? Law?"

"Student of life," Rasputin said, and drained his glass. The bartender smirked as if to say 'student of bullshit.'

"How did you do it then? I've seen plenty of guys up here after the audition. They all say it's hard, harder than the show. No one tells me their score, but they all say they'll be back."

Rasputin leaned forward. "Can I tell you a secret?" he said, negating any privacy his posture afforded by whispering like a deaf octogenarian. The bartender played along, and leaned closer as the froth neared the lip of the glass.

With a deadpan face Rasputin said, "I cracked my head open and now my brain doesn't make mistakes."

The bartender roared with laughter.

Rasputin suspected he should be offended, but the blanket around his legs had become a recliner and slippers. He took it philosophically.

"I know that's crap," said the bartender. He placed the drink by Rasputin's elbow. A runnel of foam snaked down one side and pooled on the coaster. "Here's your third mistake in half an hour. You're no drinker, and tomorrow you'll wake up feeling like the Devil's pressing a steel-capped boot into that special brain of yours."

"I'm serious," Rasputin said. "I remember everything I ever saw. And I can draw! Do you wanna picture?" He patted his pockets, hunting for a pen.

"Maybe, mate," the bartender said. "Do it again, and maybe I'll believe it." He left, evidently having lost interest in yet another drunk.

Rasputin didn't notice him leave.

Again. Yeah, that would show them. But by the time of the next audition he would be a regular in the dole queue. *If* he was allowed to audition again. Which he probably wasn't. His gaze meandered past his cane propped against the next stool. He flung a foot at it and missed, and instead almost knocked the stool over.

Mercifully, his conscience rallied. It gave him a glimpse of how pathetic a creature he must appear, drunkenly perched atop the stool. He folded his hands in his lap and resolved to sit until his cheeks felt less rubbery.

A couple came and leaned on the bar nearby. Their conversation mixed exuberance and nervousness, unable to abide a second's silence. Rasputin guessed they were a dating service hook-up, before chiding himself for indulging in speculation. Pop psychology seemed to fill every time-slot and genre nowadays.

He sat with his back to the bar, listening to the chatter next door, eyes on the blackjack table three feet away. His ears pricked when he heard the couple talking about clans and murders, before he realised they were referring to an online game.

Internet romance, then. Close enough.

A man joined the blackjack table. He slumped into a seat like a dropped sack of potatoes, tugged his tie away from his neck, and arranged both hands before him ready to receive cards. A yellow stain marked the fingers of his right hand, and they curled as if remembering a cigarette. He made the third player at the table.

The dealer distributed cards from the fifth of eight decks in the shoe. Rasputin admired the efficiency and fluidity with which he slipped cards from the deck and slid them to the waiting hands. The player nearest him had plenty of colour showing.

The Internet Romance switched to the housing market. If that wasn't the bottom of the barrel, it had to be close.

At the table, the hand finished. One player left and was replaced by another. A machine emptied and reshuffled the shoe.

Rasputin had only seen blackjack played in the movies, but soon got the gist of it as hands fell in rapid, unromantic succession. He began to take pleasure in the ebb and flow of fortune around the table. One of the players—a heavy-set, balding man with nostrils big enough to cache chips—had polar reactions to each hand. When dealt a poor hand, he hunched down on the table and brooded, and when the hand held promise he pushed his chest out and quipped with the dealer. Rasputin thought it was good the guy wasn't playing poker.

The conversation next door hit bottom and kept going with "Who's hot," but Rasputin's attention was stuck on the blackjack table. Without realising, he began nodding or frowning at bets, smiling when a player made a haul, and tut-tutting big losses.

The third player at the table, a stick-thin woman whose hair was so long it brushed the felt, bet $20 on Queen and Four.

"Bad move," Rasputin said, so loud the dealer and players looked at him. The dealer frowned. Rasputin attempted to shrink.

When he felt safe to move again, he turned to the bar and swigged lukewarm Guinness.

He continued to watch the cards fall and reappear with growing boredom until a strange sensation crept over him.

He wasn't sure when it began, but all of a sudden he was conscious of a sense of the *weight* of the decks left in the shoe. The feeling was the synaesthesic offspring of his eyes and grasp. He weighed the remaining cards with his gaze, and found them heavy. He was certain of it, without the remotest clue why: the shoe was hot.

It was on this knowledge, he realised, he had been critiquing the players. The dealer had to hit on anything under seventeen, with the object being twenty-one, blackjack, but no higher. But on a top-heavy deck, chances were that he would bust. The dealer busts, the player wins.

The player wins.

With rising excitement, he watched and kept a loose count of card values as the shoe was played down to the last deck and a half before being reshuffled. It was hard to follow. Each hand consisted of two or three cards for the dealer, and the same again for the three players, which made up to twelve cards, and more if there were double-downs or splits or improbably low sequences. And all of these cards appeared quick-fire on the end of the dealer's arm-cum-machine, and were just as rapidly swept away.

All the same, by his rough tally, the remainder of the card pool had indeed been high. His gaze had weighed right.

He leaned against the bar and let his arms slide out either side, resting on their length, and exhaled. He still felt tipsy. His smile remained, as if it was the only shape his lips made.

To the casual observer, he probably looked borderline catatonic. But his mind was churning. He quested inward to interrogate himself for the source of the intuition about the cards that had proven correct.

Within, he found the memory of the preceding twenty minutes. He focussed on the game table. As suspected, and to his delight, he saw there every hand that had been played, indelibly printed. Every cough, every call for drinks, every polite smile from the dealer, every sniff from the man with the nicotine-stained fingers (*Fourteen in total. On drugs?*), and most importantly, every dealt card.

Every card. Here was his lever.

Each of the eight decks that made the pool of cards from which the game was played had a known make-up: four aces, four kings, four queens, and so on. When the game began, the chance of dealing a given card was fixed. But over time, as cards were dealt, the make-up of the card pool changed, and so did the chance of dealing a given card. If early rounds were thick with royalty, later rounds would be thin.

It was this knowledge that could be exploited to gain an advantage over the House, whose every move was prescribed. But only if you knew the cards remaining in the pool, and only if they were favourable.

All of this was obvious to Rasputin, and it came as no surprise that he could trawl back through the hands as easily as paging through a spreadsheet and tally the totals. What anchored the grin to his face was the realisation that his brain had birthed this information quietly on its own. Somewhere in the shadow of his attention, a little program had run, tallied the card values, calculated their distribution, and floated this into his perception of the game as an intuition.

He sat watching the fall of cards with euphoria reminiscent of Christmas mornings. The couple next to him left in an embrace. He didn't notice. He glanced at the shoe often. It wriggled in his vision, a small, frightened creature until, all at once, it pushed upward against his gaze, curiously buoyed. The shoe was light. He was sure of it.

That does it.

He stood, turned, and called to the bartender for a drink, he didn't care what. The bartended poured him a pear martini. A woman's drink, his brain informed him. *Fine. No fat tip for you, sideburns.*

He took the drink, winked, said, "Dutch Courage," and sculled it. The alcohol already coursing in his veins would soon have reinforcements.

His eyes watered as he made his way to the cashier, feeling like a stork wading through lily-pad game tables. He converted most of his credit into chips, leaving enough for another dose of courage, and headed back to the blackjack table. His path took him by a roulette wheel, where he was struck by a sudden impulse to bet the chips heavy in his hand.

He paused. He would need a bankroll to stay alive at the blackjack table. *And,* a voice whispered within, *if you blow the lot now, you can slink back to the hotel and forget the whole idea.*

He took a third of what he had, $120, and threw it on Red.

The croupier called the drop and the ball bolted round the rim, skipped a few times on the hot coals, and sat on Black 26. It was over so quickly he had no time to react.

He dropped his remaining chips onto Black. The ball sped round the wheel's rim again, tapped at the slots, and settled on Black 2. The croupier slid a stack of chips at him, his winnings. He had doubled the bet.

The pear martini was evidently not sexist. It began to trickle into the byways of his brain. With a lurch of excitement he pushed the entire stack back onto Black. The ball took forever to settle, and when it did, sat snug in Black 10. His bet returned, multiplied, and after a brief battle of wills, he retrieved it and returned, bankroll in hand, to the table by the bar.

He took his old stool, and sat observing the game, now conscious of trying to look uninterested. The shoe in play finished and was reshuffled, and the dealer chewed through another without it moving far from balance. But on the third it dove fast and soon sat on the table like an immovable little Buddha, offering its cards with the promise of plenty.

Rasputin opted in.

He wore a nervous smile, but the croupier had apparently forgotten his earlier gaffe and returned the smile.

His first hand was Jack/8. The dealer dealt himself 6/9, hit again, and was busted by the Queen of Spades. In under a minute, Rasputin had won his first hand, a whole $5.

The only other player still at the table was the man with capacious nasal passages. He slouched so low he might have been eyeing a putting green. Rasputin needed no mental magic to weigh his fortunes.

The win became a run and Rasputin was beginning to feel untouchable when reality bit into his winnings, and then began gnawing on his bankroll. Three hours later, having jumped in and out of the game as much as he thought he could without drawing suspicion, he was back on par.

He excused himself in disgust and emptied his remaining credit into another shot glass.

I'd make more flipping burgers.

His gaze roamed the floor while he sipped the liquor. When the glass was drained he squinted through its bottom at a kaleidoscope of colour like a sailor with a protuberant monocle. The liquor held the room at bay, but his stomach had begun to churn with rumour. Had he been sober, he would have recognised the signs of impending mutiny.

He wandered unsteadily past the roulette wheel, conscious of having passed it earlier with about the same amount of chips. He kept walking.

On reaching a row of one-armed bandits, he paused to watch their electronic tumblers spin, but had to look away when a wave of nausea swept over him. He waded on into the calmer atmosphere of the poker room, slumped onto a stool and rested.

Nearby a game of Texas Hold'em was in high dudgeon. Another table hosted a game of 7-stud. A handful of spectators cradled drinks and commented on the play. He knew he couldn't count either game. Both were played from a single deck. He relaxed and waited to feel at home again in his own flesh, steeping in the room's hum.

Consequently he didn't recognise the synaethesic sensation when it returned. It tugged at him like he needed to pee, and he had risen to search for a toilet before it occurred to him what it was.

He sat again, brow furrowed, and concentrated on the 7-stud game. The first of three cards, 3rd street, was dispensed in a fresh round, making two down and two up for each player. As the bets began to fall, he felt the familiar flutter of heft. He hunted for the source.

He found it, not in the cards, but the *players*.

Another card was dealt face up to each player, 4th street, and again for 5th and 6th. Bets fell on each, getting heavier as the dealing progressed. It was as the last card, the eponymous 7th, was dealt, and the final bets were placed, that he had a disconcerting sense of inversion: the amply-proportioned blonde festooned with gold jewellery felt light as a feather; the wiry man sporting handlebar moustaches and a zirconium-inset ring felt heavy as a whale.

This tangible sense of two strangers disturbed Rasputin. Beyond that, he wondered if he had finally split the bag and spilled his marbles.

The hands were sprung. Goldilocks won big, Handlebars picked his teeth, and the feeling of weight all but evaporated from every player.

Rasputin ran his hands through his hair and rallied his spirits. By nature, he wanted to investigate, to uncover the why of it. But it was late. He was tired, tipsy, and queasy. He had also just witnessed the lady rake in over $300 in three minutes.

He bought into the game.

The first round came and went without any unusual sensation. He kept his head down, and folded in the 4th on fish food. Another hand passed, and he was beginning to wonder whether he had wasted more money when, on the fall of 3rd street, Handlebars' stocks plummeted. The sensation was much stronger now, charged by his investment in the game. He turned over his card, the Ace of Diamonds, and Handlebars and Goldilocks both gained fifty pounds. The fourth player, a quiet, elderly gentleman in a grey, Sunday-best suit conservatively folded.

Rasputin tossed chips onto the table, upping the ante. The others followed. 6th and 7th cards fell, bets were placed, and Rasputin felt as if he were a sideshow strongman lifting a barbell of human flesh, Goldilocks and Handlebars each to a side. He bet everything. Goldilocks folded, and Handlebars saw him.

With the slightest tremor in his hand, Rasputin flipped over his hidden cards, which included the Kings of Spades and Hearts. They made, together with those already exposed, three of a kind, Ace high. Handlebars grimaced, scratched at his gingery two-day growth, then flipped his cards. He had called what he thought was Rasputin's bluff on two pair.

"You're in the game, young blood."

And so he was, to the tune of $500.

On cue, Radio Rasputin aired Kenny Rogers' Gambler. But the chips he clawed to his chest sure felt real, and eminently countable.

As the game continued he gave his gut the reins. He lost on occasion, but more often got it right. At the back of his mind he chewed over how this new mode of intuition worked, and bit by bit the answers came.

He was still mining probability, but this was a much more lucrative lode. Unlike blackjack, 7-stud rounds draw from a single pack, which renders card profiling pointless. But there is one complex of information that accumulates with time: the profile of a *player*. Perhaps he registered nuances of posture and expression, but that wasn't necessary. Each new card evoked a response from every player, fold or bet, and if betting, the amount. Each card supplied another piece of data, dependent on the preceding cards and those of the other players. Each of the five sequences of a 7-stud hand added a quantum of information, a piece of profile, a datum of behaviour, with which to judge a player's position. All this accumulated like blocks in a tower. The trick was to predict who was building on shaky foundations.

He was playing a guessing game, but with guesses that acquired the robustness of statistical estimates as evidence accrued, just as card-counting blackjack revealed the contours of the remaining cards. But this estimate was further warped by the players' varying skill, emotion, fatigue, and blood alcohol level—and, unlike the dealer, the players couldn't get fired if they failed to follow House rules.

Comps started flowing after he won his eleventh round, halting his dangerous slide toward sobriety. But, even drunk, he could see the limiting factor at the table was Goldilocks. She knew what she was doing, more than Handlebars at any rate. She brooded over the largest stash of chips. Everyone struck good hands, but she nurtured them best. So Rasputin concentrated on her, and when she faltered, he struck.

And his winnings mounted.

"Youngblood's a shark," Handlebars said sourly. The more he lost, the more he talked. Rasputin wondered if the man was trying to break his concentration. *Good luck. I'm not.*

When the penny finally dropped for Goldilocks, she surveyed her reduced pile of chips and excused herself with a tight smile. She was replaced by a young guy in a slick suit. Thereafter, Rasputin and Handlebars shared his wealth, until he too left, leaving Rasputin to clean Handlebars out.

When Rasputin took his last chips, the man muttered, "Swings and roundabouts," and stalked out of the room. He didn't return to the table.

That left only Old Joe at the table, but Rasputin didn't have the heart to take his money. Joe had spent most of the night practicing his folding technique. Taking money from him would be like pulling splinters: tedious and painful for embarrassingly small results.

Rasputin rose, stretched, and knew the time to be just past three in the morning. A glance around the room confirmed there were plenty more punters overly burdened with cash. He had cleared his debt. Time to firm up on permanent studenthood. He secured his chips and went hunting for the toilet.

He exited the games room into a small foyer, where he spotted a toilet sign, and walked smack into Jordy.

Rasputin rocked back on his heels and smiled.

"Monk!" said Jordy. "What in God's name are you doing here? It's the middle of the night, and—" He wrinkled his nose. "You're drunk."

"As a skunk, and rich as a finch," Rasputin slurred, then paused to consider. "I said 'finch' 'cause it rhymes with rich, but it doesn't actually."

"What happened at the audition?" said Jordy. "That's why we're here, remember?" He jammed one hand in a pocket, and glanced over Rasputin's shoulder into the room as he spoke. He moderated his tone and said, "We were supposed to meet in the foyer. I tried talking to the staff but they didn't want a bar of me. Only a girl, said you'd gone off pissed."

"Master plan had a flaw," said Rasputin.

"I'm listening."

"They accused me of cheating."

"Cheating," Jordy said flatly. Rasputin couldn't tell whether he didn't believe him or them.

"Deceit. Turpitude. Improbity. Villainy. Perfidy. They said I'm a naughty boy."

Jordy took a moment to process this, then visibly relaxed. He sighed.

"You're drunk."

"As a skunk."

"Hang on." A glint leapt into Jordy's eye. "You said rich."

"Long story short: crime does in fact pay."

"What?" Jordy looked troubled.

"True story. It pays. Tax free stipend. Actually, that's crap. The part about crime. At least, I don't think it's illegal. Unless maybe you need a warrant to carry," he fingered his temple. "Warning: packing three pounds of hot grey matter. *Caveat Gamblor.* Like having to say on your car license that you need glasses. Except the opposite. Would Superman have to carry a warrant for laser vision? Like those warning stickers on DVD players, 'Class 1 Laser Superhero.' Or X-ray vision. You could get into a lot of trouble with X-ray vision."

Jordy's lids had lowered, and he said, "In English, Monk. Please." So Rasputin hefted the bag of chips in front of his face.

"How?"

"Not sure exactly. Not card-counting blackjack." Jordy waited for him to go on. Curiosity had beaten out all contenders. "7-stud. Turns out the thing that's better than card-counting is chap-counting. Chaps and chappesses."

Jordy levelled his gaze. "Monk, I can't tell whether you're serious or it's the booze talking. Can you give me a straight answer?" Jordy leaned against the wall and Rasputin followed suit, moving a little way down the corridor.

He held the chip bag up again and shook it a couple of times.

"What've you got?"

"Over twelve grand."

Jordy sprung off the wall.

"Then let's get out of here before you blow it."

"Listen," said Rasputin. He frowned and squared-off to Jordy. "You dragged me over here, and I'm the one copping the abuse. Now I should run home just when things are picking up?"

Jordy raised a conciliatory hand, but he kept on, "No way. You were right. This is the money train, and I didn't come all this way to get off at the first stop."

He strode the length of the hall as best he could and beat open the toilet door. When he reappeared a minute later, Jordy was gone.

He returned to the game room, but at least one of Jordy's shots had hit home. He got off the booze. A storm was well and truly brewing in his bowels, and Jordy's anger, which was so rare, had been a slap in the face.

But he was still determined to milk every last drop from the night. He began to prowl around the tables, stopping now and then to observe, hunting for plump targets. (Being mobile also staunched the flow of comps.) He avoided the weekend gamblers and tracked the fat cats, a modern day Robin Hood. The ideal table had two or three players, and although these tables had smaller stakes, the bleed-in on statistics, the time it took to bootstrap his mental machinery, was shorter. His stocks went two steps up for every one down like a good day on Wall Street. He just hoped to quit before the crash.

When it came, it was not so much a crash as a freeze on the exchange. Two black-clad bouncers, each with a worm-like earpiece affixed, approached him and asked for a word. He thought they meant to offer him a perk, maybe an invite to the high-stakes room or a plush suite. Instead, one bouncer politely informed him to cash his chips and leave.

He couldn't believe it. He almost laughed.

"Why?" he said.

"Card counting blackjack."

He didn't ask how they knew. They probably had software to detect suspicious activity. He was so green the pit boss probably spotted it. Fine. But it wasn't cheating. He got angry, but when the bouncer said he could leave without his winnings if he preferred, his temperature dropped from equatorial to arctic. He suspected that wasn't legal, but he wasn't going to risk it.

His two new friends escorted him out of the room, without stopping at the cashier, but he didn't protest. His thoughts were forming too slowly. He was drunk enough to be tipsy until dawn. When they walked past the lifts, fear spiked his belly. By the time they were handling him across the threshold of the heavy fire door they had given up any pretense of politeness.

They stood on a landing alone. Grey concrete stairs folded out of view above and below. One bouncer remained at the door. The other turned to Rasputin and said, "Just so you remember," and punched him deeply, deliberately, in the gut. They left before his cane slapped onto the naked concrete and sent echoes bounding up and down the stairwell.

He had never been punched by a grown man before. In place of his stomach, there was a stone of granite. It sat sucking his breath away, like a cloth soaking up water, gathering pain latent in the surrounding organs. He gasped, finally, and fell to his knees.

Senseless from pain lancing through the drink-haze, he grasped his cane with one fumbling hand, and the railing with the other, and began inching his way down. He didn't dare walk back onto the floor. Everyone would stare. No, he would gather his breath and cash his chips on a floor below.

He reached the first floor with a carpark exit, a black hole cut into the stark interior of the stairwell. He had just pivoted to descend the next flight when he heard a footfall behind him.

A hand gripped his shoulder and slung him around. A fist smashed into his face.

Time compressed beneath the force of the blow. The world broke into pieces. Sense came in juddering packets.

He lay on the concrete landing. Words hung in the air, whispered in echo: "Swings and roundabouts."

He heard footsteps. A figure emerged from the car park's gloom. It was the boy who had caused his accident, his first assailant. He was crouched over him, shouting something.

—No, he was confused. It was Jordy.

The boy again.

He took the opportunity before it was lost. He slugged the kid full in the face.

And then he was seated on the cool concrete. Jordy sat opposite him, leaning on the guard rail. He was holding his nose. Blood had streamed down and arched around his mouth. Someone offered Jordy a cloth.

Rasputin patted his pocket that had bulged with chips. Empty. The money train had left.

A day later, when Dee arrived at the airport, she found them sitting forlornly in the arrival lounge, sporting complementary shiners. It was the second time in as many months she was struck speechless.

6.

CAIN

Sixty years. Just look at me. Some beauty sleep.

When, all those years ago, I lay down to sleep, I did so secure in the knowledge of careful preparation. I had spent many Deutschmarks of the Schürmann fortune stocking Europe against our future needs—mine and my brother's. Safe houses, ciphers, food and marks. All connected in links guarded by redundancy, and obscured by cut-outs. I secured silence with the carrot of vast wealth, and the whip of certain, slow and sticky death.

Sleep took me, I confess, feeling rather self-satisfied.

But when I woke and stumbled from Central Park to be struck dumb by New York's glitter and speed, I knew my plan had developed a nasty kink. I had counted on the need to thaw my network after sleep. I had not counted on that sleep being so long. Thawing the cold of death doesn't yield much but stinking corpses.

But the same years that had eaten away my provision had given me another. A *different* kind of network.

To my rescue: the Internet. TV taught me about that too.

With the Internet's help, the world was delegate, awaiting my typed instruction. I set about learning how to invoke that power. How to find information, people, and—once found—how to command them.

But first I needed money. Enough to cast into the furnaces of mens' desires.

The Internet passed this first and crucial test. A password and account number sufficed to connect me with some of the wealth of France and Belgium I hid following the invasion. Time and interest had been kind to me, and while I was forever cut-off from the wealth of my family, my nest egg proved sufficient.

To lay hands on that money, though, I needed an American bank account. And for that, I needed another identity. My bass-playing mask had become noisome, as had the hotel in Hell's Kitchen.

So I went collecting. I got 'upwardly mobile', I believe the phrase is. I searched for single men in well-to-do apartment blocks, where neighbours didn't seem to notice, much less care about, each other. (One such apartment was near the Metropolitan Museum, where I had lain all those years gathering dust. I spent many a philosophic spell gazing along Fifth Avenue through the bulging canopies of its trees at the steps of the museum.) I particularly hunted men with a near resemblance to me—the more easily to *change* to and between.

Before long I had assembled a small deck of identities with which to enter the game proper. Passports, driving licences, payslips, everything I needed to become Bank of America's newest customer. I opened an account and wired in enough cash to requisition myself, put out feelers, and, ultimately, travel.

All the while, my education continued. I consider myself a life-long learner, but the abrupt, dark epoch I had just exited contained sixty years of missed frivolity and foment. While I slept, nations died and were born. Some were even resurrected from Europe's well-trod earth. These had lain, the unquiet dead of old wars, like vast golems of earth, river and forest, and been beckoned into life again by a latent vitality.

Nationality had never much fussed *the Imago,* but it was vital I be aware of any ethnic tensions that might have grown in my absence.

The war of ideologies too had had its winners and losers. National Socialism, clearly, had been a casualty. And so, I guessed, had Fascism. But what of the Bolsheviks? Which ideas were vogue? Which had been forever repudiated?

This might all sound esoteric for a man of my, clearly, *operational* gifts, but I needed to know which questions would put me beyond the pale in drawing rooms, which beneath bridges. Besides, I am an artist, and Art is handmaiden to Philosophy.

And Technology is the cannon of Science. As my education continued, I was besotted by one technology: the cell phone, which enabled instant communication between two people located on opposite sides of the globe. Marvellous!

To put that achievement in perspective, I recall my grandfather's story of Reuters filling an eighty-mile gap in the telegraph line connecting Paris to Berlin with carrier pigeons. Those pigeons carried stock prices. Today Reuters keeps gate on the world's news. And for the cream, make the cell phone carrier of the Internet. This is the apogee of technology—*inorganic* technology, at least.

I wanted to leave New York. Not that I had a concrete plan. I felt uneasy. Perhaps it was something to do with having been freighted there while asleep, my rest interrupted. Perhaps that was why I slept so very long.

In my fertile mind, prospects opened like the petals of a flower, vast and multi-hued. Again I had to impose the military discipline of priority. At the top of my list were what I thought to be two distinct items, which time proved to be one: my brother, and *The Imago*. You yourself were instrumental in me realising that. Doesn't life weave a funny web?

Before I left New York I visited the museum. I was curious to know what its staff had made of my disappearance, but more so, what had happened to my *dweoming* mate, my brother. Dead or alive, he was unfinished business.

I cornered an attractive young archivist and plied the stolen charm of my upstate New Yorker. She had jet black hair with a gloss like lacquer, and the most creamy skin stretched over the tendons forming the hollow at the base of her throat. From the hitch in her breath, and the way she feigned not hearing me to lean close, I knew she was mine if I wanted her. Mine like the truffle I'd eaten that afternoon at San Domenico.

She took me back into the archival rooms, which were dark and dry, and much like tombs. We passed shelves of Near Eastern pottery and coins and she told me well-worn anecdotes. While I listened to her, I rehearsed her form in my mind, in case her identity accrued value; I was always driving myself to become the perfect chameleon.

When I judged the time ripe, I enquired of the "stolen piece".

"Stolen?" she said.

"Yes, only weeks ago. A terrible loss, by all accounts."

The first hint of suspicion crept into her eyes as she said, "Whose accounts? Our insurance provider has a four week embargo on press about any theft while it conducts initial investigations."

That was a new one on me. It forced me to think a little harder.

"Ms Rawley," I said, "I was part of the team that rediscovered that artefact. Would *you* not keep a close eye on your baby?" And I proceeded to tell her what I had already learned of how 'the artefact' came to be transported across the Atlantic some sixty years prior on a US Army Liberty ship returning from the Second World War, to be dumped and forgotten in a warehouse of the Pennsylvania State Museum, then rediscovered in the new millennium, donated to the Metropolitan Museum, and promptly re-forgotten and left to rot in one of its many archival rooms.

The explanation seemed to satisfy her.

She showed me the shreds of part-petrified flesh I had torn from myself on waking. My memory of the pain was like a ghost in the room. The rags of desiccated flesh had already been re-archived in a plastic box, to await a scholar's opinion—decreasing in priority in proportion to their diminished mass.

The museum had lost the artefact without ever having taken the trouble to determine what on earth it was.

She gave me her theory about the stolen artefact: an aborted mummification. I had been so inconsequential, apparently, they had not even bothered to carbon date me. She lamented the vandalism and theft.

Her emotion moved me. I was tempted to tell her the secret, that there before her in the flesh I was—me!—not some object clouded by time and subject only to the groping speculation of archaeologists, but the best of man, a divine object.

Thinking of my brother I asked if the other artefact had also been 'stolen' or simply moved. But my question met with confusion. I left the museum, too pre-occupied to take up her unspoken invitation.

I learned later that my brother perished when the Allies made it into the Alps, as far as the ancestral home of the Schürmanns. Bombardment breached an aquifer that then emptied into the castle's basement, where we lay side by side in stillness. My butler managed to save me only. My brother drowned in his slumber mere feet from me. I wonder if he dreamed of water.

Deep down I think I knew he was dead. Had known since I'd awoken days before, in pain and confusion. But the news still came as a shock. I dropped my guard. That was when I got my fingers burnt the first time.

I was rotating through my guises for security, and returned to my favourite den, an apartment on Fifth Ave opposite Central Park. I was peeling off a collared shirt, longing to soak in the apartment's colossal bath, when in the bedroom I stumbled on the scene of a murder.

The man whose identity I now wore had owned a beagle. To be honest, it was the dog that had inclined me to him. He wasn't that near a resemblance, and it cost me noticeably more to shift to him than any of the others. It was the beagle I found splayed in vivisection on the bed atop a two-foot rose of blood. Its still-slick jaws were clamped on a note.

It read: *Wilkommen.* Welcome back.

No doubt the dog had been butchered by a nobody. I was angry about that. I also knew the method was par for the Imago. Their chains of communication have layers of cut-outs. I vowed to slaughter the next *dog* they sent across my path. Not that the messenger would have any idea of what the message meant. But then, neither had the beagle.

How did they know I had awoken? Perhaps they had posted a watch on the museums, a sixty-year watch. Quite an investment. That would explain not only how they knew I'd returned, but that I had assumed the power of shape-shifter.

What was still dark to me—and the thing I feared—was that they might have discovered I had not only known what I would become, but had actively *effected* it. That ranks with the most expensive secrets the world has ever known. The Imago don't like secrets they don't own.

So that left me with a dead dog and a blood-stained sheet. My fingers were burnt. I had two choices: flee the fire, or put it out.

You can't run from the Imago.

So I left for Newark Airport that night, stopping only at an apartment block on Staten Island to locate and assume a new identity. From there I headed for Europe and its story-saturated soil.

7.

PURITANS

Knots occur in unlikely places, from the feet-thick ropes that moor super-tankers with bulges like giant ganglions, to the microscopic, sub-cellular tangles of DNA strands.

Knots can snap a man's neck on the gallows and stifle the blood in an umbilical cord, or tether a space-walker against the sucking infinitude of space.

Knots can mean life or death.

Rasputin was seated, bent over his knees, peering at a stubborn knot in his shoelace. He had merely meant to undo it, shake a pebble loose, and retie the knot. But he had yanked the wrong bulge, become angry, pulled harder, and made it worse. How was it possible to obfuscate so simple a structure?

He twisted to retrieve his knife from his jeans pocket. He hefted it a few times. It was heavy and cool, its handle inlaid with a pearlescent white substance. He had never fancied himself a pocket-knife carrier, but had picked it up on reflex with his keys.

He flicked it open, and dug the knife's point under a tight loop of shoelace, half-hoping it sliced the lace in two. The Gordian solution had a brutal elegance.

Instead, the knot came loose. He levered his shoe off, shook the pebble free, and retied the knot.

He leaned back into the bench and took a draught of the view. A swath of grass sloped down to the foreshore, and beyond it an ebb-tide was dragging the river seaward. The gumtrees overhead were silent in the pre-dawn lull. The sun was beginning to leach the deep-purple to orange above the buildings silhouetted on the far bank.

He watched a flight of pelicans as they sailed like avian cruise liners and disappeared beneath Shelley bridge. Beneath it fishermen plied the dark water and perhaps the pelicans were after their rubbish fish.

With a sigh, Rasputin returned his gaze to the water lapping near his feet. He folded the knife blade until it snapped shut and put it back in his pocket. From the same pocket he retrieved a piece of paper and gently unfolded it. The sun shone through it like a candle, and suffused the portrait he had sketched on a Melbourne balcony with a warm glow. He propped his elbows on his knees and stared at the girl's face, allowing his awareness to sink inward.

The memory came like a crate bobbing in the sea, legacy of an old shipwreck, stained from years adrift, and sealed.

He pried its lid.

An azure sky teemed with gulls, wheeling and crying like a market of lunatic hawkers. Laughter drew his attention, and he saw *her*.

She ran past him, and he turned on stubby three-year-old legs to watch her pass. She glanced over her shoulder and smiled. He had seen it before. Groundhog day. It still punched a hole through his heart.

Then she spoke—a crack opened. *There is more here.*

"Come on, Tintin."

Tintin: her name for him. Something utterly new, something always known.

Hope flared and sent him scrabbling after this new scrap, yearning for more. He clutched at the memory, and it wriggled from his fingers as if scared of the pressure, a slippery fish.

The world began to spin around him, Rasputin the pivot. A scream tore the air, but he was already backing out of the memory, letting it fade, knowing he would get nothing more.

A zephyr caressed his cheek and he awoke fully to the world. The portrait still lay in his lap. The pretty face gazed back at him.

"She called me Tintin."

"She's beautiful. Who is she?"

Rasputin didn't start. Perhaps as Dee had come near he had sensed the breeze curl around her.

He folded the portrait and slipped it back into his pocket, beneath the knife. He stood and stretched at the band of tightness running down his back.

"I make it 7:32," he said.

"You missed your follow-up with Thorpe yesterday," she said.

He shrugged.

"He called me," she said.

He waited for her to go on, and when she didn't, he lifted his cane and began to stump toward the bridge. Rush hour traffic hummed like the mingling crash of breaking ocean swells, without being relaxing. Cars thumped on the bridge's expansion plates like distant artillery.

They walked without speaking while he fancied her mind made a dozen false starts, until at last:

"If it's the money—" she began but stopped.

It piqued his interest. Dee was disturbed, and it went beyond the M word.

"If it's the money," she said, "he asked me—begged me—to tell you he'll waive it. He promised to handle your debt too."

He stopped and squared up to her. "Why would he do that?"

"Why are you being so pig-headed?"

Anger, finally.

"This is serious, Monk. Look at you." Her eyebrows drew down and he felt the weight of her gaze. She didn't even look at his cane.

He decided he didn't want to know what had her worked up, but had to ask. "Okay. I'll play. What's the catch?"

"Catch?" she said. Then, quietly, "You're the catch."

She stepped into the gloom beneath the bridge. He followed her. Without verbal agreement, they halted near the first fisherman.

She continued in a whisper, "He didn't say it, exactly, but he's interested in your case, in you. He wants to study you."

"What does that mean, precisely?"

He saw her shrug in the gloom.

"But he'll take care of the money? All of it?" he said.

She nodded.

He stumped down the bank toward the angler, leaving Dee to merge with the darkness. The tide had left a lip of sand, which crumbled under his foot. He staggered and caught himself on his cane. The man turned at the sound and gave him a curt nod.

Rasputin peered into the bucket by the man's tackle box. Three small whiting floated in an inch of bloody water.

"Why do you break their necks," Rasputin said.

The beanied head of the man didn't turn. He said, "Better for the fish. Better eating. Doesn't stress them so much."

Yeah, thought Rasputin, they look pretty happy.

The sun's heat was beginning to reach through Rasputin's t-shirt to his back when he and Dee walked away from the river. He was perspiring by the time they had travelled the couple of hundred meters to his door. Sweat cooled his arm as he swapped his cane to his left hand, retrieved his keys, and opened the door.

Dee said goodbye from the front step. He closed the door until only a strip of her face showed through the crack, her expression unreadable.

He paused, gathered breath, and said, "She is ... she *was* my sister." He closed the door before she could respond.

Sitting in curtain-wrought darkness, he brooded on Dee's message from Thorpe, while visions of fish floated about the ceiling, their heads flopping on slivers of flesh.

At noon the clock on the lounge room wall chimed. The sound was fake, from a speaker. It buzzed as the volume stepped down in stages rather than fading like the real thing. It pried him from the couch.

He called Thorpe's room and found the receptionist to be almost obscenely eager to reschedule his appointment to that afternoon. She informed him a taxi would pick him up at 1:10. It was all taken care of.

At 1:37 he sat alone in a waiting room, acutely aware that he was hunched over, arms crossed, fingers tucked into fists—the postural equivalent of Defcon 5. No one came in or went out. A speaker embedded in the ceiling was piping in an easy listening station. Dire Straits were playing Sultans of Swing, and Rasputin willed the sweet, rolling licks to enter his body and relax his muscles. Nothing doing. Fleetwood Mac was no better, and when the song finished, the announcer called the time at 1:45.

"Professor Thorpe will see you now," said the receptionist, prompted by no signal Rasputin had seen. Perhaps it was a telepathic practice.

Rasputin found Thorpe seated behind a desk that ran the width of the room. It was a large room, yet Thorpe looked in proportion behind that desk. His chair was at a tilt, and his hands were locked behind his head. He sat as if in a dream, gazing at the ceiling.

He straightened abruptly, and rose from the chair in one motion, and skirted the desk to where Rasputin stood. Thorpe raised both hands, leaving Rasputin's right hand hovering in the space between them. The surgeon's hands locked over Rasputin's head like a cage, and drew it under his gaze. A faint odour clung to the man's skin, thin like the atmosphere of a dying planet. Rasputin wondered if it was cologne or surgical swab.

The hand-cage tilted his head one way then the other, focussing, Rasputin realised, on the surgery site. Only when he had satisfied himself, apparently, did he take Rasputin's hand, which had hung in the air forgotten.

"Your scar is healing beautifully," he said, and sat in one of two chairs arranged for patients. Rasputin took the other. Thorpe leaned forward, hands on knees, and smiled.

"I am glad you have decided to observe your follow-up regimen. It is wise. It would be silly for a little money to get in the way of something so important as your health."

Rasputin sifted his thoughts. Half his nerves stemmed from a fear he would have to pretend to be whatever it was Thorpe was looking for. *Cut to the chase, then. Let's see how many hubcaps fly off this sucker.*

"What's the deal?"

Thorpe's eyebrows shot up, but he responded smoothly. "I will handle your bill, and provide pro-bono everything needful for your rehabilitation—physiotherapy, neurologic assessment, and access to this country's finest neurosurgeon."

No prize for guessing who that was, but Rasputin was tempted to ask. Instead he said, "What am I chipping in to this deal?"

"Nothing significant. Simply your brain."

"I was hoping a few urine samples would do it."

"I can see the humour," Thorpe said, leaning further forward over his knees, great joints that even through his suit pants were chiseled like a statue of Zeus. "But the reason you are here, the reason for this unorthodox arrangement, is my grave concern for your health. Yet you do not seem to grasp the gravity of your predicament.

"I spoke to your girlfriend—" Thorpe said.

"She's not my girlfriend."

"Excuse me. When I spoke to your lady friend, my concerns grew."

So he had pumped Dee for ammunition. No, not pumped. Tapped, like an oil reservoir.

"You have missed physiotherapy, which I now understand. You are sleeping late—"

"Late's normal for me."

"And getting into fights. Is that normal for you too?"

He let that pass.

Thorpe leaned back and let the silence stretch. Rasputin's gaze hunted the room for something to remark on, to break the mood, but nothing in the cookie-cutter clinic room appeared to belong to Thorpe except the monolithic desk. His search completed a lap of the room and came to rest on the cane angled across his lap.

Thorpe's face twitched as he narrowed his gaze, a movement incongruous with his great frame, like a Lion at cat-play. "Have you heard of ALS? 'Lou Gehrig's' Disease in the vernacular."

Rasputin couldn't help but meet his gaze.

Thorpe steepled his fingers. "It can be triggered by motor neuron death." Rasputin was pinned by the surgeon's gaze. It was watching for any telltale sign of what he was thinking.

"But the hammer can fall months after the trigger has been squeezed. And the bullet comes on slow."

(Impact washes through cerebral matter in shockwaves that temporarily displaces them, as with any fluid or elastic material)

"First sign could be weakness, just plain garden variety lethargy."

(Some of them don't appreciate the ride. They are stretched to breaking point—)

Rasputin inwardly cursed the prescient machine his memory had become. It was spewing facts and he yearned for ignorance.

"Then your tongue might begin having difficulty wrapping itself round words."

(and pop—)

"And before long, you can't swallow."

Rasputin swallowed on reflex, forcing his Adams' Apple down like a tyre-tube in water.

"All comes of secondary biological cascades, you see," Thorpe said, and spread his hands as if the Christmas party committee had been informed the budget would only stretch to finger food. He jabbed a finger toward Rasputin's temple. "Your injury was a smash and grab. But the rest will be the work of a genuine psychopath, and he has you locked up, stretched out and naked, and is in no hurry to decide which morsel of your humanity he will take now and which next: mobility," his hand cut the air, a scalpel strike, "speech, and finally breath."

Thorpe emptied lungs like bellows into the silence and became still.

(Time is all you have now. We'll see if it's your friend or not.)

"This is no hypothetical, Rasputin. I witnessed this case. His name was Reginald Palmer. And the worst of it? To the very end, he was *aware*. He lay there, warm and living by physical indications, but buried alive in his own flesh. We have a clinical name for it: Locked-in-syndrome. The French have a name that captures its essence better: *Maladie de l'emmure vivant*. Walled In, Buried Alive, in his own flesh.

"A French journalist entombed in his own body wrote his memoir by winking each letter. It was called: The Diving Bell and the Butterfly. I'm sure you can discern the metaphor."

Fear ballooned in Rasputin. He had never wanted anything more than to wind back the last few minutes of life, to before this behemoth of a man had spoken, and start over in a world that split from this and knew nothing of any Reginald Palmer.

Then he wanted to laugh. He was the one who had wanted to cut to the chase, little knowing he would end up the burning hulk.

Thorpe had fallen silent and stared with unfocused eyes. He seemed tired. At last he gave the faintest nod as though he knew Rasputin's thoughts exactly.

Rasputin fingered the groove he had carved into his cane. A glint of silver caught his eye. Its source was a triangular nameplate sitting on the desk. It read: Alexander Thorpe, MBBS(Hons), FRAC, PhD. It lay at an angle to the desk's edge. On reflex Rasputin aimed the butt of his cane at it and nudged it straight.

"Why did you become a neurosurgeon?"

The weariness fell from Thorpe's face like a sheet unveiling a sculptor's masterpiece. He rose, leaving his chair spinning with imparted momentum, and bent his head in thought. He was not, Rasputin thought, searching for an answer—he lived and breathed the answer. His problem was where to begin.

Abruptly he rounded on Rasputin and said, "We should take a drive."

"I've got nothing better to do." It was true.

They left Thorpe's office at Rasputin's top speed. Thorpe told the receptionist to cancel the remaining appointments as though it were the easiest thing in the world. (Rasputin imagined the *ka-ching* of a cash register coughing out a $1,000 refund.) The receptionist appeared confused, and Rasputin was struck by the intuition she had already been told to clear the afternoon. He was sure of it.

Minutes later Thorpe threw his Jaguar onto the freeway on-ramp with little regard for its gold-plated suspension, but his face registered detachment not joy. His mind seemed elsewhere as the car growled up to 100kph with a pulse of the throttle.

They crossed a tributary of the Swan river on the Mt. Henry Bridge. The freeway was clear. Noise flowing off the Jaguar bounded back from concrete walls in weird patterns, tinny and melodic, as though the radio had tuned an alien channel. The car ate the distance to the CBD with ease. On their left, a vista of the bay unfurled. It was littered with yachts, which from the car's low elevation appeared bunched into dangerous clots. Ahead loomed the green buttress of King's Park, and opposite it Perth's skyline.

Thorpe's grimness fell away with the miles, but Rasputin knew he was not joy riding. Surfacing in the surgeon's posture was eagerness to be somewhere. Rasputin wished he knew where that somewhere was.

Rasputin recalled the handful of times he had been driven blind. His brain offered a billion-faceted breakdown of the experiences, but it needn't have bothered. One statistic spoke to his need: all bar one had ended badly. The exception had occurred one time he lanced his hand on a knife. His father's idea of first-aid had been to drive him to a McDonald's for ice-cream. He suspected Thorpe was not going to buy him ice-cream.

They exited the freeway left onto Mounts Bay road, a thin strip of asphalt frowned over by the steep, rocky bluff of King's Park on one side, and threatened by the hungry lapping of the bay on the other. Rasputin felt doubly enclosed by land and sea as the Jaguar hugged the bluff's skirt.

When they emerged from the bluff's gloom, the view broke open, and Rasputin knew at once their destination. The tower of Winthrop Hall poked squat like a Norman keep above trees bordering the University of Western Australia, his university, and home of the Bletchley Chair in Neuroscience, a chair that strained beneath the weight of the man behind the wheel.

Rasputin had asked him why he had become a neurosurgeon. The answer, apparently, lay not in a clinic room, but in the halls of academia.

The fat, green, wobbling back of a bus expanded as Thorpe closed to within feet of it. It was familiar to Rasputin. He had known the route's timetable by heart even before the accident. It would trundle through the traffic lights, pull over, and disgorge a clot of students. His life had moved to that deep rhythm for years.

Thorpe swung the car left and circled the campus, past the curve of Matilda Bay, arcing around the back of the campus. A minute later he manoeuvred the Jaguar onto a one-way lane bordered by masses of shrubs, and drove under an arch and into an alcove formed by the complicated backside of a building. Rasputin didn't recognise the place, and was struck by the idiotic thought he had been abducted by Batman.

The back entrance to the building was barred by a stout wooden door. It had been retrofitted with an electronic lock. Thorpe swept a card through a slot and held the door open for Rasputin, waiting as he took the steps one at a time down to the small landing.

Air from the old building funneled through the doorway. Rasputin caught a whiff of age-browned paper and cold tiles and urinal cake: a familiar *parfum*.

Thorpe shut the door, and strode into the gloom with an ease born of habit. Rasputin waited, propped on his cane, while his pupils dilated. A hall emerged grudgingly from the gloom. Its walls were a gallery of posters, some faded by age, containing more Latin than English, depicting fuzzy tri-colour cross-sections of what Rasputin guessed were brain scans. Each poster bore the impress of the Department of Neuroscience, and many listed a Dr. Thorpe among their contributing authors. One poster his eye happened across was a mere three years old. It credited two authors: a Scott McIntyre and the Professor A. Thorpe. The work was titled: Analysis of the motility rates of skull-anchored 50nm micro-electrodes in ambulatory patients. It was English, but might as well have been Latin.

Thorpe disappeared up a flight of stairs, leaving Rasputin to stump over to the lift. He punched the call button with the butt of his cane and waited.

He rode the lift to the only floor above and disembarked into a hallway that was a copy of the one below but for the different posters that wallpapered it. A door was ajar partway along the hallway, spilling light in angled shards across the floor and up the opposing wall. Rasputin drew level with it, took a deliberate breath, and entered.

His first impression of the surgeon's office was of the sheer weight of clutter—the absolute antithesis of the spartan clinic room. But before he had a chance to analyse this brute impression of filled space, to resolve it into ground and figure, a lower part of his mind yanked his attention toward an object that Thorpe threw at his face.

His free hand flew upward. Something slapped into his palm, jolting his hand backwards as it absorbed the thing's momentum. He opened his fingers to reveal a ball of waxy substance.

"What the hell?" said Rasputin, as the insult registered.

"Your reflexes are shipshape, which is good. But your tongue is what my mother would call a loose rudder."

"And what does she call a guy who takes cheap shots," said Rasputin, and wound his arm back to return the ball with change.

"Uh, uh." Thorpe shook his finger in a stalling gesture. Even so, Rasputin marked the way the man's knees shifted his centre of mass lower, and he doubted he would be able to strike him, despite being so close.

"Calm down. I was quite sure you would make the catch, and worst case, it's really quite soft. Take a look."

Rasputin did. There wasn't much to look at. As he had suspected, it was some kind of wax. It had probably been white once, but was now dappled shades of grey from dust and the oil of hands that had worked it.

"You asked me why I became a neurosurgeon. Well, I am that, and more. There are two breeds that study the brain: neurosurgeons, who are surgeons first, and then specialise; and neurologists, the armchair philosophers of the brain. But I took the road less travelled. I'm that rare bird who is both at once. I first became interested in the brain, and only later became a surgeon, out of necessity. I am like Henry Morton Stanley, who was not content to ponder maps of Africa and talk of Livingstone, but was compelled to toil in the continent's heart in order to shake his hand, and search for the Nile's source.

"That wax you hold there had a part in my story."

Rasputin examined it again, but gained no further insight into its significance. The urge to pelt it still lingered in his arm.

"Surely you can see that you hold in your hand a memory."

A memory – the utterance made him want to laugh. The very notion of being able to hold a single memory seemed each day to slip further into the realm of nostalgia. Memory was *supposed* to come in episodes, wasn't it? And those episodes your mind chose to keep were supposed to be the stuff of daily life that jutted out—from pain or joy or novelty—like a grown man pelting you with a ball of wax. That was novel, and might have ended in pain but for his reflexes (which, truth to tell, he was inwardly all warm about because they were firing nicely). But his memory machine didn't seem to care for episodes anymore. It operated instead on the packrat's philosophy of why chuck it if it might be useful some day.

He felt like saying, 'Yeah, I see this thing in my hand. But you know what else? I haven't had a good look yet, but I bet I've also got the *entire room* pegged. I could go home right now and put all of your books, the 2129 books on the walls facing me, in reverse alphabetical order. In my head. Or, shit, I could do Dewey decimal, or if Dewey is too American for you, then the Universal Decimal Classification. It was invented by a Belgian named Otlet (*Hello, Information Science elective!*). Or let me just daydream a little and I'll sort this library of yours by the sum of the letters in their titles divided by the number of spanners in a Sidchrome tool set. If I just watch and wait—there!—a little peristaltic movement beneath the currents of my thoughts. Books begin to shed their weight. At any moment they might begin piling off the shelf and swimming through the air. What a machine. Oh my God.'

"Rasputin?"

Rasputin came to himself, realised he was staring at the ball of wax. He glanced at Thorpe, thinking of the train of thought that had just derailed. He had imagined saying it, but dared not. Something was dug in deep and held his mouth shut.

Thorpe spoke again. "That ball of wax has become a memory of your hand."

Rasputin peered at it. The wax had been crushed out of its sphere when his hand tensed. Shadow pooled in grooves where his fingers had been. Even the creases of his palm were imprinted in the wax, coarse trenches made by the muscles that caused his hand to cup, and the gentle arcs of his life and heart lines.

Thorpe watched with eagerness. "You see?"

Rasputin shrugged. "Not much of a memory." He squeezed the deformed ball into a sausage that leaked out either side of his hand. "This stuff makes the tabloids look like a Roman inscription."

He tossed the wax sausage underhand to Thorpe and began threading his way through glass-fronted cabinets and waist-high tables laden with all manner of objects. The room was rectangular, and halfway along its length vestigial stumps of a removed wall faced each other.

Evidently Thorpe's office had consumed an adjacent office to grow to its present size.

But 'office' wasn't quite right—the books and debris made it a hybrid library-museum. He paused to lean on a stone pedestal that supported a bust of something vaguely human. He read the object's caption—*Rujah, frontispiece from the Markaal temple*—and took a nervous step backward. No need to add to his already overblown bill.

Thorpe roamed through the clutter, gaze lost, roving over the collection.

"What's wax got to do with all this?" said Rasputin, burning instead for the answer to what it had to do with his head.

Thorpe looked up from a mechanical device he held. He placed it back on a table, and said, "Nothing, but the power of metaphor."

Great, thought Rasputin, *The more I want from this guy, the more he sounds like an Arts lecturer.*

"When I said that wax is a memory, you dismissed the idea. Rather contemptuously, I might add."

"Sorry. It just seemed, well, low tech. You're a neuro-guru, after all. It would've seemed quaint, but ..."

Thorpe raised an eyebrow, waiting for the rest of the sentence. When it didn't come, he finished it himself: "And I don't seem like a man who does quaint?"

Rasputin closed the distance to the surgeon. Thorpe watched him come, drew breath, and raised a stolid finger.

"What impression did I make on you when we first met? Cast your mind back."

Rasputin knew no simple description for what he had felt the first time in his presence.

Thorpe fired him a quick smile. "Never mind. Keep your impression. But observe that our language is littered with metaphors of memory. *Impression*, for one." Rasputin began to understand. "Ever had something *seared* into your mind? *Etched* indelibly on your memory? Impress, sear, etch: all words that capture the idea of leaving a mark on your memory, like the shape of your hand in that wax."

Thorpe lowered the finger, and thrust it toward Rasputin's chest. "I guarantee you that the great men that strove to understand the mind at the beginning of Western history—Socrates, Plato, Aristotle—did not use this language to be *quaint*. They initiated the greatest quest ever undertaken by man, to understand this three-pound mass of flesh." He jabbed his finger into Rasputin's temple. "To understand how it does what it does."

He swung the finger toward the far wall. "My colleagues of an astronomical persuasion, one building over, get all excited by the discovery of a new galaxy. But I tell you, that's child's play compared to unlocking the secrets of the human brain."

"I wasn't implying it was stupid," said Rasputin. "We stand on the shoulders of giants." He knew. He had written an essay on it.

"Better to say we *pimple* the shoulders of giants. That goes for the great mass of humanity, save a select few."

Thorpe turned his back to Rasputin and began stalking through the room. Rasputin followed as best he could.

"It is a curious fact that when men struggle to conceive of the mind, they reach for the cutting edge of technology for familiar concepts with which to describe it. Hence mud, then wax, take an impression, and 'remember it', after a fashion.

"Following that dawn time, men borrowed other objects from everyday life with which to compare memory. Some pictured it as a cage of timid birds. Into this cage the mind plunges its hand to lay hold of a memory. At times it plucks out the very bird it wants. At others, it snatches a bird of the wrong plume, or merely feathers. And at still others, the hand comes away empty.

"In time people compared memory to subterranean grottos, riddled with dark, twisting tunnels, where experiences were secreted like treasure to reward the questing mind—if it knew the way."

Rasputin was watching his feet as he navigated a chicane in the furniture when the room was plunged into darkness.

"But one easily forgets the way with age. And even maps are of little use if we do not remember where we put them."

Rasputin looked up, startled, but all he saw was the fading afterimage of the cabinet he had been skirting. The darkness was near complete, and into the silence came the throb of the blood coursing in his neck, rising until he felt sure Thorpe would hear it.

Then he saw a faint nimbus of light blossom in Thorpe's hands. It grew and caught the underside of his face, staining it green. The ghostly, unanchored face began to speak again.

"Fast forward to the 16th Century, and this substance"—the green bloom dipped once—"was the cutting edge of technology. Europe was aflame with the quest to turn lead into gold. It was the age of the Alchemists. But not everyone was thrall to their spell. It was not hope of riches that stirred Sir Robert Hooke, protégé of Boyle, when he saw what I am about to show you."

Rasputin could just discern Thorpe dabbing a finger into his palm. The finger floated for a moment, a small green nimbus, a will-o-the-wisp, and then began to write on the wall. The word it wrote was obscured by Thorpe's silhouette, an indistinguishable piece of the room's shadow. When he finished, he stepped away from the wall, and the word appeared whole, glowing green, with a light intense enough to illumine the busts of dead men arrayed along the desk below.

"Domini?" said Rasputin. More Latin.

"Yes, Domini. It means *Rule*. It was the word used by the German, Johann Crafft, to impress Boyle and his compatriots in the Royal Society." He sniffed. "A party trick really."

"This is Phosphor, of course. A philosopher's fire that burns with neither heat nor air. But Hooke immediately saw in this strange substance a new and powerful metaphor for human memory." Thorpe leaned forward and breathed on the glowing word. It dimmed until Rasputin wasn't sure whether it lingered or whether his imagination was being mischievous in the dark. Thorpe continued in a whisper, "For isn't it just like memory to behold the sun at day, and ..." He paused, waiting. Then like a ghost galleon called from the Deep by full moon, it shone again, faint but undeniable: *Domini*. "... call it forth in the mind's eye in the cold of night as one lies in bed?"

Thorpe threw the light switch, with a loud, hollow *clack*. Rasputin jumped, his muscles having grown painfully tense without him realising.

"But the best the Royal Society made of this miracle substance, typically, was to invent a method of producing it that did not require thousands of litres of German urine—which was Crafft's method—so they could parade their discovery around England and boggle the illiterate."

Rasputin said, "I guess that means you really don't want my urine," wondering, not for the first time, at the pivotal place excrement took in all spheres of human endeavour.

"By all means, if you feel compelled to give me a sample, do it. Just not on the rug," said Thorpe, and for the first time they shared belly laughter.

Thorpe moved further into the room. The tour continued. "Alchemy died, ill-begotten son that it was, to be succeeded by the young and energetic stripling *Science*. Which proved very fertile soil for memory matters."

His large hand trailed over the edge of a cabinet. Not a square inch of its sheen was dimmed by dust.

"But let me wrap it up for you quickly," said Thorpe over his shoulder. "I'm boring you, and you have more pressing concerns."

"I'm not bored." The earlier mention of tunnels had reminded him of his first journey into his memory, in search of the preface to Churchill's book. His companion then, the shaggy un-nameable thing, had hunted in the twisting passages of his mind. Hadn't it felt very much like searching for treasure? The attempt to connect half-remembered fragments of sense, follow them like spore to where Churchill's book had been secreted until needed.

Rasputin thought of what had come after that hunt, the sun and the eye. "This history of yours, does it have a telescope?"

Thorpe paused, thrown from his flow. "No telescope exactly, but Hooke—the Hooke of the phosphor—did elaborate a view of the memory as planets in array, illumined by the sun of the mind's attention. In his model, remembering was like the sun's light striking distant planets, and forgetting happened when that light failed to strike a planet, because it was occluded or had over time dwindled into a far orbit."

He pinned Rasputin with a stare. "Why a telescope?"

"I thought it might fit with the landscape metaphor, is all."

He didn't buy that, thought Rasputin. *Loose lips sink ships.*

"The Golden Age of Science produced two technologies long coveted: artificial reproductions of our two primary senses, sight and hearing. I'm talking, of course, about the photograph and the phonograph. They were invented in 1838 and 1877, and the modern mind finds it difficult to feel the shock and rapture they caused."

Thorpe indicated a framed picture. "Here is a copy of one of the first photographic, or *Daguerreotype,* exposures."

Rasputin looked and saw a street scene caught perhaps from a first storey window. An eerie light pervaded it. Trees anchored shadows in more than one direction. Ghosts walked the street in vague, humanoid smears.

"That exposure took four hours."

Thorpe moved on. "Following that, just a few short decades later." He paused by a flat machine with a vertical appendage like a massive brown coral growth. He flicked a switch, and a voice spouted from the coral-horn, sounding tinny and far away.

Rasputin lowered an ear into the flange and strained to hear what was being said. He caught one word, *lamb,* and then, as if that one word were the key to a cipher, the rest of the speech became clear. "Mary had a little lamb. Mary had a little lamb ..." And that was all it said.

"That is the first demonstration given to Benjamin Franklin," said Thorpe, "Many people thought it a trick. Franklin did."

"But it's a memory, isn't it," said Rasputin. "Of the voice of a man now dead." What a marvel an iPod was.

Thorpe nodded, detecting, Rasputin thought, that he had finally lit a fire in him. They neared the desk that buttressed the far end of the room.

"In the next hundred years every new artifice of man was co-opted to explain memory and the mind: It was a beaker of chemicals, a steam engine, a calculating machine, a telephone switchboard." He paused to flick another switch. "Even a hologram." A three-dimensional image of a skull burst into sight, revolving, with a glimmering tangibility.

Behind Rasputin, the faint buzz he knew to be Mary having yet another little lamb, cut-off with a snapping noise. A relay had closed on a timer. Rasputin wondered how many times a year Thorpe gave his tour.

Thorpe rounded the edge of his desk, without sparing the rotating skull a glance, and sank into a chair. He spread his arms wide. "And, as you've probably already guessed, we arrive at the present here." He indicated the sleek laptop lying on the desk.

He pried its lid open and Rasputin heard the soft buzz of a hard drive spinning up.

"By the time we got to the computer, scientists had finally become conscious that what they had been trying to do all along—attain total mastery of the physical world—had an ultimate demonstration: to replicate man, artificially. Then the metaphors began working backwards, from man to machine. My computer's hard drive is its long term *memory*. It is pulling bits from a platter spinning thousands of times a second into its RAM, recalling who it is and what it was up to, into its short term memory. Like a waking coma patient." The hard drive's whirring stopped. "Now it's thinking about what it found."

Rasputin cocked his head. "You can call it thinking, but that's a fair stretch."

"Maybe. But I bet the last time you used a computer you spoke to it."

Yes, thought Rasputin. *It was a four letter word.*

"But you're right. It is more than a fair stretch. A computer may simulate a human in some respects, but it is worlds away from the real thing. This," he tapped his own temple this time, "is a Bach canon, compared to that"—he flipped a derisive hand at the laptop—"child with a recorder."

Didn't Rasputin know it.

"The computer boffins build more and more complex models. Neural networks of thousands of 'cells', parallel systems that process billions of small instructions per second, networks of semantic association that can be analysed to effect a kind of problem solving. But ..."

Rasputin recalled his audition and the fright he had received when he touched the sticky tendrils that seemed to glue parts of his memories to others. They were associations, coupling memories in countless ways: Peter Jackson's name to his image; the letter A to every instance Rasputin had ever seen or heard; and, mind bogglingly, the very *concept* of separateness and beginning. He recalled how the sticky idea-glue had separated in finer and finer strands, and how he had known intuitively that they kept forking no matter how close he looked.

Good luck building a network to reproduce that. A billion-trillion nodes wouldn't begin to cover it.

Rasputin said, "Kudos to them for trying, but I reckon the wet-ware has the edge."

"How perfectly put," said Thorpe, and Rasputin again noticed the hunger in his eyes when he looked at the wet-ware sitting on Rasputin's slim shoulders. "That wet-ware, as you put it, is my domain. And I promise you, Rasputin, that I will help you navigate into safe waters. The regimen I prescribe for you will be bothersome at times. There will be many and varied assessments to endure. But endure them you must if you want to be sure to avoid the fate of Mr. Palmer. Do I have your promise that you will do all I ask, and be completely honest with me?"

Rasputin didn't trust himself to speak. He nodded.

Thorpe paused as if assessing Rasputin's response. Finally, he said, "Good." He rose and rounded the desk to shake Rasputin's hand, engulfing it with his own. "Come tomorrow and I will give you a detailed plan for our time together. Until then."

All of a sudden Rasputin found himself dismissed. He suppressed the urge to fish for a lift home, and left.

It wasn't until he exited the lift at the ground floor that he realised what had been nagging him about Thorpe. The second time Thorpe had seen him in hospital had been after his interview with Bert Hills, the forensic artist. Rasputin had spent the time between visitors playing with his newfound artistic flare, sketching hospital staff or ransacking his memory for subjects. So his room had quickly filled with sketches.

Surely that wasn't normal for post traumatic head injury patients? But Thorpe had made no remark, hadn't said a thing.

Hadn't he been even a little curious?

He stepped from the building's foyer into air yellow with mid-afternoon sunlight. It slanted into the oaks bordering the lawn in front of the building. Rays struck their leaves, enflaming them luminescent green. The light that pierced the tumbling mass of foliage fell impotently on the grass, dappling it amidst the gloom in patches like Rembrandt's dying Christ.

He crossed the lawn. A quick mental check assured him he had credit enough for the bus home. He headed for the highway slowly, winding through as many of the campus's green places as he could, enjoying the haphazardness of its life, the clots of students sprawled on its lawns and in train for lectures.

He stopped at a café, bought a drink, and sat at an ancient table-top arcade game. It all felt so familiar, so *normal*. The past months faded, and he savoured the smell of the drink and the sense of being adrift. He fished in his wallet for a twenty-cent coin to drop into the machine's slot. He found one and slipped it home.

The game sprang to life. It caused his heart to flutter with euphoria, which was soon crushed beneath a realisation. The game, when stripped of ghoulish adornment, was a pattern. The player progressed by learning that pattern (when did the skeleton drop from that ledge?) and executing movements at the right time. Therein lay the fun: observing the pattern, improving the response. Only, his brain—the Rasputin T. Lowdermilk Super-Brain (tm)—had seen the entire pattern before, and now drove his control of the joystick and buttons perfectly. It was the forensic sketch all over again, but this time it occasioned a strangely deep sense of loss.

He played for five minutes more to confirm it wasn't a fluke. It wasn't. He forsook the game, leaving it to a wide-eyed and thankful freshman, who immediately evoked the machine's failure sound effect—something Rasputin had been unable to do.

His journey to the bus stop took him toward a tunnel under Stirling Highway. Its mouth gaped dark—darker than a tunnel of twenty meters should be. It had always felt like the kind of place he would avoid if not for the near constant traffic running through it.

He crossed the tunnel's lip and heard his footsteps rebound from the tiled walls. Simultaneously he felt a tug on his head. It came from inside, as if he had lost balance. But his ears were fine. He wondered if the darkness had disoriented him.

Then he realised his mistake. The feeling was familiar for a different reason. The same kind of sensation had guided his short blackjack career, and then again for 7-stud, a turbulence in his mind bubbling into his perception.

The tug had been to his left. He stole a glance that way, before his feet carried him too far into the tunnel, and caught a glimpse of a man leaning against the tunnel entrance.

He was not remarkable—too dapper, perhaps, for a student—and there were a thousand better places to read a paper on campus. Nine tenths of his paper were peeled back, which meant he was reading the classifieds or sports section. That thought jarred with Rasputin's impression of him, but so what? *It's a free world.*

But that sense of mental *pressure*, that inner feeling of heft extended out into the world, had put a lot of money into his pocket, however briefly. The least he could do was show it a little respect.

While he walked, he dove into the eye and slapped a snapshot of the man onto the eye's wall, like a homicide detective briefing his team. What followed stunned him to a standstill in the dead centre of the tunnel.

The image didn't remain alone. It was a lodestone that attracted memories, sucking them from their constellations to itself like a magnet. But not every memory. The magnet discriminated, drawing only those with an affinity to itself, only those that contained the man. And he featured in surprisingly many from recent days.

Just as the memories that teemed in the void seethed with an inestimable life and logic, so too did this miniscule portion of it. The bunched memories were not all static; some crept, others raced in loops. Nor were they uniform in perspective. They captured the man in close-up and extreme long shot, in light and dark. It was a montage splattered over the wall.

Then in a surge of gestalt, something emerged from the montage. It was the man's face, a tessellation of disparate memories containing him, a Frankenstein of them all. The eye had made a magic picture of him, each memory an atom of the whole, their scattered motions lending it a glistening life.

"Shiny," he whispered, so low there was nothing for the tunnel's tiled walls to reflect.

Rasputin had not willed the magic. The eye, it seemed, had the soul of an *artiste*.

He scrutinised individual memories and the effect dissolved. The face vanished. Rasputin wondered if he had imagined it.

He picked through memories that were easy to place and came to an unsettling conclusion: the guy had been tailing him since he returned from Melbourne. He had lurked in the dairy aisle of the supermarket, drunk coffee in the chic half-light of Rasputin's favourite café, and passed him any number of times on controlled street crossings, bobbing in the oncoming throng as Rasputin laboured forward in a bubble of space opened by his cane. He mixed and matched three sets of clothes, and always wore the same aviator sunglasses. Once he had worn a fedora. *A fedora*, for crying out loud.

This was what his mind was alerting him to. How many times had it already tried, with increasing persistence, only for him to dismiss it as dizziness or indigestion?

Again he remembered the errand-carrier-become-sun, the rainbow hues washing its surface as it turned a scrutinising awareness on the constellations of his memory, autonomous. Was this its handiwork? Did it ransack his memory for patterns, detect when one crossed from coincidence to conspiracy, and force it into his conscious mind by whichever sense-conduit was appropriate or handy?

A student walking in the other direction brushed past him, talking on a phone, and Rasputin became conscious that he was stalled halfway through the tunnel. He began woodenly to walk again.

Where the tunnel disgorged, the path split in two. He took the right fork, which rose to a bus stop. He saw the bus already standing at the stop, and hurried up the slope, hop-a-step, fearing he would catch his wayward leg on the uneven concrete. He reached the end of the queue as it was being swallowed by the bus. He mounted the steps, ratcheting up, dug in his wallet for his rider card, and flashed it past the fare machine. It bleeped compliance, and he slumped into a disabled-priority seat behind the driver.

His heart was hammering his ribs, and he wondered how many people made it to the priority seat only to be struck by myocardial infarction.

The door accordioned shut and the bus's motion pressed him into his seat, only to pitch him forward again when it halted.

The door folded open and a familiar set of aviators floated up the stair. For a moment, Rasputin saw himself mirrored in miniature in their lenses. He hastily became engrossed in a poster encased in plexiglass behind the driver. He heard the bus's fare reader bleep, and sensed a shadow pass.

A temptation to bolt back down the stair seized him, but with a hiss the door closed. Besides, it would be idiotic. The aviators would follow, and then where would he be? Stuck with his shadow at an empty bus stop.

He hunkered down as low as he could, watched the bay drift by, and tried madly to arrange his thoughts.

The bus stopped once to let passengers off. As it surged away from the stop with a whine, Rasputin hazarded a glance at the convex mirror set at the head of the aisle. He thought he could see reflected in its vibrating surface, smeared and silhouetted by late afternoon sunlight pouring through the rear window, a now familiar profile.

The bus wound its way into the sun-starved canyons of the CBD. The pavement along St. George's Terrace was bustling with pre-peak-hour suits and faded lipstick. The bus stopped and he took the plunge into that bawling mass of humanity.

Minutes later he entered a lift in the city's tallest building, Central Park, and punched the button for the 43rd floor. The lift shot up like an express train and in no time he stood before a glass door he had seen on only three separate occasions. Silver lettering on its frosted surface proclaimed it to be the premises of Gödel IT Consulting Group. (The sign writer was evidently not big on umlauts.) He entered and waited at the counter for the receptionist to notice him. She appeared to be checking recommendations for hotels in Phuket, and was quite thorough.

She smiled tightly, "Can I help you?"

"I wanted to see Jordan Mitchell. Is he in?"

She picked up the phone receiver, a finger poised above the keypad. "And you are?"

"Rasputin."

The finger didn't quite drop. "*The* Rasputin?"

Short of the late-19th century monk, he wasn't sure who *the* Rasputin would be.

"Sorry?"

"From the paper. Mr. Lowdermilk. How could I forget that name. Lovely."

"I'm sorry, but I have no idea what you're talking about," he said with a sinking feeling.

"Jordan's friend. You had the accident. Terrible. It was in the paper," she said, and her gaze hunted his head for the telltale scar.

"Oh, the paper. Yeah," he said.

The paper? What paper?! Why the hell didn't anyone tell him anything anymore? Of course there had been something in the paper; this was Perth. In Perth, a farting wombat was news.

The receptionist's finger fell, mercifully, and dialled an internal extension.

"Jordan? Rasputin Lowdermilk is here to see you," she said, flicking him a quick, conspiratorial glance.

Jordy appeared moments later with the word *what* inscribed on his features.

"Got a second?" said Rasputin.

"It's nearly Five. I'm about to go home," was what he said, but his face still said *what*. "Hang on. I'll get my things."

Jordy reappeared shortly after, holding a briefcase of shiny black leather.

"Nice briefcase."

"Shut up."

As they were leaving the receptionist called after them, "Nice to meet a real celebrity." Rasputin said thanks, and guessed the cogs in Jordy's mind had turned far enough to connect her comment with the news article, because the *what* had dropped from his face to be replaced by *shit*.

"Monk, we were going to say something—"

"Forget it. I've got bigger fish to fry." What was it with fish today? "Someone is tailing me."

Jordy looked around dumbly as they entered the lift.

"You being paranoid again?" Jordy said.

"No, I—what do you mean, *again*?" Rasputin spluttered, momentarily forgetting The Aviators of Damocles.

Jordy waved the question away. "Go on."

The lift doors closed and they dropped.

"I noticed him today, but he's been hanging 'round like a bad smell since Melbourne. I've seen him everyday since then."

"Okay," said Jordy. "Why are you only telling me now?"

"I just noticed."

Jordy didn't comment, but Rasputin marked the way his eyes darted to his scar. At least one other person was beginning to respect The Brain.

Jordy shrugged. "So call the cops."

"What if he is a cop?"

"You're being a moron. Why would a cop be tailing you? Unless he wants an autograph."

"He wore a fedora."

"Ah, well, in that case, he's in amateur theatre and it *is* an autograph he wants."

"Be serious."

"How the hell can I be serious about a fedora?"

A man and a woman entered the lift, and Rasputin and Jordy fell silent while they decided where they were going for post-work drinks. By the time the lift reached the foyer, it was packed with end-of-day traffic and smelt of sweat. Rasputin and Jordy were the last to exit, and Rasputin tugged Jordy behind a nook formed by the angle of two directory boards.

"You want to camp here all night?" Jordy said. The metal feet of his briefcase rapped the tiles when he set it down. "If so, I'd better nip out and get some toothpaste."

"You're going to nip out, alright, but I want you to scope for this guy." Rasputin halted, appraising his friend's appearance. "But I bet he knows what you look like—here," he said, and tousled Jordy's hair."

Jordy slapped his hand away. "Quit it. I'm not a dog."

Rasputin stepped back, satisfied Jordy's private-school part had been destroyed. He slung his jacket to the floor and stripped off his t-shirt. Jordy didn't stop complaining as he worked his tie loose and undid the buttons of his work shirt. He swapped it for Rasputin's t-shirt.

Seconds later Rasputin gave him the once over. "It'll have to do."

"I feel like an idiot," Jordy said, plucking at the t-shirt's faded fabric, which sat rumpled incongruously above his suit pants.

"Plenty of guys go to the gym after work," said Rasputin. He retrieved his jacket from the floor and stuffed it into his backpack.

"Not in their suit pants, they don't."

"You're setting a trend," Rasputin said with a wink.

"Yeah, fashion homicide."

Jordy sighed and stepped into the open. "What's he wearing?"

"Aviators."

"Okay. Looking for a naked guy in aviators."

Rasputin rolled his eyes and spoke fast: "Short-sleeved shirt, checked with mauve and teal, a pocket over each breast. Khaki pants, but good ones. Brown leather shoes, maybe Colorados, with an inch of black sock showing. Sideburns dropping maybe one centimetre below ..." But Jordy waved him off and disappeared.

Rasputin waited, tense, half-expecting to see twin mirrored lenses intrude on his bolt-hole. But it was Jordy who appeared a minute later, his bearing changed.

"I mark him. He's on a bench, pretending to watch a bocce game. Now what?"

Rasputin pumped his fist, then became still. He realised he had no idea what to do.

Jordy spoke first. "He could be a cop. He looks like a cop."

"Why would he be skulking after me if he's a cop?"

Jordy shrugged and sucked his teeth.

"Okay. Back to the lift. There are plenty of ways out of this place."

"He'll know I'm onto him."

"Maybe. Or he'll figure he missed you." Jordy looked back, seeming to weigh the odds. "Come on."

They circled round the blind side of the lift wells. All six lifts were spewing out foot traffic. Jordy pushed the down button and they waited. Eventually an emptied lift indicated it was heading down and they piled into it. It dropped to the first basement level, where they got out. It was a car park.

"I hate car parks," said Rasputin. Jordy remained silent, but it was an inclusive silence. He waited for Rasputin to catch up, and together they mounted a ramp to the street level.

They slipped along the darkening foot of the skyscraper, mingling with the crowds that thronged the pavement. As they turned up a lane that lead away at right angles, Rasputin scanned the patch of grass where bocce was being played. No sign of the guy—the living collage-portrait his mind had wrought floated up into his thought like an apparition. Yes, he knew what he looked like. But he was gone.

They merged with the deeper shadow of the narrow lane but Rasputin felt no relief.

Quarter of an hour later he sat squashed against Jordy on a train. The multi-level blur of suburbs racing by was a hypnotic palimpsest. It combined with the swaying cabin to make Rasputin feel drowsy. He was sliding toward sleep when Jordy spoke.

"Sorry about the paper. We should have told you, but Dee agreed that you were ... well, *fragile* was the word she used. Some reporter was sniffing around for a quote from you, but we hedged. I thought he maybe had some kick back scheme with an ambulance chaser."

Rasputin mulled that over. "Maybe my tail is the reporter?"

"No. I know what he looks like."

Rasputin glanced at Jordy with an unspoken question.

"He came to the hospital," Jordy continued, seemingly absorbed with the rushing sprawl. "I told him to get lost."

"Bet you didn't. You're too polite, country boy."

Jordy smiled without returning his gaze.

Rasputin leaned back into his seat and closed his eyes, lowered defences he felt had been up all day, and let the train tug at him as if he were a rag doll. It felt wonderful.

Two letters arrived the following day. Rasputin read them as he lay sprawled in a lounge chair. One was from the insurance agent representing Mr. Hewitt, the man who had almost made his Valiant a lethal weapon. The letter held no surprises. It said that, regrettably, Rasputin had no claim. The second letter was from Thorpe. It was printed on Department of Neuroscience stationary, and unlike the insurance letter, came in an envelope stuffed to the brim. At first glance, it appeared that Thorpe had scheduled activities in every one of Rasputin's non-contact hours. On closer inspection, he saw appointments scheduled over the top of lectures.

Welfare suddenly took on a little lustre.

His new timetable had, in addition to one-on-one sessions with Thorpe, appointments for physiotherapy and occupational therapy, post-traumatic experience counselling, and psycho-cognitive assessment, whatever that was. He grew tired just looking at it. Each stream of appointments had a corresponding chunk of verbiage about where to go and what to expect. Stapled to the back of each was a privacy statement printed in a microscopic font, and a liability waiver that just needed his signature.

He flung the thick sheaf of papers down. Sections of it shot across the floor like parts of a decrepit, triangular telescope.

He felt the weight of every planned hour latent at his feet. There wasn't going to be any clean snap of the neck for him. Thorpe was going to tease back each scale and groove the flesh from his hide—Heaven knew why. He planned to savour every morsel Rasputin's head had to offer. He would lick the bones clean, every last one, and mount the skeleton in a frame in his museum of wonders: *Rasputinus Excogitas.* Rasputin the Unthought.

Rasputin jerked his shoulders square and billowed his cheeks.

Well, Professor Thorpe, you might get a surprise at what you find on your hook ...

He cupped his hands around his skull, normally a reflex of over-tiredness, and held it gently, with control. He had the feeling that what lay between his hands was only beginning to wind up. He fancied he felt it sucking in force from the aether like a driven magneto.

This time you hooked something with teeth.

Reluctantly he retrieved the papers and set them in order. He read the cover note properly and realised with a start that the bold print was alerting him to the fact that his first appointment was today. This morning.

No longer was he a comet gliding through the morning on a trajectory for rendezvous with a Mediaeval history lecture that afternoon. One short burst of laser, courtesy of the morning mail, had knocked him onto a collision course with a nearer, nebulous body: psycho-cognitive assessment.

He heaved himself out of the lounge chair and jog-hopped into the bathroom. There was no time to accumulate the normal routines of showering, shaving, and (de-)perfuming. Pinched for time, tooth brushing trumped them all. Personal hygiene was more *Bridge* than *Battleship*. He brushed like most people mow a lawn, touching every surface once, and only once.

So when a knock at the door came with his lower jaw untouched, his whole day felt threatened. By the time he finished, and sent the toothbrush careening off the sink, he was sure whoever had knocked had given up and gone.

He needn't have worried.

"Dee?"

"Hi." She bustled past him, and put something in the fridge.

"What are you doing?"

She reappeared, strangling an empty plastic shopping bag. "Taking you to uni."

"Does Jordy know?"

"What?"

"That you're having a phone affair with Thorpe?"

Rasputin thought she might have steeled herself against his bad mood. If so, it didn't seem to have had much effect.

"So sorry I happen to give a shit," she said, with tears in her voice, and went back out the door.

Rasputin picked up his backpack from the floor where he had dumped it the night before and went after her.

The silence was like clear glue packed around them as Dee moved through the peak hour clog on the freeway, stabbing forward only to stop again. The radio was off. A nameless rock anthem leaked into the car from someone else's jacked-up stereo.

Rasputin desperately wanted to say something, anything, to dissolve the glue that fixed his face forward, and cut them off from each other. He felt like a boa constrictor that had swallowed a goat and now decided what it had really wanted was the salad.

With pain, he regurgitated the goat. "Sorry." And that was all he said, but the air became air again.

"I like the new car," he said.

"So do I. It followed me home, so I kept it."

He snorted. "Good luck with the vet bills. You kids never think about the bills."

They were silent again for a time. The traffic cleared a blockage and began to flow. A car was parked in the emergency lane. It hadn't obstructed any other lanes, but its hazard lights had enough people rubber-necking that it may as well have sat in the middle of the freeway. A young boy sat in the back of the car, head in hands, staring back at the passing traffic, while his mother spoke into a mobile phone, painting her predicament in large brush strokes with an arm laden with bangles.

"Did you ever wet your pants in school?" Rasputin said.

"What?" Dee neighed, spraying spittle at the car's spotless windshield. "No I never wet my pants in school."

"Bet you did. You just blocked it out."

Dee was shaking her head.

"Okay then, " he said. "What's the most embarrassing thing you ever did as a kid?"

She checked his expression, evidently to gauge whether he was serious or winding her up.

"I don't know about most, but I could compile a top five, maybe even a top ten."

"Pick one."

"I killed a hamster once."

"That's tragic, not embarrassing."

"No, it was embarrassing. I was told a minute before to watch where I sat."

"Tragic and negligent, then."

"Okay, okay." She paused while allowing a car to merge ahead of them.

"I sat in a urinal once." When he said nothing, she explained. "I took a piss in a urinal. *Comprende?*"

"How old were you?"

"Seven. Dad was always on call, so Mum usually took us out. I'd never seen a standalone urinal before."

Rasputin tried to imagine it. Dee took a hand from the wheel to slap him on the chest.

"It's not that funny," she said. "It was a school excursion." Then, lower, "My teacher, Mr. Gilbertson, walked in."

Rasputin suppressed a laugh. "More tragedy. The only way that could have been more tragic was if you'd peed on a hamster in a urinal."

Dee pressed her lips together. Rasputin predicted he would hear nothing more from her top ten.

He drew in more breath than needed, then said, "What about regrets? Is there anything you really regret doing?"

They passed beneath an electronic billboard telling them the freeway ahead was crawling. Useful information once you were on it.

"There are so many of those. I regret *not* doing something. I regret it every day."

Rasputin could not look at her face.

"I never told my Dad I loved him before he died. Not in words." She glanced at him apologetically, "That's kind of cliché, I know."

He couldn't believe it. Of all the people he knew, Dee was the one who said that word the most.

"But we're not talking about me, are we?" she said. And Rasputin immediately found himself uncomfortable in the trap he had laid for himself.

"Hey, I'm not the hamster killer," he said, and propped himself against the arm rest and gazed at the far-off silhouette of Winthrop Hall's tower. It was thrust into the sky, an axle about which the wide bay seemed to turn as they drove.

"You can't shrug everything off with a joke, Monk. That's no way to live."

"Seems to work for most," he said, sounding mawkish in his own ears. Perhaps to raise the tone, he reached for an authority: "What is life, but a tale told by an idiot, full of sound and fury, signifying nothing." Did he believe that? He guessed not. "But, I suppose it takes one to know one, and there we hit a paradox," he said, feeling the childish bookend slot home with pleasure.

"Whoever said that?" said Dee.

"Some yob. It doesn't matter. I just concluded he was an idiot."

"Why did you ever get into philosophy? I swear it's corrosive, for you at least."

"Why did you get into microbes? They can be pretty corrosive. Why did Hitler get into genocide? Ditto."

He sensed she knew he was just playing with her now. He hadn't meant to. Deep currents within him were doing everything possible to draw him away from what he really wanted to say.

He sought to bring it back to the level: "Someone else said: 'It's perilous to the mind to reckon up the mind.' He was right. You're right." He examined a lonely cloud, its wind-wrought warp and woof, but saw nothing in it.

He sighed. "But you might as well tell a crack junkie that the stuff eats his organs."

"What do you regret, Monk?"

He looked at her along his eyes. The eastward sun cast her profile in shadow, and limned her silhouette a luminescent gold. In that moment he knew Dee to be beautiful, and in the same moment was deeply happy that Jordy loved her. He wondered when Jordy would tell her.

She continued, eyes on the road, hesitant. "Is it your ... sister?" She spoke the word as if her tongue were navigating the contours of a foreign word.

Sister. It would have punched a white-hot spike through his head, if he were genuinely synaesthesic. But he had wanted it. Wanted it to be out there, in the real world. Now it was.

The car wound off the freeway exit and onto the bay road, the same he had travelled with Thorpe not twenty-four hours before. He thought he had been scared then. He let the silence stretch.

They were soon banked up behind the wide backside of a bus about to bomb the university with live students. Dee edged the car forward, attempting to ease past the bus and into a car park.

"My sister, yes," he said, as the car slowed. "It has to do with her. That I can't even call her by name, because I never found the courage to ask what it was. I regret that."

Dee pulled the car over by a disabled parking bay, and stared at him unblinking.

He opened the door and stepped out. He shouldered his backpack and settled his cane by his side.

She said, "Wait," and reached out a hand.

He thought she meant to grab him, said, "Don't," and was startled by the ferocity in his voice. "That I don't know her name is a fly on a pile of shit the size of Mount Everest."

For the second time that morning he breathed air in like a man stealing his last lungful. The goat had been hard. This felt like turning himself inside out.

"I never asked if I was the one, the one that ..." Tears sprang into his eyes. They blurred Dee's face, fractured it. "And the kicker: I can't bring myself to regret that. I've tried. I can't. I'm terrified I never will."

He failed to shut the door properly, leant on it with his hip to squeeze the mechanism home, and walked away.

He had worried what Dee would say. That she had said nothing was worse. Her bleary, pale face had just looked at him as though he were a stranger who had opened a vein in front of her.

He walked through the leafy campus without seeing it. He had agonised about mingling Dee with the memory of his sister, which roiled within him. Her reaction clung to him like a fog. He waited for the sun to burn it away.

He mounted the steps to the psychology building still trying to shake his mood. Worse, he feared that to a trained eye, a psychologist's eye, he was broadcasting his thoughts like a signal fire, his head ablaze in a flaming column of self-revelation.

A sudden fear wedged itself in among the others: Thorpe had sent him here, for psycho-cognitive assessment, to lay him open like a cadaver. Hollywood portrayed psychologists as modern day magicians, able to pluck the very thoughts from a man's head from nothing more than a telltale twitch. Rasputin had always scoffed at the idea; who knew the thoughts of a man but the man alone? But today he couldn't find comfort in that assertion.

He followed the signs to the clinic up a flight of stairs and was soon shaking hands with his assessor, Lloyd. It helped that *Lloyd* was not a name Rasputin could easily imbue with magical aura.

Lloyd handed him a clipboard holding a form and a pen.

"Put your name and details there, Mr. F. Meat." He laughed at his own joke, then pointed at the bottom of the form. His fingernails were clipped in precise arcs and unnaturally white. "Don't worry about that part. It's for subjects receiving remuneration. Usually you get $25 a session—which is pretty good if you ask me. Better than McDonalds. But I was told these sessions won't be covered by a grant."

Rasputin said, "I'm covered. It's fine," thinking that Lloyd didn't know the half of it.

"Did you receive the waiver in the mail? They get sent out so that subjects can read the fine print if they're really interested. If you didn't bring it, no problem. You'll just have to sign again. "

So that's what I am, thought Rasputin, a *subject*. A subject in the encyclopaedia of life. He imagined his entry: Rasputin Titian Low-dermilk, male, twenty-five, permanent student, permanent disability. Suspected ongoing mental cataclysm. Imports goodwill and friendship. Exports moody wisecracks. GDP in freefall, Trade deficit terminal.

He indicated to Lloyd that he hadn't brought the form. Lloyd produced one and Rasputin splashed his signature over the line at the bottom of the sheet.

Lloyd then showed Rasputin to the *Media Room*. It was a stark white cube, three meters to a side. One wall was taken up with a projection screen, and the opposite wall was inset with a mirror that Rasputin guessed to be two-way. In the centre of the room sat a chair that looked transplanted from a dentist's clinic.

"It's a bit Orwellian, isn't it?"

"That's why we call it the Media Room. I don't think folks would be keen to help if it were called the Orwell Room. But don't be put off. We have to take care to satisfy certain protocols in psychological experiments."

Lloyd held out a hand, inviting Rasputin to sit in the chair. "Now, if you'll please?"

Rasputin sat, feeling the cool of the vinyl penetrate his jeans and numb his skin. Lloyd lowered an apparatus hanging from a segmented metal arm that sprouted from the back of the chair, and settled it on Rasputin's head. The apparatus resembled helmets he had seen in Sci-Fi movies from the Sixties: it was thick at the back and reached forward in three tapering extensions that curved over his skull, past each ear and over his crown. Lloyd explained it would keep his head in roughly the same place for the duration of the experiment.

Lloyd stepped away to verify all was in place.

"The guide," said Lloyd, and rapped a knuckle on the helmet, "also has built-in microphone and speakers, so we can communicate as we go."

"You're not staying?" said Rasputin.

"No. I'm in there," said Lloyd, indicating the mirror.

"Alone?"

Lloyd smiled. "Does it matter?"

He left the room and soon Rasputin heard a faint hiss and crackle come through the headphones.

"Quick sound check. Can you hear me?"

"No," said Rasputin.

"I actually have to mark this down. Can you hear me?"

"Affirmative."

"Good. Let me tell you what we're doing today. You're going to see a sequence of images appear on the screen in front of you. I need you to say the first thing that comes to mind for each image. Don't worry. There are no right or wrong answers."

"So if you show me a picture of a spatula and I say 'urine monkey,' that's okay?"

"If that's the first thing that pops into your head, yes."

If only exams were that easy.

Question: Name the principal event that catalysed persecution of the French Huguenots.
Answer: Why, Buttermilk, my dear fellow.

... but then, he supposed exams were that easy, now.

Lloyd was speaking again. "That's the first phase of the experiment. I'll explain the second when we get there."

"How long is this going to take?" said Rasputin, feeling the cold of the chair colluding with his bladder.

"About an hour."

I can do an hour, thought Rasputin, and attempted to locate whatever muscle clamped his bladder shut to give it a workout.

"Ready?"

"Bring on the urine monkeys."

He heard a faint click from above. Colour burst onto the screen in front of him. It was the projector's test image. A moment later it was replaced by a photo of a vivid green hillside set against a clear sky. The grass on the hill's flank was speckled with yellow wildflowers.

"First thing that pops into your head," said Lloyd through the head-phones, sounding as if he were speaking from within Rasputin's head.

"Juicy," said Rasputin, and straightaway feared Lloyd would think him a nutcase.

Rasputin mentally audited his answer. He traced the word, *juicy*, backwards through the fading residue of his line of thought, like the flight-path of a pinball that had rattled and bounced with light speed logic through his mind's machinery. The connection that had prompted his answer was the memory of a cow licking up wet tufts of green grass. He had been close enough to hear the great, moist smacks of its hairy muzzle. Crisp dawn air, the smell of manure, and that sucking sound. And green grass. All of these senses bundled up organically into a single memory.

The image changed to a photo of a skyscraper.

"Lift," said Rasputin, now fearing Lloyd would think him simple.

The sequence of images grew. Rasputin and Lloyd settled into a rhythm, each couplet of image and answer taking about seven seconds.

Rasputin stopped worrying about what Lloyd thought of him and focused on capturing the first word to flutter from the cage of his mind.

Lloyd had photos of trains, faces, animals of all kinds, clouds, crowds, and shopping malls. Rasputin responded with an equally varied range of concepts. Once he had warmed to the task, it was as though he had pulled a plug from the bottom of his mind, and all sorts of rubbish was draining out of it through his mouth. He gave up trying to trace the source of each answer, concluding his head was a hopelessly tangled mess.

At 37 minutes and 13 seconds into the experiment, according to his internal chronometer—which he now knew to be the equal of any watch—a photo hit the screen that shocked him, broke his rapid-fire responses. He had seen it before. It was a famous photo. In it, in the middle ground, was a child hunched low over its knees. The child's sex could not be discerned, obscured by a belly bloated by malnutrition. Its head was large, too heavy for one so small, its limbs an ineffectual accretion of tangled branches. Death was drawn near enough to touch. The parched earth and bleak vista told of a land familiar with death. The one spark of vital life in the scene dwelt in its sole witness, beside the camera operator: a vulture.

Rasputin's face became hot with held-back tears.

"Suicide," he whispered finally.

Lloyd must have heard. Another image mercifully obliterated the once-living child.

But the reprieve was only momentary. An image of a carnival wheel was replaced by another photo Rasputin had seen before: a napalmed Vietnamese girl, running toward the observer, her eyes wild with pure terror.

Rasputin pulled his gaze away. "Robin Williams," he said.

Two more images in succession pictured hell, the first, Nazi ovens, and the second, a dog that had been beaten to death.

Rasputin burst.

"What the hell is this?" He swivelled to look into the two-way mirror, feeling the helmet tug against his head. The walls amplified his voice to a shout.

Lloyd's voice held its own tremor. "I'm sorry if you're finding this distressing, but these are the images given me by Professor Thorpe. We're almost done."

Grudgingly, Rasputin settled back in his seat and gritted his teeth to face the final images. For an anchor he looked to his promise to Thorpe and his hope for a cure, and grasped it. But his hand shook with fear. Each of the gruesome images had passed through his eyes and fallen on his mind like a hammer on fired metal, sending sparks skittering in every direction, threatening to kindle wildfire in his mind. Most of all he feared that one such spark would alight in the memory of his sister—that spark would find not tinder but dynamite.

The images came. With each, he felt again an inward pull not of his willing, as though he were not himself to command. It tugged in every direction at once. Each answer he gave dispelled that exploding force, but he suspected his head didn't come back together in exactly the same way, like a child's Tupperware ball, tugged open and left to spring together askew. (And wasn't the purpose of that action to allow the letters inside the toy to fall out?)

Another image, a photo of a man whose face had been horribly burned. Another maelstrom of pressure. Another answer: "Wax."

The photo winked out, replaced by the projector's test image.

Rasputin panted quietly.

"We'll begin the second phase, if that is okay with you," said Lloyd.

"Is it anything like the first?"

"I can't answer that," said Lloyd. "But your instructions are to observe the screen. Images will be presented to you in batches of eight. In each batch of eight there will be one image, and only one, that you have already seen today. You need to indicate to me which one. If you don't know, say so. Don't guess."

Surely the worst images wouldn't be making a reappearance. Who would forget them? What would be the point?

The first set of eight images appeared. They were all photos of cars. Red cars, to be precise. Rasputin knew immediately which photo he had already seen.

130

"Third down on the left," he said.

"Okay," said Lloyd, "Let's call that number 5, numbering left to right, top to bottom."

The next set of photos were of skyscrapers. Four of the photos were of one skyscraper taken from slightly different points of origin. The other four, similarly, were a set of another skyscraper.

Again, Rasputin knew within a split second which photo he had seen before—which skyscraper, and which perspective from among the cluster of close vantage points.

But caution held his tongue. Any fool could have spotted the correct red car in the previous set. And a good observer with a healthy memory could spot the right skyscraper, even with the close red herrings. But would he know them *all*?

Rasputin would. And that would be giving the game away.

"Number Three," he said, sparing a glance for Number Eight, the correct skyscraper. It galled him to flunk the question.

The sets of eight came, and as predicted, he knew the correct answer for every one in a fraction of a second. He sprinkled his false guesses and I-don't-knows with correct answers. The last few sets were of shopping malls shot from the same vantage, flooded with people—so similar only someone with a photographic memory could have aced them. He patted himself on the back for having so quickly smelled the rat.

"How'd I do?" he said when Lloyd entered the room.

"I'm not at liberty to discuss your results," said Lloyd. "That is for Professor Thorpe."

Rasputin thought Lloyd sounded relieved about that. "But we have an appointment on Thursday, don't we? That assessment is a more conversational, sit-down affair. Maybe we will be able to dig into ... things then."

Lloyd pried the helmet from Rasputin's head.

Rasputin rose, kneading stiffness from his shoulder, wondering what kind of a chat he and Lloyd would have. Would Lloyd be drinking Earl Grey, and would Lloyd be asking him about his father?

"See you Thursday," said Rasputin, and went in search of a toilet. His bladder was screaming broken pact, and he didn't want to see if it was bluffing.

"Straighter!" she commanded. "Now hold it. Give me another twenty seconds."

Rasputin had liked the hospital physiotherapist better. The physios at the University clinic, where he was now strung out on a mat, struggling to keep a tremulous leg in the air, were decidedly more fervent. Their veins still coursed with the ideology of the scientifically-manipulated body, untempered by life's messiness.

Dee had picked him up again that morning, and he had succeeded in keeping the banter light. He had daydreamed in the car about what physiotherapy might entail. His fantasies had featured hours of remedial massage and talk about his 'mobility goals.' When he said as much to Dee, she seemed to go along with it. In hindsight, perhaps she had been tactful.

Physiotherapy, in the event, had turned out to be more boot camp than day-spa. His physiotherapist, Donna, had given him a breakdown of the anatomy of his leg, from big toe to hip. Her briefing had featured a lot of Latin. Latin, in turned out, was the language of not Rome but pain. Donna's plans for their hour together had boiled down to turning his "piece-of-jelly of a *Vastus Medialis Oblique* into iron," and she had delivered her decree uncomfortably like a coach from a gridiron movie.

But it turned out that gridiron coaches were pansies.

Rasputin's internal clock registered every last second of the hour-long appointment. Each was an age.

"You're done," said Donna, at last. And he was. Sweat slicked his body. He realised it had been minutes since anything above a grunt had escaped his lips.

Between gasps, he asked what was all of a sudden an important question: "If my problem is neurologic, how does this help?"

132

"It helps me plenty," she said—only, that wasn't what she said. His head wasn't altogether together. Sparks danced in his vision as he hauled himself off the mat. It took him a moment to recollect what she had said: "In the past, we might have agreed with you. But we now know the body is very complex. We talk about the brain as if it is a static lump that drives the body, but evidence increasingly points to it being quite plastic."

The word *plastic* made Rasputin think of China-made toys.

Donna went on. "Think of the body as being a car. The engine drives the wheels right? Break the engine, and the wheels stop. Well, no. Apparently, sometimes driving the wheels on a broken engine propagates change up the chain, and fixes the engine—or, it would be better to say, finds another way to get the engine to work the wheels."

Rasputin couldn't shake the vision of a world populated by beings running on Chinese-built brains. He nodded, more to end the conversation and escape than indicate understanding.

"I'll see you again on Friday, Eight sharp," she said and smiled. Her teeth were big, and very white, and reminded him of the carnival clown game, where the object is to knock its teeth in with a thrown ball. She gave him an efficient little wave in the waiting room before introducing herself to her next victim. Rasputin contemplated slipping the guy a warning note.

For the rest of the day he found walking harder than normal. He felt sapped of strength, and his legs quivered when they bore his weight for more than a few seconds. He realised he must have been grimacing with pain when the girl at the checkout counter asked him if he needed help.

He declined, slung his backpack engorged with two-minute noodles over his shoulder, and headed for an exit. His route through the mall took him below the foodhall where he had eaten his last meal on two good legs. The cocktail party chatter of the hall, and the smell of food sitting in *bain-maries*, rolled over the lip of the mezzanine and engulfed him. He suddenly tasted Chinese spices in the back of his throat.

Beneath the food hall lay an exit that led to the enclosed car park where he had confronted a child jimmying his car door. He approached the automatic doors, feeling his pocketknife's weight press against his backside with each stride.

His mind was a cauldron of thought, had been all day. As he had scraped along supermarket aisles for press-button food, the week's tumult had swirled in a never ending stream of recall: Thorpe, and his room of wonders; the photos like cannon fodder he had given to Lloyd; physiotherapy and an exhaustion that was a new kind of pain. It left him feeling like the meat in a monstrous sandwich. To make matters worse, he wasn't sure who was intending to eat it.

So when the automatic doors clapped shut behind him he stood and fixed his eyes on the stairwell at the far side of the car park. Below it, he knew, was the bay where he had left his car that sodden night. Scant feet from that bay was the asphalt across which a Valiant had sent him careening. Maybe there was a divot in the surface there, and maybe, at the bottom of that divot, fused with the bitumen, there was even a little piece of his epidermis.

His mind reimagined the concussing blow, sending a fierce frisson of pseudo-pain scuttling over his scalp.

He shook it off, and squared his shoulders.

"I'll be damned if that punk is going to eat my sandwich," he hissed, and stumped toward the stairwell.

When he made it to the scene of the accident, he found the road surface to be entirely normal, entirely unlike his nightmares. Nothing suggested it had witnessed anything worse than garrulous shopping trolleys and sugar-hyped children. No divots, no blood stains, not even a lick of police chalk. But then, he hadn't died, had he?

He searched a moment longer, feeling the dull weight of anti-climax, and then mentally erased the carpark from his list of places-to-see-before-I-die.

Beside the stairwell a throughway right-angled past a strip of fast-food shops. He entered it, heading for the bus stop. As he rounded the bend, he collided with a man coming the other way.

Rasputin staggered back a step, an apology forming on his lips. Then he noticed the fedora on the man's head.

The man's lips parted in surprise, eyes hidden behind mirrored lenses.

Immediately Rasputin's nerve network lit up with a signal: it screamed *flight*. But he stood, rooted to the spot, adrenaline backing up against his will, like a flash flood surging behind a dam wall. His body was taut, primed to open the floodgate, needing only the order to fly.

But rumour of a countermand paralysed him. The new message came from the same deep place as the command to run, but was nurtured by the anger that had simmered in him since morning. It began to boil. He decided to *fight*.

He drove his foot into the path's concrete and plunged forward, pinning a finger into the man's chest.

"I know you," he said, anger spilling into his voice. "You want a piece of me too?" He stretched his arms wide. His cane rapped against the wall, sending reverberations up his arm. "Well here I am." He raised his cane in front of him like a sword.

Rasputin wasn't sure what he expected, but it wasn't an apology and an about-face.

The man glanced over his shoulder, tugged the fedora down over his ears, and strode back along the walkway.

Rasputin watched mutely. When he saw the man meant to leave, he cried out, "Well? ..." There was a plaintive note in the cry. In response, the man only quickened his pace.

Conscious of the ludicrous reversal, Rasputin began to chase the retreating figure. They emerged into open carpark, Rasputin jog-hopping after the man in a fedora and aviator sunglasses, who faced resolutely forward. Shoppers began crossing their path.

Rasputin raised his voice to shout: "You like making fun of cripples?"

That drew looks.

The man missed a step, stopped. He turned around, let Rasputin close the gap, and said in a harsh whisper, "I don't know what you're talking about. Please stop following me." He said it politely, but Rasputin saw he was flustered.

He turned to leave again, so Rasputin said in a voice that carried over the hum of traffic, "You were stalking me at the university, and on the bus."

The man kept walking.

Rasputin fired another barb: "And lurking in the supermarket. You an identity thief or just a pervert?"

Bingo!

The fedora executed a swift pirouette and bore down on him. He stood his ground. The man had a height advantage, but Rasputin held the mirrored gaze until it loomed over him.

The man removed the aviators and folded them in one movement.

He spoke quietly but quickly. "You've got me all wrong. Trust me. Stop making a scene." As he spoke, his gaze darted about. Rasputin couldn't tell if it was nerves or something else.

"Why should I trust you? Maybe I'll call the police. What are you going to do?"

The man swept a hand over his chin. He was thinking fast.

"Come here a minute," he said, and manhandled Rasputin backwards.

Rasputin shrugged him off, and stood his ground.

The man held his palms up, a conciliatory gesture. "Just get out of sight and I'll explain."

Rasputin relented, and moved back into the enclosed throughway.

"This is far enough," Rasputin said. "Now explain."

The man drew breath, then spoke: "I'm an insurance investigator. I've been employed to audit your claim and ensure it's legitimate."

"Nice try. My claim was rejected."

The way the man's face fell was comical.

Rasputin went on. "Your credibility stocks just took a major dive. What's your next story?"

The man's shoulders slumped.

"Alright. That was crap. But I am an investigator ... or would like to be."

It was a good act, or the man had finally spilt the truth.

"You're a vigilante? If so, your underwear is supposed to go *over* your pants."

"That's very funny." The man slipped the folded aviators into a pocket. "I work for ASIO. I'm an information officer," he said, and then seeming to remember where he was, "Or rather, would like to be an IO. I'm on probation."

ASIO, Australia's very poor cousin to the CIA?

Rasputin didn't like where this was heading, but had to ask. "What do I have to do with your probation?"

"You're my assignment. I'm meant to be surveilling you."

Rasputin was stunned, but his mouth kept running.

"I'm guessing this little tête-à-tête means that isn't going so well for you."

"No, in intelligence parlance, this is being up the faecal creek without a paddle."

"Or canoe."

"What tipped you off? It was the fedora, wasn't it."

"Yes," Rasputin lied.

"The officer in charge of my probation thought it would make an interesting challenge." He tugged the hat's brim self-consciously, and, Rasputin thought, a little protectively. "He's a bit of a hard-ass."

"Smart-ass, more like."

"My name's Sam," he said, and extended a hand. Rasputin shook it.

"Spade?"

Sam shook his head.

"Smith," he said, not quite able to say it with textbook solemnity. Sam doffed the fedora and spun it on one finger.

"If it makes you feel any better," Sam said, "surveillance ceases in a week." The hat stopped spinning, and hung lop-sided. "I don't suppose you could pretend you hadn't caught on to me? I'll send you a carton of beer when I return to Canberra."

"I don't drink."

Sam smirked. "You did a fair bit of not drinking in Melbourne."

"Melbourne?" A shock wave of fear rippled through his stomach. "I never saw you in Melbourne. That was weeks ago. What do you know about that?"

Sam seemed lost for words again.

Rasputin went on: "Forget the beer. The deal is you tell me exactly why I'm being watched." He held an index finger up in Sam's face. "But if any of it doesn't add up, and I mean to the hundredth decimal place, I'm on the line to your smart-ass boss."

"Calm down. I can explain. You'll probably laugh—it's quite ironic."

"Sarcasm fits my mood better just now, but go for it. I'm all ears."

Sam weighed the fedora in his hand, seeming to weigh his words. "That I'm here in Perth, watching you, is the fruit of coincidence. We don't know what you did before the audition in Melbourne, but as luck would have it, there was an ASIO officer at your audition."

"ASIO sends agents to Temptation auditions?" Rasputin screwed up his nose, incredulous. "The government is either paying you guys too much or not enough."

"He wasn't on duty," said Sam, a touch offended. "ASIO employees are smart. It makes perfect sense to me."

Sam might be on probation, thought Rasputin, but in the brain-washing class he was head of the class.

Sam continued, "He made the last cut, but it wasn't until after his interview that he heard a rumour that someone—*you*, as it turned out—got a near-perfect scorecard. So this agent sniffed around and got your name. Your profile looked promising, and here I am."

Sam fell silent.

Rasputin felt he had missed something. "I don't get it."

"ASIO is legislated to double over the next five years. Cyber-crime, counter-terrorism, you name it. We're supposed to keep our ear to the ground for potentials."

The picture was resolving, but the antenna needed one last nudge: "Potential whats?"

"Recruits."

Recruits.

So the shadow that had hunted him, nameless behind mirrored lenses, had overtaken him and snagged him in its claws ... to offer him a job?

"Okay," said Rasputin, "that is ironic. If my English teacher had explained irony that way I might have remembered it."

Sam switched into salesman mode. "Information Analyst is a great job—"

"Analyst?" said Rasputin, cutting over the spiel. "Aren't you an Officer?"

"Almost, but the Officer role is the 'man of action' type." Rasputin noted Sam's athletic figure and poise, with a grudging admiration. "You, however, were targeted for your intellectual prowess."

And my youth, my singleness, and my motivational indebtedness.

There was a thought: how much did they know about why he was fortune hunting in Melbourne? As far back as the accident? As far forward as Thorpe?

Sam was still talking. "Analysts sift through mountains of data and distil it into intelligence. You get paid to research. You have to be awake to nuances of culture, companion to zeitgeist, in possession of prodigious powers of recall. When does a missing bag of shit become a terrorist bomb?" He paused for effect. "Your intel might find its way under the Prime Minister's nose.

"I can put shit under the Prime Minister's nose?" said Rasputin idly, still mulling over what ASIO might know about him.

"One more question," said Rasputin. "What do you know about why I was in Melbourne?"

Sam sobered immediately, to his credit.

"We know about the accident. We know about your predicament. We know about your surgeon."

He *is* my predicament, thought Rasputin. But Sam hadn't mentioned anything about sketches or immaculate memory, what Rasputin had been listening for beneath his words.

"Actually," said Sam, "we've started a file on him."

"Are you going to start a file on my cat too?"

"You don't have a cat."

"*Touché*," said Rasputin, and smiled for the first time that day. "Okay. I give. I'm moderately interested, and I promise not to dob on you."

Sam cast the fedora onto his head. "Thanks. What can I give you, if not beer?"

"Your phone number."

Sam baulked, so Rasputin added, "I won't call you up every night for a deep and meaningful. It's just in case I need to reach you."

Sam relented. "You need a pen?"

"No."

"That's the way," he said, and recited the number.

"Your number is three away from a prime," said Rasputin.

Sam frowned in confusion, turned and left Rasputin leaning against the wall, wondering what the hell his head was doing plucking prime numbers—those rare jewels of the limitless mathematical caves—from phone numbers.

Rasputin stepped off the bus and into an afternoon that wanted to make the mysterious shift to twilight. It was held back, like the watched kettle, only by his observing eye. A moment's pause to resettle his backpack and hitch his pants was all the shy afternoon sky needed to shrug its deep blue and slip into burning orange.

The bus stop was a mere hundred yards from the dilapidated letterbox that tilted over the path in front of his flat. If the box had lately borne more than bills and form letters he might have done his tenantly duty and fixed it. But daily it gestated and birthed trouble, so he had come to loathe it.

What caught his eye, though, was the sleek, low shape of the Jaguar parked at the curb in front of it. A figure turned at his approach, seeming to materialise from the half-light. Thorpe caught his eye and strode to meet him as he reached the driveway. His eyes burned with the twilight fire.

"Our deal was predicated on complete honesty."

"What are you talking about?" said Rasputin, racking his memory for the source of the pang of guilt that struck at Thorpe's words.

"You lied during your assessment."

Ah. Yes, that was true.

But curiosity overcame the sense of shame that blossomed at the accusation.

"How did you know?"

"There is a pinpoint camera that monitors the subject's eye movement, and tracks which image is looked at. If a subject recognises an image, he dwells on it first. The behaviour is almost involuntary if one is not aware of being observed."

Sneaky bastard, thought Rasputin, but couldn't help smiling. It was cunning.

"By mouth you got two-thirds right. By eye it was a whitewash." Thorpe stepped closer, pushing over the wall at the boundary of Rasputin's personal space. He seemed to grow a foot.

"But the point is: you lied to me. And I can't help you if you lie to me. The road to hell is paved with lies. Is that where you want to go?"

The mention of hell recalled the images he had been made to see. He rallied that stale anger to his defence.

"Alright. I wasn't square with the test, but why did you make me endure those photos?"

"What photos?"

"You know damn well what photos: the dead, the dying, and the despised."

Thorpe shifted his weight onto his back foot, and was silent in that way that gave Rasputin to think he was choosing his words carefully, like an artist colours from a palette.

"It is common practice to seed the images in a memory test with … noise. In your case, disturbing imagery. It is like asking someone to sort a deck of cards, when what you are really interested in is what their legs are doing."

"Lloyd didn't seem to think it was 'common practice.' He practically apologised."

"Lloyd is a deck hand; I am the captain."

And, thought Rasputin, in short order Lloyd would be scrubbing the poop deck.

Sounding childish in his own ears, Rasputin couldn't help but add: "You could have picked another distraction. Sorting cards would have been preferable. There's enough crap in the world. I don't need to live in a toilet."

"You're right. And I haven't told you the complete truth yet."

Rasputin's ears pricked up.

"I could have chosen a different distractor, but I chose those images for a reason. To kill two birds with the same stone."

"I'm listening."

"A common side effect of your condition is depression," he said, leaving the word hanging alone.

Rasputin jammed a hand into a pocket and let his gaze roam the lichen-encrusted tiles of his flat.

"You needn't have bothered. I can tell you straight out I'm depressed. I owe money, and what job prospects I had are crippled by a leg with a chronic identity crisis. Who wouldn't be depressed?"

"You don't owe anything anymore."

"Yes I do. My debt just changed currency."

"Feeling depressed isn't the same as *depression*."

"Depressed. Depression. Why do you care either way? What's it got to do with the time-bomb in my head?"

Thorpe's gaze relented. He scuffed a leaf from the driveway with an expensive leather shoe.

"Potentially, much." He looked up and to the east. Perhaps with those clear eyes he saw Venus, the Morning Star, waiting in the wings for its curtain call.

"Depression is one symptom in the constellation of woes that accompany the progression of ALS. The earlier I mark the appearance of any symptom, the better I can gauge the trajectory of the disease, and the more effective at the end are the steps we take now." He smiled at the sky. "Nudge a missile as it leaves the wing—just a child's shove—and see it fall wide of a village of children."

For Rasputin, the thought of forestalling his disease conjured a different image. He saw a butterfly beat opalescent wings over tropical waters and invoke a cascade of chaos that grew into a city-killing hurricane. He saw the heel of his shoe smear the insect's gizzard and avert disaster.

The scrape of shoes on pavement drew Thorpe's gaze. Someone approached. Rasputin turned to see Jordy walking from the bus stop. One shoulder was pulled lower than the other by the weight of his briefcase. A shirt flap hung over his pants, which were creased above his thighs. The thin end of his tie was peeking out. His appearance was what Rasputin called After-Jordy, what a day in the office did to Before-Jordy, who he sometimes bid farewell to in the morning.

Jordy straightened up as he put the briefcase down and greeted Rasputin, "Monk." But his gaze was on Thorpe.

"Mr. Mitchell, I presume," said Thorpe, and extended his hand. Jordy took it, nodded, but said nothing. He held it long, and Rasputin noted how the skin about their knuckles went white as they compressed each other's hand.

Their hands swung apart finally, and Jordy said, "Why are you standing in the drive. Didn't this punk offer you a drink?"

"I can't stop," said Thorpe. "I merely called past to tell Rasputin he was a liar."

Rasputin wasn't sure if it was meant as a joke.

"You could do me a favour, being his flatmate, by keeping an eye on him."

"Like a brother," said Jordy, without humour.

Jordy's reply worked a curious, fleeting change on the surgeon's face. It was suddenly animated by distaste or frustration. Whatever the cause, it stifled whatever else he had to say. He rounded the front of the Jaguar and bent to open the door.

"What am I looking for, exactly?" said Jordy, when Thorpe had one leg planted on the car's floor.

"Irritability. Moodiness. Slurred speech. Seizures." He sank into the car. Its engine wound and caught. The car heaved forward, as the engine whined up an octave, and was gone.

"Check. Check and Check," said Jordy, catching Rasputin's eye.

"Seizures?" said Rasputin. "Shit."

"Relax, Monk. He's trying to get your goat."

"He already has my goat. In hock."

"He's just grumpy. It's an occupational hazard for surgeons. All those narcotic-propped hours. Plus the god-complex."

It was the kind of thing Jordy said to diffuse a situation, but it lacked the needed edge of humour. The net effect was negative.

As Rasputin left the next morning, in a rush to make his appointment with Lloyd, he nearly stepped on a package left in front of the door. It was a yellow envelope about the size of a milk carton. It lay in line with the mat's WELCOME message, occluding the LCO.

"WEME to you too," he said to the morning. He stooped to retrieve the package and tore off the sealing strip. The weight of the package lay at one end, so he tilted it. An object slid satisfyingly down its length until it took flight into his hand. It was a mobile phone. He jammed the envelope under the door, and kept walking, navigating by peripheral vision while he examined the phone.

He wasn't up-to-date on mobile tech, but it looked shiny. He turned it on, and noted that it had signal and a full battery. Someone had sent him a flashy phone that was ready to go.

He punched Sam's number into it as he drew level with the bus stop, and gazed back down the road in the direction the bus would come as the call worked its way through the network, found Sam's phone, and blipped confirmation of the connection.

When Sam answered he sounded put out and tense. "Yep."

"Honey, could you pick up milk on your way home from work?"

A short pause elapsed before, "Rasputin. You promised me you wouldn't dick around with my number."

"True, true. First and last time unless the situation is dire. I promise."

"Go on."

"Do you go in for hunches?"

"Did you say 'lunches' or 'hunchbacks'? Because that would be 'yes' and 'no' respectively. But I'm guessing I misheard."

"I was wondering, given you've opened a file on Thorpe, if you knew if he has siblings. In particular, any brothers. No biggie, but I'm feeling like cannon fodder, and it would be nice to have something to return fire with. If it's not too much to ask."

"I'll look into it. But please don't call me again unless it's serious."

"Okey dokey. And, hey, thanks for the phone."

As Rasputin snapped the phone shut, he heard Sam's tinny voice say something like "What?"

The office where Rasputin met Lloyd was downright homely compared to the Media Room. Nestling a computer were photos of a woman, presumably Lloyd's wife, and two little-Lloyds. Lloyd's immaculate fingernails shone up at Rasputin from hands resting splayed upon an open folder.

"So," Lloyd said, drawing his hands up into a shell under his chin. "Tell me about yourself. Start wherever you like. Whatever comes to mind."

"Thorpe admitted those photos were his attempt to depth-charge some kind of latent depression."

"Ah, yes," said Lloyd. He had been briefed. "He told me you asked about them. I thought you would. He also told me he explained their dual purpose, to detect and *distract*."

"I bought that when he said it," Rasputin said, and watching Lloyd's face stiffen, regretted he wasn't a smoker; it was the perfect juncture to stub out a cigarette and enjoy a *beat*. That's what a screenwriter would have done. "But if that were true, you'd sprinkle those photos through the test, not drop them in a glob at the end."

"But your response is the pressing issue," countered Lloyd.

Rasputin wondered if Lloyd felt comforted that he could easily shift to a career in politics if psychology failed.

"Okay. My dad never bought me a bike and that makes me really sad."

"Do you get on well with your father?"

"Like a house ablaze. When he's around." Rasputin lifted his left hand to look at the faint freckles that patterned its back. So familiar. He noticed a faint tremor in his fingers, something not familiar, and gripped his cane to stifle it. He shot a glance at Lloyd to see if he had noticed, but the psychologist was staring out the window. "He's not around much."

"Oh. Where is he?"

"Abroad. With Mum. They're in Europe now, probably doing something with a vulgar boatman."

"You know," Rasputin continued. "It occurs to me that it's my parents you should be talking to. They'd be much more fun. I mean, who just floats around the globe subsisting on novelty? That can't be healthy, can it?"

Rasputin sensed Lloyd was trying to seem nonchalant as he spoke. "Why do you think they spend so much time away?"

The answer leapt into his mind, and nearly from his mouth in the same instant: *to avoid me.* But that couldn't be true. They loved him. He knew that deeply. Why would you avoid someone you loved? That didn't make sense.

"I guess they're of a cosmopolitan bent. My mum always has her head in fashion magazines, art magazines. She loves Europe, in particular, as the throbbing heart of all that. And I think Dad is quite happy, in parallel, to conduct a gastronomic experiment on a grand scale. The man just loves croissants."

"When did they begin this ... lifestyle?"

"The symptoms appeared while I was in primary school, and exploded into full blown contagion about five years ago."

"When was your last contact?"

"A little while back, after my accident."

Lloyd's silence invited Rasputin to continue. When he didn't, Lloyd said, "What did you talk about?"

"We didn't talk. It was a letter. My mum wished me a speedy recovery. Told me to put betadine on my scratch and eat some chicken soup."

Lloyd's bent arms formed a square with his shoulders as he leaned forward. Rasputin had the distinct feeling Lloyd had found a lever and was about to lean on it.

"How did that make you feel?"

"You cried?" said Jordy.

Rasputin nodded and busied himself making a cup of soup.

"Wow," said Jordy quietly. He slotted a frozen meal into the microwave and pressed instant cook. The kitchen filled with the noise of the oven's decrepit fan as the food spun and its plastic sheath ballooned with heat.

"Maybe there is something to what Thorpe says," Jordy continued. "You have been a bit moody."

Rasputin fished in the soup for dry lumps, and sought to trap and crush them against the cup.

"Then again," said Jordy. "Who could blame you. Right now you're playing with a crap hand."

The microwave emitted a beep and fell silent. Into the silence came another beep, fainter and plaintive. It took Rasputin a moment to realise it came from the phone in his pants pocket. He drew it out and noted its charge was almost spent.

"Since when did you own a phone?" said Jordy, coming over to inspect.

"It was on the doorstep this morning. I think it's from my ASIO angel." He held it up for Jordy to see. "You got a charge cable for one of these?"

"I'll check the tangle in the bathroom drawer after I've eaten."

Jordy took a closer look at the phone. "Shiny. You finally enter the 21st Century and jump straight to the cutting edge."

"It's just a phone," said Rasputin, but had secretly fancied himself James Bond with the tech cached in his jeans.

"That thing isn't even in the country yet—GPS standard, Zeiss lens. ASIO boys must have some perks. Bit of an oversight not to send the cable."

"It might be fancy, but its battery life sucks."

"How much credit is on it?"

"No idea," said Rasputin, to which Jordy shook his head.

He slid the phone back into his jeans pocket, and took his soup out onto the back steps. Jordy followed, swapping the hot container holding his dinner from hand to hand.

"I'll ask next time I talk to Sam. But he was pretty jacked off I called this morning."

"Why would he give you a phone if he didn't want you to call?"

"Don't know. At least my contact list isn't empty now." He pulled the phone out again and accessed its contact list. Sam's number was alone, listed under *Tracey, Dick*. "Almost a prime."

"Are you that bored you checked to see if his number is a prime?" Jordy stabbed a chunk of potato with a fork and held it before him. Steam coiled up from it into the early evening air.

"*Checked* nothing. I knew straight away. It isn't. It's three off, as it turns out."

Jordy rested his fork in the plastic tray as he turned to look at Rasputin.

"Hang on. Are we talking about the same thing. Prime, as in prime number? The maths prime, divisible only by one and itself?"

"No, prime fillet. Sam's number is just shy of the barcode on a juicy-looking porterhouse I saw yesterday—"

At the mention of barcodes and primes a tremor shook him, within the eye. Remembered barcodes mushroomed like an underwater explosion in a cluster of cauliflower florets. Yes, there were primes in there ... and, if he really wanted to know, more exotic beasts a hairsbreadth away. But he didn't. Not now, anyway. Inwardly, he gripped the ballooning cloud and extinguished it.

"—of course I'm talking about prime numbers."

Jordy placed his meal on the step and clasped his hands.

"Then you're officially freaking me out."

"Good. I've been freaking myself out for weeks. It's nice to have company."

"I didn't get it when you explained what happened in Melbourne, with the cards and the players," said Jordy. "But this, this is more ... pure."

Jordy's meal sat forgotten as it vented its heat into the atmosphere. His gaze seemed fixed on the tangled branches of a bougainvillea that reached over the back fence in perennial escape.

Rasputin sipped his soup. His desire for the salty broth bordered on craving. At length, he ventured to interrupt Jordy's reverie. "What do you mean, *pure.*"

"Pure *calculation*. When you were gambling, you were weighing odds with a mix of evidence—cards, people—and came out on top. But, to be honest, I thought you just got lucky. That's part of why I wanted you to get the hell out before you blew it like all the other suckers."

"Apology accepted," said Rasputin.

Jordy smirked, but sobered as he continued. "But there aren't odds with a prime calculation. The House takes all: a number's either prime or not. End of story. And to work it out, you have to factor the number until only two numbers remain: one and the number itself. You have to run an algorithm, and that algorithm gives you a definitive result."

"So what?"

"That phone number is twelve digits. Minus the leading zero gives you something of the order of forty billion. A brute force search for factors, starting from two and going up to half the number amounts to twenty billion checks."

Rasputin blinked. Twenty billion was only three times the Earth's population. No biggie.

"That's the worst case," said Jordy. "The best known algorithm reduces the number of checks to the quadratic root, a piddling amount in this case. But that only swaps one problem for another, because that algorithm isn't exactly a walk in the park. More than that, you found the *nearest* prime. That's even harder."

Jordy looked at Rasputin for the first time since he had put down his dinner.

"Either way that's a prodigious piece of calculation in ridiculously quick time for a human."

He paused to retrieve the now-cold chunk of potato and jam it into his mouth.

"Prodigious piece of *calculation*, not memory," he said, chewing noisily. He swallowed. "Or *computation*, if you prefer."

He stabbed another potato, held it up to emphasise his point.

"Question is: why is your head increasingly emulating a computer? What's it planning on computing?"

Rasputin recalled Thorpe's comment about how metaphors for memory had begun to work backwards when it came to computers, from life to machine. Just now, the relationship felt more like an Irish dervish.

Rasputin licked up more soup, savouring its load of salt.

"No comeback?" said Jordy, coaxing. "That's not like you, Monk."

"Could you do me a favour?" Rasputin said.

Jordy shrugged *of course*.

"Could you think about it?" Rasputin tapped his temple. "Every time I go in here I find something new. It's like returning home to find I've been the target of *Surprise Renovations*. Only it happens every day, and they haven't just painted the walls and hung curtains, they've joined the basement to the attic, and turned off gravity in the kitchen."

Jordy had become still, his gaze fixed on Rasputin.

"You know what my memory is doing. Maybe now you get what my mind, my sub-conscious—I don't even know what to call it—my *deeper* mind, is spewing to the surface." Rasputin swirled the remainder of his soup to dredge the sediment and skulled it. He said, quietly he guessed because Jordy drew nearer, "But it's growing, like rats in a sewer. And I have no idea where it's headed."

It was the closest he had come to describing the thing in his head in autonomous terms. He wondered fleetingly if Jordy thought he was slipping over the edge.

Jordy said, "Your driver's licence renewal came this morning. I paid it."

It didn't matter that Rasputin could no longer drive. He said, "Thanks."

They sat in silence as the temperature fell. A breeze began to ruffle the bougainvillea, lending its silhouette a B-grade Horror look.

Rasputin's phone emitted a sound for the second time that evening, but it lacked the pleading bent of its earlier cry. Rasputin drew it out to investigate. The screen read: You have one new message. He followed the display prompt to retrieve the message.

It read: "CompuCorp makes sense of your data."

Jordy leaned over to read it, and said, "You've had a phone one whole day and you get spam. Welcome to the future. Not as rosy as prophesied." He rose, stretched and went inside.

"If that's an ad, it's an epic fail," said Rasputin to the gathering darkness. "There's no contact number."

The phone emitted a pathetic, accusatory bleep and died. Rasputin shivered and followed Jordy.

As Rasputin lay in bed that night waiting for sleep, with the smell of flannel sheets too-long-gone in his nostrils, a wind rose and began to play upon the chimes beneath the eaves. To his ears, the knock of wood had the taste of Asian tones and structures, something exotic and beautiful if only he could understand its motions and relations. His mind sifted the random noise for intention, looking for order and retrospectively altering his anticipation when it was not satisfied. The only sense to persist was of its alienness.

Behind closed eyes, a place that felt more like a harbour each day, he gazed at the eye's constellations. He watched for the glistening threads strung between memories. He felt both fearful and drawn to these telltale signs of the deeper structure of his mind.

Sleep was crouching at his door. But before it slipped through the keyhole, his gaze tripped over something he had *not* seen before.

As he watched glistening ribbons sprout and reach forth from the day's freshly minted memories—the rack-shouldered girl at the bus stop, the interview with Lloyd—he saw motion beyond them, out in the deep dark, like a wave rolling through an oil spill. The wave caught the silver light and threw it back in fleeting sheen.

The moment passed and the patch again became a uniform black. *What the hell was* that?

It wasn't a memory. He couldn't simply ask the eye to pull it near.

He let his gaze roam across the twinkling vault. A handful of times he caught a flicker of motion in his peripheral vision, but when he looked square-on it vanished.

He returned his attention to the patch of sky where he had first seen the motion, gritted his teeth, and concentrated on it.

A stomach-dipping jolt shook him. He staggered and nearly fell. He groped for his centre of gravity as if he were aboard a boat come adrift of its mooring.

When he looked up again, his mouth hung open.

His little observatory had pulled its anchor. The globe of the eye was in motion. In response to his desire, it had lifted into the void like a gondola riding a silver thread.

He crouched and splayed his arms in search of something to brace himself. He watched, terrified, as the eye travelled toward a tracery of silver filaments—the skin of his hand tingled with the memory of the sticky stuff. He feared the tendrils would collapse around the eye like a spider's web. Instead, they bowed against its surface—and slipped behind it.

He sighed with relief and stood up straight.

When the bobbing, swaying motion of the eye finally soothed his nerves, he looked out again and tried to guess at the distances between the memory clusters all around him. But he lacked even the cues to gauge how fast the eye moved. He felt like a skier lost in cloud, where all is white and he knows not what bumps his legs and buckles his knees, nor if he moves at all.

But he was moving. The patch of once-disturbed darkness continued to take shape, a snatch of black velvet hanging in a jet sky, until a tug forward told him the eye had come to rest.

Rasputin waited for a sign or explanation.

He got neither. The thing simply hung in space, rippling occasionally with a telltale glint.

"What is it?" he said at last.

From somewhere someone spoke, "Manna."

A moment later he recognised the word was spoken with his own voice. It wasn't an answer, merely an echo of his question in Hebrew.

He tried again: "Show me what this is."

In response, a faint glow began to radiate from the eye itself, as if it were a submariner firing lamps on the deep ocean floor.

The light struck the thing and revealed its curves. He saw now that it was puckered along one side. A seam ran down it like a tipped smile.

He pointed at the flaw: "Go there."

The horizon swung to bring the seam centre. The eye moved forward. The seam stretched at once, each end disappearing out of view above and below. The smile widened. But would it widen enough for the eye to fit?

He was about to find out.

Feeling a mild pressure on his eardrums, he crossed the threshold and was swallowed by the smile.

His first thought on reaching the other side was of finding an air bubble in a pot of ink. But what set his skin tingling was that the bubble appeared to be larger than the bottle. He had entered a wardrobe only to find it a portal to a snow-bound world. He had slipped into a fold in space.

Walls of deep black arched above and below, and colours like oil upon water swirled over them and strobed their surfaces like searchlights. As far as Rasputin could see, spires the size of planet-axles punctured the walls, thrusting inward. The place looked like an inside-out sea urchin.

The spires all converged on an object that he could not recognise. A riot of light was riding each spire to clash and coruscate around the object, so intense it baffled his view.

Shielding his eyes, he willed himself toward it.

As the distance shrank he began to pick out details of the object amid the flashing brilliance. But they were little help. The thing resembled the skeleton of a skyscraper fallen to its side. But its girders had an *organic* look—they were tangled and restless.

His gaze travelled along one such elastic girder, until it tripped, and stopped, rooted to a point.

He blinked, and stared. There, dwarfed by the scale of the object but unmistakable, was the likeness of a man.

As if Rasputin's gaze had announced his presence to the man, he rose from a crouch, turned, and stared up at the eye. An instant later he stood before Rasputin.

Blood drained from Rasputin's cheeks.

The man stood still, staring at Rasputin in frank appraisal.

Rasputin made his own inspection: the man appeared the purest stereotype of the mad inventor, with pinched brows couching eyes that shone with the lustre of cut sapphire. Unnervingly, his fly-away hair seem to wriggle like the girders of the thing outside.

When he spoke, his voice sounded borrowed from the forensic artist, Bert Hills. It rumbled as though some mechanism of his voice box had worn bearings.

"Mary had a little lamb," said the inventor, "and everywhere that Mary went, the lamb went *if so inclined?*"

Rasputin smiled despite himself.

Ambient colour stained the inventor's white coat. He thrust his hands deep into its pockets.

"You're far from home, little lamb," he said, and Rasputin felt he was being weighed in the man's gaze.

"Who are you?" said Rasputin.

He gave no response. Colour continued to moil over his coat, but strangely not his face. If anything, that looked paler.

Rasputin changed tack. He turned and looked out on the colossal super-structure. It reminded him of the bamboo scaffolding that sheathed buildings in Asia, only this was in the grip of a hurricane.

"What is that?" He barked, suddenly carried on a sense of proprietaryness. After all, it was *his* mind. Wasn't it?

The inventor followed his gaze. His face lit with a smile. The wriggle of purple veins beneath his temples showed through his now translucent skin.

"A beginning."

"Of what?"

"The greatest construction ever made."

"But what are you building?" Rasputin said, riding a wave of indignation that died when he looked again at the man.

His coat had turned black, and its cut had thinned and lowered. His hair, which had not stopped moving since he had appeared, was now curling in on itself, tightening and drooping down either side of his face to rest on his shoulders. His face began positively to shine until Rasputin was forced to squint.

The man's expression was unreadable beneath the strengthening glow as he said: "I am building a case."

Rasputin saw at last that the inventor had become a judge.

When the judge spoke his voice seemed to come from his feet.

"But you are not ready to be here yet."

He swept a hand toward Rasputin. The gesture picked him up, picked the eye up, and thrust them backwards, across the cavern, and through the lip of the fold in space. The gap closed and was gone.

The part of Rasputin that might have asked if this was a dream had long since fallen asleep.

With the blinds drawn up, Thorpe's room looked less like the den of a Mediaeval collector of antiquities, but only a little less.

For an hour they had been talking, or rather, Thorpe had been trying to dredge up the history of Rasputin's family life, and Rasputin had been fending off the probes, and telling half-truths.

Rasputin felt stiff from tension. He was sunk so deep into the leather of his chair he fancied, were he to rise, his buttocks would produce a double-beat syncopated sucking noise.

Thorpe had been genial throughout, but Rasputin guessed he was frustrated. Their conversation had been a play-act. Both knew it, neither was admitting it.

Now Thorpe was simply watching Rasputin. Finally, he sighed, as if coming to a resolution.

"Can I get you a drink?" said Thorpe.

Rasputin recalled the pleasant warmth and looseness Guinness had worked in him at the casino. He nodded.

Thorpe rose and turned to the sideboard behind his desk. He poured an amber liquid into a tumbler and passed it to Rasputin.

"Top shelf, or so I'm told."

"You not having one?"

"Can't stand the stuff."

Rasputin sipped at the liquor, and felt its warm length slide inside him snake-like. It sought his stomach, and when it fell there radiated warmth outwards. He imagined tension evaporating, and thought, after all, he might leave his chair without acoustic accompaniment.

"You're the first professor to give me grog."

"Brain cells are my specialty—healing and killing."

Rasputin was beginning to get Thorpe's humour, and its lack of conventional markers.

He took another sip. His chest hitched on the verge of a cough. He waited it out, then said: "So, am I depressed?"

"You are raising an alarming number of flags, including signs of depression."

Flags, signs, constellations. Wasn't this supposed to be science? It sounded more like gizzard reading and tea-leaf augury. He yearned for a definitive pronouncement. He wanted facts or figures that put him on a trajectory that someone had trod before, which gave shape to his future, which offered even a little hope to dispel the dark, suffocating cloud that thickened every day.

"Can't you scan me or something?" There was a hint of hysteria in his voice. "I know you said cell damage can be undetectable, but surely *something* will show up?"

"Have you ever held a baby?" Thorpe said.

Rasputin, now used to Thorpe's segues, answered promptly. "No. Never."

"Fantastic creatures." He pointed his finger at Rasputin. "Just after you were born, lying in your mother's arms, still smeared in birth-white, possibly dribbling, probably crying, and uglier than a puppy, your brain was already a more complex and powerful machine than any endeavour of man, in all the marches of civilisation, has ever produced: a bloody, needy, baffling miracle—if I may use such a quaint term. Look beneath the surface of that wrinkly little pate and you, were you able, would see a brain building 250,000 new cells every *minute*. A biological big bang less understood than its cosmological cousin."

Thorpe had rested his hand again on the table as he spoke and his attention turned inward, but his gaze snapped back to Rasputin as he fired questions at him.

"Why did those cells reach out 100 arms to their neighbours? Why did they gradually shrink from that contact as you grew into a man, until only five remained? Why did those that remain fight to exist, and why did they win? And how did they find their way in the first place, through the primordial sea of Rasputin, through tangles of other beginning, growing, organising cellular matter."

Thorpe flicked his hand at Rasputin's foot which had perched unremarked on a corner of the desk after he had begun to drink.

"I know you curse your leg at the moment, but isn't it a marvel that a single cell extrusion, the longest nerve in the human body, reaches over a meter from the base of your spine to your big toe: a single cell that carries the pain message of a stubbed toe all the way up your leg to hand it off to your spinal cord."

Rasputin suppressed an urge to squirm.

Thorpe leant forward on his elbows, and his fingers interdigitated. "Your brain is knit together like all the world's highways a million times over according to the blueprint of a mad genius poet."

He stood and reached above his head for a heavy-looking book. He flipped it open, placed it on the desk, and rotated it the right way up for Rasputin. The open pages depicted the brain, littered with overlaid labels and text describing its features. While Rasputin examined it, Thorpe rose and navigated to a massive world globe set in an intricate metal stand. Rasputin glanced up and saw Europe in miniature, dotted with towns and lined with rivers.

"Students open that textbook, see that figure or others like it, and think *Europe:* mapped, travelled, and, barring the details, understood."

Thorpe spun the globe and stabbed his finger down, halting it.

"Not so."

Rasputin squinted to see what Thorpe had fingered. It was Africa, but there was something wrong with it. He knew immediately that its shape was askew in places—the eye could show him precisely where it varied against every map of Africa he had ever seen. But what drew his attention was its dark centre. The heart of Africa was a shaded apology, an embarrassing stain of ignorance, compared to the complete picture of Europe and the dominion of which it spoke. Hedgerow versus vine-tangle.

"There lies the brain," said Thorpe, and spun the globe idly as he walked back to his seat.

Something buzzed in Rasputin's pocket and he nearly leapt from his chair in fright. He retrieved his phone and saw an incoming call from Sam. He killed the call and replaced the phone.

"So, in answer to your question," said Thorpe, "can't I just scan you or something: no. The cutting edge of brain scanning technology is not unlike a satellite floating thousands of kilometres above Africa. From its images you can see how much of the Congo has been eaten by desert, and whether the Nile is in flood, but not where the Ebola virus is reaping its bloody harvest."

Rasputin's searched the cross-sectioned brain lying open on the desk before him. The page contained fifty-seven features that were named, many of which had accompanying descriptive text. He desperately wanted to believe in Europe.

Thorpe's eyes twinkled, and there was a smile in his voice.

"You don't believe me. Look here," he said, and pointed to the illustrated brain. "Do you see this feature? *Nucleus reticularis tegmenti pontis Bechterewi.* Impressively long, isn't it. But I prefer these." He pointed out a series of features, naming each as his finger rested on it. "*Substantia Innominata*: Unnameable substance; *Nucleus ambiguus*: Translates itself; *Zone incerta*: Uncertain area." His voice rose the further he went, until at last it bubbled over into laughter. "But, my dear boy, the entire brain is *Zone incerta*. And as long as we continue to approach it the same way, that is what it will remain. Scientifically named, but no closer to yielding the mysteries of the philosopher's fire within.

"Let us instead simply call it, *Par Inust*: the Burning Within."

Something deep in Rasputin cracked under the pressure of his words. His mind wailed, a plea that escaped in whisper: "Isn't there an answer for me?"

Thorpe drew near in the silence that followed, and the room shrank to the space between them.

"Yes, there is. But it will take more than satellites."

Rasputin did not have to turn to see the dark heart of Africa. It was mirrored in Thorpe's pupils.

"We need a landing party. We need the spirit of the explorers who trod the ground to open the great frontiers. We need to get beneath this globe of bone so vital for life, yet so resistant to understanding of that same life, to the treasure held in its bony protuberances."

Thorpe leaned away, as if sensing the mood that had fallen over them like a leaden shroud.

"We're very near the heart of my calling now. You understand I am a rare bird, Rasputin: neuroscientist, neurologist. But the best description is the one I've alluded to: explorer." He reached into a drawer and placed an object over the drawing of the brain. "And this is the landing vessel."

His hand withdrew to reveal what at first glance appeared to be a bullet. It had the dull, clean shine of all instruments at the business end of clinical medicine. At Thorpe's invitation, Rasputin picked it up. Its weight and tubular shape were very like a bullet casing, but complications at its butt pointed to a different purpose. Rasputin raised the rear of the device to his eye and tried to decipher the meaning of the small, regularly spaced holes.

"They look almost like—"

"Terminals, yes," finished Thorpe. "That is an electrode. Its purpose is to apply electrical stimulation directly into the cerebral cortex." He arched an eyebrow. "But similar devices have been in use for decades. To see what is novel about this particular specimen, you need to examine the other end."

Rasputin did so and, at first, saw only the terminus of the electrode.

"I see a curling wand for the sticky side of your skull, but—" he began, then noticed the head of the electrode was not a simple point. From it bristled a tuft of impossibly thin wires. It sent a shudder wriggling down his neck and over his shoulders. "So it curls *and* buffs?"

"Those wires are a micro-array of electrodes. Each wire is only 50 nanometres thick. Small enough to read the electrical impulses fired by a single neuron."

Rasputin became conscious, for the first time during their interview, of Thorpe's breathing.

"This electrode is to neurology what the microscope was to biology."

"Did you invent it?"

"No. Electrodes capable of reading at cell resolution have been in existence for some time now."

"Why the excitement then?"

"There's a rub, you see. Applying electrical stimulation to the brain is a long-accepted treatment for certain neurological disorders. But *reading* electrical charge has no immediate clinical benefit. The ethical watchdogs will maul anyone inserting an electrode for merely experimental purposes. The beauty of this device—"

"Is to smuggle one in with the other." Rasputin's gaze was fastened to the tiny star-burst of wires.

"*Smuggle* is a rather negative term, but you have put your finger on it. This device delivers aid to stricken Egyptian villages, while allowing the mission to search for the source of the Nile; a patient's need for therapy becomes the researcher's opportunity to advance science. And you can see now why neurology must leave the lab and take a machete to the jungles—why I call myself, above all, an explorer."

Rasputin's phone belched. Annoyance rippled his brow as he pulled it free and glanced at the screen. It heralded a new message. He called it up, conscious of Thorpe's gaze. The message was from Sam, no surprise there.

It read: *Thorpes bro. U o me a case now.* It was followed by an address.

He crammed the phone back into his pocket and met Thorpe's gaze. "I have to be somewhere, sorry."

"Remember what I've said. If we are to unravel this knot," said Thorpe, threading his fingers again for emphasis, "we need a pioneering spirit."

"I will," said Rasputin as he rose, and let himself out.

As he rode the elevator down, the word *knot* rolled like a marble around his mind. It occurred to him then that Thorpe shared his first name with another who had been interested in knots. The association was not encouraging.

Outside, standing in the spill of afternoon sunlight, he recalled the address in Sam's message. Thorpe's brother lived in Shenton Park, a suburb that bordered the university.

He dug a coin from his pocket, a twenty-cent piece.

"Tails I go home. Heads I hunt the Jabberwocky."

He flipped the coin. It bounced out of his palm and rang on the concrete. He stooped to retrieve it. *Tails.*

He decided to pay a visit anyway. Thorpe needed some family to fix him in the tissue of human society. Beyond that, spontaneity was fast becoming a virtue for Rasputin. He began walking, and wondered briefly if he ought to examine that trait, but the thought was soon banished from his mind. Bars of sunlight were falling through the tree canopy as if in cloud burst, causing the chosen few of leaf and flower to burn in the arboreal gloom. The earth under foot smelt rich with moisture.

He left the campus via the same tunnel he had taken the day Sam appeared on his radar. An irrational fear of the then unknown stalker closed over him momentarily. He fought the emotion to reconcile it with his knowledge of Sam, the ASIO agent tasked with monitoring his movements, but his mind clung to the first impression as though that dark man was real, possessed of independent life.

It was not the first time he had felt this fracture in reality, a bifurcation of first impression and subsequent familiarity.

Jordy—the Jordy he knew—was a far cry from the creature Dee had introduced years before. Clinging to Rasputin's memory of that party was the smell of pot. The music had been loud, stripping all subtlety from conversation. And that Jordy's eyes had crawled over every dress in the room. Later, Dee had pleaded his case: he had lost a long-time friend to a brain tumour. Her judgment of his character had been vindicated by time, but it had not erased that first impression.

The wash of traffic noise receded as he got away from the highway and into suburban streets. It was an expensive postcode, but the houses were modest. The homes he passed were clad in brick and corrugated iron rooves of subdued, earthy tones, quiet beneath the drooping branches of peppermint trees, and presiding over niche courtyards and neat patches of lawn. Each garden had a unity imposed by an economy of space not money—*laissez-faire* English cottage gardens, Japanese pebble features, and Australian natives biopsied from the Bush. But over the pastiche, the peppermints asserted their aura, which for Rasputin was of summer holidays, salt, sand and flies. This was as *old money* as Perth got, a contrast to the *nouveau riche* mansions on the riverfront, which puffed out their chests to challenge the view rather than steep in it.

He had been walking for half an hour when his leg began to murmur with pain. He knew the precise location of the street he was after, but had underestimated the distance—that is, the distance on foot. When it came to learning to take account of the limits his leg imposed on him, he was proving a slow learner.

Two things about the house he found at the address struck him as peculiar. It rambled backwards over a double block, and it was gated. He might have turned around then and there if his leg hadn't screamed blue murder.

He approached the intercom and pressed the hail button. A woman's voice answered immediately. "Walsham's. Yes please?"

Walsham's? That wasn't right. He wanted Thorpe's.

What the hell.

"Joachim Thorpe. I'm here to see Joachim Thorpe."

A pause.

"The nature of the visit?"

"I'm a friend." Was that half true? What was the enemy of an enemy?

"Your name, please?"

"Lowdermilk. Rasputin Lowdermilk. I'm a friend of Alexander. A family friend, really." He grimaced as he said it.

Another pause.

"Come through," she said, and a metallic snap reverberated through the grillwork of the gate as it was remotely unlocked.

He passed through the gate and descended a short flight of stairs to the front door. He opened it, entered and found himself in what appeared to be a small foyer, complete with counter. Behind it was seated a woman, presumably the one with whom he had spoken. She acknowledged his presence with a weighted glance before returning her attention to a computer screen.

He scanned the room.

"Do you need help locating Mr. Thorpe?"

"No, no. I've been before."

"I have no record of you having visited," she said, searching records that rippled upwards over the computer's screen.

Then why, he thought, didn't you just tell me where he is. You are tricksy. He said, "Perhaps they got my name wrong. It happens a lot," and sidled closer to the counter to absorb the records flowing over the screen.

"Never mind," he said, and wandered into a corridor that appeared to be the thoroughfare out of the lobby.

The place was a puzzle that his mind worked furiously to fit together before someone realised he was not meant to be there—and of that he was sure.

The foyer had been furnished with expensive but discreet taste. There was no sign of 'Walsham's' anything, nor any other markers identifying its purpose. The building was gated to keep riff raff out, but exactly what kind of riff raff?

The clues began to gel as a familiar smell tickled his nose. The perfume of industrial strength cleaner wafted under his nose, the kind that killed germs and blanketed the odour of urine and worse, and at that moment a door in the corridor opened to admit a woman wearing nurses' whites.

"How is Joachim?" he said on impulse.

His question startled the nurse, and he wondered if she was used to being addressed. She replied, apologetically, in English buried beneath a heavy European accent, "Oh. Mr. Thorpe. He is three doors down." She pointed the way.

Upon entering the dim room, the first thing Rasputin noticed was the noise—a scraping, juddering that became thick with liquid noises and then aspirated with indrawn air. Was someone perking coffee in a self-contained espresso machine? But he saw his error immediately, before the machine cycled from silence to grind again. The rhythmic sound was coming from a life support device connected by wires and intubation to a man lying on a bed.

Only the man's head and shoulders were visible above a linen sheet. He was of colossal height. His legs overhung the end of the long bed. But the sheet clung to his form in valleys and peaks that gave it the look of a death shroud covering a skeleton. Converging on the man's face were support lines from the machine, but enough of his pale, sunken flesh, which sat upon his bones as the sheet sat upon his frame, was visible for Rasputin to know beyond doubt that this man was Thorpe's brother.

Rasputin pulled a chair up to the bed's side and sat facing Joachim Thorpe. He tried to decipher the meaning of what was in front of him, his thoughts beginning in a number of false starts, like fire taking to loose tinder. But each flared only to find it had consumed the evidence, and starved and died as quickly as it had begun.

The room was luxuriously appointed and carefully tended. What light there was slanted through a gap in the heavy curtains. It fell in a bar across the carpet and then over Joachim's midriff. Fresh flowers were bursting from vases placed on space-filling furnishings and a mantel that ran parallel to the bed's foot. Between them nestled numerous photo frames, too dark to make out from where he sat. Even the door standing ajar on the opposite side of the bed, revealing a disabled-ready shower and toilet, was of thick and expensive-looking hardwood. A cigarette tray on a bedside table was the only item out of place. A sprinkle of ash sat in its rim like salt and pepper, and he fancied he could smell smoke lingering in the air.

What ambience the room might have had was crushed by the machine's unceasing rasp. And *that* smell.

He mused aloud. "What is this place, Joachim? And what are you doing here?"

He rose and crossed to the mantle forested with flowers. Their blooms cast shadows over the photos beneath, which could have been headstones nestled in undergrowth. He leaned closer to better look at them. Figuring in most was a younger, much healthier looking Joachim. The second most popular subject was a woman with a strong resemblance to both brothers, their mother. Alexander appeared in one photo, back bent, skin glistening with sun-struck moisture, hauling a catamaran from what looked to be Crawley Bay near the university. In the foreground was Joachim, laughing at someone out of frame. Both men were near 30 perhaps, and Joachim had then had a physique to match his brother's.

Rasputin turned to look again at the stricken man in the bed. How long had he been here, like this? Walsham's provided some kind of palliative care, that much he had decided. The kind that cost a lot but delivered privacy and a kind of dignity.

He scanned the photos again, examining Mrs. Thorpe. She had an easy elegance about her. No doubt the family tree had deep roots in money that went beyond any need of Alexander's professional wealth. Did she put her son here?

He thought back to when the woman in the foyer had searched her computer for a record of his name. The log of visits appeared, clear as day, intact in his mind's eye. In it, the name that figured most was a *F.*

Worthington. It recurred in great slates of Worthingtons, pockmarked by names he didn't recognise, and one that he did: A. Thorpe.

But F. Worthington intrigued him more. He scrolled to the record of the last visit under that name, and took a moment to realise it had been that very morning. Perhaps F. Worthington smoked, and it was he or she who had left ash in the tray and the ghost of smoke in the air. He was struck by the intuition that F. Worthington was the woman smiling out of so many of the photos. Perhaps she was divorced and remarried, or widowed and had reverted to her maiden name—no, the first, he decided; this woman would not orphan her sons, at least, not this one. Yes, she came, daily he realised. He imagined her lighting up and reading from a book to her bedridden son. A faithful mother.

He turned his concentration to the other name. What did Alexander think of his brother? He visited him. But why? To grieve? To gloat?

Rasputin looked at the mask strapped like a muzzle over the prone man. He could see the shadow of condensation through the translucent, ribbed plastic of the tube, a lifeline to the atmosphere and its billions of tons of oxygen—oxygen as useless to this man as to a stranded fish but for the pump forcing it into his lungs.

At that thought another association struck him: the mask reminded him of a scuba diver. The modern equivalent of a *Diving Bell* ...

And then two things happened simultaneously. Rasputin realised that, according to the visit log, the last three by Alexander occurred straight after he had met with Rasputin. And Joachim opened his eyes.

Rasputin caught the faint movement in his peripheral vision, just beyond his tight circle of focus on the mask. He started backwards with intaken breath, startled as if a tarantula had crept from the man's ear. He would have caught himself before falling in a previous life, but hampered by the sluggish response of his leg, he fell, splayed over the chair, which collapsed onto its back. The carpet mercifully deadened the sound of its fall.

The eyes—brilliant blue, not grey like his brother's—trained on Rasputin. But Joachim made no other move or sound.

The last piece of the puzzle slotted home, and Rasputin cursed himself for an idiot. Joachim was buried alive in his own skin. *Maladie de l'emmure vivant. Eingeschlossensein.* Perhaps Alexander had seen a patient named Reginald Palmer, but he *certainly* had a patient now suffering from the very disease he feared for Rasputin: his own brother.

And still the eyes stared. A blink, then another. Two blue jewels, spheres of complexity having the appearance of simplicity, alike shipwrecked, stranded in the ruin of the vessel that had once carried them in a world that was a never-ending visual banquet.

Emotions clashed in Rasputin. He was engulfed by fear and pity. The being before him was a monster; he was a child; he was neither. Rasputin lacked categories for the thing in the bed.

Then Joachim began to glow, and Rasputin's thoughts clutched again at *monster*. Joachim's face effused a red aura that spread slowly, enveloping his whole body. His trunk and legs shone through the sheet as though X-rayed. Light gathered at his extremities. A feeler of solid red light began coiling off the tip of his nose, as though it were a smouldering wick. Soon a forest of ribbons of light were twisting up from his body, and meeting with the roof were baffled and began to writhe and clot together into clouds like storm heads at sunset.

He sat frozen, straddling the fallen chair. Joachim seemed unaware of his own transformation. The blue eyes simply gazed at him, while they let loose geysers of blue, which turned to mauve as they wound up into the red haze.

Other colours began to mingle with the red, and Rasputin realised that it wasn't only Joachim bleeding his aura into the room. Everything was. Every object, living or not, was giving up its colour into the mix. The room was a watercolour sinking beneath a wave, each colour relinquishing its fixity in one object, sharing it with all others. The room was becoming an impressionist image of itself.

Then an odour assaulted him: ozone from a lightning-rent sky. Then another, liquorice so strong a smell it was a taste. Smells strobed him like lights, tugged at him like a fitful breeze.

Pain finally pried him from the floor. It stabbed him somewhere in his brain, made him gasp and stagger to his feet. It struck again and again, each time in a new place, a percussionist with roving hand. It struck in the corner of his right eye, where the upper and lower lid met, drew to a point and pressed inwards—his tear duct felt punctured by heavy gauge fence wire. It slid through his ocular cavity like a skewer through fat as it was fed in, and punctured his cortex, before curling down in an arc. He could feel the full length of it, a heavy, cold line of fire carving a channel in his grey matter.

He wanted to say, "I'm having a seizure," but his lower jaw was locked onto the upper as though there had never been an opening there.

He lunged off the floor, cramps pulsing through his muscles from head to foot, and landed a glancing blow on the wall above Joachim's head. The emergency button clacked against the wall with the impact, and Rasputin passed out.

... his eyelids opened a crack. Light burned in darkness, stark white on black, sunrise on a planet without atmosphere. He felt his mind gather up the sense of his body, gather nerves as a loom gathers skeins of wool. He listened in on those nerve pathways for word from the field, blinded by the fog of war, anxious. He heard a sound like an approaching rain front on tin rooves and the nerve endings writhed in his grasp. He was aware enough to sense another seizure coming. Before it struck, he let go the frail grasp on his body, nerve-endings snaking from his hand lest they whip him, and fell back into blackness.

Radio Rasputin came back on the air. Hidden in the dark beneath his eyelids, he heard Dee speaking.

"—so why isn't someone doing something?"

Voice of an unfamiliar woman: "Please try to calm down. We're—" Break in transmission.

"—need to kill these rolling blackouts. He's not California. He's not even in the First World." Thorpe.

"But he only just presented. You want to—" Another woman.

"I don't *want* to. I need to. His brain will pull itself apart if I don't operate."

The word *operate* was neural adrenaline. At the cost of sudden intimacy with every one of his aching muscles, he gained control. He forced his eyes open. Shock registered on the face of the nurse with whom Thorpe was arguing. Thorpe saw it and turned to Rasputin.

"Quickly now. Do you remember our discussion?"

Speech was impossible. He grunted just to connect with the man.

"You are being hit by waves of self-reinforcing seizures. I must operate to provide a cut-out, break the circuit." He glanced at the nurse. "Do I have permission—"

Rasputin found voice, cut over him. "I see now. You and me. Not so different." Thorpe, anxious as he was for Rasputin's answer, bent nearer, confusion on his features. "Your brother. My sister. We just want an answer." Rasputin's hand stumbled across his sheet like a deranged spider, seeking Thorpe's, which rested, fingers splayed on the edge of the bed. "It hurts, doesn't it."

But then he was gone again as all frequencies were hit by a blanket jam, and *Rasputin* became a synonym for pain.

He rode a bubble, heading for the surface. Its payload: his consciousness and just one word, a simple word.

It hit the surface and popped. His eyes opened and it was as though someone had thrown the light switch.

Jordy, Dee and Thorpe looked at him as one. They spoke over each other.

"Monk, what—"

"Please, just keep your eyes—"

"Focus, Rasputin." Thorpe won out. "Give me permission to insert the probe."

Rasputin hunted through a fog for Thorpe, shrieked—and miraculously delivered the precious payload: "Yes."

Then he was falling again, having let go of the air that buoyed him. He sank, a dead weight.

But not into oblivion. He fell into the eye—but the eye as he had never seen it. Ripples roamed its surface, and where they passed it fluxed and erupted into liquescent vortexes, which grew and shrank and were absorbed again only to burst forth in another place. All over its sky was wracked by a storm of lightning. Great many-fingered slivers of light burst forth and travelled its breadth in a blink.

He cowered at its centre. The transparent sphere encasing him was a lens not a shield. He was a bug, and a million far-flung suns vied to burn him beneath the ray of their gaze.

With effort he raised his head. The memories nearest, half-seen in the chaos, were blurred, and to look at them turned his stomach. They quivered in the midst of the storm. He clasped his head with his hands, wishing they were big enough to encase his whole skull. He bent his knees to sink farther, willing an implosion. But something frustrated it, tugged at his attention, wouldn't let him fold.

One memory, a brilliant red dwarf in a mad sky, burned with singular clarity. It was as though the eye had given up all attempt to render any other memory clear for the sake of that one.

Rasputin pulled at it with what shreds of will lay in his power. He drew it on a cord that felt too thin to hold—it was a shark on light gauge line, and he feared any moment the line would snap and the shark turn on him.

The blazing anomaly drew near, filling his vision, and blossomed. He saw Thorpe's office. But something was off. There had to be a spanner in the machine, because there was not one Thorpe sitting across the desk from him but two. Two Thorpe's moved and talked in almost the same space, almost. But each vied for corporeality in turn, becoming a ghost of the other, like moving images of doubly-exposed film.

He realised the eye had taken two distinct memories—his first visit to Thorpe's office, and his last—and smashed them together. Each memory was eater and eaten. It was stellar warfare. No wonder they burned red.

As each replica of Thorpe became opaque, his voice strengthened as though carried on a wind. The fading Thorpe likewise quietened before rising again as the wind swung to his quarter.

It took Rasputin's overwrought senses a moment to realise the scenes playing out were looping. As one worked forward, the other was reversed, returned to its beginning. He strained to understand what the Thorpes were saying before complete unconsciousness took him.

And then he heard.

One Thorpe, at the peak of clarity, and with hungry eyes, saying, "... be sure to avoid the fate of Mr. Palmer."

Then, as that Thorpe was wound back, the other swelled. His back to Rasputin, he poured a drink, turned, and said: "Top shelf, or so I'm told."

They wove again, now swelling, now diminishing, in counterpoint:

"... be sure to avoid the fate of Mr. Palmer."

"Top shelf, or so I'm told."

... be sure to avoid the fate of Mr. Palmer.
Top shelf, or so I'm told.

... avoid the fate of Mr. Palmer.
Top shelf ...

Rasputin's attention lanced behind the twin apparitions, no longer listening. He looked, and saw, behind a perpetual motion machine whose ball-bearings beat spastically in the wrinkled, spiralling fabric of time-space, the sidebar from which Thorpe had served the drink. Rasputin waited for that Thorpe to rewind, to return the drink to the bottle. He passed, causing the hair on Rasputin's neck to stand. He gripped the bottle, let it suck the glass dry, and replaced it.

The bottle containing the amber liquid Thorpe had decanted stood like a glass skyscraper in a miniature glass city. Something glimmered in it, like a naked flame seen through a far-off window, two-thirds up its side, where the liquid's level rested. Rasputin strained forward to see it. The quavering light was coming from where the liquid's meniscus curved up to cling to the glass. It clung in two places, quivering between them. Now one, now another. And its motion caused the incident light to shift and sparkle. It had clung at one height at Rasputin's first visit, and another for his second. But the difference was not enough to account for even a sip of drink. Something had been added to the liquid. Something small. Something from another kind of shelf entirely.

He spiked my drink.

Rasputin let the conjoined memories implode. He looked up into the eye's seething sky, an inner reflection of the anarchy let loose on his body by the seizures.

Thorpe authored this, to get inside my skull again, to plant his precious probe.

Panic took him. He had to get word to Dee or Jordy. He needed to speak. But unconsciousness was closing over him like a midnight tide. He could hear them talking, but their voices were waning ever fainter. The gulf between the real world and his inner world was widening. His body was dragging him down into sleep, a defence mechanism against the pain.

He pushed upward. He needed only a moment to wring obedience from his body to speak. The voices grew louder, and as he broke the surface, his eyes opened.

Thorpe was the first to notice. He approached the bed and his shadow swallowed Rasputin.

Rasputin's gaze darted about the room hunting for Dee or Jordy— they had to be there. But all he could see was Thorpe's trunk, clothed in dark blue surgeon's overalls.

There was nothing for it but to shout the countermand.

But as the word rose in his throat, his jaw snapped shut on it. Rasputin had time enough to see a corner of Thorpe's mouth lift in a half-smile, before the seizure rolled his pupils up into his eye sockets.

The last clear image to flash across his mind was of an electrode biting into his grey matter.

When he came to, he was aware of his body—not because it screamed at him in pain, but as one feels the purring of a well-maintained engine. He sensed its eagerness to respond, to leap forward at the merest pulse of the throttle. He promised himself to never again take that feeling for granted.

He opened his eyes. He lay in a different room, but still a hospital room. It was washed in daylight and he was alone.

Was it all a dream? Have I only just woken from my coma?

Moments after pressing the call button all doubt was dispelled, for accompanying Dee and Jordy to the summons was the loping form of Sam.

"We've got to stop meeting like this," said Rasputin to Dee.

Dee leant to hug Rasputin, and he saw a uniformed police officer stride past along a corridor.

He pushed Dee away and said to Sam, "Please tell me the cops are here to nail Thorpe." Then, reminded by the surgeon's name, Rasputin shot a hand to his temple. It met nothing but skin and hair, intact and responding with no sensation other than quiet acknowledgment of the touch.

Sam nodded.

"You got it. And don't worry. We got him in time."

"Just," said Jordy, and raked his hair back with both hands.

"Can we find some fresh air?" said Rasputin. He rose. His body felt like it had been through a stone-wash rinse cycle.

Jordy found Rasputin's cane in the pile of belongings that had been stripped from him on admission. Evidently the staff hadn't been expecting him to need it any time soon. A little way down the corridor they found a sun lounge, with meter-wide windows thrown open on gardens and the arc of a lake's shore. Rasputin fell into a chair, closed his eyes and basked.

"How?" he said at last.

Sam laughed, and said, "With the opposite of precision," he said.

"I called him," said Dee, indicating the agent-in-training. She continued, in response to Rasputin's unspoken question. "Right after you woke briefly this morning. I didn't *see* you wake, but I could tell from how he acted." She paused, closing her eyes a moment. "I saw *his* face, and it scared the hell out of me. I can't describe it, Monk, but he did not mean you well." She became silent, her face contorting with fought emotion.

Rasputin had to look away.

Jordy took up the story. "So we had the idea to call Sam," he said, turning to him. "And, to be honest, I had bugger all idea how you could help. But it was clear we weren't getting anywhere with the staff here. They were all subject to his charm."

"Fear," corrected Dee, having composed herself. "I found Sam's number in your phone."

Rasputin noticed Sam cock an eyebrow, and said, "What did you tell him?"

"It was Dee's idea," said Jordy.

Dee's face held a mixture of shame and grim pleasure—an alien look for her.

"They called me," said Sam, "and told me a mad-heroin-addict surgeon, who was bragging of having taken a hit this morning, was about to open your skull and jam a probe into your brain, and could I do something."

"We hoped drugs would put it on his radar," said Dee. "Plus, you're ASIO's latest protégé."

"He's not that," said Sam, and Rasputin repressed the urge to ask why not. "I told you what interested me more." He looked at Rasputin. "Remember you asked me to work up a brief on Thorpe?"

"I asked if he had a brother. Thanks, by the way. I think."

"We don't do things by halves. The data boys built a full profile, including financials. One point in particular captured my interest, retrospectively, of course. Thorpe had patents pending on electrode signal analysis technology—not uncommon for an academic—but, in addition, the company owning the patents, his company, had another partner.

"So?"

"The partner is a criminal lawyer."

"What does that mean?"

"No idea. But it's odd isn't it? And odd often turns out to be interesting."

Rasputin stifled a yawn.

"That's a bit of an anticlimax."

"You haven't heard the rest yet," said Jordy with mischief in his eye.

Sam continued, "I called up my boss for permission to involve the police. It was a risk. It would blow our little understanding, and he might've blown my ear off, but he bought it enough to give the okay."

Thank God, thought Rasputin.

"We almost blew it, though," said Sam. "One of the cops sent here to check our errant surgeon was a green stick. Thorpe was the coolest customer, apparently. He asked to visit the toilet first, and the young gun let him go. When his partner found out, he bolted to the loo and burst into the cubicle." Sam stopped.

He, Jordy and Dee were beaming at each other.

"What?" said Rasputin. "He flushed the heroin?"

"No, you idiot," said Jordy. "There never was any heroin."

"But there was Chlorpromazine. Six ampules of it, in fact. Two were empty, and, funny thing, empty ampules don't flush so well: the cop found Mr. Thorpe frantically watching over a few floaters. Some smart folk can be really dumb."

Rasputin enjoyed a moment's Schadenfreude.

"Chlorpromazine?"

"An anti-psychotic. But give it to someone with a lowered seizure threshold and bingo: more seizures."

Rasputin said, thinking aloud. "Then he got me in here, doped me up, and set himself up as the only saviour in town."

"I knew he was no good," said Jordy, "the moment I first met him."

"Why so?" said Sam.

"Women's intuition," said Rasputin. Then he turned to Dee. "You were lucky he had the stuff on him. What were you going to do if he was clean?"

She shook her head. "I hadn't thought beyond buying time. Anything to keep you out of the operating theatre." She went on in a whisper. "That look, Monk ..." She gazed out into the gardens and shivered.

They were silent then for minutes, as though taking a collective breath. Dragonflies flew and pinballed among reeds at the lake's edge, and just then were the most interesting sight in the world.

"What now?" said Rasputin.

"Home and rest, is what now," said Dee. She hovered nearest to Rasputin, perched on the edge of a reclining lounge.

Rest, thought Rasputin. What a funny word. He wondered if rest was what unicorns did in castles of cloud.

"Where's Thorpe now?" he asked Sam.

"Being questioned at the station in the CBD," said Sam. Then added, "Behind locked doors." Rasputin fancied Sam thought him afraid.

Jordy's pants emitted a belching sound that startled him.

"You still have my phone," said Rasputin.

Jordy dug it out and handed it to him. The display indicated a new message. It read: MediCrypt—locks away your medical records.

Rasputin furrowed his brow.

He spoke to Sam. "Did you give me this phone to dick around with me? It's getting a little trite."

"What? I didn't give you any phone."

"But—" He halted. He thought back to the night he had sat on the steps with Jordy as night closed in.

"Do you remember the message I got the other day?" he said to Jordy. "You said it was spam. It said 'makes sense of all your data,' right after I'd unloaded on you about the crap going down in my head. I bet it was *him*, toying with me."

"You're being paranoid," said Jordy.

"How would he have known that?" said Dee. Rasputin smiled at her; she couldn't help defending the absent party.

"No idea, but now he's taunting me from beyond the grave."

Sam said, "If you mean Thorpe, you'll have to settle for 'professional' grave. He might lose his license, but don't count on him getting time for today."

Rasputin rose, feeling the large muscles in his limbs twang and settle like new guitar strings. Everything hurt, but he forced himself to walk. "Would it be too much to ask for a pound of flesh?" He stumped toward the corridor leading back to his room, and his clothes. "Downtown, you said?"

Jordy pulled Rasputin's rusting coupe over to the curb. He listened as the engine died. "That's your valves. You do need to service this thing, you know."

"With what?" said Rasputin, his gaze fixed on the facade of the police station.

"You want me to ... come in?" said Jordy.

Rasputin swung his legs out, planted his feet on the pavement, and heaved himself onto them.

"No. Thanks." Before he could change his mind, he pushed away from the car, swinging the door shut with his free hand.

"Pick you up in an hour," Jordy shouted from behind the glass. He started the engine and sliced into the traffic flow.

Thorpe was alone in an interview room. His jacket was off, shirt cuffs rolled high as though he was doing rounds. Rasputin peered through one-way glass set into the door and bided the return of his courage. Thorpe was locked in and all but defrocked. So why did he look more the lion than ever? He held his great maned head level as he strode in neat circles around a table at the room's centre.

Rasputin reached for the door's handle, felt the cool touch of its metal, and paused. He had been offered ten minutes with Thorpe by the officer in charge, reluctantly, and only because he had threatened to frustrate charges against the surgeon. Right now, he wasn't sure he even wanted ten seconds.

Thorpe halted at the far side of the table as Rasputin entered. His question caught Rasputin off guard. "So, do you have a death wish or are you a moron?"

Rasputin reminded himself he was at a police station, not Thorpe's office.

"You first: sadist or criminal?"

"No, I'm serious. You've sabotaged your only hope."

177

"Sabotaged? What the hell do you call spiking my drink and stoking seizures?"

Thorpe rounded the table. Rasputin circled it to keep him opposite.

"Collateral. And besides, the seizures will leave no permanent damage. They became necessary when you persisted in fending me off." He stopped, and so did Rasputin. "I got lucky first time. The particular concoction you drank causes seizures in less than one in five people— of healthy mind, that is." The surgeon's brow drew down. "I'm curious about you Rasputin. What thing in your past is so potent to goad you to fight with such energy?"

"I could ask you the same question."

"Oh? My brother you mean?" He laughed, an unhealthy, forced sound. "I've no idea how you found him, but you're wrong, whatever you think."

Thorpe turned away for the first time since Rasputin had entered the room. A thin band of sweat stained his shirt between his shoulder blades. The room smelled of scared men.

Rasputin pressed him: "What would cause a man in your position— wealthy, respected—to risk so much? An ailing brother, perhaps? It fits."

Thorpe spun to face him. His voice was even, but he gripped the chair in front of him with such force the tendons over his knuckles blanched.

"Spare me the playroom psychology. My brother is an interesting case, nothing more, and if you say our veins run with the same blood, I say I don't care for the mystical significance placed on what is cellular detritus—*nothing more*. Blood might be thicker than water, but so is sewage."

Thorpe released the chair, seemed to relax. "Is that really the best you've got?" he said, humour in his voice. "Yes, I begin to believe it is. What a contrary young man you are. You want light, but then you think you are the moth and fear the flame all at once. You fear me. But know you need me, or why else would you be here. You're not the gloating type, Rasputin."

Thorpe sat, and invited Rasputin to do likewise. He remained standing.

"All that talk about pioneering the new frontier," said Rasputin, "when all you wanted was another schmuck carrying your hardware so you could turn a buck."

"Turn a buck? Turn a buck? I—" he said, and stopped as if choked by too many thoughts wanting voice.

"I know about the patents," said Rasputin, hoping Thorpe didn't press him on the depth of his knowledge, which he had exhausted with the statement.

Thorpe dismissed the comment with a wave. "A man must protect his intellectual property, but it saddens me to think you've formed the impression I'm some kind of entrepreneur." He leaned forward and caught Rasputin's gaze with his own. "On my honour, money is my least concern. And my offer was sincere. To pioneer a genuinely new frontier is perhaps the most rare of all opportunities—a chance not to be missed. So forgive me if I went beyond the pale to include you. I wouldn't have done it if I didn't think you would benefit.

"Please sit and let me put you in the picture. As I said, it's a grand one, and will suffer little from this annoyance." He waved a hand at the walls. Rasputin relented and sat. His leg was hurting. "You were part of it. Grease to the wheels, but ultimately not crucial. I don't mean to be rude. I'm just being honest."

"I'm listening."

"I find it ironic we're finally having this discussion in a police station, of all places." Rasputin felt the cloak of conspiracy drawing down around them, but found himself hanging on Thorpe's words. "Because, if I succeed, I will render this place obsolete. Or, at least, unrecognizably transformed."

As the words left his mouth, Rasputin forgot any concern for his own sanity. This guy had slipped down the black slope of Mount Sane.

He went on. "Imagine if you could read a man's mind, infallibly."

"I saw a movie about that. It had hover cars."

"It will be reality. The seeds already exist. Don't believe me? Look up an article titled, "Single-Trial Learning of Novel Stimuli by Individual Neurons of the Human Hippocampus-Amygdala Complex." The authors found in humans something never found in primates: neurons encoding familiarity."

Rasputin must have looked nonplussed, for Thorpe barked, "Use your imagination!" His arms swept outwards as though carried by the explosion of his breath.

"Their experiments used electrodes like the one I showed you to find neurons that fired or didn't fire based on whether the subject was *familiar* with an image. They deciphered if a subject had seen an image by directly reading it from their brain—just like taking their blood pressure, no need to ask! In fact, they found subjects often knew better than they thought, got it wrong when their cells got it right."

Thorpe paused.

Rasputin tried to let what he had said sink in. He thought back on Thorpe's comment about the police station, and speculated.

"If what you're saying is true, you could know for sure if a man knew a place, a thing, or a person."

"Yes. But say, instead of man, 'the accused', and for place and thing, say 'crime scene' and 'murder weapon.'"

"... and victim."

"Yes! This is not possible yet, but we're close. If scientific discovery is a man groping in a dark room for the light, his fingers have brushed the switch. It is only a matter of time before we throw that switch and light up the brain to not just familiarity but complete disclosure. We will find cells that code for like and dislike, desire and intent, love and hate. All that sums up to humanity will be found on the end of a very small wire."

Can he be telling the truth?

If Sam's information was right, Thorpe had managed to convince at least one person to back his research with cold hard cash, and a criminal lawyer no less.

Rasputin pondered the image of silvery tethers, too many to count, streaming out into his inner universe. Could you eventually tag them all? Would it be possible to list every one and their relations one to another, to transcribe *Rasputin* to paper, to silicon?

He had a revelation: Thorpe had found in him not just any guinea pig, but *the* guinea pig.

Electrode or no, Thorpe seemed to read his thoughts.

"Yes, Fate was kind to bring you across my path."

Rasputin snorted. "'Grease to the wheels,' you said."

"Let me repair that sentiment."

He leaned back in his chair as if to appraise Rasputin afresh. "You are the Mona Lisa, when all I had before were finger paintings."

"The sketches gave me away, didn't they?"

"Yes. There was a host of other signs that fit with my theory, but the sudden appearance of that prodigious ability was diagnostic."

"Diagnostic of what?" said Rasputin, over the rising volume of his heart beat.

"Oh, I'd say a member of the class of Sudden Savant Syndrome."

"I'm becoming Rainman?"

"No. Rainman was an attempt to portray Autism. Savant Syndrome centres on the presence of a deep shard of genius. Savants sketch, sculpt or compose like the greatest masters. Some can recall scenes with camera precision. Others calculate equations or find primes faster than computers. Savants redefine the limits of human capability. Some are born that way, some become that way as they slide into senescence—one day Uncle John forgets to dress, but can sight-read Mozart."

He looked pointedly at Rasputin. "And some are birthed by disease or traumatic injury."

"But?"

"The gift is usually at the expense of higher cognitive functions. It's as if the very shard driven into the brain to tap this power destroys the fragile balance of inputs required to read the emotions of others, have empathy, socialise. And in the case of injury, as I have said all along, the risk of neural breakdown is real, whether it be motor system dysfunction, hallucination, or schizophrenia."

Rasputin cast his eye inward, an eye that feared to own what it saw. This was his house, and he had just been informed it had seen a murder. Was his mind a train wreck in motion, slowed a thousand times but inexorable? Were the girders of his sanity buckling and breaking just beyond sight?

His mind answered with the memory of a photo. The photo was from Joachim Thorpe's room. It pictured his mother. Rasputin looked at Thorpe and noted his resemblance to his mother, in the curve of his cheek bones, in his eyes.

"Three times you visited your brother straight after seeing me—to gloat or console, I don't know which. The one exception was the day we met in the *morning*. That day you didn't visit until the afternoon. Why was that?"

Thorpe became still.

"See, I knew there was something special about you ..."

"You didn't answer the question."

Thorpe patted his shirt pocket and seemed surprised to find it empty. He rose, turned his back to Rasputin, and appeared to examine a spot on the wall. The band of sweat down his back had thickened.

Rasputin stood and, putting aside his fear, drew near the surgeon on a thread of curiosity. Thorpe had not moved. He stared not at the wall, but through it.

"Your brother is locked up in his mind, prisoner in his own body, and you expect me to believe he has nothing to do with this, with me? That would be some coincidence. And, forgive me if I'm wrong—I'm an Arts student—but I thought scientists shunned coincidence."

Thorpe remained still, barring the rise and fall of his chest as he took in air, pulled the oxygen from it, and expelled the spent gases, the instinctual, creature motions.

Then the creature summoned the ghost. His eyelids snapped over glassy eyes. When they lifted, his eyes had pivoted to pin Rasputin with their glare. Surplus tears gathered at the rim of their lower lids.

"You're clever," said Thorpe. "Tell me, what does one find at the bottom of a hole?"

"Is this a trick question? I often find myself at the bottom of a hole."

"No tricks. Your answer is right, after a fashion. I would say: whatever one puts there."

"Glass half-full, half-empty. I get it. Which am I?"

"Neither. You are: where's my damn Coke? It's not your fault. It is generational."

"And what was your brother?"

"That is my point. It depends on who you are asking."

"I'm asking you."

"He was a vacuum, a black hole that sucked life from everything near it."

Rasputin paused before asking the next question. He felt like a kid toeing a coin on a ledge high above a city street.

He nudged it over the edge.

"And your mother, what would she say?"

"She has always been such a positive person, bless her. She pours only the purest motives into holes, wherever she finds them; my brother is all holes."

Rasputin spoke his thought without meaning to: "And you want to lift the lid on his darkness and show her."

Thorpe's face contorted a moment and Rasputin thought he meant to do him violence. But the dynamite going off in him was that of the precision destruction engineer, taking him down from the inside.

Part of Rasputin wanted to lay out a picnic blanket and watch the show. But he could not enjoy it. He pulled open the door, twelve seconds shy of the allotted ten minutes, and paused at the threshold. He reached into his pocket and retrieved his phone.

"Thanks, but you can have it back now."

Rasputin balanced the phone in his hand, as if it were a skipping stone. Thorpe's gaze drifted to it, slowly, as though drugged, and then returned to meet Rasputin's with the same torpor. His expression lacked any trace of having recognised the device.

Rasputin let himself out, easing the door closed, and tried to believe that had been the surgeon's parting shot, his last psyche-out. But the calculating part of his mind was having none of it. The man was scooping water to stay alive; he had no thought for idle guns. He hadn't sent the phone.

Before going to bed, Rasputin inserted the charge cable into the phone, the newest addition to his steadily accreting nightly ritual. He examined his reflection in the bathroom's mirror, between the mirror's age-blemishes, which grew at its edges like brass-coloured lichen. His eyes were sunk within hollows of blue, and marbled with red veins.

"Hours of seizure will do that."

He tilted his head and swept his fringe up to reveal his scar. It shone a lurid maroon in the fluorescent light.

"Still, better a battering than a chunk of metal in my brain."

The phone bleeped acknowledgement of the charge flowing into its battery.

He picked it up, found Sam in the contact list, and called him.

Rasputin's thumb was hovering on the cancel button when he picked up: "Rasputin?"

"Sam, my heroine. Tell me you're not in bed. You sound like someone died."

"No ... no, not bed. Just dotting the t's on today—the i's, I mean. Covering my arse."

"Bugger." He had hoped Sam would get a boost from his success. "I was just thinking I look better without a pound of metal stuck in my head, and wanted to say thanks. Seriously."

"No problem, Rasputin. I'm pretty stoked I could help," Sam said. He sounded tired.

"Am I still on the watch list, or have you guys decided to trust me?"

A pause, then "About that ..."

About that ... The words were taken by that part of his mind concerned with prediction, and became the seed for a tree. It burst from the ground in seconds, its branches ramifying in thickness proportional to the probability of what Sam might say next. By far the thickest, the most likely, was not what Rasputin wanted to hear. He stared at himself in the mirror, becoming a stranger to himself in the seconds it took Sam to continue.

"About that. You're off the books. I mean, completely. ... I'm sorry. There won't be an offer from ASIO. Best to keep at the study, hey."

"Because of today?" Rasputin said numbly.

"No, nothing to do with today. I reported to my boss on how today finished, and he said someone pulled your records from the server two weeks ago. They only found out yesterday. Whoever hacked in covered their tracks pretty well on the way out."

Rasputin heard now that what he had mistaken for tiredness in Sam's voice was uneasiness.

"But that must happen all the time. What could they have got, anyway? What do you guys collect? Hobbies? Shoe size?"

"It doesn't matter what they got. The problem is what they didn't get."

"You're not making sense."

"Of the thousands of records the hacker gained access to, he pulled one set: yours."

"But—"

"It's no good. I tried. They won't touch you with a barge pole now." An awkward silence followed, and then, "I'm still good for that beer if ever you make it to Canberra."

Rasputin mumbled thanks and hung up. As he did, the phone buzzed in his hand once, announcing a new message. Unthinking, he called it up.

It read: On sale now at Sanity Records—The Nutcracker Suite.

He turned the phone off and lay down, wishing for unconsciousness.

8

CAIN

It might have been a gas giant that enfolded my plane as we touched down rather than Munich Airport's vapour-wrapped tarmac, a wall of white, strobed by landing lights and pin-pricked blue.

From the US I had headed home, Germany; while it is a different wine that runs in my veins now, I still count it a *Deutsch* vintage.

I passed customs, where it appears the *Reich* lives on.

First contact came swiftly. The beagle, I knew, had been a summons.

A chauffer was waiting at Arrivals with a placard seeking Gottfried Schürmann. He escorted me to a black Mercedes S-class limousine. He held the door open and I seated myself in an interior with only a little less leather and legroom than Lufthansa's First Class. He told me over the intercom he had been paid for the whole day and would take me anywhere I wished to go. I hunted for my own intercom switch, depressed it, and told him to head for Marienplatz. The cabin fell silent and the tug of motion told me we were in transit.

I noticed two things immediately. My seat was warm. I assumed, despite it being before dawn, someone had recently occupied the cabin.

And on the seat beside me lay an envelope. I tensed, fearing foul play. The envelope buzzed. I opened it and found a cell phone. It was ringing.

As I reached for the phone, the limousine cornered again, and this time I noticed the seat support alter pressure to cradle my body. The entire seat reacted to the inertial forces of motion, automatically by some pneumatic machinery. (Fitting end to the innovations of Germany's oldest automobile manufacturer: triviality.) I assumed, correctly, that it was therefore a small matter to pre-heat or chill the seat to an occupant's satisfaction. Thus I dispelled the ghost of a drop man, and grasped the phone.

I picked up the call.

A hash of white noise assaulted my ear, and then I heard a voice.

"*Herr Schürmann? Cain?*" It was a woman's voice.

"*Ja.*"

"*Gut. Ein moment.*"

That same white noise stole over the end of the woman's speech, and when it subsided a different voice spoke, a man's voice.

"Good morning, Cain. Welcome back, and thank you for accepting my hospitality."

"Who is this?" I said, "And with whom was I just speaking?"

"Clotho—and Clotho. We are all Clotho," he said, and laughed. "You must remember me?"

Yes, I remembered the name Clotho, and I needed a moment to think, to recollect.

"A moment," I said. With my free hand I poured a cognac from the minibar. *Schnäpse für die* Synapsie.

A wave of static overtook the call, but beneath it, just audible, the laughter continued unbroken until suddenly, distinctly, it tripped up a register and again became a woman's voice. Another unfamiliar voice.

"Forgive me," that lady's voice said. "The autobahn from the airport has many cell towers and many opportunities for me to pander to paranoia."

Paranoia: that clinched it.

I was speaking to Clotho, whose original name was lost to the ravages of time. Clotho, a name borrowed from the Greek Fates, the

Moirae, who preside over the destiny of each life. Clotho, spinner of life's thread; Lachesis, measure-woman of the life-thread's span; Atropos, wielder of the blade that severs that thread.

This Clotho had taken the name as I took Cain. This Clotho was the surviving dweom-mate of one who took the name Atropos, it is believed. But the story of Clotho's origins is woven from rumour.

I know that Clotho, when asked by the Imago why two names—Clotho and Atropos—had been taken from the canonical three rather than a pair, as is customary, had demurred that one version of the Greek myth held only two *Moirae*.

(One could speculate, were he a believer in myth, what the death of Atropos by Clotho's hand following the dweoming means for Clotho's lifethread. Is it left to spool out, forever unchecked by the death blade?)

Paranoia. If there is a single word that characterises Clotho, it is paranoia. And as he/she/it/they began to tell me, this call was being bounced through many cell towers, under different voices, genders, accents, and occasionally, languages, to stymie accidental or intentional surveillance. Clotho, I'm sure you've guessed, had acquired a gift for technology, and was using it then to hide behind a digital curtain.

I decided openness was the best policy: "Should I be afraid?"

"You have nothing to fear from me."

I had hoped this. Clotho and I had been on good terms, or, at least, the best available in the penumbral world of that coterie of Imagines.

But one cannot assume.

She went on. "I thought a sixty-year old homecoming merited a welcome"—the voice slipped down an octave, like water over faceted rock, from a twenty-something to an elderly man of smoke-ravaged throat—"and a warning: they will demand you complete the dweoming ritual."

I've told you I expected this. It did not bother me, though I do not share their compulsion for that ritual.

"Thank you," I said.

I desired to probe at my true concern: "What reception should I expect?"

There was silence on the line. When Clotho spoke again, the voice came for a moment as through a fan, ribbed and baffled, before it cohered into a child's.

"Some will be interested in your, ah, *prophetic* abilities—shifter desired, shifter become."

The statement sent a shiver down my spine, but in and of itself it was no admission of knowledge. I brushed the thought aside. There was nothing I could do about it in any case. I had been summoned. I would appear.

Clotho giggled and hung up.

I pressed the intercom and spoke to the chauffer. "Where are we?"

"Approaching the E52 ring road, sir. If I may presume to direct your attention to the navigation monitor above the console to your right."

I looked, and, as indicated, there sat a small screen displaying a map of greater Munich. The map was centred on a red dot, which I assumed to be our position. We were indeed approaching the bisecting line of the E52.

"Who else knows our position?"

"Sir?"

"The intelligence indicated on this map—who else knows it?"

I believe he stifled laughter at that. When he spoke again, his mood frayed his professional facade.

"That's the GPS Sat Nav. The car reads a signal from a satellite, like a radio I guess, and plots our position. It can be used for fleet management, but we don't send the information anywhere: we pride ourselves on client privacy."

I bade the chauffer take the ring road until further notice. We duly swung off *Kreuz-Munchen Nord* and began to circle the city. You would think I would have been chomping at the bit to get out of the enclosed space, off my derrière and into the fresh air, but the car's motion was soothing and conducive to thought all at once. Maybe it was the second cognac begun to work.

When at length I had the chauffeur drop me at Marienplatz, I felt my plans were well in order. I checked into the hotel I had booked while in transit, and strode the perimeter of the square in search of a foaming stein.

On returning, the concierge informed me a telegram had arrived for me, under the name Finchley, the passport I was currently using. I took it to my room and opened it.

It read: REQUEST YOUR COMPANY STOP STEPHEN WC MATIN III STOP

No dead dogs this time, but the missive still annoyed me. Translated, it was a command to be at St. Stephen's Cathedral, Vienna, in the war chapel beneath the building, at Matins on the third of the following month. That was less than a week away.

I booked a train for Zurich under another name—no passports necessary within the EU, happily—and in the meantime attempted to initiate contact with Clotho.

I had no luck with Clotho at that time.

Zurich was a personal indulgence under the guise of tactical necessity. I first found a suitable Swiss identity for the onward trip to Vienna, and then visited one of my safety deposit boxes in the *Suisse National*, accessed under the number and password protocol I had specified so many years before. I was overjoyed to find within, shrouded and snug, and looking as though it had only just been left, a little Renaissance portrait of dubious provenance. The light was poor, and sadly I could not take it with me. But I gave it an hour of my devotion and was amply rewarded. My memory had not falsely augmented its virtue.

I arrived in Vienna on the third, and took the subway from the Hauptbahnhoff to Stephensplatz. I ate dinner at McDonald's, which I have discovered agrees with my palette, and waited for the day's light to fail.

Stephensdom, once the tallest structure in Europe, still takes my breath away. I watched her as night fell, and only half the stars came out. The rest were blotted out by the cathedral's vast roof. It was different to when last I'd seen it. It is now diamond-patterned in glazed tiles of primary colours, a canvas for the largest Mondrian in existence, and within their weave, Habsburg eagles are resplendent and staring into the past at a now-faded glory. The original roof was burnt when looting broke out at the approach of the Russians at the end of the war. But its sheerness, so steep snow rarely clings to it, what impressed me as a child, remained.

I entered and joined the few faithful, in the hushed silence hunched beneath their favourite shrines.

A guard was set over the entrance to the catacombs beneath the sanctuary. I approached and he informed me there was a private function that night, the tour was not in operation.

"I am of that party," I said, and gave him the name of the American by which I had registered at the hotel in Munich.

He executed a deft bow and ushered me to the stairway before returning to his post. His first instinct had been to salute me. I saw the impulse rise before he resisted it; my eye is now attuned to such miniscule movements. I doubted it was the church employing ex-servicemen.

As I descended and the darkness swallowed me, I experienced a surge of visceral fear, the first in a long time. I remembered who I was and conquered it.

The cathedral has an underground existence impossible to perceive from above ground. It is under-mined by countless charnel houses and ossuaries filled with the harvests of plague and war. I squinted at one through a rusted cast-iron grate to see femurs stacked neatly, end-on, like an ancient library of scrolls, each with a story simple but powerful.

The war chapel is carved into the eastern arm of the subterranean complex. I paused, yards from its entrance, when I heard the susurrus of voices in conversation echo along the passageway. The murmur was punctuated by the occasional bark of a raver.

I hesitated, then recalled the truth I had armed myself with, against the contingency of second thoughts: to make an end of it, I had first to be accepted. The only way to be free of the Imago was to become one in body, spirit, and—what I lacked—*law*.

"Cain, welcome back to us." It was Remus.

"Why did you kill my bloody dog?" I said. I refused to let their script play out as written, like some fresh-faced Hollywood protégé.

Remus didn't buck an inch.

"*My* dog?" he said. "Which *me* goes with that *my*, shifter? Besides, it was an American dog. I thought you would appreciate a parting shot in a long-cold war."

"Dogs don't own a nation," I said. "Apology accepted"—nothing in his bearing had indicated one—"I'm here. What do you want?"

A snarl erupted from a man standing in a corner of the room, and bounded back and forth in the small sanctuary. Its owner continued to stare at the grit-speckled plaster as if it were the portal to heaven. A raver.

I wondered, and saw the same thought behind other eyes, why Remus had invited a raver to this meeting, one who had drunk too deeply from the dweoming well, drowned or dissipated in it. Was it too much to ask for a sane quorum?

"The premature death of your brother is lamentable," said another I knew, Heloise. She had murdered her lover to enter the ranks of the Imago. No wrinkle of regret marred her timeless skin.

Her voice, creamy as her skin, lifted goose bumps on my neck. But Heloise took lovers the way most take a fine meal, so deeply was the pattern of her dweoming stamped.

I snatched my gaze from her.

She continued, "But you must find another."

I had been right. They demanded the contest, the killing. But in my case, I knew this standing on ritual was a thin pretext. They wanted me leashed. Or better yet, dead. Shifters are rare, and feared. None dared say it, or else my corpse would already have been floating in the Hudson.

Happily, no one there remembered or, if so, cared I had desired this very ability. Had they, they might have pried up my little secret, and the only ritual to involve me then would have been the *coup de grace*.

"This brother," I said. "Must he be wild or cultivated?"

Remus shrugged, magnanimous: "The lore doesn't proscribe." He smiled. "Brother, sister, found, made. It is up to you."

The Imago claim mystical significance for the pairing. But, at best, it is an accident of history; at worst, a vetting mechanism. Every man and woman in that room was guaranteed a murderer. The ties that knit. It made the strangest congregation the War Chapel has ever seen.

"But if you decline to try," said Remus, "you will submit to *patronage*."

Patronage. Benign word for death-in-life. The patron, so called, held title deed over the life of the Imago consigned to him. This relationship was enforced by the collective and incalculable might of the Imago. One of few cases where that might was united. Violation meant death to the consignee. And worse, what constituted a violation was *defined* by the patron. The consignee was effectively in thrall to his patron.

"And who would be my patron?" I said to Remus. "You?"

His smile grew, drawing his lips taut.

"I would have that honour, yes."

I shuddered, and cursed myself inwardly.

My eyes darted to the raver who was tracing an imaginary line on the wall, a loop of spittle arcing between mouth and shoulder. All ravers were assigned to patrons, without exception, lest they be walking dynamite among the brute populace. Not that the Imago cared for people. They cared not to be hassled. This raver, who barked just to hear his echo, was owned by Remus. One of many under his patronage. No one knew why Remus kept so many. Rumours swirled that he unpicked them, mind and body, for amusement. But I suspected he kept them like oysters. For all their froth and grit, they occasionally turned out a pearl. That is, until they had dived so far within themselves that their brains ceased to bother with such mundanities as the body's autonomic functions of digestion and heart beat.

The sight of the pathetic creature fired my blood.

I thrust my face forward until it was inches from Remus, then slowly, deliberately, tilted my head until I could see the tips of his Oxford Wingtips poking from the cuffs of his pants. I spat.

"You couldn't keep me, scrawny wolf," I whispered into his face.

With a snarl he wrapped an arm behind my back. His hand took hold of my jacket and with great force he bent me backwards at the hips. I was caught off guard, finding my balance again, when he thrust something like a gun into my stomach.

"Maybe not, but the Imago can and will. And until that time, we're watching you."

With a flash of insight I realised it was not a bullet chambered in the gun. I locked my hand over the hand holding the gun and, against Remus's protesting muscles, raised it until I was staring down the black hole of its aperture. It was rectangular, no wider than the edge of a coin. A tagging device.

I pulled the trigger.

Pain burst in my eyeball as though I'd stuck it with a burning brand. Pain that made my whole body clench. But contrary to my expectation, the eye screamed with light. It went supernova, not black hole.

When I mastered myself again, I looked out of my good eye and was delighted to see the shock on Remus's face.

I heard Heloise breathe, "Such a waste." She sounded genuinely disappointed.

Then, summoning the latent power of my sublimated biology, I commanded the flesh of my eye to expel, to draw blood, to seal, to scaffold, to knit. To restore that jellied orb.

If possible, this pain was worse.

As the newly minted lens, complete with corneal cap, surfaced to sit snug in the regenerated tissue, something popped free. I caught it in my palm and saw the quarter-inch square tag that my healed eye had extruded.

I held it in Remus's face and crushed it to dust.

"You already watch me. I won't be tagged like livestock."

Remus recovered his composure.

"That is an interesting gift," he said. "I once knew a man with that gift. Before he died I tested it, organ by organ, by means chemical, radioactive, and combustive." He stroked his grizzled jaw, seemingly lost in reverie. "But I don't know why I bothered. Each morsel of flesh came to the same end. Dust and ash."

I hesitated a moment. I envisaged my fist crumpling the cartilage and bone of his nose. The fingers of my right hand were curling into a ball when a hoarse shout rang in the small room.

"Shifter, shaper, flesh-twist-maker!" sang the raver, eyes aflame, in a mockery of nursery rhyme. "Seed sown well and grew a faker! The

194

Eye it sees—" and he broke off and turned back to inscribe his invisible fancies on the wall.

But he'd lifted the hairs on my neck. Like I said: the occasional pearl. It was time to leave.

I turned to Heloise and, avoiding her fey gaze, said, "I will find a brother then, in the wild."

The hunt for a naturally-occurring Imago might give me the time and scope to find a way to be rid of the Imago for good.

We dispersed, dust into the air, to homes all over the world, and many in Europe. The Old World felt most like home to these men and woman who had lived such long lives.

But I headed for Hong Kong, for that was where Clotho—who found *me*—would supply the resources I humbly requested.

On route, somewhere thirty thousand feet above baking Arabian sands, I pondered a riddle: what threat can one hold over those without care for money, power, or experience—who possess it already in super-abundance? The Imago, united by nothing save what they *are*. What lever would pry them from my back forever?

In Hong Kong I learned the true extent of the web of information crisscrossing the Internet. Clotho taught me. He showed me the trap-doors and swinging bookcases that led to the hidden web, the Dark Web, where whole economies flourish that will not come into the light for fear of shame or retribution. He taught me how to tap it. I learned, and adapted. That is what I do. I sifted the hay and found my needle. ... and here I am.

The last thing I did before leaving Hong Kong for Perth, Australia, was to transfer my liquid funds into HK Shanghai Bank. I swapped my Swiss account and password for the lumpen touch of an authenticating *chop*, the Asian equivalent of a signature—a seal, carved from wood, signifying its possessor is entitled to draw on my funds. My chop was carved in the shape of Infinity. The swap was a precaution. Clotho had taught me not to trust to digital codes in the aether. And, truth to tell, the feel of the chop's grain transports me to another time. Perhaps I too am of the Old World.

9.

PAST RUIN

The night sky is a double illusion.

Powerful telescopes pointed at the tiniest wedge of sky—any wedge—find it filled with galaxies of stars in the billions. If the naked eye could see so well, night would be not a star-speckled void, but a sheet of light. Day would be the darker half.

To count every star in the known universe at one second a star would take a quadrillion lifetimes stretched end to end. More time than has elapsed since the Beginning, since dumb matter shrugged dumb shoulders and slewed off worlds and life, or the hammer of God's voice fell upon the anvil of His will.

The night sky is a *double* illusion because, of the few stars visible to the naked eye, many are long dead. The light striking our retina is old and stale, every photon a letter from a dead friend.

Rasputin was hunkered down in the angle made by a bookshelf and a window, in the nook that served him and Jordy for a library. It was the first day to top 30 degrees Celsius since the previous summer, and he could feel the sun's rays warming the curtains. He was soothed by the dark quietude.

"The universe is bathed in orphaned photons," he said to no one.

Flakes of gold glimmered in the periphery of his vision from the bookshelf. They were trapped in a souvenir flask, but Rasputin's brain informed him that these too had been born in the sun's colossal nuclear furnace.

His hands held a copy of Pride and Prejudice, taken from the same shelf on which the gold sat. It was closed. He knew the book's publisher, *Red Saturn*, without having to flip it over, something he had in common, unaccountably, with Rasputin-from-before-the-accident. His eyes rested on the dark bar the book's removal had left in the shelf.

He scanned the shelf, then those below. He had read most of the books. The millions of words they contained hovered in clusters beneath the surface of his vision. He could summon any or all into sight at will. (How long would it take him to read each word?) The only black holes in the textscape came from books he had not read, such as Jordy's manga and computing texts.

In the weeks since his showdown with Thorpe, the ability to merge his inner vision with everyday life had exploded. But the pull of that inner world had grown too. He had spent whole days within, in the eye's quiet harbour. He would play games with its machines and ransack his memories, emerging only to visit the toilet, and eat. His appetite had doubled. Sometimes, if feeling brave, he would search for warps in the fabric of its sky, for telltale signs of activity.

He toyed with the idea of writing an autobiography. Andy Warhol had made a movie of a man sleeping for eight hours; Rasputin could more than one-up that. Every memory since childhood lay within his reach. Even those from the very first years, he suspected, were coming beneath the eye's aegis, its silver feelers tireless in their work of cataloguing, associating, and connecting every sense-bundle he had ever recorded.

That growth was why, when bored of playing games and rediscovering forgotten experiences, he went fishing for the memory of his sister. It was slowly, but undeniably, becoming crisper, fresher.

All of this convinced him Thorpe was wrong. He was no Sudden Savant. He had researched Savantism with a fury, and found it fascinating—the lives lived under its blessing or curse read like fiction. One boy, following an hour-long helicopter flight, had sketched vast swathes of London, complete with pillar boxes and fountains: a super-human memory and the muscle control to transcribe it to paper. A man Rasputin read about could perform mental arithmetic to arbitrary decimal places, and, most interestingly, was able to describe the mental contortions he performed to do the math. He described his mind as being like a fantastic landscape ruled by numbers, where every digit had a peculiar shape and feel, and each calculation was a journey through that land. The answer lay inerrantly like a pot of gold at journey's end.

But no case bore more than passing resemblance to his condition.

His search had widened perforce, due to the rarity of true savants. He had stumbled across a most interesting case in a neurobiology textbook. It described a man able to control, by force of will, autonomic functions of his body. He could raise his heartbeat by imagining running, dilate his pupils by thinking about a dark room, and lower his temperature by picturing himself in a blizzard. Yet more bizarre, he could turn off the sensation of pain, take the agony of a burn—that most acute and insistent pain—wrap it in cloth and sequester it in the attic of his brain, just another possession, devoid of the power to hurt. Rasputin had wondered if the man could do the same with grief.

But as amazing as this catalogue of abilities was, it did not square with his experience. Yes, the accident had gifted him an immaculate memory, a memory so organically connected to his nervous system he could effortlessly translate it to paper. His sub-conscious could perform calculations that took computers dedicated to the task hours. But unlike a Savant's gift, which is fixed, his was an ever-renewing forest. Who knew what timber was yet to thrust through the canopy into the light, and what creatures were still to crawl from hidden places in the sylvan gloom beneath.

His thoughts drifted back to earth to the book in his hands. He flipped it open to the first page, needlessly. His eyes scanned the first line. He read aloud: "A truth universally acknowledged," and wondered how many of those there were.

Staring at the phrase, he bent his mind around it with the slightest effort, cupped it in his attention with a squint that didn't touch his eyes. Letters wriggled under the pressure, and exchanged places to form a new sequence: *Austen wrecked lavatory dunghill.*

"Profound, Rasputin," he said into the mid-morning silence.

A knock at the door startled him. He fought himself a moment over whether to answer or lay low. His conscience won. He found Dee standing on the mat outside the door wearing an apologetic look, which had become habitual.

"I'm not going in today," he said.

"I'm not picking you up. I thought we could hang out."

"Don't you have work?" he said, eyeing the large book tucked under her arm. Dee seemed unable to move about the world without taking some part of it with her.

"My rats were wiped out by a disease."

"Ironic."

"It's not funny, Monk. That's a month of work."

"Sorry. Come on in."

She stepped past him, allowing him to see that what he had thought was a book was a photo album.

She turned to him, her nose wrinkled.

"It's pretty ripe in here. When did you guys last clean?"

"Clean?" he said, knowing Jordy would cop the lecture despite being the hygienic one.

"What are you reading?"

He held Pride and Prejudice up for her to read the cover.

"Not reading, as such."

The wrinkle jumped from her nose to between her brows.

"Juggling, then?"

He walked back into the front room and sat again with his back to the window. She followed and sat across from him. He flipped the book back open to the first page.

"I was playing a game. I pick a sentence or phrase and anagram-ise it."

"Is this a nerd thing?"

"Look," he said, and ran a finger over the phrase in the opening sentence. "This has the anagram—" he said, and paused to mind-squint at the text. The words wriggled and regrouped again with a different result: "Vowed Austen, lethargically drunk."

The knot between Dee's brows thickened before it released and she smiled.

"You're kidding."

He shrugged.

Dee dug into her bag and found a loose receipt and pen. She turned the receipt over and copied out the original phrase and the anagram, and then began to work her way through the phrase, letter by letter, crossing each off when she found it in the anagram. When she had struck through the last pair of d's, she looked up.

"That's cool! How long did it take you to work that out?"

He grunted dismissively, and warped the phrase again: "Austen: Vocally wrinkled daughter."

She bent over the receipt to check the anagram, but evidently thought better of it when she caught his eye.

"How long a phrase can you do?"

"Don't know. It's not exactly useful, though, is it. Maybe a notch above belching the alphabet." He looked at the text and warped it one last time, spoke the result: "Crude, unloving, wry: Death takes all." Yes, there was a candidate for a truth universally acknowledged.

He looked up and was surprised to find tears in Dee's eyes, shimmering in the frail light. She put the paper and pen down, and lifted the photo album into her lap. She set one hand to the edge of the cover, but sat poised, as though steeling herself to plunge into icy water.

"Your dad?" he probed. She nodded, drew a deep breath, and folded the cover open with such reverence, he guessed it was the first time she had looked at it since her father's death. He set a guard over his tongue.

The album's hinge complained as she lay it flat. He imagined she had opened his coffin.

He watched in silence as her gaze wandered over the first page. She pulled a handkerchief from her bag and blew her nose into it wetly.

He studied the ceiling where cracks in the paint radiated from a water damage stain. He remembered the summer storm that had caused it by filling the gutters too fast. He had sat at the same window in darkness and watched lightning connect earth and sky again and again, a message without content but full of power.

Dee stirred.

He said quietly, "Why are you torturing yourself?"

"It's not torture," she said. "Don't you ever feel the need to draw off a little poison? Grief is a kind of poison."

"What is that photo, there," he said, and touched its corner. The photo was shot into the sun, silhouetting a man and two girls against lush heath and the arc of a craggy bay.

"Us holidaying in Albany. We were always there in summer, but have precious few photos of Dad. He was usually behind the camera."

"Do you ever go down there?"

"You mean to holiday? No. I visited once, just once. We must have spent the best part of seven summer holidays there. It was tempting to hope, having spent so much time there, that the place would be imbued with a little of him. That the pavement might have taken the imprint of his thongs, the caravan park a little of his smell, or the locals the rub of his character." Her finger touched the man's silhouette. "But I found none of that. The tourist crowd swells and ebbs each season, and has no memory of its own. Even the locals eventually fall out of orbit into the bigger cities."

She turned the page.

"Going back was a mistake. I came home with less. I only found what I already knew, that what I'd enjoyed as a girl was the people, to be there with my family, with Dad. It wouldn't have mattered where we were. The substance was the warm bodies nearby, the pick-up games, the cuts and sunburn, the Milky Way, and the laughter of board games played well past bedtime. It's just a town now that doesn't know me."

His heart ached. Her tears had dried, but her voice had become distant. Drawing poison, she'd called it; it felt more like vomiting it up. He rued answering the door, and then, in the time it took for the thought to flash across his mind, felt guilty. He buckled down and resolved to ride it out with her.

She turned another page, and her sudden laughter banished the shadow that had gathered over him.

"I remember this," she said, and angled the book to afford him a better view. He took a moment to interpret the scene. Her dad occupied most of the photo. A camera obscured his face. He appeared to be taking a photo of himself in a bathroom mirror. His brown arms, winging out to either side of his face while they propped the camera before his eye, contrasted with the pallor of his naked torso, which was relieved only by a scribble of chest hair. Above his head sat a white towel, which hugged his scalp and spiralled up to a point that had folded under its own weight.

"He said he was a soft-serve ice-cream. He thought he was so clever."

She flipped through more pages, pausing to pore over each and comment. Rasputin watched her as much as the picture show. Her face was a shifting study of the tracks of human emotion. Each photo she scanned summoned an immediate echo of the event in her expression, which then played out in changing nuance as she recalled the event and explored its nooks and crannies. The tears came again, as often as not, but he thought he detected tension leave her frame.

He couldn't help contrast the number of photos Dee had of her father with the lone touchstone he had of his sister.

Without meaning to, he began calling up her memory.

It came slowly, first with the cry of gulls invading the quiet room. He drew it near without taking his attention from Dee and the photo album. The room remained dark and still, while the sensation of a breeze began to play up and down his arms, and midday sun kissed his skin, over his arms, and beneath his jeans. Its warmth finally pulled his attention away from Dee. He only realised when her question broke through to him: "Monk, are you okay?"

"No seizures," he whispered. "It seems some part of me believes in your poison therapy."

"Can I," she said, hesitant, "Can I come with you?"

"Please."

She slipped a hand over his and squeezed it once. With that skin to skin contact as an anchor in the real world, he let himself fall into the blooming memory.

"Can you tell me what you're seeing?" she said, sounding both far-off and near.

"A Falcon station-wagon. Its tyre wells are spattered with mud. We must've been on unsealed roads," he said, then realised he was only noting what was new since he had last explored the memory. He began again. "I'm at a beach. The surf is pounding, and the sea is stirred up. There's a line of white water out there. It must be breaking over a reef."

"Is it a town beach?"

"I don't know. I can't just turn around. Memories from when I was a kid are ..." he paused, groping for the right word, "disjointed, like your photo album. And worse, many are blurred or skewed, or like they're under-developed. I don't just mean the sights, either. Sounds too. Everything is like that—"

He broke off. His sister ran behind him, down the grassy shoulder of the beach, off the lip and into the sand. He felt the bluster of her motion pass across his shoulders, and he turned in time to see her look back.

"My sister. She has ... green eyes, like me. And she's missing a front tooth, but it doesn't hurt her smile. She's calling me: Tintin."

His toddler's reaction, delayed, was to turn to her. A giggle bubbled out of his throat and he began clumsily to chase her.

"We're playing a game," he said. "I'm trying to catch her." Suddenly a view of the beach opened wide. It was strewn with people. Metres from the car a family clustered under an umbrella. He didn't recognise anyone.

The view faded to black and was replaced for a moment with a pure sensation of dizziness. He was chasing his sister around the car, and this was not the first circuit.

"I'm in the car," he said, his voice falling to a whisper. "I think I'm looking for her." But it was hard to tell. Time had slowed. He was on all fours in the passenger seat, and children were visible through the open driver's side doorway, taking an eternity to cross the gap. The sharp cries of the gulls had dropped octaves to become long, low howls; it was a pack of wolves out there, on the hunt.

A final, static image appeared before he felt the first, familiar wave of disorientation, of screaming, assault him again. It was of the car's handbrake, depressed to the floor, and, closed over its shaft, his hand.

His mind turned and ran from the memory as though from a primed bomb.

He opened his eyes, but the memory clung to him like nightmare.

He looked at his hand, the one still enclosed by Dee's. He yanked it free and stared at it.

"You're sweating," Dee said. "What is it?" She tried to take his hand again, but he snatched it away. "What did you see?"

"I ... She ..." he began, then fell silent. He balled his hand into a fist, then extended his index and middle fingers. He walked them over his drawn-up knees. "I was chasing her around the car, I think—hard to piece it together."

Dee nodded, coaxing.

"She must've been out of sight too long," he said. "I crawled through the car"—his fingers crouched and slowed—"maybe thinking she was in there, maybe trying to cut her off on the other side ..."

Dee kept nodding, but his fingers stopped. He couldn't get them moving again.

"What happened in the car, Monk?" she said. "Was she there? Was she sick?"

"No, no," he said, and examined his hand again. He curled his fingers around the imaginary shaft of a handbrake lever and mimed dropping it. Her face wore an expression of confusion, but he continued to lift the lever and drop it, lift and drop, as though he were playing charades with an imagination run dry. The deadlock held until she suddenly sat back. Her pupils had nearly eclipsed her irises.

"The *handbrake*?" she said.

"Me. I must have disengaged it, and—"

She came forward, grabbed him by the shoulders, and said in a rush: "No. Don't go there. You don't know that. Did you actually see yourself do it?" He shook his head. "Then it could have been anyone—*anyone* Monk—or anything. It may have broken. Or maybe it was someone else. There must have been plenty of people around. Maybe the brake had nothing to do with it."

(*The car rolled, just a foot, and stopped*)

He nodded at her words, smiled, and tasted salt on his lips. He felt a perverse need to comfort her. She looked so small and weak.

(*Screaming. Is there a worse sound?*)

Dee was still speaking, but he was watching her face. So animated. One minute she was pleading, then her brows drew down in determination.

He spoke, finally, and she froze. He needed to give her a job, something to take her mind from the discovery that her oldest friend had taken a life. He said, "Would you help me?"

"Anything, Monk."

"I need to find the source of my gift," he said, holding her gaze. "I don't want it anymore."

She was still a moment, then shook her head, not in response to his question, but as if to shake off an irrelevant thought.

"Oh, that. Yes, of course." She twisted to retrieve her bag. "I've been thinking about that too." She pulled out a diary and flipped to its last page. She tore it out. It came free from the spiral spine with a rattle. She handed it to him. On it was a phone number, and what looked like hours and a building number.

"What's this?"

"An old lecturer of mine, Professor"—Rasputin suppressed a shudder as the word passed into his ears—"De Groot. He lectures in biology, but researches biomarkers for neurological disease. At least, he used to. I think he's in semi-retirement. Give him a call."

205

He forced a smile, out of respect for Dee's concern, folded the paper and stowed it in a pocket.

"Sure."

"More importantly, he's a nice guy. He helped me out no end in my honours year."

Her brow furrowed in concentration. "Monk," she said, drawing his gaze. "Promise me you're not going to load yourself up with guilt for what you think happened."

"Guilt? I was three. I hardly knew the girl."

"Promise me."

"I promise."

Dee gathered up her things, hugged him, and let herself out.

He went to bed in his clothes. He searched for the memory of a U2 concert, and dragged it like bedclothes over his head. Soon he was standing by Jordy in the pit below the stage. He picked through the band's set until he found *Fly on the Wall* and set it to loop, loud. He sank into smothering, flashing darkness, the bump of strangers, and the overpowering smell of sweat.

At 2:55AM his phone, lying on his bedside table, buzzed. The sound reverberated on the wood, magnifying it. It woke him, not from sleep—his mind was just beginning to wander in valleys that led there. His hand shot out into the night-gloom, groping. It missed the mark once, rapping the table, then found the phone.

He switched it on and tiny letters appeared, blazing with an intensity heightened by the darkness. It said: You have 1 new message(s).

Leave it, he thought. Then called it up.

Different words burned in the dark: Murder? Food for the soul. Builds character.

Fear licked the nape of his neck.

He replied, in a fury fuelled by his fumbling, too-big fingers: Who r u.

When his reply was confirmed sent, he threw the phone into the darkness. He heard it strike the wall and fall in at least two pieces.

Rasputin's footfalls echoed in the foyer of the biology building. He faced the far end of the tiled room, which contained two doors. One was propped open, and through it came a voice. He could not discern what it was saying, but it rose and fell with the cadence of a lecture.

He turned, approached a board of photos of the biology faculty, and scanned the rows of dour men and women. He imagined how the photo shoot had gone: "Face the camera. Now imagine you've been diagnosed with cancer—SNAP!"

He was deciding on the best way to tell Dee, "Thanks but no thanks,"—*academics don't mix well with my personal life*—when his gaze was hooked by a photo in the bottom row. It held a man whose hair was swept back from the camera as if by the flash, in a style Rasputin coined on the spot, *hedgehog-attempts-land-speed-record*. But his expression was warm. His eyes were engaged, as though the exposure had interrupted a lively conversation.

Rasputin knew without reading the nameplate that here was Dee's Professor De Groot.

He trained his ears on the vocal rumbling escaping the lecture theatre. Twice it was drowned by a noise that finally resolved into the sound of many people laughing.

He crossed to the propped open door, his shoes clapping on tiles, and snuck into a seat at the rear of the theatre. He made it just as the last peals of laughter were dying away.

A student two rows below Rasputin raised his arm. The professor took the question: "What's the point of polymerase? Why the fuss? The cell simply has to copy the protein sequence, right?"

Rasputin shifted his attention to the information on the large screen behind the professor. It broke every rule of presentation. In place of succinct assertions, was something like a mediaeval illuminated manuscript penned in crabbed handwriting. The sea of text was relieved by a chain of circular islands connected by lines. This island-chain wormed downward, doubling back at the screen's edge a number of times. He guessed the diagram was an example of the slide's eponymous *Protein Sequences.*

The professor cleared his throat. "You are wondering, *mijn jonge,* about the need for complex error-correcting facilities of the cell, of every cell? Why does the cell ... *fuss?*"

The student nodded, and the professor continued. "I'll give you the answer," he said, and then did something decidedly strange.

He bent to the ear of a girl scribbling notes. She jerked upright, belatedly coming up to speed with events. He whispered in her ear, and when she simply stared at him, winked and whipped a hand parallel to the front row. She caught on, leaned toward the girl seated beside her, and whispered in her ear.

Murmur grew as understanding of the impromptu game rippled through the audience. A few laughed. The message passed with increasing speed to the end of the first row, skipped up a row, and bounded back in the opposite direction. Its track reminded Rasputin of the protein chain woven through the text on the screen. The message passed from head to head, each pair converging to exchange the secret.

If it hadn't been for the way the professor tracked its progress with twinkling eye, Rasputin would have suspected him of time-wasting.

More than a minute had elapsed when the baton-pass entered the final leg, and bore down on the student whose question had ignited the game. He retrieved it from a girl with ash-blonde hair, who didn't seem to want to get too near him. Rasputin, mere feet from the final exchange, barely heard her murmur.

"If you'd please," called the professor. "The answer? Speak up."

The student stood, and, twisting a belt-loop self-consciously, said: "We doubt we need be all matched up." His voice rose as though he were asking a question.

The professor laughed, a generous sound, and the audience responded in kind.

"Couldn't have said it better myself. Please sit down."

When the noise had died away, he said, "What I actually said, as some of you already know, was: Without it we'd all be so much soup."

"Every cell in our body is a little drug factory. Without its error-correcting machines, they would slowly but surely begin turning out junk proteins. Your veins would run with sewage, your tissues be awash in garbage."

He raised a finger for emphasis.

"Worse! Do not forget that these little factories also turn out other little factories, replicate *themselves*. Every cell holds a complete blueprint of your entire body: DNA. And DNA is simply another protein. The message written in that DNA is just as susceptible to corruption when copied as any other protein. Remember our game? Some of you mumbled, some didn't listen, some forgot, and some were too concerned about the body smell of their neighbour to get too close."

He waited for silence, and said: "But, for your body, the stakes are higher than our game. The loser gets cancer."

He turned to look at the screen.

"That protein chain—" he began, then pivoted to ask a question: "Who will hazard a guess as to what it is?"

Conversation broke out like spot fires. Rasputin examined the figure, not caring what it was. But as he looked, it became animated. The clumsy drawing was suddenly sublimated into a neat representation of the protein. Each island in its chain was replaced by a textbook-precise rendering, stolen from his memory of biology lectures.

It became a many-coloured snake. He suppressed a gasp when it lifted its head from the screen and into the room. It swung a moment above the audience, and then did something no real snake could do: it folded back on itself, at many points along its length, at seemingly random locations. It folded acutely, in a way that would have snapped the spine of a real snake. It continued to fold and interlock until its beginning and end were lost within an irregular, three dimensional cluster of protein islands.

Recognition lit his mind and flared from his mouth: "It's an alpha chain of Haemoglobin."

Unfortunately, the hubbub had died prior to this ejaculation, in anticipation of the answer. But no one appeared to have expected it from the rear of the theatre. The professor took it in his stride.

"Correct. It is indeed one of four chains that make up Haemoglobin, the protein that even now is carting oxygen about your body, fuelling your hungry brains."

He replaced the slide with another. "Here is the full and folded molecule."

The picture on the screen was computer-generated rather than drawn. It showed a molecule comprised of hundreds of small building blocks. When folded into a three dimensional structure by its inherent potential, it looked, to Rasputin, like the knobbly, plastic balls found in supermarket two-dollar bins.

Part of the molecule pulsed with light, the part Rasputin had recognised—*scanned, folded and recognised*, he amended. The light limning the protein faded, leaving him feeling as if his mind were making sure he believed it. Self-indulgently, smugly, making sure.

"One mistake transcribing this," the professor said, "and you get, instead, this." He replaced the slide with one depicting a warped Haemoglobin molecule. "*Sickle-cell anaemia*. Great for malaria. Not so good for living beyond thirty." He held up a finger. "Just one mistake," he said, and, curiously, chuckled.

The lecture was over, and the theatre emptied in a squall of scraping chair-legs and talk. Rasputin made his way against the flow down to the floor.

The professor was collecting his transparencies when he noticed Rasputin out of the corner of his eye.

"Ah, Mr. Haemoglobin," he said. "I must have forgotten your name."

"I'm not sure you'd know it, sir," said Rasputin.

"I'm not British, *mijn jonge*. No 'sirs'. I assume this is not the first time you have taken my course."

"I haven't taken your course. I'm visiting."

The professor's brow drew down in consternation, his eyebrows bristling like two grey caterpillars facing off.

Rasputin hastened to add, "I must have seen Haemoglobin's sequence before. Funny how some things stick in your memory."

The professor nodded. "Funny." He piled his slides into a battered tinned-soup box, and said, "Help an old man. I'm sure your muscles match that memory of yours."

Rasputin tried to imagine a body that *would* match his memory, and failed.

He lifted the box with his free hand, propped it against his chest, and waited for the professor to lead the way. The professor switched the projector off, the snap of its plastic switch echoing in the now-empty theatre, and walked up the isle to the exit with a sprightliness that belied his age.

His office was on the same floor as the lecture theatre, a short trip down a corridor connecting offices and a lunch room to the foyer. On entering it, Rasputin rested his cane against the wall, and lowered the box with both hands to the floor.

Without a word, the professor sat and began to check email. Rasputin used the moment to survey the office. Aside from the computer, the only electrical appliance in the room was an ancient bar heater. Despite the sun-drenched day outside, its single bar was bright red, radiating heat at the professor's back. The heater's warmth seemed to have raised aromas latent in the thick carpet—boiled lollies, tea, and liniment. A bowl nestled between keyboard and computer was filled to the brim with paper clips, broken staple blocks, and drawing pins, an old magpie's hoard. A half-size bookshelf was crammed with birthday and Christmas cards, nested for lack of space.

Above the cards sat a corkboard covered with photos and postcards. It had been filled, and photos were pinned to its edges, hanging into space like the fringe of an *avant-garde* rug. At some point, when the board had been filled, new photos had been overlaid, carefully, to avoid occluding faces. The professor had been happy to cover anything from the Grand Canyon to London Bridge, as long as the smiling faces of his children—for that was clearly who they were—were exposed to the gentle radiance of the bar heater.

The creak of the professor's chair as it rotated signaled to Rasputin that he had finished.

"The world is not ending today," he said, and rose. "So. A coffee, I think, and then you can unload that trouble from your breast."

"Sorry, sir—Professor?"

"Call me Reim. A young lad shouldn't have dark circles around his eyes. Makes you look like a racquet."

"Racoon?"

"Racoon, yes. So, come. Indulge an old man in an entrenched habit, and keep me company."

Reim left the office without waiting for an answer, and presently Rasputin was hobbling next to him, straining to keep up. They emerged from the building, descended a flight of stairs, and joined one of the many thoroughfares riddling the campus. Reim struck out east, head thrust forward over his paunch, which rolled over his belt buckle, obscuring it. With his hands folded together at the small of his back, he looked to Rasputin like he was embarking on a safari. He lacked only a pith helmet and elephant gun.

Reim travelled as the crow flies. He lanced between packs of students playing kick to kick, not breaking step as his gaze tracked a punted football arcing overhead.

Rasputin began to fear Reim's 'entrenched habit' was power walking. They had walked for barely three minutes and his leg was burning. His spirits sank further when they crossed Hackett Drive, and left the campus behind.

Before them the silvered waters of Matilda Bay stretched left and right, framed above by the canopy of gum trees, and below by grass that grew almost to the water. Nearby, a restaurant commanded a view of the bay, and farther round the bay sat the Royal Perth Yacht Club.

Farther still, the riverscape was boxed in by the prominent knoll of King's Park and the city. Cars crawled like so many species of beetle across the Narrows Bridge, which plumbed the city's main artery into the heart of downtown.

The professor made a bee-line for the restaurant, and Rasputin followed on his heels. Inside, while Rasputin stood, feeling self-conscious about the tattered and dirty hems of his jeans, Reim ambled to the bar and was greeted by an attendant. He ordered and rejoined Rasputin to wait. Presently the attendant reappeared holding two tall paper cups. Reim took them, thanked the attendant, and disappeared outside. Rasputin found him waiting on the grass.

"This place is getting too fancy for its own good, but then," said Reim, surveying the bay, "with a view like this, who can blame them?"

He offered one of the cups to Rasputin, then, squinting to find the hole in the lid of his cup, drank. Rasputin didn't need to taste the cup's contents to know it held coffee. He drank and enjoyed being still. The coffee was good.

"Has this been your coffee haunt for long?" said Rasputin. "Thanks for the coffee, by the way."

"Don't mention it. And to answer your question: yes, if you count sixteen years as long, though I don't think I do any more."

They were silent again, watching the bob and sway of yachts tethered to the club's jetties.

Reim moved off. He walked toward the water, then began to follow the curve of the beach. Rasputin reorganised himself and followed. He stepped in the clean, treadless prints left by Reim's battered leather loafers, puncturing every other one with the butt of his cane. A minute later he was standing on a jetty, looking into the obscenely small hold of a 16-foot yacht. It bobbed in the wash reflecting from the jetty's pilings. Rasputin read the vessel's name, which was painted on its side in a curling script: Van Leeuwin III. The gaze Reim fixed it with was full of possession, and it caused Rasputin a sinking feeling.

"*This* is your habit?" Rasputin said.

Reim winked, and then squatted with that same youthfulness, and dropped into the boat's stern.

He proffered a hand to Rasputin, and said, "Come. I promise you won't regret it."

With one longing glance at the shore, Rasputin passed his cane to Reim, and then awkwardly lowered himself off the jetty and into the boat. It rocked alarmingly as he shifted his weight. Reim stood by the tiller and rode the roll without seeming to notice it.

Rasputin looked at the yacht in the next pen. It had to be close to 40 feet long. A miasma of money clung to it, in its spit-polished fittings, moulded hull, and leathern seats. By contrast, Reim's wooden get-about was in dire need of fresh paint, and the bilge smelled as though it held a drowned rat.

"Must cost a penny to moor here," said Rasputin.

Reim turned from fussing with the sail.

"It's not my pen," he said in faux shock. "I'm Dutch! Don't you know my uncle argued with a Scotsman over a penny and invented wire? No, it is a loan from a colleague—absent and esteemed." He added with a chuckle, "One day he'll return and be neither."

Reim cast off, pushed the yacht clear of the jetty, and raised its single sail. Its cloth billowed and pulled them away from the gleaming 40-footers. Rasputin fancied their little vessel blowing a raspberry at the proud craft left staked behind.

Rasputin noticed the water darken as the silty riverbed fell away. His heart beat faster.

"Do I need a life jacket?"

"No. You need to not fall in."

Reim trimmed the sail, and Rasputin began to relax. He shifted on the seat to a more comfortable position, and began to take in the vista spreading in every direction. He recognised the landmarks: the old boathouse, sticking out into the bay from the Stirling Highway side; the tumble-down buttress of King's Park; and its faint echo to the South, Heathcote bluff, once an asylum for the insane, now an asylum for picnicking families; the grey strip of the freeway to the east, and the bridge where it arced over Narrows Point. He knew and could name them all, but was struck by how unfamiliar they looked. He had never been *on* the river. It had always been scenery slipping past on the other side of a window.

Reim was silent, and only moved occasionally to trim the sail or nudge the tiller in response to some change in the wind or current to which Rasputin was insensible.

After a time, when, for Rasputin, the silence became more uncomfortable than his desire not to intrude on Reim's reverie, he said: "Have you been sailing for sixteen years, too?"

Reim responded without a sign he had been interrupted. "Longer. I used to come out here with my boys when that freeway over there still smelled of the asphalt. Now it goes nearly to Bunbury, over a hundred kilometres."

"That must make you feel old," said Rasputin.

Reim took his eyes from the water to squint at Rasputin.

"Old? No, there are no end of roads. They don't make me feel old," he said, tucking one leg over the other. "I feel old the third time I take a piss before sunrise. I feel old when my kids call me and give me advice." He pinched the bridge of his nose then, and Rasputin realised he was making a show of moroseness.

"It's a funny thing," Reim said. "I am conscious of having gotten old, but that happened without me ever feeling grown-up."

"Where are your kids now?"

"Uh-huh," said Reim, and unlocked his legs so he could face Rasputin. "The De Groot Diaspora." He chuckled.

"All safely married," he said, and Rasputin smirked at the odd description.

"My oldest, Pieter, does law in Toronto—and he's welcome to the weather."

Rasputin raked through the memory of Reim's photo board and found the older-looking brother. Toronto's iconic CN Tower loomed impossibly high in the background.

"Then comes Jop, my next boy. He got my wife's brains, and researches in the mathematics at Stanford."

Rasputin found him on the photo board too, a dark-haired man with a pleasant smile and a slim build—*like me*, thought Rasputin. He was standing at a pier.

"And last, my princess, Ineke. She lives now in Burma. She and her husband have fifty-six children at last count." Reim took a moment evidently to savour Rasputin's incredulity before delivering the old punch line: "Orphans."

Rasputin found her easily, for half of the photos of her were filled with the smiling faces of children, every one brown-skinned, cheeks daubed with a white substance, and clustered about Ineke as though she were sitting in the middle of a meadow in flower-burst.

"And here you are," said Rasputin, "flogging freshmen. Positively tame by comparison."

Reim inclined his head in acceptance, but his smile lingered.

"And Mrs. De Groot?"

"Is with the Lord," Reim said, and silence followed his words but for the occasional snap of the sail.

Rasputin peered into the water as their craft crossed into the channel. Ahead, breaching the shadows beneath the Narrows Bridge, came the sleek bulk of a ferry. It swept past, and Rasputin craned his neck to look at the cluster of antennae bristling from the roof above its bridge. Seconds later they were rocked by its bow wave, and Rasputin went rigid, clutching at the gunnels.

When the boat had ceased rolling, Reim yelled, "Lee ho!" startling Rasputin, and tacked to the south, on an angle that took them near the freeway shore.

Once Reim had trimmed the sail, he turned to Rasputin and said, "Would you like to learn?"

Rasputin answered out of habit. "No."

"Just hold this for me then." He handed Rasputin the mainsheet, which had not left his hand since they set sail.

The breeze blustered in his ears, ebbing and flowing, and Rasputin felt the mainsheet become taut and lax in echo. The coarse rope tugged at the skin of his palms.

Their new course put what angle the sun's rays had directly into Rasputin's eyes. Reim suddenly stood and then sat next to Rasputin, giving the boat a decided lean.

"Take my seat. I can't bear you squinting like that. I'm used to it. You kids spend too much time in front of computers."

Rasputin obeyed. He rose gingerly, pivoted, and sank onto the seat by the tiller. Anything to restore the boat's equilibrium.

"You might want to grab that too," Reim said, indicating the tiller. "So we don't hit that 30-footer," he said, jabbing a thumb over his shoulder without looking. "Just a thought."

Rasputin gripped the wooden arm of the tiller and yanked it over. The boat swung and spilled wind. The boom began to swing fitfully.

"Pull her back," said Reim, "before you brain me."

Rasputin did so, and the boom swung back to where it had been, like a compass needle finding north.

"And tighten her up a bit," Reim said, nodding at the rope still clutched in Rasputin's hand. He did, felt it thrum with the strain. "We'll make a salty of you yet."

"So long as there's no scrubbing of the poop deck," Rasputin said, attempting to sound sardonic, yet struggling to contain laughter perched at the top of his throat.

He relaxed as he got used to the feel of the rope and tiller. He began to sense how one played off the other, and how both were influenced by the breeze. When there was a lull in the wind, the roar of traffic flowing from the freeway penetrated to their boat, and when it died altogether, even the hiss of the bay's choppy waves breaking struggled out to them. The stench of rotting seaweed, the same smell that filtered into the bus on the way to university, only more pungent, filled his nostrils, but the lap of water on the boat's hull and the caress of nature-made wind transformed it; it smelt like life not death.

"Why did you come to me today?" said Reim.

The abruptness of the question made Rasputin withdraw from the feel of the boat. For a moment, it ceased being an extension of him. He eased himself back into it, through rope and tiller, while he tried to formulate a response to Reim's question.

"A friend of mine, Dee Morgan, said I should look you up." Reim's brow crinkled. "She was a student of yours, a few years back." When the professor still gave no sign of recognising the name, Rasputin said, "She said you helped her in her honours year."

"Oh. Deanne?" he said, "With the little spiders?" He held his hand up, palm down, and wriggled his fingers in imitation of a spider.

"That's right," Rasputin said. He plucked the Latin name of the spider species from the tip of his mind like a ripe blueberry, "*Lampoda cylindrata.*"

Prior to the accident, his best guess at Dee's honours topic would have been beetroots, and not from lack of her telling him. What a jerk, he thought, and made a mental note to apologise for not being more supportive during that year.

"I remember," said Reim. "Half of them died in the first month. Dear little thing. Dee, I mean, not the spiders. I hate spiders."

Spiders, rats. Rasputin scratched the mental note, and replaced it with a reminder to needle her about her resemblance to Dr. Kevorkian, the doctor of death.

And then he realised there was nowhere safe to go with his answer, and it was a long wade back to shore. He cast his gaze up into the sky's spotless vault and, for an instant, drew down the stars he knew to be beating on that blue blaze with spindles of lonely light. He saw them all, arrayed in perfect position for the time of day, waiting for night.

Then, with a faint pressure like a compulsion, the eye sought to swallow everything, the bay, the blue, stars and all, in its own fantastic sky, and make Rasputin the centre of everything.

"Not now," he muttered, and steeling himself as if for a needle prick, pushed it away.

He returned Reim's clear-eyed gaze.

"I've an odd tale to tell," he said, with presence of mind enough to play at sea dog. "It began when my head was split open, and since then I've come to yearn for something as mundane as bloodletting."

He went on to tell Reim everything that had happened since emerging from a coma until that morning, when he had squeezed silently into the back row of the lecture theatre.

Reim interrupted him twice. Once to tack northeast, taking them back toward the freeway shore, which had drifted away as their southerly course continued to pull Heathcote bluff nearer, and again, to jibe on a direct course downwind toward Matilda Bay, their origin.

By the time Rasputin had finished, shadows had tightened beneath the sail, and the shore had drawn near enough to make out the park benches and barbecues that dotted it.

Reim regarded him, expression unreadable.

"And you want me to—what?—assay your blood?"

"Yes," said Rasputin, unable to gauge Reim's response to his brief history. "Dee thought you were working with blood-borne biomarkers of ..." He stopped mid-explanation, struck by the sudden fear the idea was ludicrous.

Reim finished the sentence for him. "Neurological disease. That is true, although my expertise lies more with the animal than the human. My team is diverse ... But surely a neurologist—"

Rasputin's gaze dipped at the mention of neurologist. Reim paused.

"Well, no harm in giving me a blood sample. Visit the pathology lab on Broadway. It's a collection point for our trials. I'll put your blood through our arrays, and see if anything turns up."

"But do you believe me? Test me. Ask me something. Ask me how many windows are in that apartment block over there," he said, jerking his head over his shoulder.

"Rasputin, you are either a liar, mad, or telling the truth. I doubt very much Dee would have sent me a liar, and if you're mad, that makes two of us—the dish and the spoon." He smiled. "Mr. Haemoglobin, I believe you're telling the truth, no matter that I find it incredible."

Rasputin wanted to kiss the old man.

"But I would love to test you," Reim continued. "Not to reveal a lie. I'm interested in what you can do."

Rasputin rolled his shoulders, laced his fingers, and stretched them. "Go for it."

"Picture a chessboard, but one that is initially white-on-white, and stretches in every direction without limit. To this board add two players. We'll call them the Angel and the Devil."

"Spooky," said Rasputin, smiling while he formed the image in his mind.

"The rules of the game are simple: the Devil's sole aim is to trap the Angel. Each turn the Devil blackens one square, which is henceforth cut-off from the Angel. The Angel can flee up to a fixed number of squares each turn. Let's call that number *jump*. The game ends when the Angel has no white squares close enough to jump to: he is captured."

"Got it," said Rasputin, as in his mind two figures, one dark, one light, faced off on an endless grid.

"Here's the question: regardless of how big *jump* is, is our Angel forever doomed to fall into the Devil's clutches?"

Rasputin gave the image of the grid and its lonely-looking figures over to the brute force of his mind. His sub-consciousness became fluid and crashed over the grid from every direction in a flood that swept up grid, Angel, and Devil.

Rasputin was struck by fleeting images. The grid extruded into three dimensions and become a maze. The Angel, trailing a hand against its wall, moved through it swift as a mouse. Then cinders fell like snow, and he saw the Angel feint back from a wall suddenly engulfed by black flame—only to squeeze through an escape opening in the flame's wake.

Rasputin blinked. His lids had hooded his eyes without him realising. Scant seconds had passed since Reim had asked his question.

But Rasputin had the answer.

Reim watching intently, said, "Who wins our game of celestial cat and mouse?"

"The Angel."

"My, my," said Reim. "And so quick." He pressed further: "For bonus marks: Do you know the smallest value for *jump* at which our Angel survives?"

"Two," said Rasputin, surprised to find it sitting on the chessboard like a rock left by the tide. "But don't ask me to explain the proof. I have no idea why two jumps is enough."

"Bravo!" said Reim, and clapped his hands. "Nice to know you only need two steps to stay ahead of the Devil."

Or two friends.

"Do you have a real question?" said Rasputin.

Reim's brow puckered in a frown. "Don't be coy. It took no less than three PhDs to solve that problem earlier this year."

He leaned back, still surveying Rasputin with fresh regard. "But you want harder? Try this: Picture in your mind a circle of diameter one foot. Now square it for me. Make a square of that circle. What length are its sides?"

"I said hard, not impossible," said Rasputin, without bothering to focus on the question. "Even I know the sides of such a square would be a proportion of Pi, an irrational number; the digits after the decimal point go on forever."

"Forever, yes. As does anything that matters."

"You believe your wife still lives, don't you," said Rasputin.

"Yes."

"She was a good woman?"

"She is a forgiven woman."

Rasputin couldn't help but look away from Reim. When he looked back he noticed a small brooch affixed to Reim's lapel. Engraved into its centre, just visible at a few feet, was the symbol for Pi.

"I thought you were a biologist."

Reim caught his glance, and said, "When I was young I considered a career in maths. I think that is where my boy Jop caught the disease. But biology has a lot of maths, especially when one looks at the molecular level."

Reim tilted the brooch so he could peer at it. "Pi is my favourite number, a prince among beggars. It is the key that opens the portal for so many seemingly intractable problems."

He unpinned the brooch and handed it to Rasputin. Reim nodded: "Open it."

Rasputin found a tiny catch at its side, unlatched it. The brooch split. He prised it open on its hinge, and found within a grainy photo that had lost its colour. A face looked out at him, a woman's face—lined and fleshy but beautiful.

Reim took his gaze from the river long enough to touch the brooch with it. "Within the lesser love, is set the greater." The words sounded well worn on his tongue.

Rasputin closed it gently and handed it back.

Minutes later they drew up to the jetty. Reim scrambled onto it.

"Throw me that mooring line, Jop," he said.

Rasputin quelled the urge to correct him and passed him the rope. Rasputin noted how the old man's hands, leathery to the touch, were yet supple and swift as he tied off. He decided it was not any sense of condescension that prevented him correcting Reim.

"It's not broken," said Jordy. "The battery is missing."

Rasputin couldn't meet his eye. It was obvious the phone's cover had come loose by blunt-force trauma.

"It did feel lighter when I put it back together. Hang on."

Rasputin went to his room and searched behind boxes he hadn't unpacked in two years. He found the battery lying under the flap of a box, sitting on lecture notes that were beginning to fade. He retrieved it and returned to the kitchen, where twin fluorescent tubes cast the brightest light in the house. Jordy took the battery, slotted it into place, and snapped the cover back on. The phone bleeped.

"There. Happy phone," he said, and handed it back to Rasputin. "That'll be $150."

"You can have the equivalent in options on my brain," said Rasputin, and made for the front door.

"Where are you going?" Jordy called, not following.

"For a walk." *Or a whatever it is I do now.*

Rasputin made it as far as a park that abutted the local primary school. The sun was unobscured, drawing the sap of every tree, and the air smelled of clipped lawn. Summer was come.

Rasputin surveyed the park quickly. It was empty. "What an indictment," he said, but was pleased.

He switched his phone on, holding his breath while it booted: Power, good. Signal strength. Network …

Messages.

You have 2 new message(s), it said.

He called up the first.

It said: For psycho readings call 1800-C-R-A-C-K-E-R-S.

More of the same. He eyed a nearby bin, a yellow 40-gallon drum pinioned between two posts, and was tempted to toss the phone into its dark mouth. Instead, he flicked the phone's display to the second message.

It said: Who r u?

He froze, then frowned, thinking he had mistakenly called up the last message he had sent.

He hadn't.

He began a new message and thumbed it in, "U 1st or r u chkn." He sent it and reclined on the bench with satisfaction, only to be startled a minute later when it buzzed in his lap.

He snatched it up and retrieved the new message: "I'm willing. Are you Abel?"

Rasputin muttered to himself, "Text or write, but if you're going to write, at least try to spell," while he typed a reply: "I'm all ears."

A response arrived seconds later. "I'm your looooong lost brother ;-)"

A rapid-fire exchange began.

"Bullshit. I don't have a brother."

"Like you don't have a sister?"

That made him pause. It had begun to feel like a game. He wondered if he was imagining his unknown interlocutor to be the news reporter he had never met, trying something lateral. But it didn't matter who it was. Whoever it was knew something about Rasputin's past that he himself had only recently uncovered, something dark. And that scared him.

Another message arrived. "OK. Brothers, close brothers, know each others' thoughts, no?"

"I wouldn't know."

"Explore your memory for insults and wounds."

Something about the choice of the word *explore* made Rasputin uneasy. He began to knit together skeins of speculation into a nascent theory.

He tested the theory's strength: "Today's? Yesterday's?"

"Don't be coy. I mean ALL of them. Drop the coin stamped with injustice's image into the jukebox in your head and see what plays."

Fast as a bullet, shock bifurcated into hope and fear. His theory held this much. Did he dare believe he had found someone who understood the workings of his mind because they had witnessed the same first-hand, from within?

He pushed harder. "Speak plainly. What jukebox?"

"You know exactly what I mean: the Miracle Machine in your Head that connects Memory and knits Knowledge, new from the fragments of old."

Rasputin collapsed back onto the bench. "My God," he said. "He knows."

He texted back, "Wait," and then did as told. He reached for the remembered sensation of insult's injury, of physical blows and shame's sting, distilled them, bound them into an organic bundle, and dumped that bundle into his mind's eye, a query.

The torrent of hurt that broke over him in response struck like a physical blow, beat him down upon the bench. It pushed him inward, into the eye, and held him there.

The eye's wall was thronged with mockers, an unrelieved gallery of antagonists. From the left he saw, a moment too late, a 12-year-old's fist close on him. (Why he had goaded a boy twice his weight he couldn't fathom.) The memory of the punch landed on his cheek, not crisp as the real punch had been, but fluid like a jet of water, passing through his skin, carrying the alien feel of violence within. The punch—brute instrument of pain—was followed by a memory melange of half-seen smirks and half-heard quips at his expense. Ghosts haunted the eye, girls he had liked, year-mates he had wanted to be like. They slipped through him, seemingly oblivious to his presence, leaving his skin prickling with embarrassment and burning shame at his impotency.

He arched, grimacing, as a different kind of pain tore at his back. He turned to see the form of a once-friend. He knew his name, though he had scrubbed it from conscious thought—Haydn Stone. Haydn walked hand in hand with a girl of unmistakable gait, Katy. (Rasputin had never quite blotted out *her* name.) The couple receded into the distance, fading to silhouette, blurring, touching, and merging.

The clamour rose and pressed on his ear drums as though he were descending from a height. He shrank under the combined weight of so much remembered ill will.

He wanted to escape back into the park where his body sat. He glimpsed grass and trees and sunshine, but they drifted on the fringe of consciousness like memory—good old-fashioned memory. Instead, it was the eye-become-tortureplex that felt real and inescapable as fresh grief.

He strained toward the surface, but fell, flailing, in a dream of flying that was failing—

When he found an advocate.

He saw a face hitherto unnoticed in the tumult of this sensory assault. It was Jordy.

He clutched at the memory. It was fresh, barely a year old. Jordy had rebuked him for the way he spoke to Dee, for his caustic tongue. Rasputin had brushed it off. It hadn't helped that Jordy had bottled the reprimand so long he was angry himself. (*He spat while talking*—spat!) Then, in the cool of night, Rasputin had seen what had been invisible to him, and repented.

225

It had stung. That was why his mind had summoned this memory alongside the others. But it had been the surgeon's wound, the wound of a friend. To recall it was to remember he was not alone. It leant him the strength to reach for the real world, touch it, and break free.

He blinked, in command of his body again, and relished the afternoon's cooling air.

A message was waiting for him: People are real shits aren't they.

"Some are," he replied.

"Now try this. It's fun. Pick someone—you'll know the one—and let your mind loose on them."

The message's idea woke a suspicion in the depths of his mind, a faint claxon. But it was too near and full of flame. He grabbed it before the claxon rallied the rest of him to its warning.

He sat again within the eye, but this time he was not alone. Seated before him was the summoned ghost of Haydn Stone, or, rather, a hyper-real recreation of him, a patchwork memory construct. The one flaw that threatened to jar Rasputin's suspension of disbelief that this was indeed Haydn Stone (assuming he still lived) was that *this* Haydn Stone, sitting staring sullenly back, was 14 years his junior. This doppelganger was built of old parts. But it would do.

The eye too was altered, but no less a torture chamber. Cluttering its walls were every tool for evoking pain ransacked from Rasputin's experience—actual and vicarious. The brass knuckles of every lip-splitting punch; the iron maiden of Fiction's ghouls; the rack of slow-burn, mental dismemberment (Orwell's 1984 stood front-and-centre); and the Water Torture of the daily grind for bread that turned to ashes in the mouth.

He surveyed the array of apparatus and then cast a speculative, sidelong glance at Haydn's clear skin and square jaw.

Knuckle-dusters, he thought, and reached for them.

The shadows of the eastward trees were reaching deep into the park when he surfaced.

Haydn Stone the memory-construct sat beside him on the bench, a mind-excrescence exuded into the real world. He had aged, a simple trick learned in the preceding hour, of applying patterns of aging deduced from many observations of the process. He had matched Haydn to his own age, and then driven him into senescence.

Haydn, the senior, sat hunched on the bench, dragged earthward by pound upon pound of fat. His scalp was a pattern of bizarrely young-looking pink skin and yellow liver-spots, relieved only by a fuzz of white hair that clung in patches. This Haydn was half-way to losing his identity to the ravages of dementia, and, above all, lonely. Abandoned.

As Rasputin considered his one-time friend, he noticed on the wall of the eye a tool he had not yet wielded. It was rare for being a lived experience. It was the knowledge of having killed one's sister.

He glanced at Haydn and weighed adding *that* burden to a mind already smothered.

"And, no," said Rasputin. "You don't get to change places with her, make it right. No matter how much you want to."

Haydn's glassy stare remained fixed on Rasputin, peering out from the wrinkled craters of his eye sockets, a canine stare. He seemed to sense Rasputin's thought—something possible, Rasputin grimly knew, because he was *of* it.

Instead, he put the weapon down, and let Haydn rise, to wander across the field, and disappear.

Rasputin wrapped his arms about his torso and cast a furtive glance about the park. Still empty.

A message waited on the phone.

"Heady, isn't it."

He didn't reply. The shadows had already swallowed the far side of the park, and now the sun dipped below the horizon, ceding the sky to one of summer's long twilights.

Another message arrived.

"Till next time. Enjoy the park."

A moment passed before the import of those last three words struck. He sat bolt upright and searched the limits of the park for an observer. He found only the same trees, bins, and benches, looking forlorn in the second-hand light.

He rose and hobbled home, feeling like a child straining toward lit places against the suck of a dark room.

Rasputin floated in the void.

He was there because of something Reim had said that morning while sailing, their fifth voyage in two weeks. It had given him an idea. It had set up an itch.

To scratch it, he had chosen the main café on campus. He had sat at an unoccupied table by a window overlooking the cricket oval, and ruefully let his belt out a notch. (Dee was right. He *was* putting on weight.) He had steeped a while in the chatter, enjoying the anonymity, and picked at the calluses thickening on his fingers. Then he had wrapped his awareness in the eye's sky.

Reim had mused on *genius*—a favourite topic, and one Rasputin thought was the old man's attempt to normalise him. Specifically, Reim argued that what was deemed to constitute genius changed like fashion.

To prove his point he took two men: Thomas Aquinas and Albert Einstein. Aquinas's genius was ascribed by his mediaeval contemporaries to his prodigious memory. He could absorb and recall any text he had read, and thus synthesise new knowledge. Einstein's genius, on the other hand, was ascribed by his colleagues to a powerful imagination. His flights of fancy jounced him from the ruts of conventional thinking, and let him ride a beam of starlight while wondering if he would be able to see his face in a mirror.

Both kinds of genius bore fruit. Aquinas's scholasticism led to the creation of the first universities; Einstein's fancies sparked the Quantum revolution that gave the world transistors, computers, lasers, and instant, global communication.

But must it be memory *versus* imagination? Surely each needed the other. A ballerina cannot lift herself into the air, and the ballet dancer needs her crowning grace.

Memory and imagination.

Rasputin's journey through his memory had been wrought by his imagination (so went his train of thought) and what had he found at journey's end? An inventor. A judge. One to make, and one to assess.

Therein lay the itch. Making what? Assessing what?

Perhaps the inventor-judge was only a dream, but even dreamlings had intentions, albeit indecipherable or absurd.

Rasputin wanted to know what they were.

Curiosity burned in him as he drew near a glistening patch of darkness that indicated a pocket in the void. He had found it within seconds of searching. They appeared to be multiplying in new constellations of blisters, swollen and tinted by the opalescent pus of whatever lay beneath their surfaces.

He willed himself to enter through the crack to the pocket's interior. He had no way of knowing if this was the pocket he had visited before, but he tensed against the prospect of finding someone within.

As he crossed the threshold, and the view spread out impossibly, he saw that the place was unfamiliar. This was a cavern such as one might find at the root of a mountain. Its floor was carpeted in a thick mass of vegetation like curling fern-frond. Currents ran at cross-angles in the green sea with no apparent cause.

The curve of the eye vanished, dispersing like a mist rather than rupturing like a bubble. Rasputin stepped into the flora, and sunk knee deep. It felt wet, but when he ran a hand through it, he found it bone-dry.

Light swirled over distant walls, and rode spires to clash and coruscate over an object in the cavern's centre. But already he could see this object was not the quivering, intricate construction he had found in the other pocket. That had reminded him of an oil rig, turned on its side, and probed and stretched by currents of an unseen ocean.

This thing looked alive. Like the stuff through which he waded, it was *biota*.

He was wading toward the thing in the centre when he halted. Fear more visceral than the threat of discovery gripped him. Through splayed fingers he saw at last that the object in the middle of the cavern was a creature, a vast mass of flesh. Waving above its body like dock-side cranes were cylindrical growths, which gave it the appearance of a many-headed hydra. Each head suckled on a spire connected to the cavern's wall, gulping down great swallows of light. Bulges of it travelled down the necks in peristaltic waves.

As he watched, a lump formed on the beast's flesh. The same light playing beneath the creature's skin gathered in the protuberance and intensified. It rose, lengthened, and thinned. A bulb formed at its base and rose up the neck until if popped free like a snail's eye arriving at the end of its distended stalk. A crease split the bulb, and all at once it opened in voiceless cries of hunger.

Rasputin crouched down among the fronds, wondering if the thing ate human.

Far above the new hydra head, at a point on the wall directly above it, something else was happening. Tatters of many-coloured light came streaming from every direction, spiralling into that point. The light mixed and grew bright, waxing until it seemed the naked sun had broken through.

And then something else broke through.

The silhouette of a man showed briefly against light. As he fell toward the cavern floor, something long and thin spooled out behind him.

Rasputin threw himself face first among the fronds. He fancied he heard a shout of glee.

The man dropped among the vegetation, tether in hand, the other end of which appeared anchored to the centre of the portal of light above.

When Rasputin had summoned the courage to raise his head and peek again at the man, he confirmed his fear: it was the man he had met before. Here, in this cavern, he wore a pith helmet and safari suit, but he was unmistakable.

Tugging the tether along behind him, the man approached the creature. Its new head bent low, and snuffled at the ground before the man.

Rasputin's skin tingled with anticipation.

The man reached up and patted the creature's flank, then lifted the end of the tether to its gaping maw. It drew back a moment, then snapped its jaws over the tether.

A tremor shook the cavern floor. The tether poking from the creature's mouth drew thin as though it were a straw sucked on by an immense force. Above, where the tether threaded the eye of the portal, it began to glow and widen. Light trickled in droplets and runnels down the tether and it widened to accommodate the flow.

The creature seemed to sense it coming. It sucked harder until the tether became a solid line of light. Its neck swelled with succour. Its mouth fused with the thickening tether, bonding with it as with a teat, and, like its mates, became one with it.

The man watched a moment, as if to ensure the connection secure— or perhaps to enjoy his handiwork. Then he walked to within touching distance of the creature's flank, reached out, took hold, and began to climb. As each of his hands and feet touched its flesh, light eddied and seemed to wash over them, as though he crawled in luminous water.

He climbed as far as the base of one of the creature's necks and halted. The neck was as thick as an ancient redwood, and its head towered far above him, grafted to a tether that stretched in a bowing line to the distant side of the cavern. If the height and thickness of the neck were any judge of its age, this had to have been the first to sprout.

The man reached a hand toward the surface of the neck, and Rasputin wondered if he meant to climb it too.

To Rasputin's shock, the instant the man laid his palm upon the flesh, he shrank to a pinpoint of light. His body deflated as though it were a plastic bag rapidly evacuated of air. Appearing exactly where his hand had been, an angry whorl of light bloomed and fled up the tether, too fast to track, and was gone.

Rasputin breathed easy again, and stared at the creature in wonder. He had been too afraid to reveal his presence and ask his question, but he would make learning by observation his new mantra. He approached the newest neck.

Up close he noted the young skin's translucency. It reminded him of raw squid. Beneath it, light pulsed, down into whatever gullet the creature had, and up in smaller amounts, pumped there by whatever served it for a heart. Such a great quantity of the stuff was in motion that he could hear it—the slow thunder of swallowing, and riding over it, the faster rhythm of its pulse.

His heart throbbed too, competing with the creature's noise.

He reached out his hand but paused. He remembered when he had touched the silver memory-stuff, the cloying despair he felt as it began to catalogue him. The sense of staring into a bottomless shaft, and an inescapable loss of balance. He shuddered.

Steeling himself, he took his palm and, as the man had done, pressed it against the translucent skin.

It felt soft and elastic, and sticky, and only then did he realise he had not disappeared as the man had. But the realisation was swept away by the sensations that began to tingle in his fingers and ride up his arm.

He struggled to understand what he felt travelling beneath the creature's skin—not shapes, but something like shapes. They flowed across the plane of his consciousness like the stream of a shade-dappled road seen from a car. There were distinct forms, connections, and relations, but he could not hold them long enough to really see them. They were only the shadows of something else—shadows on Plato's cave wall, and out beyond his grasp, their substance was blooming into being.

He concentrated harder. He swiped his hand across the skin in an attempt to track the flow of images, if only for a moment to arrest them for inspection.

For a moment he saw clearly. He glimpsed the abstract beauty of a Mandelbrot set, the weird art rendered by incestuous mathematical functions. It looked like an alien insect.

But no sooner had he seen this than the sensation in his finger tips faded. He felt the skin lose elasticity and toughen. Scales formed over the tender flesh, and, just before it lost all translucency, he saw a branching filigree of veins spreading up the neck.

He squinted up at the head, which still sucked single-mindedly on its supply line, and to his surprise saw the veins bursting upward beneath the still-translucent skin of the tether. The red marbling raced away until distance diminished it. He had the feeling it reached all the way to the cavern wall.

Something nudged him. With a start he realised the creature had grown. Its girth had thickened and its flanks were pressing against his legs. No real creature could grow so fast.

He stepped backwards, only to bump against something else. He spun and stared straight into a gaze of cut sapphire.

It was the man.

"You still shouldn't be here," he said.

Rasputin woke.

In the short weeks of his friendship with Reim, Rasputin had grown to read the subtleties of emotion revealed in the skin like sun-split riverbed around his eyes. The man smiled easily and his words were always lofted on an air of geniality. His was a vibrant inner life that spilt outwards, its super-abundance flowing to the benefit of all with impartiality.

But there was something unreadable in his face today.

Rasputin ordered at the counter on autopilot, wondering whether he had at last pushed this opportunistic friendship too far and become a burden to the old man.

He paid, retrieved his order, and walked out into the alfresco area of the café. He found Reim sitting at a table overlooking the moat at the base of the university's Reid Library. His gaze was lost to some point beneath the scummy water, not drawn to and fro by a pair of busy ducks.

"Cracking the HIV code?" said Rasputin.

Reim took a moment to reply, as if his abstracted attention was a heavy weight that first needed recalling. He smiled deliberately.

"No. I leave that to greater minds, or more stubborn, than mine. Besides, HIV is a whole family by now, each strain having its peculiarities. Domestic courts are the worst."

Rasputin sipped his tea. Over the rim of his cup, he saw Reim's gaze resting on him. Gone was the detachment that had been there that morning. He seemed to be examining him now.

"You are tired."

"I would love to be just *tired*," Rasputin replied. The thought of waking in the morning and rising refreshed had taken on the feel of myth. It had left the realm of reality long ago, hand in hand with Santa.

"The world is run by tired people."

Rasputin paused, cup half-lifted to his lips. "It shows."

"I got your blood work back this morning."

Rasputin tightened his grip on the cup.

Reim continued, "I should say, this morning I got your final set of results."

"I only gave blood once."

"I requested the tests be done again."

"Why would you do that?"

It was Reim's turn now to drink.

"The first made no sense."

"They were botched?"

"No, I don't think so."

Reim reached into his satchel, which was made of the skin of some long dead animal, and hunted for something. Presently he laid a stapled stack of paper on the table between them.

"Because these make no sense either."

Rasputin nudged his phone aside, which had become something of a fetish since his text-conversation in the park, then swivelled the paper the right way up to read. It was a report, congested with numbers and abbreviations, but light on explanatory text. It was nonsense to him.

He said the only intelligent thing that came to mind: "This looks more like a game of Sudoku than a path lab report."

"It's not from a path lab," Reim said, and, in response to Rasputin's unspoken question, continued. "It's from my lab."

"Your lab?"

"Yes. Both of them, to be precise."

"Now you're not making any sense."

"Then let me be sensible," said Reim, in another of the unintentional mis-utterances in his idiolect that Rasputin found endearing. "I submitted the sample of your blood to my lab that enables my work on biomarkers of neurological disease. We have developed a battery of tests, well worn by now, and cheap. I won't bore you with the details—"

"Bore away."

"The lab ran your blood through DNA microarrays targeting specific genes. A single strand of DNA has a sequence of three billion base pairs. Our tests only fish for a fraction of that amount. It's like trawling alphabet soup with a sieve that only catches a specific letter."

"But the bowl holds a billion litres?"

"Yes, and, to be pedantic, we're actually looking for phrases not letters."

"What did you catch?"

"Something Greek."

"Okay."

"We use an English phrase book."

"Oh."

Reim flicked the edge of the report with a leathery finger as though it were to blame.

"So, of course, I assumed someone had not followed the recipe, and asked for the tests to be repeated: same result."

Reim looked askance at Rasputin before continuing. "I took charge personally, then, and upped the ante. I subjected your blood to a more expensive, a more comprehensive, test."

"Your other lab, right?" said Rasputin, trying to track Reim's flow.

A thought occurred to him: "Did I get you in trouble?"

Reim's eyebrows popped up, a bushy exclamation, as if he had just then perceived Rasputin's concern. He laughed.

"No, no, *mijn jonge*. The test was expensive, but that lab has a budget bigger than the GDP of some countries."

Reim's hand idly stroked his leathern satchel. Rasputin smiled at the juxtaposition it created with the confession of a man driving a lab with a GDP-sized budget.

"So this other other lab—is it the cross-dressing lab that goes out with the ladies on Thursday nights?"

Reim smiled. Rasputin sensed it was because he had been waiting for the question, had invited it.

"Have you ever seen a babushka doll?"

"Of course. Hollow wooden dolls. You crack the first and find nested within a smaller copy, and on it goes until you reach the solid little babushka at its heart, no bigger than a pea."

Reim looked mildly put out before continuing. "Yes, well, my analogy is not perfect. My lab, the expensive one, is actually a lab within a lab within the department of biology."

"How does one crack open the facade?"

"My voice will do it. Or a numerical code—standard security for a C2 bio-hazard containment facility." Reim's hand brushed the lapel of his coat, absent-mindedly, the way a child might tug at a lock of hair.

Rasputin was tracking Reim's revelation mentally. He imagined the first babushka doll cleaved in two, and emerging from within a smaller, meaner looking woman, perhaps with a recurved blade in hand.

A memory rose, of wandering past the research lab situated on the basement level of the physical sciences building, a stone's throw from where they now sat. He saw the signage hanging on its frosted glass front, and furrowed his brow.

"Wait a minute. That lab is only C4."

"The neuro-genetics lab is. Its protocols keep out any but staff and visiting bureaucrats, and it serves as a kind of—" Reim hunted for a word, his hands wheeling over each other, "—*poortgebouw*. In English, a gatehouse, protecting the inner sanctum. Only the initiated are even aware of the inner lab's presence, let alone equipped with the information to authenticate themselves and enter. The neuro lab is the perfect rind, protecting the sweet fruit within."

The penny dropped for Rasputin. He lowered his voice to a whisper. "You're serious. You have a secret C2 lab hidden within your research lab?"

Reim laughed. "You can speak up. Whispers are guaranteed to draw attention, but I think you can relax. No one here is going to care. That's the beauty of the arrangement. The lab sits right in the middle of a university, surrounded by students with their heads lost in ideas or life, sharing the high priority power grid with nearby Charles Gardener hospital, geo-stable, and covered by the facade of a live research lab that camouflages the comings and goings of staff such as myself and much of the supplies and equipment required to keep it running, while screening off the vast bulk of the public and would-be nosey parkers. My lab is the little clownfish living in the anemone—living just down there." Reim prodded a finger at the lawn surrounding the moat.

"Down there?" Rasputin said, incredulous. Reim just flexed his eyebrows in confirmation. "Except it's your clownfish has the sting."

The sheen of humour fell from Reim's face as he nodded. "The worst kind."

Reim took a swig of tea and stared at the spot on the lawn beneath which Rasputin imagined must lie the secret lab.

Rasputin waited for Reim to go on. He was eager to learn what kind of sting Reim's fish had.

"I have always been attracted to universities," Reim said. "Here ideas pile up in eclectic layers like office detritus, and no one is ever sure if anything can be thrown away."

"Don't get me wrong," he continued. "I'm not enamoured of ideas for ideas sake. Intelligent men can say dumb things. The most intelligent the dumbest, it seems. But I like that here they don't quite die."

Reim and Rasputin sipped tea in sync. Rasputin waited. Reim talked on.

"The university also receives impressions from outside on a more mundane level. Did you know there was a bomb shelter beneath that lawn?"

Rasputin shook his head.

"Bit of a white elephant as it turned out, thankfully. Another plus for Western Australia. Part of it became a marshalling area for cabling and plumbing. It now houses the most sophisticated protein sequencing equipment in the state." He winked. "But if you look closely, you can still find evidence of its original purpose. See, history preserved."

"It was built to keep bombs out, small conventional ones at any rate. Then co-opted to keep power and sewage in, and in that it comes much closer to its current purpose. Because not so long after the cold war thawed, concerned scientists saw that the humane genome would be mapped, and that that mapping would be to biological weapons what quantum theory was to the development of nuclear weapons."

Reim drained his cup and placed it down with a clunk.

"My lab houses some of the most potent microscopic killing machines known to man—natural and man-made. Old and new. My job is to imagine the missile, and create the anti-missile."

"Earlier I put HIV in the family court. The viruses I deal with would be tried at Nuremburg."

Rasputin had wanted to know what the sting was, and now he knew, he was profoundly disturbed at the revelation. Why would Reim be telling him such sensitive information? He had known him barely a month.

"The first test," said Rasputin. "What was wrong with it, precisely?"

"It indicated either, as I said, error, or that you are a mosaic of improbable—I could say *impossible*—degree. Your blood is that of a chimera. It is as though the sample were drawn from a vat into which had been poured blood from every person in Perth."

Rasputin smirked. "I'm a complex guy."

"This is serious. The DNA of every single cell in your body ought to be identical. In rare cases, there is a mix of two or more sequences. Sometimes a chance mutation in the developing foetus gives rise to two distinct DNA patterns. Other times it is the result of two embryos merging, or one eating the other"—Rasputin shivered—"but *never* is the variety of practically endless extent."

"And yet, here we are," said Rasputin. He felt the familiar surge of contrariness that took him when he felt at fault.

Reim fixed him with his eye. "You should be dead. You should be a bag of blood, going rigid in your skin."

"Your test must be wrong."

"It's not."

"Then your logic is."

"Clearly."

There was a pause as Reim surveyed the test results, as if they might change beneath his gaze. Rasputin dismissed the fleeting notion that Reim was grumpy because he didn't fit with the world as Reim knew it. He wondered if he glimpsed in Reim's face the younger man beneath the layers deposited by time, an academic at the height of his powers, not willing to cede defeat, to suffer being baulked by dumb matter. But no, he realised, not every academic was stamped with the image of Thorpe. The contrast between the two men was stark, and who cared if their differences had lain dormant in their substance at birth, or arisen contingent on a procession of accidents of history, writ 'power' or 'kindness' tabula rasa.

"To put this in perspective," Reim said at length. "A single mutation in the LMNA gene causes Hutchinson-Gilford Syndrome, and accelerated aging to a life expectancy of 13 years."

Rasputin put his cup down and flexed his hand into a fist. The veins in his arm stood up. He could see the blood coursing beneath, flowing in a confusion of red and purple worms, every surge and ebb driven by the fist of muscle that had beat in his chest thanklessly for two score years and more.

Motion caught his eye, and he glanced upward to see the shifting dapple of the moat's reflection on the ceiling. Dark bands moved through it in waves, reflections of ripples on the water disturbed by an enormous koi that had breached its surface. He recalled a remarkably similar pattern, a mesmerising thing, seen on the skin of a cuttlefish. It had been a warning sign.

Reim said, "I can see you're troubled. I know my boys, and I think you are a little the same. You put on a brave face, but you are scared."

Rasputin hunched over, made a study of his hands so he didn't have to look at the old man as he replied. "I've been scared so long it doesn't register any more. I guess I must be terrified."

"We'll nut this out."

"I've heard that before."

Later, as Rasputin trod the lawn adjacent to the moat, he visualised the lab he now knew to be sequestered beneath it. He resented knowing it. Yet another sign that something stank in the state of Denmark. Yet another harbinger of doom that would forever be part of him, part of his memory, unejectable as the grit that invades the oyster. But unlike an oyster, he knew of no defence with which to target the unwelcome invader. There was no substance he could bind this knowledge with, quarantine it. On the contrary, he felt it, even now, reaching out and connecting with the rest of him, unceasingly informing and being informed by the universe of his experience. Reim's lab and he were now forever welded.

Rasputin took a bus home. He was seated, head juddering on the window's glass. He watched cars pass, streaking by in the freeway's rightmost lanes. He knew the speed at which each was travelling. Time and displacement idly married in his head to yield this. He mentally issued a ticket to a Commodore pushing 114kph—human speed camera, yet another career he might pursue. Provided he didn't become a dead 'bag of blood', ossified, to sit forever at the road's side, a memorial.

He retrieved his phone and, in a fit of pique, typed a message to his unknown interlocutor: "You called it a *Miracle Machine*. I'm a human multanova. Some miracle."

He sat back and waited for a reply, fearful and eager. Was this how a crack addict felt when calling his dealer? This dealer only dealt information, but Rasputin had a prescient sense that it had the same potency of life or death.

Minutes lapsed. He issued two more tickets. Then came a reply.

"Whoever said that was a miracle?"

Rasputin jumped to reply. The stilted, conversation-through-a-straw of texted communication began again.

"You."

"No I didn't ... Try this: Imagine an alien observing the front yard of a Mr. and Mrs. Jones. In the drive is the family car, engine idling, lights on, and radio blaring. Seated behind the wheel is Mr. Jones, twiddling his thumbs while he waits for his wife to finish powdering her nose."

Rasputin waited for the next burst of text.

"Question: What would our alien make of the Jones's car? What would he perceive its purpose to be?"

Rasputin had no idea what the question was driving at. He waited, praying for more.

It came.

"Answer: A small dwelling, perhaps for pleasure, supplying heat, sound, and light."

"I get it. If he didn't see it move, how would he know a car is for transport."

"Good boy. I never said what kind of miracles the machine makes."

Seconds stretched into minutes. Nothing more came. Rasputin abandoned his resolution to remain silent. He typed again.

"That it? No more pearls?"

The bus crossed the Narrows Bridge and was swept by a dark band of shadow beneath an overpass.

Finally, a reply: "Next time, wait the extra minute for the 97. It doesn't wind through Bentley like a drunk old maid. You'll get home ten minutes sooner."

Rasputin's head whipped up. His gaze strafed the interior of the bus, and then, ridiculously, the cars passing on either side.

His fruitless search brought home the fact he had no idea with whom he had been talking. Was he young, old? Was he a he? Why had he assumed he was a man—just because he had said so?

He hunkered into the seat and willed the bus homeward.

"That shouldn't be there," said Jordy.

His attention was focused on a point just above the finger he had planted on the computer monitor.

Rasputin watched, uncomprehending but alert. He had done nothing else since arriving home to find Jordy waiting on the other side of the door, hovering in the lounge room.

Jordy had followed him through the house as he shed

accoutrements—keys, phone, a pen he had forgotten to return to Reim. At the first sign of agitation, Jordy had made a shushing motion, and led him down the hall and into the office, where they now sat.

"A dangling hook. Innocuous enough, but I wanted to find what had put it there. It has the whiff of a virus. Something inveigled."

"What are we looking at?"

"Your phone."

Rasputin glanced in the direction of the kitchen, where he had left his phone on the counter, charging. The thing was barely making eight hours per charge.

"My phone is in the kitchen," said Rasputin. "Have you been drinking?"

"Don't be pedantic. This is an image of the software running on your phone. A virtual copy. I downloaded it last night. I couldn't cope with your belly-aching about its crap battery life, so I thought I'd see if it was running any programs that could be culled."

"Okay. Pretend I understand. What's got your knickers twisted?"

Jordy's eyes lit as he turned back to the screen. He was enjoying this.

"Software is like an ecosystem. Getting about in it, solving a problem, is like hunting. This thing here"—he tapped the screen—"is spore."

Rasputin picked up the analogy, with the first glimmering of understanding. "What are you hunting?"

"Maybe nothing."

"You already know *something*, otherwise why the cloak and dagger."

Jordy's fingers scrabbled over the keyboard.

"First rule of the hunt: find out what the beast craps. Gives you an idea of what sort of animal it is and, more importantly, what it eats."

Jordy opened a terminal window, and deftly executed a series of commands. A clot of text appeared at the bottom of the window, and was then thrust upwards and out of view as more text—numbers, letters, and snippets of English—began streaming upwards.

"Packet sniffer," said Jordy, flicking a hand at the flowing characters. "It's our Beagle Hound. The computer is running a virtual version of your phone, and the sniffer will tell us if it is excreting anything abnormal."

"You mean besides my conversation."

"Yep. In addition to that."

Rasputin trained his attention on the torrent of text streaming over the window. It was a wash of zeros, punctuated by small clots of other digits and characters.

"What am I looking at?"

"These," said Jordy, his finger tracking a clot of text racing upwards, "are typical mobile telephony protocols. It's called handshaking. The phone is trying to talk to a cell tower, tell it where it is. It isn't getting a reply though, so it's trying extra hard. It doesn't know it's only a pretend phone living in my computer."

"And that," said Rasputin, nodding at the wall of zeros, hands laced over his expanding gut.

"A whole lotta nothin'." He turned to Rasputin, and grinned evilly. "The transmission of which is sucking on your battery like a plague of mosquitoes on a Shetland Pony."

"Poor pony. Can't you just kill whatever is doing it?"

"Don't you want to know what it is?"

Jordy turned back to the screen. "I'll admit, it had me stumped for a while. I couldn't find where in the protocol stack it was being spliced in."

"Then I remembered that I was on the hunt. Sometimes hunting is passive, sometimes you need to act. You need to beat the bush, startle your prey out. You see?"

"I see a nerd going to metaphorical extremes to extract a little excitement from what is—let's face it—glorified accounting."

"I'm ignoring you, because in a moment you're going to hug me."

Jordy's hands played over the keyboard again as he spoke. "So I thought: let's poke the beast. This virtual copy of the phone is living in a zoo. Let's put it outside, in its natural habitat. So I gave it a location." Jordy punched a key and his hands fell still.

Rasputin watched the screen for any change. Nothing.

Then something caught his eye. A change, almost too small to notice. A clump of non-zero characters drifted in the wash of zeros, a log amid the stream, floating between the larger islands.

He continued to watch and soon saw another one. They repeated, regular as the handshakes Jordy had identified.

"I see them. What are they?"

Jordy brought a different window into focus. It contained a map of Perth. In the middle of the CBD stood a red marker, a virtual tack.

"This app outputs location as latitude and longitude co-ordinates. I'm piping them straight into the virtual phone. I'm fooling it into thinking it's outside." Jordy lifted the tack marking the phone's pretend location with the mouse cursor. "Watching?" he said, and pinned the tack to the middle of the Swan River.

Rasputin returned his attention to the packet sniffer. He saw the small clot of non-zero characters rise. They were very nearly the same.

But not quite.

"That," said Jordy, tracking the changed cluster of characters, "is a GPS co-ordinate."

Jordy swivelled to face Rasputin, and only now did his demeanour sour.

"Your phone is tracking you."

"And telling someone," said Rasputin.

"Why didn't I notice the GPS indicator?"

"The same malicious code removes it unless you're using a program that uses the GPS, like, say, the navigator."

Rasputin sat back as his thoughts knit together. This was how the guy had known he was in the park, on the bus. He had been tracking him the entire time. It comforted him that he had not been surveilled in person, but the comfort was fleeting. The train of his thought crashed on.

"Why would someone give me a phone to track me?"

"There's worse," said Jordy.

The thought occurred to Rasputin: *What about the other zeros?*

Jordy evidently saw the realisation dawn on his face. "That's right."

He began calling up more windows.

"I've put your phone on earth, but it's still lacking realism. For that, I need"—he clicked a button—"sound."

From the computer's speakers sprang the ever so familiar sound of John Cleese arguing with a pet store owner.

"Now, pipe that into the phone ..."

And voila! thought Rasputin. He saw the packet sniffer's river of zeros flee, followed by a mess of characters, an oil slick chasing clear water.

Jordy sighed. "Your phone is splicing in whatever it hears, and transmitting it who knows where."

Without verbal assent, they rose and trod the hall back to the kitchen. The phone lay on the bench, its charge light a happy amber, as it sat supping contentedly on the current flowing from the wall socket.

Jordy lifted it from the bench and switched it off.

"I found the beast," said Jordy. He held the phone up for Rasputin to see.

"A bug," said Rasputin.

Jordy agreed to keep trying to crack open the phone's parasitic code, to see if he could discover where it was sending transmissions. All he would venture was that the modification to the phone involved hardware. How else was it tunnelling data over standard mobile protocols? He didn't need to add that it implied considerable technical skill.

Rasputin couldn't help wondering if the instigator was Thorpe after all. Rasputin had been his prize pet.

Then there was Sam. He had the technical resources to do it.

Both men had reason to surveil him. One to confirm his investment, the other to purchase his desired career.

But he dismissed both in quick succession. Thorpe had not been faking it in the dying moment's of their last encounter. His defences had been down, and, when proffered the phone, he had registered a complete blank. As for Sam, Rasputin counted him a friend—that, or the world's best liar.

Reluctantly his thoughts released their hold on these suspects, and drifted into the void of unknowns. Even his brain refused to make headway on this mystery. It simply spun without traction in darkness, binding it like a web around him. It weighed on his mood, and dulled his senses.

It unleashed a torpor that enervated his every limb and organ.

As summer's onslaught began in earnest, he took to dwelling in the relatively cool darkness of his room. He told Jordy he was catching up on course material he had missed since the accident.

Christmas approached, but he spared it scant thought. It was a celebration, a ritual to be done in the world out there.

Sometime during a string of sweltering days, when rats began scuffling in the roof cavity above his bed, shedding nightmare into his sleep, and the heat was seeping in unrelenting waves through the double-brick, he forsook the waking world altogether, save to eat, toilet, and to keep up appearances for the watchful Jordy.

He learned the trick of catching his mind in the act of waking, and shunting it, instead, into the eye, whereupon he would play for hours among his memories, or in built worlds of fantasy. Sometimes he would meld the two into a hybrid and rewrite the script of his life.

He kept well away from the memory of his sister. It had become a neutron star, sucking his will toward it in an irresistible embrace if he strayed too near. The only escape then was to wake. And then his body's claims would fall upon him, and leach away all desire.

Jordy was too polite to break in upon him—something Rasputin counted on. Dee was another matter. She entered his room mid-afternoon on a Friday.

Rasputin was within, walking an urban canyon built of a mixture of fancy and found-object, whose sides rose high enough to block the rays of two westering suns. The canyon walls were made of the same substance as the object he had found in the first pocket void. The street he trod was not hard stone or asphalt but faintly elastic and moist. It was thronged by all manner of creatures, none of them known to the annals of zoology. Many-headed hydra plodded, necks craned, heads lofted, incessant and aloof. Smaller creatures scurried in the shadows they cast. Beetle-like beings canted from side to side in head-high domes of iridescent tortoise-armour, and bristling with antennules and flagella that curled, split and coiled tighter still.

Other beings swept the thoroughfare about his feet, creatures that only became manifest when viewed askance, and vanished if watched. They whorled, with the appearance of condensed clouds of colour-tinged air, and bent the dying sunlight like floating lenses, warping the image of organic surface beneath. They appeared to be atmospheric disturbances, but for their own peculiar susurrus they contributed to the ambient conversation on the street.

He had conjured this place the previous day, and populated it with creatures stumbled upon in the festering places of his mind. It was his zoo; he was warden. But today unfamiliar creatures moved in it.

Something thumped against his leg like a dog's tail, and passed him in a tumbleweed spin. It was born along on many stalks sprouting from its central mass, a nucleus in the form of a perfect cube. Before he could study the creature, a shadow eclipsed them both as a twisting, serpent-like shape masked both suns. It was the size of a bus, rippling in the sky. Its hide appeared to be covered by interlocking metal plates, but as undulations rode the length of its body in ponderous waves, the plates warped and flowed, and wrinkled like skin.

He halted, unable to shrug a suspicion that had been growing for days. Had there been a shift in the atmosphere? Was there a taste in the air?

The place felt ... *heavy*.

Dee's presence seeped into this inner world. She was the moon that chased the withering suns from the sky. Rasputin surfaced.

She was seated in a lazy chair salvaged from a roadside. He had no idea how long she had sat there.

"Why have you locked yourself away?" she said.

He shrugged, not game to trust his freshly conscious mind to form intelligible speech.

"Is this your monastery, Monk?"

He laughed. His room was the opposite of a monk's spartan cell. It was a magpie's nest, piled with collected things.

"Give it a rest. This is an indulgence."

Dee surveyed the room again, the drawn curtains, the bed clothes twisted around his prone form.

"It feels more like penitence," she said.

He propped himself up on his elbows. His head hurt.

"What do you want? I want to sleep."

"We're going to the farm for the weekend. I want you to come."

"No thanks," he said, and slumped back onto his pillow. The brief separation of his skin from its material was enough for him to feel his sweat on it.

"Please?" she said. "It isn't far. If you don't like it, we'll drop you back. The air is fresh. It's quiet. We'll build a fire in the stove."

He let his eyelids fold over his eyes, and heard the creature-murmur of the strange street swell.

"Monk, what are you doing here?"

He whispered, wanting her to leave. "Study. Rallying my strength. I just need some rest."

She whispered then, but her words came lancing through nevertheless. "This is no staging camp. You're giving up."

He heard a faint rustle. She had risen. He heard the door open, a moment of silence, then, "We're packing the car. We'll wait for you till four."

She eased the door shut and was gone.

Susurrus rose in his ears. He began to bend his made-world around him, on a whim thrusting a third sun into the sky. But the will necessary to sustain the simulacrum wavered, and fell. He had been infected with fear.

He woke fully. The source of the fear crystallised.

Dee had intervened, as usual. But she had not pried him out, had not man-handled him with her iron-tough concern. She had spoken, yes. But not with sureness. Her voice had carried despair.

Minutes later he emerged into the dining room. It had been agonising, to stand, to move.

Surprise registered on Jordy's face.

Rasputin dumped the bag he had hastily packed on the floor, unable to hold its meagre weight any longer.

"Fine. Show me this farm. But if I get bitten by something, I'm biting back."

248

An hour later Dee's hatchback was struggling up the scarp that overlooked Perth. Its young engine whined as it bore them up the last winds of the road, unaccustomed to carrying three adult bodies and sundries. Dee opened the throttle to overtake a road train whose spent inertia had left it crawling. They crested the final rise, and the car, let loose from gravity's pull, stepped up through its gears. The embankments hemming the road folded behind them and occluded the Swan Valley and its city.

Rasputin felt enclosed by forest. Spreading out before him, over the hills that terminated at the scarp behind, were rolling waves of green—a vast blanket turned back at the sea.

He checked his phone was off, surreptitiously. Dee didn't know of its sinister character, and Jordy had agreed, reluctantly, not to tell her. He couldn't bring himself to part with it, not his only link with ... what? Never mind. He would make it his talisman.

He slumped low in the back seat, and wound the window lever a notch to ward off car sickness. Wind blustered around the gap and drowned the conversation in the front. Their destination was an hour out along the Great Eastern Highway, a couple of hundred hectares of land tilled by Jordy's family for generations. Jordy was the weak link, a country boy with an affinity for computers, and averse to getting soil beneath his nails. The land was now leased to a local farmer who, depending on the market, ran sheep or cropped canola.

Rasputin steeped in the gentle roll of the car and hum of its engine. He watched the thickets of trees come, separate and pass.

But what began as a soothing, liquid sensation soon became a drowning flood. Every passing leaf, every twig, every stone, stalled mid-motion. All deviated from their neat, orderly lines of parallax, and rushed at him, as though he were the singular focus of a perfect perspective. Every physical object shed its material guise, and became a naked datum of information. They became a blizzard, each flake stinging not his eye but his mind, falling like a hand upon his shoulder—an interruption, a request, a message, a warning. The car dragged him through a landscape that may as well have been the collected output of the world's news presses, shredded, dumped in a paper downpour, and left for his mind to tease back together.

He experienced a burst of empathy for the madman doomed to decipher messages in Morse tapped out by wind and branch on the asylum window.

He quailed, and slid as low as the seat would allow, and crooked an elbow over his ear. He closed his eyes to shut out the torrent.

He was awoken by the noise of the tires thrumming over the grill of a sheep-brake. He peeled his sweat-stuck cheek from the door's upholstery to raise his head and look out the windscreen. The sun's orb had fallen below nearby hills. The sky above their black backs was on fire with its passing. Evidently Dee and Jordy had stopped on the way without waking him.

Nestled beyond a shallow valley was a house. The car slowed as Dee navigated a dirt road that led to the house. It had not rained for weeks. Dust was a brown vapour boiling off the wheels. They crossed a bridge of crushed rock over a shallow, seasonal creek, whose bed was still inscribed with last winter's flow. Rivergum branches hung low over the track and scraped the car's roof as they passed. Finally, Dee turned the car in at the back of the house and halted. They were greeted by the forlorn gaze of an old tractor's headlights. It was stowed in a shed that might have served for a car port in years past, and seemed doomed to stare at fields that no longer needed it while it rusted back to its elements.

Dee killed the engine and Rasputin felt engulfed by a vast silence. Slowly, his ears found the level, and he discerned sound: the slow drip of water falling ten feet from a tank stand beside the car, the whisper of leaves from an aged almond tree standing in the yard, and, far off, frog and cicada calls.

No one spoke, and Rasputin found the mood of solemnity catching. He swung his door open and was bathed in a breeze streaming down over the shadowed hillside. It felt deliciously cool, and only then did he realise he was drenched in sweat. He tried to rise, and succeeded on the third attempt. An exhaustion that had been dormant as he lay on the seat woke and fastened itself to him.

"Can you get the house open?" he said. "I need to lie down."

He fancied he saw Jordy bite back a remark.

Dee dug the house key from its cache, and within minutes they were in the house. She began to lay a fire in the stove for hot water while Jordy fetched their luggage from the car. Rasputin concentrated on putting one foot in front of the other. He crossed the kitchen's linoleum floor, feeling the wood beneath flex and creak.

"Where am I sleeping," he said, feeling the effort cost him.

She straightened.

"Second room off the hall," she said. "Monk, you're drenched."

"Must've got a bit hot in the back."

"I'm sorry," she said. "I had the AC on full. I thought you'd be okay."

He shuffled out of the kitchen and found his room. The single bed had linen folded at its foot, but it was all he could do to collapse onto its bare mattress. He shut his eyes and heard the fire in the kitchen click and pop as it fed on kindling, and over that, the ticking of the iron roof as it settled in the dropping temperature. He fell directly into a deep sleep.

He awoke to darkness.

Someone had covered him with a sheet. It was slicked down over his body with sweat. He peeled it back and sat up. He was still, listening to his breathing, while his eyes adapted to a faint light. He looked and through the room's only window saw a square of star-shot sky. It beckoned.

He rose, struck by a sudden portentous feeling. Perhaps it was the sensation of waking in an unfamiliar place. He groped in the dark, and found his phone on the floor by the bed. He turned it on, and waited, knowing there would be a message for him.

There was none.

He put the phone away and hugged himself; the old house had clung to a remnant of winter's chill.

He eased the door to the hall open and navigated by feel into the kitchen. The fire had burned down to coals. Their deep red light shone through the grill and lit the room with a surreal glow.

He let himself out onto the back veranda, easing the screen door shut behind him to mute the shriek of its aged spring.

A path split the back yard, a grey bar in the darkness. He followed it, navigating by feel past the yard's fence until his feet bit into dry grass. He kept walking, mindless of the stalks of wild oats that slipped between his toes, to be stripped of seed with a faint *thrip*.

A hundred metres from the dark house he halted. He was staring, as he had since leaving the house, into the sky, enthralled.

Above him the Milky Way blazed with a glory that stunned him. Instead of the few, scattered stars he was used to seeing through Perth's haze, he saw the wide band like a dense mist whose every droplet was a massive primeval engine, the brightest like diamond studs.

He tilted his head and twisted to follow the galaxy's axis from one horizon to the other, and was struck by a sudden inversion. All his life the night sky had been only a backdrop. But in that moment, their roles reversed. The dark hills lost their rondure and shrank to a paltry two dimensions, while the stars dilated into three. How parochial was the Earth! It was the Milky Way that stretched below the horizon. Continued beyond. Had no end. Figure and ground were swapped.

How vulnerable was his little island of warmth in the face of that vast sea of cold? In time it would quench the sun's fire, and the Earth become a dead rock roaming space. No soul would remain to remember Earth, let alone one called Rasputin.

Then another inversion.

He felt the sky draw down, as if to listen.

Warm currents suddenly flowed, branched, and reformed in that dark sea. It became at once vast and cosseting.

The Milky Way's band brightened as the stars began to crowd each other. Shadows sprang from beneath the field's grasses and spun like needles on a million compasses. But as the stars continued to swell and merge, the shadows bled away—and disappeared altogether as the sky became an unbroken sheet of white.

Rasputin wheeled, and saw an endless plain of grass beneath a sky that ought to have burnt his eyes to charcoal. Gone were the hills. Gone was the house.

He knew then that he was *within*.

Striding across the plain toward him came the figure of a man. He threw no shadow beneath that sky, nor would he have if there had been but one sun. He glowed brighter than the sky.

The horizon dogged his steps. It was irising, closing upon Rasputin, consuming the plain in silence with its white-hot fire.

Rasputin knew before the man reached him, before his effulgence dimmed enough for Rasputin to discern his features, who it was that approached: the inventor, tamer, judge. In another guise he had been the orb that had melted a hole in his mind and laid bare his inner world.

Fear rode Rasputin's body like electric current, but he stood still to meet him. What had he come to claim?

The horizon shrank to within meters as the man came to rest before him.

"Now am I allowed to be here?" Rasputin said, trusting once more to the joke's ready defence.

The man smiled.

"Allowed, and required," he said. He wore a cloak, and with one hand opened a flap. "Hide here."

Rasputin took one look at the silent fire closing from every side, then hunched forward, crouching to enter the space made for him. He turned to look out.

"What are you doing?" Rasputin said. The fire was so close he could have reached beyond the cloak's fold to touch it.

"Remaking you."

"Will it hurt," Rasputin said, as the white-fire licked the cloak's cloth.

"Childbirth always brings pain. And sometimes joy."

The flap of cloak fell, shutting out the light, and Rasputin knew no more.

10.

CAIN

It's late, but I can see you are eager to know how my journey began, when the man who walked this road was called Gottfried Schürman.

I walked it, then, in boots with inner soles a fraction thicker than standard issue. Five foot ten inches was the minimum height for soldiers admitted to the Waffen-SS. I fell short by only half an inch, but wasn't taking any chances. I wanted to be where my brother was, and that was poised alongside three million men on the Western Front, not in the halls of the Prussian Academy of the Arts in Berlin (where I knew more than my lecturers, in any case).

You might wonder why, with my blue blood, I chose Himmler's pet army rather than the *Wehrmacht*. The Navy was out of the question. I piss enough water, didn't need to make my home in it. *Luftwaffe?* Perhaps, but they would not have accepted me. I had a slight astigmatism in my right eye—I say *had*. They would take me now, would take ten thousand of me. *Das Heer* then? *Der Herr*, more like—yes sir, no sir. Not like the SS.

The SS aimed to build a different kind of soldier, in the words of Felix Steiner, "a supple, adaptable soldier".

In what is now well worn history you'll recall how, with a few thousand tanks of the Panzer divisions, we punched a hole in the front fifty miles wide, through the Ardennes, a landscape, according to the French military experts, through which no modern army could manoeuvre, an area 'of no danger'. In a matter of days, the north of France was sliced clean through to the channel, the famed French Armies shattered, the British Expeditionary Force of 400,000 men thrown into the sea minus their equipment, and Holland and Belgium conquered.

My brother and I celebrated in Brussels, before beginning the specially assigned task of digging up native Belgians of SS quality.

We were barracked in what had been the residence of a wealthy Belgian. The former owner had exquisite taste in art—paintings, sculpture, and antique furniture. The foyer had a Rubens.

One day a man came to survey the art. He valued it, locked some items away from the encamped men, and took others. He was a member of the *KunstSchutz*, the Art Protection Force, so-called. It was a revelation.

I contacted my father and had him arrange for me to be honourably discharged back into civilian life as rapidly as I had left it, and employed by the *KunstSchutz*.

The *KunstSchutz* ostensibly existed to care for art caught in the cross-fire of war. The Great War had erased many irreplaceable works of art from the face of the earth. What's more, the trenches of that style of warfare had unearthed ancient treasures long hid, of Celtic and other origin.

In reality, it was the inventorying and clearing house for the Third Reich, the agent of Hitler and his planned Linz Museum, and collector for the private estate of *Oberkommandant* Goering.

I didn't care. Rarely does an art historian have such wealth pass beneath his gaze. And if you were careful, there were some sweet pickings to be had.

I did not expect sweet pickings the day I was assigned to the Palace Mondial, to something called the Mundaneum, the grand information fetish of a librarian named Paul Otlet. The rooms of this Mundaneum were to be cleared to house fresh troops, and an exhibition of Third

Reich Art—the flower in the fist, and first shots fired in the cultural war for the minds of Europe. I was tasked with assessing the worth of the Mundaneum's material.

Now, it is important for my story that you understand something of the temper of those times. Only a few years prior, H.G. Wells published his information age manifesto on the *World Brain*. I love Wells. The Time Machine is one of my favourite books. But he believed the salvation of man lay in the synthesis of knowledge. There was such a mess, he said, of knowledge scattered throughout the world, in different journals and languages. Work went unheeded, unknown, and the wheel was destined to be invented many times over. Wells' answer was a society built upon an encyclopaedia—*the* encyclopaedia—alive, growing, interconnecting experts around the globe. "A new all human cerebellum. A cerebral cortex, for which university research departments would be essential ganglia," laying bare "the whole of human memory ... to every individual." Not to mention the basis for a global, totalitarian government, a socialist utopia.

Wells was not the only Encyclopaedist, merely the best known. Many scholars and statesman caught the vision of Solomon's House propounded by Bacon centuries before. Among them was Otlet. Indeed, he met Wells in 1937. The novelist was much impressed with the little Belgian. But Otlet saw further than any of them.

And it was his apparatus, and its corpus, that lay before me that autumn day in 1940. It was an imposing sight. The Mundaneum contained cabinets of 3 x 5 inch cards in the thousands, hundreds of thousands, summaries and cross-references to information in quantities beyond conception.

It was so imposing I flirted with the idea of putting a match to the lot, in favour of a certain Belgian vintage I had been enjoying.

As fate would have it, or accident—the milkman of invention—the first card my fingers found at random was the stub for an article that appeared in the British Medical Journal in 1886. I slid it from among its cousins to inspect it. The article it represented was titled: "The 'Elephant Man'".

I had heard of him. My nanny had used his name as a threat for naughty children.

The card I had stumbled across piqued my interest.

(There was at that time a renaissance of that field of bio-medicine called Eugenics, a renaissance limited in scope to the Reich. Eugenics attracted the interest of many Encyclopaedists too, for what was the good of the perfect society without the perfect human?)

Then I noticed a curious feature of the card system devised by Otlet, implemented by untold hours of human labour. At the bottom of the card was an allowance of space for recording queries that touched that card, and, intriguingly, the address of cards a querier subsequently consulted.

What a fantastic little game! I soon followed the link to the next card consulted by the only querier of that article, simply noted as a Mr. G. It was for an article in the British Journal of Dermatology published thirteen years later that claimed the Elephant Man had suffered from von Recklinghausen's disease. Seemed straightforward.

I hunted for the next link in the chain, while the clamour of that Belgian vintage rose to press its claim on me. Just one more card, I thought.

I had a time finding the next card as it was located in a different cabinet. I pulled it from its place and examined it under the flickering light of a war-torn power grid. It was an enigma.

The card was a stub for an account of a patient with prodigious mental capacity. Pasted to the back of the card was a photostat of the abstract from the original letter to the publishing journal. The patient was remarkable for the ability to remember forty-two numbers in sequence after hearing the sequence only once. That gift was courtesy of a brain lesion.

I was impressed.

But what did this have to do with the Elephant Man, and von Recklinghausen's Disease? I began to wonder about the identity of Mr. G., and his motives.

For the remainder of that day I followed his trail through this library of libraries, as it brachiated, reaching across wide swathes of Knowledge's domain, and circled back upon itself infuriatingly: from salient cases reported by Harley Street's chirurgeons to accounts of witch doctoring in African tribes in the annals of anthropology; the herbology of the opium poppy and synthesis of the new psychedelics; X-ray crystallography of the two dimensional structure of DNA; and the lifecycle of the Asian salamander. At times I thought I could see Mr. G.'s mind working, and even divine beforehand where next his search would lead. Many times he slotted into the ruts of trails blazed by other researchers, passing along their routes, a shadow come days or years after—as I was now treading in his tracks.

Eventually daylight failed. My eyes were sore, my fingers dusty, with deciphering cards. I left, but not to the drinking hall. I went to my barracks, to my pallet, and pondered.

I didn't know it then, but I was suffering the first ague of an addiction, an addiction to knowledge.

I dreamt that night of an image I saw that day. It was a lithograph, printed on an invitation to a conference announced by Otlet. I found it amid paper covering the floor like leaf litter, a storm trooper's boot print tattooed over it. The image depicted a stylised ship, sailing toward the setting sun on a dark, wind-tossed sea. Emblazed on its billowing sail were entwined ellipses, the symbol of the globe. Books were its only cargo. It seemed to say: here is the Ark, and its precious cargo is not man but text.

On rising the next morning I decided the library must be mine. Vested with the power of the *KunstSchutz*, it was a simple matter to declare the library worthless, and have it packed—all materials, journals, photographs, maps, and the invaluable index to it all—for freighting to one of the many bonfires burning in Brussels; vested with the power of the Schürmans, it was simpler still to redirect that freight to our schloss in the Alps.

A small part of it escaped my notice. Still today it is housed in a museum dedicated to it, and moulders there, a relic, a curio, with barely the patronage required to keep the lights burning.

Before I left Brussels I met Otlet, a little bespectacled man of grief-dimmed eye. I thought him a genius and told him so.

From the Alps I summoned my brother. I trusted him in the martial field, and he trusted me in the cognitive. I sold him the idea of a grand game, a complex riddle. It would require him to scour Europe, behind and beyond the Front, for books, items, who knew what. As boys we had played at secret missions, and hunts for lost treasure. Here was the mission par excellence.

The first item I had him fetch were the only samples of tissue preserved from Joseph Merrick, the Elephant Man. Following autopsy they had been taken by his friend and doctor, Treves. I wanted them. I didn't know why. Perhaps retrieving them was a test of strength for Hans (they lay in London). Perhaps they were my symbol, my icon, a banner beneath which I would pursue the quest to discover what great secret was evidenced by the search of Mr. G. For there was a secret, I was sure of it.

Three weeks later, I was screening staff for the lab that was to be the core of the apparatus of my quest, when a package arrived. I assumed it was from Hans. I had dispatched him to the university museum at Koln in search of an idol, a small stone totem with peculiar grooves in its head. But upon opening the package I found instead a machine that looked much like a typewriter. The following day a telephone call was made to the schloss. The caller claimed to be from Intelligence, and I thought at first I had run afoul of the Gestapo. I soon learned the man believed himself to be part of a sanctioned intelligence operation. He was mistaken.

He asked me: "Herr Schürmann, have you received the machine?"

I said, "Yes."

"Good. I will dictate a message to you, and you are to enter it verbatim into the machine."

I wondered what he was playing at, but retrieved the machine.

I sat alone in my library, the only sound the muted roar of sleet and the crackle of fire. I informed him I was ready.

He began to speak words that made complete gibberish: fish, gristle, tidal, puncture ...

I typed each word into the machine, slowly, hunting the keyboard for each letter, pecking with my index fingers. Every time I entered a space to delineate a word, the machine hummed and spat out a word of its own, a different word, onto the paper I had slotted into it.

The first statement to emerge was: burn immediately following consumption.

Ah! I thought, a simple word-cipher. But no, for I found that a cipher word did not produce the same clear-text with repeated use. Decryption seemed to depend on the context of the word, what came before.

In this way, a message formed with glacial speed.

You might have guessed the man on the telephone was a cut-out. Without the coding machine, he could not know what message he was transmitting, and I never heard the voice of the message giver.

I told you Clotho was paranoid.

You see it was Clotho's peregrinations through the tracts of Otlet's informationscape that I was shadowing. Why "Mr. G.?"—perhaps for *Gamma*, the third letter of the Greek alphabet. I don't know. When transmission of the message was complete and the caller hung up without further ado, the sign-off was Clotho. It sounded like what it is: another cipher.

I sat back to read the message in its entirety, which I had been unable to do while rushing to keep up with the spoken cipher.

It was in three parts: an introduction, an explanation, and an offer.

Clotho introduced himself as one who was aware of my researches, and a friend. His offer was to sponsor my induction to an order called the Imago.

By far the largest part of the message was the explanation. This I read many times over. It claimed to be the reality I was groping toward in the fog of Clotho's stale tracks. Its assertions baffled me, and stung me with a fierce zeal to confirm them.

The explanation began in the popular idiom of Nazi Germany. Its first line read: You don't know it, but you are looking for the key that unlocks the master race.

He had my attention there.

It ran on: Better to say not *race* but *phase*.

It claimed that every human has dormant within them prodigies. If we would only open the sluices to release the biochemical cascades that inundate this fertile plain, we should be gods on earth.

11.

SBTQVUJO

"Caesar."

"Pardon, sir?"

"I'll have the Caesar salad please, *mijn jonge*." Professor Reim Tieke De Groot stretched, and settled his belt more comfortably beneath his paunch. "The heat of summer here always catches me. So: the salad."

"Yes, sir," said the waiter, smiling despite having failed to comprehend the connection, and bustled out of sight.

Reim reflected on the fact his father would never have paid good money for a salad. His father had not been fond of parting with money, period.

A dignified murmur of conversation soothed his ears. He sipped from wine he had ordered before the meal—something his father *would* have done—and let his gaze fall on the window his table abutted. Reflected in it was the restaurant's low, warm mood lighting. He relaxed his focus and let his gaze find the channel lights pulsing red and green over the river. He relaxed it further, to the dark mass of King's Park, the moon hanging above it, then beyond the world, as he ceased to see and tried again to corral his scattered thoughts.

They centred on Rasputin. In more ways than one, he was an enigma.

Reim's history was littered with attempts to play father to those who were without. For some few he had, he felt, successfully given a little of himself. He had a history, too, of wrestling with stubborn problems of biology, and there had met with much success. But now, in the twilight of his life, he found both powers called upon for the sake of the same object: Rasputin—in the twilight, when powers fade.

He scratched a tuft of hair his razor had missed.

Rasputin the problem: greater than the sum of its parts.

Deanne had called on him. She had confessed to sending Rasputin, and alluded to a buried grief she believed was eating away at him. Reim had probed him about it gently, and knew, from his terse answers and abrupt re-directions, the contours of that grief, if not the content.

That was one part. The other was his physiology. His blood work was unique. He should be dead, or at the very least in the process of being eaten alive by his own immune system. Admittedly, the lab tests weren't infallible. They were susceptible to corruption. They could be skewed by incorrect blood collection. The same chain-reaction mechanism used to amplify a genetic line into testable quantities could amplify, instead of the target DNA, some contaminant. Mice, cockroaches, even plant life, could muddy the waters beyond recovery. But for each of these threats, there were protocols that caused suspicious results to throw flags. None had risen.

So he should be dead. That he wasn't, troubled Reim's professional equanimity at a profound level.

And yet ... Something niggled him. Some *things*. If he viewed his understanding of human biology as a pattern within the larger pattern of the knowledge he had synthesised of the larger animal kingdom—a pattern woven, unpicked, and re-woven over many years of theory applied in experiment—he felt there was a repetition, a connection, he was failing to see. Some feature of the precise detail of Rasputin's singular blood waited, in the penumbra of his perception, like a spider web hung behind wire mesh, to be resolved by a change of focus. If only he could effect that shift. It hovered just beyond conscious thought, like the shape of a word without the sound.

With a sigh, he lifted his glass. He swirled the remaining wine, preparing to drink it. The burgundy liquid eddied, momentarily revealing an ellipse of glass beneath.

Reim froze. Wine pooled again at the bottom of the glass.

Again he swirled the liquid, watched it ride up, pressed by centrifugal force, to reveal that lens of glass beneath its centre, and then, when his hand became still, revert to its original form.

"Your Caesar, sir." The waiter eased a bowl filled with a mountain of lettuce and smelling of garlic before Reim.

"*Idioot!*" Reim whispered hoarsely.

He thumped the glass down, slopping wine onto the table, rose, and left, leaving the waiter to watch a red stain spread across the tablecloth, wondering what he had done.

The call tone cut out as the connection went through.

"Rasputin? I've been an idiot! I know what is happening to you. I scarcely believe it, but you are entering—"

"Professor De Groot?" Dee cut over him.

"Yes," he said, as though having to check. "Who is this?"

"Dee Morgan, and you were going to say *Hibernation*, weren't you."

"Yes," he said, even more baffled. "How did you know?"

"It's happening. We found him last night outside, lying in the grass. He'd passed out. We put him to bed, but this morning ..."

"This morning?" Reim pressed his ear closer to the receiver, as if he could come nearer to Dee.

"Professor," said a man's voice, Jordy's. The static on the line increased as he pressed the phone's speaker button. "His skin. It's toughened, cracked. His mouth is sealed with it." His voice sounded on the verge of hysteria to himself, though he felt an odd calmness.

"Jordan—it is Jordan isn't it?" said Reim. "Rasputin is not just hibernating. He is entering a chrysalis."

"A chrysalis," Jordy repeated, as if checking off items on a shopping list.

264

"He is entering a process of change. He is metamorphosing."

Jordy's calm broke. "That's ridiculous."

"It is. And it's true. I checked his tests again last night and saw what has been staring me in the face. No, I have never seen *exactly* this before, not in humans. But the paradigm, yes. In insects, amphibians, even fish. The systemic changes. The cascading expression of genes that control for the enzymes needed to"—he swallowed—"consume the animal's body, take it down to the skeleton, back to the blueprint, before rebuilding it."

Reim paused, waiting for some reply, but the line just fizzed with static.

"It is either this absurd truth," Reim said, "or our eyes deceive us, and he is in fact dead already, has been for weeks. I'd hazard you prefer the former explanation, as do I."

Reim ran on, speaking to himself. "I see at last, a little light. To perform this transformation for a creature so large, to assemble the necessary genetic machinery, not simply to survive but to change. It is to play a million games of chess blindfolded against a million grand masters, at the highest stakes, and win them all. It is the most improbable event. Or the product of a calculation of singular complexity ... And a change into what?"

Dee spoke again, her tone warbling a little. "We're calling an ambulance."

"No!" Reim cried, and feared he had startled them when the line went momentarily silent.

"No?"

"No. Let me come first. What will doctors do? You know what happens to creatures for whom the process of metamorphosis is aborted."

He wanted to laugh, expecting at any minute a reprieve from this practical joke, a camera crew and host, smiling at a fooled old fool. This is your life, Professor De Groot. But still the phone ticked and popped.

Dee spoke again, and still wasn't laughing.

"I can't even take his pulse any more," she said. "What if he's dying?"

"If he is, he is beyond our science." He pleaded with his hands, a useless gesture. "Wait. Please. I will come."

12.

CAIN

Every human has dormant within them a phase change?

I had expected a revelation from this Clotho, not garden variety absurdity. Perhaps he had been enjoying a little too much of the *flieger schokolade*?

But it was entertaining. I read on.

He traced a schema of the history leading to his bald assertion. This phase change, he said, was hinted at in records of antiquity—accidents, happy or hapless. Most hints were manifestations of aborted phase changes. Unhappy monsters. Mortally-wounded geniuses.

Now my mind was tantalised by that word *Imago*—the adult creature that emerges from the chrysalis. But the pragmatist in me still cried ludicrous.

He must have anticipated my incredulity, because he began to list specific cases, specific men. He began with Joseph Merrick, dubbed the Elephant Man by his freak-show managers.

I read the name and thought if ever there was one that proved the opposite of latent celestial power in man it was him. His form was grotesque beyond description. I paused from reading the message to retrieve the vial containing a portion of his epidermis. It floated in chloroform with the appearance of an exotic mushroom. I am used to cadavers, and, unlike so many happy citizens, am able to recognise the ex-human in whatever context I see it. But his skin looked alien to me. Many who saw him alive wondered what manner of being he was.

But Clotho told a different tale. He asserted that Joseph Merrick was the bullet that never left the chamber because flawed. He was one in whom the phase change had been triggered, but then some vital part of the complex machinery had gone awry, some chain had snagged in a gear, causing the whole thing to blow apart by the forces set in motion. Instead of the beautiful ballistic curve reaching its target, it had exploded at the point of origin. His body had exploded in deformity of bone and flesh on a scale never before recorded in the annals of medicine, or indeed any society.

For Joseph, the cocoon had failed cataclysmically. The crux of the process, the transformation of his inner man, had not even begun.

Clotho gave me more names. One I remember well, partly for the contrast he made with Merrick: Blaise Pascal.

Pascal was what we call a Renaissance man, the last caste of humanity to claim all of nature and the horizons of reason for his domain before that land was fractured by the ineluctable reductivism and specialisation axiomatic to Science. Pascal pioneered in mathematics, physics, and philosophy.

Clotho told me something about Pascal I had never heard. On November 23, 1654 Pascal had what he called 'A night of fire'. That day he and friends narrowly escaped death when their carriage careened through a barricade. Their horses fell from a cliff, leaving the carriage teetering at its edge. Pascal was so overcome by his near-death experience he fainted, to lapse for hours into a coma. So critical did he deem the experience that when he awoke he recorded it on a scrap of paper, and sewed it into the lining of his suit, to have with him at all times.

Pascal interpreted this intervention as a visit by the Divine. Clotho read it differently—or, perhaps, read more from it. He asserted Pascal had suffered merely the tremors of true change, which were capable alone of lifting the power of his mind to a new echelon, and were evidenced by the quality of the treatises that hence issued from his pen.

Clotho claimed for his hypothesis Euler's meticulous mind, Aquinas's monolithic memory, Mozart's musical genius, Tesla's mental gymnastics, and Samson's doomed strength. The list went on and on, as though he meant to smother my unvoiced objections with sheer weight of evidence.

When the transmission ended, sleet still rushed upon the schloss, but the fire had burnt low.

Clotho's explanation was an invitation to more inquiry, which I grasped immediately. The following day another call came, but this time the agent asked if I had need to transmit a ciphered message. I said yes, and while he waited silent, I tried the machine. I typed my questions, and watched the ciphered version appear before me, which I spoke into the telephone.

I was direct with Clotho. I asked for evidence of those who had "matured" successfully, then hung up.

He must have guessed my mind in advance, knowing his catalogue of oddities would not witness sufficiently to some universal and untapped potential in humankind. A third call came within the hour.

I arranged the machine before me, and waited, giddy, for more information.

The agent talked. I typed.

Clotho said his case list—his *Bestiary*, he called it—had only served him in retrospect, viewed through the lens of those who succeeded in the change. Of these he offered proof of three:

Case One was a man formerly known as Mihai Patras, a Roumanian. He suffered a blow to the head in a fight with a cousin over the will of a deceased uncle. He fell into a coma that lasted two weeks, and when he emerged began to exhibit unnatural insight. As mutterings grew about suspected sorcery, Mihai took to wandering the mountains alone. His wife watched as her husband, formerly so voluble, grew silent.

One evening he did not return from hiking beneath the alpine forests. His body, or something like it, was found lying in a woodcutter's hut. He was buried and mourned. A month later he burst from the grave, clear of mind and sound of health. The cry of Vampyr was raised, and he was driven from his home.

You will not find any record of Mihai. No documents are extant. They are all burned or lost or confiscated.

Case Two was a woman, a Scot, named Mary Ashcroft. She contracted encephalitis, showed signs of mental derangement, before sinking into a coma that lasted more than three months. On waking, like Mihai Patras, she demonstrated curious new aptitudes. She attracted the attention of doctors in Edinburgh (then a renowned centre for medical research) but as weeks passed she became withdrawn, and began to rave in what the doctors took for delirium. Finally, she succumbed to a kind of petrifaction of the viscera. For two days her doctors plied her with drugs, attempting to reverse the condition, but being unable to find a pulse, pronounced her dead, whereupon they conducted an autopsy.

The carving scalpel found her blood still ran red. But by then it was too late. She remained a mystery in the annals of Scottish medicine, until the pertinent records were lost to fire.

Case Three, and the last I will recall, was an American named Carl Rossiter. He is dead, killed by the Imago, his gift too dangerous.

His story began when a trek over the Rockies with fraternity mates soured. An early blizzard closed a mountain pass. While attempting to find shelter, Carl was struck a concussing blow by a falling rock. He entered a coma that lasted a mere three days. Within weeks he entered the chrysalis, but his friends, fearing they would be blamed, left him, hoping perhaps he would be cleaned away in the spring by an awakening grizzly.

But Carl appeared again in society for the time it took to exact revenge, before starting afresh with a new identity in South America. It was in Ecuador that the Imago tracked him down and killed him.

His was a most dangerous gift. He was an empath. A creature so attuned to the emotions of others, so able to synchronise his every reaction with his prey, that soon predator and prey were meshed like gears—but only one gear supplied the torque. Let your guard down for a moment and an empath could dance you over a cliff. And you would wear a smile all the way down.

In each of Clotho's cases, the subject stumbled upon the change by chance. Other cases told of direct intervention by the Imago.

The final case Clotho offered was himself.

For proof he directed my attention to the very machine by which we were communicating. It was his design, the product, he claimed, of a sublimated mind. A machine for automatic, word-level, context-sensitive ciphers on a large vocabulary, and a generation ahead of the state-of-the-art in use in the war. The Enigma was a toy by comparison, and already cracked by the Poles and then the British. (Knowing Enigma was cracked didn't alarm me, which serves to show how disconnected I had become from my previous passions.) Further, he claimed his design was a mere trifle, an afternoon's thought-caper, for the mind of an Imago with a suitable gifting. A mind like his.

I pressed for detail: how is the change invoked? What concrete gifts does it obtain? Who are the Imago?

He said the pathway to the change is no longer open to the natural organism—if it had ever been. It is a watercourse that must flow uphill. It needs help. It is a dry forest requiring an igniting spark, and regardless of whether that spark is hand lit or lightning-borne, the result is conflagration. He contrasted it with turning a crocodile's egg, a motion that for the embryonic creature brings death, for us life. But that movement must come from an outside agency.

That agency, for most cases, is the Imago, gatekeepers to the process of change, initiates of a new Gnostic sect; keepers of the sacred flame, and priesthood of a new religion.

And they guard their secret jealously.

He would say no more than that the procedure was imprecise, involved pharmacological and physical intervention, and was not guaranteed. The requirement for drugs did not surprise me. The body is a factory for countless drugs. Neither did the need for physical intervention surprise me. I've splinted many sundered bones. What scared me was the possibility the process could misfire, to cause a shattered mind or body. The image loomed in my mind of the Elephant Man.

He asked me outright if I wanted to, as he called it, *elevate*.

I suspected this was the choice the fox offers the chicken.

I demurred, saying I wanted time to consider.

He said, don't take too long.

I had made my choice: thrice times yes! But first I wanted to know more. To a caterpillar invariably come wings, to a tadpole legs, to a wasp nymph a sting. But if I was to change, I had to know what would be the outcome. What would be my gifting? And could I effect it? If I set the fire just so, would it burn to a pre-ordained flame?

I returned to the cases Clotho had cited and in a fever began to search in the Mundaneum's library. I found what I was looking for. Although the original documentary evidence had vanished from the face of the earth, its trace there remained.

I began with Mihai, the one accused of being a vampire. What could I discern of who he was before his change, and what he was after?

I worked backwards, beginning with his escape from the grave. The account protested he had not been dug up, but had burst from the ground by his own power. Which meant, if Roumanians dealt with their dead like their brethren of Christendom throughout the continent, a coffin and six feet of entombing sod.

My conclusion: Mihai's gifting had been overwhelming, super-human strength.

I sifted more evidence, attempting to peer through the veil of his rebirth to what kind of man he had been beforehand. Had he been particularly strong? A trait naturally his, and simply amplified by rebirth?

If anything, the evidence pointed the opposite direction. Mihai had been weakened when young by a wasting disease, which left him barely able to scrape together a living for his family. Indeed, destitution had provoked the fight over the distribution of his uncle's estate.

Next I turned to Carl. What could I glean from the other man Clotho said had emerged from the changing intact? Again my mind was drawn first to the obvious connection: a fraternity boy surrounded by a coterie of clingfasts, a leader, a social butterfly, gifted with an augmentation of natural empathic gifts.

Further inspection revealed, on the contrary, an awkward boy who became a shy young man. The fraternity tour had been something of a breaking out for him, but probably viewed quite differently by his so-called brothers. I imagined his revenge to have been sweet.

I poured myself into my task, holed up for weeks on end within the schloss. Later, when I contacted Clotho to accept his offer, I had settled on a provocative hypothesis, one I was eager to test.

During this time I shared everything with Hans. We were of one mind. He was fascinated most by Mihai's story.

It was only when the Imago's butchers arrived, armed with vials, blades and drills, that I was informed of a further stipulation, the lore I have already mentioned: two might undertake the change, but only one could seize the prize. If Hans and I both entered and emerged from the metamorphosis, we must fight to the death.

We took it philosophically. We both knew there was no longer a choice—hadn't been since Clotho had contacted me.

The Imago spoke of it not as death or termination, merely a diverging. One dweomer took flight into Eternity, while the other remained to master Infinity.

Secretly, I nursed the hope that my hypothesis was right, and that once Hans and I emerged from dormancy, we would write new lore, begin a new order.

Alas, it wasn't to be. The war, which by then seemed like so much child's play, intruded upon us in the form of a fifteen-inch shell. Hans drowned, and, as I have already explained, I was tasked to prepare an alternative dweomer or find another.

I suppose you're interested to know my hypothesis—my secret, rather, as my existence has proved it.

As I said, I formed it from evidence of the dry, textual kind, found in Otlet's library. To that I can now add the evidence, vivid and intoxicating, of lived experience.

I've told you of the common theme I found in the lives of Mihai and Carl, the contrast between what they were and what they became. I unearthed many more such tales in the indices and footnotes of Otlet's library. They led me to pose a simple question: What is the opposite of what one has?

You, given your situation, should have a ready answer.

It is: what one *wants*.

Greed is the greatest god. The stomach is never filled, the eyes never sated. The things laid at their altar are quickly consumed, and one must range ever wider for the next offering.

The god of the weak man is strength. The god of the despised is esteem. Thus were Mihai and Carl equipped by the change.

Like any other process of nature, the key is within. Inside the acorn lies the oak. The idea of a great, many-branched tree is printed in microscopic strands of DNA. Pity the acorn that cannot change itself, cannot have a new idea of itself. If it could, perhaps an acorn could become an elm, or an aspen, or an asp.

When Hans and I awoke from coma, we took stock. And then began to restock.

I noticed presently within my mind a kind of motion, a rummaging through, a cataloguing. I watched it take inventory, as if, having passed through the blackout of coma, it needed to be reacquainted with itself. I felt as if a great hand were roaming over my memories and desires, examining, probing, taking note, before returning each to its place.

My theory predicted this. I had not expected it to be so transparent. My excitement grew.

This rapid validation of my hypothesis made me wonder how aware of the process the Imago are, whether they had documented it scientifically, or attempted to systematise it. If I had learned so much so quickly, with only Hans' conversation—merely the substance of two experiences conjoined—surely the Imago, with the resources at their disposal and the examples of so many lives elevated, had achieved a mature understanding? That is, if their penchant for mysticism had not blinded the paths of Science.

I began to ply my knowledge. My volitional contribution to the process of my change was to guide that great hand toward a single goal: I desired to be the ultimately adaptable creature.

Since I was a boy, I had seen how that which adapted survived, and, in surviving, flourished. I recalled watching moths emerge into what should have been spring's quickening, only to be struck by winter's parting shot, a snow squall. Beneath the clear skies that followed, moths of the same species lived or died on the proportion of black and white to their speckled wing. If change is the only constant, it follows that changeability is the prerequisite for continuing life, regardless of what one does with the life thus secured.

I began systematically to call to mind memories of when I had effected a kind of adaptation: feigned interest in the piano to woo a vivacious fraulein; awe during my interview for admission to the Art programme at Berlin (and ebullient extroversion to obtain presidency of the guild of the same); even my affectation of a blank-faced, clean-living Nazi at Waffen-SS recruitment. In each case, though the name of Schürmann had gone a long way, I had adapted to the need of the moment.

Having looked into the past, I then turned my attention to the future. It was time to stock my hopes.

My thoughts each day, from rising to turning in, were drawn to my one desire. And I let them be drawn. Every idle thought fell into the orbit of my hope for ultimate adaptability.

As the time drew near for my dweoming, I began to dwell within my mind in a way hard to imagine for those who have not had the privilege of dweoming. I could enter at will into something like a vivid, waking dream. What's more, I could fashion dreamscapes with an exactitude normally precluded by the dream-addled mind. I set myself tests, to survive, to gather information, to seduce. I fashioned hostile environments, and cast myself in a role suited to each. I became the ill-favoured son of a dying patriarch—really became him—and challenged myself to extract an inheritance at his death bed. I plunged myself into a jungle and became the quarry in the hunt of a despot—I became a gaunt figure, barely human, and befriended shadow and silence as I eluded him and his hounds. I took the form of my brother and confronted my mother over the affair that had broken my father's health—my mother!

Day after day I scourged myself in this way as my time drew near. In my mind, I fooled them all. Only one question gnawed at me: Would my body reify this dream?

The answer, as you can see for yourself, is: yes.

I've told this tale eight times now. It has become something of a ritual. It grows with every telling, giving me time to observe, and perfect my form. I watch for all of the subtle expressions that travel a subject's face, the starbursts of reaction to each revelation, and gather the nuances necessary to fool a lover's intuition, or a mother's scrutiny.

Strange to say, the look is not sufficient to create a flawless doppelganger. We do not stand like statues for each other in real life. We constantly move. How often do we recognise an acquaintance, even at great distance, by their gait? The slightest perturbation, a leg hitched up too far, a shoulder slung to low, and the game is up.

Now it is time for you to travel on into the Great Unknown. I almost envy you. But I thirst for the endlessness of space. I shall exhaust Infinity before acquainting myself with Eternity.

13.

I, PART SUN

A boy stood atop a cliff, looking out at the ocean. In the distance, clouds spent themselves in rain upon water burnished by the descending sun. Was there a more beautiful futility? Perhaps beauty trumped futility.

He sighed—so deeply he took himself for a man.

The man shifted his gaze to the shore. Waves were hurling themselves onto the beach, climbing it, pausing ever so briefly, then listing, receding to mingle with the next. Each wave left a momentary stain upon the shore like a shadow of itself.

The man desired the feel of spume and sand in his toes. He began to descend.

He reached with his mind to fashion the brute rock of the cliff into a stairway, and then remembered he could no longer do it. The loss still hurt. He had yet to adjust to this impotence, to be unable to shape the world according to whim. He felt stuck in the concreteness of it all, a fly in amber.

He had first sensed something sapping his power as he rose from the centre of the earth, treading a stair he formed by parting and shaping the living stone. The realisation had coincided with the rumble of a far-off storm—an out-of-place sound in the grottos formed by the ballooning of his will in the uniform rock. Perhaps he had heard the storm before then, in the murmur of molten pools near the earth's core. He could not remember why he had travelled there, what quest had pulled him thither. He could not remember much at all—it was as though he were in a dream. As with a dream, he could not recall how it had begun.

Now that he had breached the surface he could see the storm standing off on the horizon. Its belly was dark, and the wind carried the scent of its menace.

The man resigned himself to picking his way down the cliff's haphazard ledges. Its rock was limestone, bored by wind and ancient waters as though it had played host to some gigantic parasite. An onshore breeze moaned in the hollows. Stunted scrub clung impossibly, eking out life in defiance of gravity and the elements.

While descending, he pondered (not for the first time) why he could not remember his name. He knew he had one. It was like a tickling at the back of his mind, just beyond the reach of his thought.

Who are you?

—Who r u?—

He was surprised on reaching the beach to see it marked with small footprints, like those of a child. Beside them ran a groove in the sand, as though the owner trailed a stick in one hand. With his gaze he tracked the footprints along the beach, just above the water line, as they shrank and disappeared behind a small bluff.

Intrigued, he followed the tracks. He could not remember the last time he had seen another living soul.

The footprints meandered left and right, always staying just beyond the reach of the water that would erase them. The groove dogging the child's heels wove to and fro across the footfalls. When the man had rounded the bluff the footprints veered the closest they had come to the waterline. The groove disappeared, and the man saw the last traces of a pattern of marks that had been etched in the sand—writing or perhaps a sketch. The surging water had removed any possibility of recognition.

He quickened his step.

Soon he saw more evidence of writing in the sand. He thought he must be gaining on his quarry, for the marks became increasingly clear. Each had been left to the ravage of waves for less time than the last.

He came across marks that were tantalisingly fresh. He squinted and tried to force them to become words. They wouldn't. When he looked up, his breath caught. There, planted in a line beside the small footprints, were large ones, those of an adult. He felt a thrill of fear.

He dug in his back pocket for the pocketknife he knew to be there. His search yielded, instead, a folded sheet of paper. He withdrew it and unfolded it. It was the sketched portrait of a girl. He recognised his sister, and, as he lowered her portrait, he saw her a hundred yards farther down the beach. She was crouched, drawing in the sand with a stick.

He hurried toward her, realising as he went that the large footprints he had feared were his own; he was on an island, had already circumnavigated it.

Seeing him approach, she stood and ran in the opposite direction. Her hair bounced as she ran, and he fancied he heard the wind carry her laughter back to him. She rounded the bluff and was lost to view.

Passing the point where she had been drawing, he had time enough to see a single letter written in the sand: H, already being assailed by the water.

The man rounded the bluff and saw that he had gained on her. She had stooped to draw, but on seeing him, ran again. Her hair flailed out in a banner. The wind was beginning to rise, sending spume flying, and sand snaking across the beach's undulations.

As he ran, he became aware that his path was curving more and more tightly. His sister no longer trailed the stick, so he could not gauge his path neatly, but there could be no mistake: the island was shrinking. That realisation brought him to a halt, and when he looked up and out at the ocean, he was appalled by what he saw.

The storm had closed on the diminishing island. The encircling ocean, far from being beaten down by the coming torrent of rain, was lifting to the cloud belly, bending upwards like a colossal meniscus.

The world had ceased to become plastic beneath his will, take its impression. It now seemed intent on ejecting him altogether.

The man watched, for a moment forgetting his sister and pursuit. The ocean's lip touched the cloud, which lowered like a curtain. Vapour and liquid moiled together until it was impossible to tell where ocean ended and atmosphere began. The island was enclosed in a rapidly constricting pocket of space. The wind, now confined, began to howl parallel to the beach in a vortex driven by preternatural force.

The man tore his gaze away and hunted again for his sister. Her footprints had broken away from the shore and angled toward a hump of sand, a dune standing now at the centre of the island. He glimpsed her crouched at its peak. He struggled up the dry sand, going to all fours, gulping air, as the water rose hungrily behind him and lapped at his heels.

He planted each foot in dry sand, only to draw it forth again from an agitated slurry of sand, water and froth. He felt wetness caress his face, and upon raising it, saw the heavens had sunk to within yards. Only a small orb clear of chaos remained, centred on the dune's peak, where his sister still squatted, and licking out from the looming wall came spiralling liquescent arms.

It was all suddenly very familiar.

The Eye had found *him*.

He mounted the last yard. The girl rose and turned to face him. She smiled once—it smote his heart—before diving into the water.

He cried out—*Tell me. What is my name!*—clutching after her but she was gone.

The orb closed in. He had to crouch, and, there before him, saw a message scrawled in the sand. Water chattered up the last feet of sand and raced to obliterate it. He dropped to his knees, and arched his arms to protect it, realising he had only seconds.

He saw his mistake immediately. The message did not start with a H, but an I. He had read it the wrong way. It said: I forgive you.

Water poured over his forearms. It clasped his head, embraced his body.

I forgive you.

Not a name. Perhaps better than a name.

The water entered his nose and mouth, from above and below. The light was extinguished and he was thrown into darkness.

Light bloomed softly into complete darkness, and with it came the realisation he was suffocating. That knowledge was not distant or academic—with animal cunning he sensed it, and with animal ferocity he fought it.

His lungs hurt, too much for him to bear. Much easier to give it away. Sink back into the numbing darkness.

But the animal would not be quieted.

He resolved to fight. He had known pain—he could recall no single memory—but he had known it and tamed it. He summoned his strength, like a king calling his subjects by an oath of fealty.

In response, he found himself. His will invested in body and limb, and with that reunion came the crisp image of his peril. He felt himself bound, head to foot, encased and unable to move. Worse, lodged in his throat was a heavy mass, as though his tongue was distended and swollen in place.

His senses sharpened and like a keen wind drove off the ghosts of dreams that had converged on him, hovering over the knot of confusion and pain he was.

He was in the process of dying. He would die. Be dead.

A soundless shriek rang through his head.

He focussed every ounce of strength on his left arm, which lay parallel to his trunk, fixed to his flank. He drew on it with his bicep, levering with his elbow, as blood throbbed in his temples and in the engine room of his chest.

The light began to fail. He felt himself slipping downward, a nameless cluster of sound and pain.

His left arm tore free.

Pin-pricks of light began to sparkle in the darkness, little constellations being born beneath his eyelids in honour of his passing.

His left hand scrabbled over his face, banging dully against his ear before finding his mouth—or rather, where his mouth should have been; his fingers found only toughened and puckered flesh. He dug fingernails under it, seeking purchase, conscious of his strength ebbing as the oxygen in his blood fell.

More stars blazed, and the throbbing of his heart rose to drown out thought with its requiem beat.

His hand, still poised above his mouth, slowed and became still.

He ceased to strive.

Even the pain gave off, and left him alone, content to watch and listen, to not hurt.

What moronic logic had led him to struggle?

Something brushed the raw flesh of his hand, something that in its foreignness felt like ice.

It was another hand. It covered his own, its fingers twining with his, and pried.

He rallied, contemplated fighting that hand—oblivion was so inviting—then strove together with it to tear open a passage for breath.

Another hand gripped the side of his face, and then something hard, like the cap of a knee, dug into his side, and pressed down on him bearing its owner's weight. He felt panic in the force of it.

Singular pain lanced his face as a clot of flesh was pulled from his throat, making him gag. In the pain's wake came a new sensation, the feel of air over raw lips and teeth suddenly chalky. His diaphragm convulsed, compressing air in his suddenly too-small oesophagus. The inrush of air, its payload of oxygen, was the closing of the master circuit breaker. His whole body sprang into life. The rails of his internal tracks were electrified, and a long dormant population sprang forth and thronged the streets. In the clamour, all he wanted was to cry.

He felt himself lifted, pulled into a sitting position. Tightness like a ripe scab resisted every movement. The hands that had helped free his mouth would not be still. They came and went, touching and testing, over his head, chest and belly.

The panic that had immersed him ebbed until it was a residue on clear thought. His heart slowed, and the hands, as if sensing this, became less frantic.

With his free hand he explored the skin of his face. He could only feel its pressure through the thickened, dry skin, as though it were anaesthetised. He climbed his fingers up and into the cleft beneath his brow, searching for his eyes. They too were skinned over. He began to pry at the dead skin. The other hand sought to help, but he pushed it away, gestured for it to stop.

His lids cracked open on what seemed to be the centre of the sun, and at last he could cry. Great tears merged, pooling between the new and the old skin, before spilling in streamers over the senseless skin below.

Into the shimmering brightness already dimming came a face. He knew her name immediately: Dee. She was crying too, and at his acknowledgement, her eyes disappeared in a smile. Her lips moved with speech, but he heard it only as a dull buzz.

He flexed his right bicep and ripped the arm free, ignoring the pain that made his flank spasm. He dug in his ear.

"Help me hear," he said, unsure if she heard him. He could not hear himself.

She seemed to understand, for she brushed his hand aside and loosened the skin stopping up his ear.

A small rupture—and a world of sound poured in: breathing, its faint echo from the walls of the half-lit room, and Dee's sniffing up of tears.

"I can hear," he said.

"Oh, Monk," she whispered, and leaned forward to embrace him.

"Please," he said, and pushed her away, square-on to him. "My name. What is my name?"

"Monk—" she said, then seemed to see something in his gaze, intent and fraught. "Rasputin. Your name is Rasputin."

"Rasputin," he said, his tongue feeling its way over the contours of the word. "Yes."

He let her hug him then.

It felt like they were clasped a long time, but he could not say how long. His mind would not mark off the seconds.

Dee broke the contact. She left the room and returned with a damp flannel. Rasputin sat curled and taut, bound by ropes of his own cast-off flesh, able to see, hear, and flex his arms, but cosseted still within the birth canal. Beneath the bed clothes snarled around his waist and legs, he was naked. But as Dee began to fuss over him, to soak the skin above his still-blind eye and slake it away, his shame dissipated. Her ministrations had motherhood in them. He was surprised by their beauty.

When at last he was free, wrapped in a towel and attempting to take some water with salt, his mind came up to speed enough to recognise where he was. The room's high ceiling, and the brass door handle glossed with a heavy patina, brought back to him the farm, and the field.

He turned to Dee, who was seated beside him on the sagging bed, and said: "Where's Jordy?"

In response, she burst into tears.

14.

PAR INUST

Rasputin fingered the head of his walking cane. It rested against his leg, jutting into the cavity beneath the car's dash. When he and Dee had left the farm, the sun had gilded the cane's glossy paint, sending a thread of fire down its length. The twilight now suffusing the car's interior wasn't able to call forth the fire.

His leg was not right. Still not right. He felt that initial realisation again keenly. Though plunged deep into the valley of the shadow of death, he was still not whole.

He had swivelled on the bed, waited as muscles took up the strain as he loaned his weight to the leg, only to feel it give, and twist dumbly like a dancer bereft of wit. It had been the image of the day he had first left his hospital bed, made worse by the weight of foreknowledge he had not had that day.

Hell. Caterpillars got *wings*. Was it that greedy to want the full use of both legs?

He caught his slip into self-pity. He had been fighting it since they had flown the farm, but it would not sit, like a ball-bearing repeatedly set on an incline. He gritted his teeth and hurled it away.

"Why didn't he take the car?" he said.

Dee replied through pre-occupation he knew did not stem from concentrating on the road. "He thought I might need it, so he walked to the highway and caught a bus." Her eyes were dry. He guessed their wells were dry too.

He chewed his lip. It had been like this since they left—a question, an answer, then quiet.

He had stopped trying to comfort her, to persuade her that everything was fine, that Reim was fine, that Jordy was fine. He didn't believe it, and he couldn't keep that out of his voice.

In the distance a knot of eucalypts were silhouetted by an orange sky, stark against vast cauliflower cloud heads forming above the scarp. The clouds made the hills look like volcanoes in eruption, but although they appeared thick and tangible, he knew they held no rain. The only sound was the engine's dull drone, and the occasional skitter of loose grit flicked into a wheel well.

Dee turned the car's lights on, revealing the occasional moth or bug that came wheeling out of the blue to collide with windscreen or grill.

And from all of this raw data Rasputin's mind made nothing. It remained just that: raw sense parsed only for animal necessity. There were no messages nested within visions.

He drew a deliberate breath, and began again to put the pieces together.

"When did you last hear from Jordy?"

"Four days ago."

"What did he say?"

"He couldn't raise Reim. He was going to have one last try at unpicking the phone."

"What does that mean?"

"He thought he could find who was bugging you."

He was silent a moment as he collated the facts.

"Why didn't you just call an ambulance?"

"Reim said they would kill you."

He chewed on that. "He was probably right."

"And you say Reim called—when?"

"Two weeks ago. The morning after you ..."

"Then nothing?"

"No. He said he was coming, but he never showed."

"Maybe he got lost?"

"For two weeks? I texted him the address."

"What did you do?"

"After Jordy left? What do you think, Rasputin? I made one mad rush into Northam for food, and then sat with you, torn."

"You called Reim?"

"Every day. It was like Jordy said: his answering machine said he was sick. His email bounced with an 'Out of Office.'"

"Did you try Jordy's parents?"

"I asked them if they could see if he'd left yet, that his phone must be dead and there were a few items I needed him to bring. They went past, but the house was dark. That was three days ago."

"It's a blackout," he said finally, to himself. He glanced sidewise at Dee. She gripped the wheel tightly, her face set dead ahead, lacking expression.

"I'm sorry."

She turned. A small smile escaped. "It's hardly your fault."

He suppressed the urge to say it somehow was. It would only provoke her.

Silence stretched out. The foothills became more tightly rumpled together, the cloud bank loomed nearer. Soon they would top the scarp.

When Dee spoke, her words lacked the proper emphasis, as though they had sat on her tongue for hours. "Do you feel different?"

His gaze flicked unwittingly to his cane. He swatted the thought away.

"Yes ... No."

Dee waited in silence for an explanation.

"Ask me what the square root of two hundred and fifty three is," he said.

She played along. "What's the square root of two hundred and fifty three?"

"Beats me."

He studied her face as she absorbed his revelation. He saw reflected there his own mixed feelings.

"You're normal?"

"Things seem familiar again. It's like I've moved back home after a decade overseas, back to the house where I grew up."

"You really don't know the answer?"

"No, it isn't floating in the wind, or congealing below to float into my consciousness."

"But?"

"But my old house, the one I've come to live in again, now has a basement."

"A basement?"

"Yes. And its door might be stiff with age, but I don't think it's locked."

She frowned and took a moment to look at him.

"You've carried that too long. Carried her too long. You need to let it go."

"My sister? Oh, no." He smiled. "She's not down there, not any longer. I think, somewhere along the line, we made peace."

Dee could not hide her relief, nor her curiosity, but she said no more about it.

"What's in the basement then?"

"The square root of two hundred and fifty three, among other things."

"Then nothing has changed?" she said in alarm.

"It has. Like I said, I'm not drowning in thoughts that seem like someone else's. Deep down, the wheel still turns, but I've come adrift of it. It's as though I've been jolted from the hub, and the machine's motive power no longer flows through me. I don't feel *harnessed*, a cog in some colossal artefact."

He paused, picking gingerly through memories of being within the eye. They felt old now, stale like normal memory-stuff ... and yet. "But it's still humming down there."

"In the basement," Dee said, like one trying to share a joke not quite understood.

"In the basement."

He wound the window down an inch. The air was heavy with summer's humidity, and larded with the smell of the sundried leaf-litter of eucalypt and jarrah. From the corner of his eye he saw Dee twitch.

"Too noisy? I can wind it up?"

"No, don't," she said. "I miss the bush."

The car hurtled up a rise, its green shell reflecting the gloaming. From a thousand feet up it was the carapace of a beetle making a bee-line for the scarp's crest.

They topped the scarp, but it was another minute before the road curved to the right and the forest fell away to reveal the bowl of Swan Valley, with Perth's skyscrapers twinkling at its centre.

At the same moment, Rasputin's phone buzzed to notify him of a message.

They stared at each other for a moment, comically frozen, before he lunged, spearing his arm into the rear passenger foot well. His hand stabbed the side of a sports bag. He found the zip, opened it and groped through its contents. After seconds that seemed like minutes, he retrieved the phone.

He pulled the message up.

He read it aloud: "I need you. Come quickly."

"Who is it?" she said, breathless.

"Reim."

The sun had left off their hemisphere by the time Dee pulled the car over to the curb and killed the engine. All was still bar the shape of a low-hanging branch that swept back and forth in the wind, like a person tracing and retracing their steps in the night. The tick of the car's cooling engine punctuated the silence.

Reim's house looked out of place. It was a relic from an older Perth, when riverside suburbs had rambling lawns riven by dirt driveways, cluttered with river-going paraphernalia. The small, single storey house was set far back on the block, hemmed on three sides by brick walls that seemed to lean off-plumb in the darkness. The neighbouring houses were two or three storeys, and pushed to the front of their blocks to create private spaces behind. As Rasputin opened his door, he heard water splashing unceasingly, and guessed at fountains and manicured lawns behind the bordering walls. The smell of putrefying nectarines wafted on the inconstant breeze.

The only light gleaming from within Reim's house came warped through bubbled-glass flanking the front door. They were halfway up the dirt driveway, a lighter darkness twisting its way toward the house, when the door opened, spilling the lone light in a bar down the steps of the veranda.

The silhouette of a man appeared in the doorway. It bent over something, and doused the light. Rasputin heard the door shut and the jangle and scrape of a key being fitted to a lock.

A smaller light flared in the darkness. It came bobbling down the stairs, its sharp beam strafing restless peppermint trees, before tracing a path down the driveway.

Rasputin and Dee halted, waiting. As the light drew near, Rasputin saw by its diffused glow a wild look in Reim's eyes, one he had never before seen. He saw also that what bent Reim's right arm with its weight gleamed metallic.

"Professor, why do you have a gun?" said Rasputin.

"Rasputin. Dee," said Reim, running his words together. "Please, we must hurry. Jordan has been here. He has my entry code to the lab. He means to steal the virus." Panic had thickened his accent.

"What virus?" shrieked Dee.

"Why the gun?" said Rasputin.

Reim ignored Dee. "Jordan was not himself."

Reim tilted the torch so that its light enveloped his face. Rasputin heard Dee's sharp intake of breath as his eyes fell on a dark oblong smudge that ran down one side of his face. Its centre was scored with a line of dried blood.

By the time they pulled into a deserted car park at the university, the harried look had left Reim's face. In its place was one of frank appraisal: Rasputin caught Reim looking at him in the rear-view mirror more than once.

Reim turned in his seat as far as it and his ageing joints would allow, and, with the ghost of a smile, said, "I was right."

Dee had told Rasputin of Reim's call the morning after he had passed out in the field, of his talk about hibernation. Now, Rasputin sensed a hum of excitement beneath Reim's mien—not even bodily assault, it appeared, could whip the academic bent from the old man.

The campus looked altogether different in the dead of night. It appeared empty, and the dark obscured familiar landmarks, and caused the outlines of buildings and trees to take on new relationships.

The foyer of the biology faculty was imbued with a faint fluorescent glow from a handful of afterhours lights. In the penumbral gloom, portraits of dead and retired academics floated, insubstantial as wraiths.

Reim shuffled ahead of Rasputin and Dee. Rasputin guessed he had received a harsher beating than he was letting on.

They descended a flight of stairs that squeaked beneath their shoes. The stairs made a ninety-degree turn and terminated in the small foyer of the bio-toxicology lab.

Reim produced an identity card from within his cardigan. (Rasputin smiled, despite everything—the temperature had to be above 20 degrees Celsius, and the Dutchman was wearing a woollen cardigan.) He sliced a box on the wall nimbly with the card, and the large single-plate glass door swept open.

"The C4 lab?" whispered Rasputin.

Reim turned and for a moment seemed confused. Then: "Yes. Just the card. Next is the honey pot." He was silent a moment, listening. "And perhaps Jordan has not been here after all. Nothing seems amiss."

They walked single file between benches strewn with microscopes and other machines whose function Rasputin could not discern. The room was lit with faint green light, as though the ceiling burned with foxfire. Rasputin and Dee were alike glancing about. Reim's head was thrust forward of his shoulders, and his gait had steadied into the purposeful walk Rasputin knew so well.

"Don't people sometimes work here at night?" Dee said.

Reim replied without turning, "Not in the holidays."

In the welter of events, Rasputin had forgotten it was New Year's Eve.

They passed a series of partitions that served to baffle the view to another room whose signage designated it to be for virology. The benches in this room held containment hoods, and more specialised equipment. Rasputin noted that though the room was within the confines of the C4 facility, only staff whose work touched on viruses would have a reason to be there. All others would be sifted out by the baffles guarding its approach.

At the back of the virology lab was another partition that looked to be a set of cubicles for book and computer work. They delved past this, turned, and were confronted with another plate-glass door. Reim swiped through this, and they entered a dim corridor. Rasputin's cane tapped on the tiled floor, echoing. It smelt of cleaning agent.

At the far end of the corridor was a thick door that reminded Rasputin of the freezer room doors he had seen working one summer at an abattoir. Those doors had been stainless steel. This was transparent.

A camera sat in the left corner above the door. Set into the wall below was a keypad. The keys glowed with that same green light.

Reim stooped over the keypad and said: "Reim De Groot."

A speaker set into the wall above the keypad gave out a desultory bleep. The door remained shut fast.

Reim repeated the phrase, with the same result.

He muttered, "This Brave New World," then turned to Rasputin and Dee. "Every time I get the slightest flu."

He adjusted his glasses, peered first over them, then through them, and began to laboriously key in a ten-digit number. Rasputin noted only the first three digits, before, belatedly, some instinct of politeness caused him to look away.

Reim finished and as he straightened up, the door hissed slightly, withdrew a fraction of an inch, and slid open.

Light burst over the room, startling Dee.

Jordy was nowhere in sight.

Perhaps this is all madness, thought Rasputin.

As the door shooshed closed behind them, Rasputin took a quick mental inventory of the lab. It was much smaller than he had imagined—a square perhaps 40 feet to a side. It was rimmed with a wide, white bench, which was spartan compared to the clutter in the outer lab. One corner of the room held a room within the room, a cube that did not reach quite to the ceiling. Silver taps with instruments protruded from one side, and were connected to hoses made of a silver and white woven material.

Reim caught Rasputin's glance. "That's the wet section." He winked. "The virus vault."

Reim strode over to a computer and brought it out of hibernation. Over his shoulder, he said: "Jordan is not here now, but it is imperative I make sure he hasn't been here."

He logged into the computer and accessed a program.

"The refrigerated vault is tied to this software. It logs all accesses. I will check nothing has been tampered with, and then"—he swivelled on his chair—"we'd best call the police."

Rasputin winced voluntarily. The bruise on the old man's face seemed more gruesome in the harsh, fluorescent lighting.

Rasputin caught Dee's stance out of the corner of his eye. Her shoulders were slumped, her head hung pendulously on her thin neck.

Shit, he thought, *I've been thinking of myself again.*

He edged toward her and rested his hand on her shoulder. She acknowledged the touch without looking up.

Reim grunted to himself. "Found it," he said. He hunted in his shirt pockets and drew out a folded serviette and a pen. He began to copy something from the screen.

Rasputin smiled. Here Reim was, at a computer in a lab that pushed at the envelope of man's understanding of the deadliest biological agents ever known, and he was scribbling with ink on an old napkin.

Rasputin watched. He watched Reim's shaggy head bent over the paper, which glanced up now and then to check the information he was copying. He watched the cardigan bunch a little as Reim's arm moved. He watched the purple veins bulging beneath his brown, patterned skin. He watched ink leave the pen and stain the paper.

Then Rasputin's body moved—almost before reason, almost. He raised his cane, fought an instinctual revulsion, and swung it at the old man's skull. It struck just behind his right temple. He slumped onto the desk, slid backwards, and fell to the floor like a sack of grain. The pen clattered on the floor, a little coda.

Dee screamed.

Rasputin stepped away from Reim's inert form, surveying the effect.

Dee was breathing rapidly. It seemed she couldn't form words.

"That is not Reim," Rasputin said. His chest was hitching with fast, shallow breaths. He repeated it twice, emphatically.

"What?" was all she could manage in reply.

He pointed at the serviette, perched on the edge of the bench.

"Reim is *left*-handed."

Rasputin looked at his own left hand, flexed it. *Yes,* he reassured himself. *He is. We are.*

"But—" she said.

"I don't know how," he said, and returned his gaze to the man who was not Reim. "But I could guess. It doesn't matter. That's not Reim."

At last, Dee's tongue began to work. "Where is Jordy?"

Rasputin shivered. "I'll bet he knows," he said, hoping it didn't sound like a death sentence, and toed the man's leg.

Dee bent over the man and dug in his pocket for the gun. When she straightened up, it dangled from her hand as though she was afraid it would turn and bite her.

"What do we do with this?"

Rasputin reached for the gun and gently took it from her. He fiddled with the breach mechanism (it always looked so easy in the movies) and finally succeeded in laying open the cylinder. Six slugs sat in their chambers, awaiting the hammer blow.

Rasputin pivoted the gun and the bullets slipped into his palm. He stared at them. He had never seen real bullets before. Now isolated, each seemed no more dangerous than a stone.

He glanced about the room. He dismissed the idea of slotting them one by one down a sink drain. Then he saw a one-way hatch on the far wall. It was placarded with a high-contrast warning about what could and could not be put through the system, in lists of acceptable classes of hazardous substance.

He walked to the hatch. "These qualify as a potentially hazardous substance," he said, yanked it open by a metal handle, and dropped the bullets into its bucket. They made a loud clatter. He slammed the hatch shut and reopened it, just to be sure they were gone. The hatch's bucket was empty.

The gun was heavy in his hand. He considered stowing it out of sight in a cupboard, but instead thrust it into his pocket.

He turned, saying, "We need something to tie him up," and froze.

The man who was not Reim was no longer on the floor. He was upright, one arm draped over Dee's shoulder, the other poised by her neck. In that hand he held the pen he had dropped when clubbed.

"Move and I'll slot this through her jugular. It requires strength, but is quite reliable." He smiled a smile that was an introduced species on the face that looked so like Reim's. "The pen is mightier than the sword, after all."

"You're probably disappointed I'm conscious. I'm a quick healer." As he spoke, the bruise marring his cheek dissipated until the only evidence it had ever existed was a line of rust-coloured blood.

The man pushed Dee into a chair, his eyes on Rasputin. He bade Rasputin to yank an electrical cable from a computer, and sit in the chair next to Dee. Rasputin complied, moving like an automaton, his mind racing but yielding nothing. Next he instructed Rasputin to loop the cable around his torso and Dee's, and then between their legs. Finally he told him to coil it round Dee's wrists, and then his own.

As the man leaned to inspect the cable, Rasputin sat up and swung his elbow sharply upward, hoping to catch his chin with its bony point. He missed, and his momentum twisted him in the chair.

The man punched him deliberately on the face. Rasputin felt hot liquid spring from his nose, and flow over his lips. The man drew his fist back again and repeated the blow. The second impact hurt his numb nose less than the first, and he drew a little satisfaction when the man cried out in pain, guessing he had cut his knuckles the second time.

While Rasputin sat dazed, the man lunged with feline speed, grabbed the cable and pulled it taut. Rasputin and Dee cried out in unison, pain forcing the breath from them. The man cinched the cable tightly, and secured them to a strut beneath the bench.

"There now," he said, and wiped the back of his hand across his forehead. He exhaled loudly, drew up a chair, and sat. "We can talk."

"Who are you?" said Dee, through clenched teeth.

"Ah!" the man said. "Just the question." His tongue darted out and licked his bottom lip—another gesture incongruous with that aged face.

He drew in a steadying breath, an orator's prelude. Then said:

"I was born Gottfried Schürmann. I was reborn Cain, one of the lucky few to walk again on History's miscarriage-strewn highway." He nodded at Rasputin. "I have called you brother."

"Before I kill you, I want to tell you my story."

Rasputin listened as Cain told his tale, and after the initial pulse of adrenaline at the portent of imminent death, sat silently, absorbing it all.

When Cain had finished, Dee was the first to speak.

"You said you've told your tale nine times now." Cain nodded. "Did you tell it to Reim last? Was he the eighth?"

Cain nodded again. "Yes. It has become my changing ritual."

Tears leaked from Dee's eyes as she said, "And Jordy before that?"

In reply, Cain's face was full of mischief. He rolled a foot closer on his chair and thrust his head forward.

Rasputin thought he meant to spit. Then he noticed Cain's left iris move—no, it didn't move: the eyeball was fixed. The sense of motion came from the iris's substance. Its colour was changing, dithering. Over twenty seconds, the iris altered from Reim's slate-grey to vivid blue. A vivid blue that in Rasputin's world was the window on Jordy's soul.

Dee sobbed and hid her face.

"You're a bastard," said Rasputin.

Cain leaned back in the chair. The iris faded back to grey.

"Of course. Surviving genes are bastard genes."

No one spoke for a time. Dee wept in silence again. Rasputin thought he detected a faint buzzing in his ears, and judged it an ironic time to discover he had tinnitus.

Cain slapped his thighs in the manner of one having come to a decision, and rose. He picked up the serviette that had sat perched on the bench since he had been clubbed, and approached the cube of the wet area.

Its access way was a hermetically sealed doorway guarded by another keypad. Cain entered the ten-digit code and the door hissed and slid open. He ignored the orange suits hanging on the wall that Rasputin could see through the doorway, and moved farther into the room and out of view. The door hissed shut behind him.

He reappeared minutes later. In his hand he held three vials. He pocketed two and placed the third on the bench, out of reach of Rasputin and Dee. He then pulled something else from his trouser pocket, retrieved the third vial, and, with his back turned, began to fuss with it.

"What's that?" Rasputin said.

"This lab works on some of the strongest, most complex antidotes and vaccines ever conceived."

A little knot loosened in Rasputin's chest.

Cain went on: "The study of which is provoked by," he turned and lifted the vial up for Rasputin to see, "the most abominable holocaust machines ever known."

"That?" said Rasputin numbly.

Cain looked at the vial. "This."

Cain turned his gaze upon Rasputin again. "And to think, it was you who put me onto this little caper. You presented me with the solution to all of my problems."

Rasputin's brow wrinkled in confusion. Then understanding broke open like a boil. His retort died on his lips.

Cain saw it die. "That's right. You and your loose-lipped Dutch uncle. Tsk, tsk."

"You're going to kill us with a virus? Seems a bit roundabout."

"It's not. Time is short—I've got to nip, change, and be back—but I'll explain it to you."

Without warning, Dee spat at Cain.

He was startled. He raised his hand, and Rasputin thought he meant to slap her. Instead, he wiped the spittle from his face.

"Understandable," was all he said, before turning his attention again to Rasputin.

He sat.

"I told you the Imago don't like changers. We're too dangerous. They're hoping you'll kill me. But when that doesn't happen, they will contrive some way to do it themselves. The only thing that will stop them is a deeper danger. That's where this comes in." He held the vial up again. Rasputin saw that he had attached a small metal device to its side.

"This is the perfect genocide machine. I beat that information, with the help of some expensive drugs, out of your professor, along with his pass code. Imagine a virus that has a ninety-nine percent mortality rate, an incubation period of two weeks, an airborne vector, and, most importantly, no vaccine yet in existence. Imagine the fun we'd have with that. Dropped in the right places, it could have pandemic reach."

Cain gestured as if framing a scene. "Mary arrives back in New York. JFK is a busy place—a hub for world-spanning travel. Two weeks later, she leaves work early with a niggle in her chest. The flu season has come early, she thinks. That night she wakes gripped by stomach cramps."

Cain seized his stomach, his features contorted by a theatrical grimace.

"The following afternoon she is found by her flatmate—dead, her skin a pouch for a soup of systemically failed organs. The pathology is done, and the medicos realise they're dealing with an unknown. They quarantine. But the bull has run the gate."

Cain tapped a finger against the vial. "How many people could you infect in two weeks, death cloaked and stalking by your side?"

He leaned back into his chair. "Pretty much everyone, I'd say."

"You want to kill the Imago?"

Cain's eyebrows popped up. "What? No! Haven't you been listening? The Imago can buffer themselves well enough, hide away for years, little nodes isolated from the social network that spans the globe."

"I don't want to kill them. I want to scare them off me forever. I want to threaten them with a fate worse than death."

"Which is."

"Boredom."

"Boredom?"

"Yes. Can't you see that all of the Imago's power, all of their freedom, all of their interest is inextricably tied to a world *peopled*. It is the bulwark against terminal *ennui*. They play their games, and live whichever life of luxury or perversity they desire. But they all, at bottom, depend on the toil of others. Without *others*, they are no better off than the next man, than an animal in the jungle."

He paused, his gaze became direct. "I forget who said: Millions long for eternal life who do not know what to do on a Sunday afternoon."

Cain stood.

"There is one thing that intrigues me still."

"I couldn't care less."

"You should. It is your gifting."

"My gifting?"

"Yes. What is it? My only fear in all of this was that I'd encounter, at the last, an empath. That would have been a tragedy. But you're clearly not that; I'm not the one tied up."

"Beats me," said Rasputin, and the truth stung.

Cain shrugged with genuine disappointment.

"It's time for me to go."

He placed the third vial, with its metallic parasite, on the bench.

Cain indicated the metal device, "This is a simple timer with a sprung mechanism. When the timer runs down in," he moved a switch on the side of the device, "fifteen minutes, a little hammer will strike the vial—that's 10:23 by that clock. There is a species of lobster that does something similar when predating prey holed up in bottles. The contents will disperse enough, I think, to infect you both. I daresay you will get loose from that cable eventually, but it has only to hold for a quarter of an hour."

He strode toward the door that led to the outer lab. Before leaving, he pivoted on the spot, and pointed behind himself at the glass door.

"That's where the camera crew will set up. I dare say they will contrive some way of giving you sustenance, but there is no one in the world will let you leave this room. A televised death is perhaps not what you had imagined for your future, but it is something. The Imago will watch, and know."

Cain entered the pass code, his fingers obscured by his back. The door opened, he looked back, tipped an imaginary hat, and left.

The silence that then descended was the heaviest Rasputin had ever known. It would take diamond to cut it. He wasn't sure he was up to it.

Dee had not moved since she had spat at Cain, not even to watch him go. She looked crushed. That alone was agony to see.

Rasputin shrugged his arms up and down. He had been going at it a for seven minutes that seemed like seven hours, enough perspiration gathering at his temples to drip down his cheeks, when Dee stirred.

"For how long has Reim been dead, do you think?" She said it so detachedly.

Rasputin kept shrugging and writhing. He matched her tone: "I guess from sometime after he called you at the farm."

"And Jordy?"

He didn't reply.

"What are you doing?" she said, with the same apathy.

He saved his breath, kept working at the cable.

"You'll never get it free in time."

He glanced at the vial. Before the blood had begun to roar in his ears, he had fancied he could hear the mechanism ticking. He pushed it from his mind, and shrugged more violently.

The cable was slipping ever so slightly. In seven minutes it had perhaps gone an inch down his trunk. (He wondered if this was what an antelope felt like as it beheld the boa's gaze.)

He needed another foot to free his arm.

He needed millimetres to reach his pocket, the pocket containing his knife.

With one last heave, stretching the cable to the extent his strength allowed, and with the slightest slippage, he was able to tuck his hand backwards and fish in his pocket. His fingers felt the smooth texture of the folded portrait of his sister, and below that, the cool surface of the knife's handle.

He drew it out, panicking for a moment as it slipped—to drop it now meant death. He manoeuvred it in his palm, his fingers working to turn it like a series of autonomous armatures, until it lay along his hand. He worked at the collapsed blade, awkwardly, pinching and pushing up with his thumb and index finger. It came open with a faint snapping sound.

He spent a handful of seconds to steady his nerves, and then began sawing on the cable.

Cain had looped it three times around their trunks. He felt each strand go—one, two, three—then the whole cord went lax.

He sprung up and untangled himself.

Dee sat, unmoving.

He began to speak, but, instead, put his arm around her, drew her up, and walked her away from the bench. She stood standing where he left her.

He went back to the vial, approaching it as if it were a coiled cobra.

"Better get this thing off," he said and picked up the vial.

He gripped it and was about to tug when Dee spoke.

"Wait! You don't know that it doesn't spring if tampered with."

That was true. He *hoped* it wouldn't, but hoping was not knowing.

"Okay. Then let's just get out of here."

As one, they whirled and hurried to the door. By the clock, they had six minutes left—if Cain had been telling the truth. But at the same moment they realised, absurdly, comically, that the ten-digit code was required not only to enter, but exit.

Rasputin laughed. *Is this what hysteria sounds like?*

Dee spun on the spot.

"Can we put it in the wet room?"

"Needs the code."

"What about the hatch?"

"I'm guessing it isn't air tight. Cain was right: that thing goes off in here and they're not letting us out."

"Fire alarm?"

"Probably lock-down."

She turned back to the door.

"Do you remember the code?" she said.

"The first three digits only—I didn't see the rest."

"How many goes do you get?"

"I don't think it matters. Couple of weeks ago I could have told you the odds on guessing a seven digit number."

"A couple of weeks ago you probably would have known the number."

His rueful smile collapsed as he saw the truth in that.

"Okay," he said.

"Okay, what?"

"Get the vial, and get ready to rip the timer off."

She ran to the vial, picked it up, holding it the way she had held Cain's gun.

"What are you going to do?" she said.

"Try the basement door."

Her look of puzzlement vanished as she evidently recalled their conversation in the car.

"What if it is locked?"

"We'll have to find a key."

He began to focus inwardly, not knowing how he could crack that inner world he could *feel*. It hovered, near but beneath an impermeable barrier through which his will would not seep.

"Wait," Dee said, interrupting his attempt to calm his mind.

"What?" he said, irritation riding over panic.

"What do you know of Reim? Perhaps there is a key."

Precious seconds merged with the past, as the clock's hand hastened around its face.

He knew he didn't know Reim's birthday, and even if he had, he wasn't sure how it could be turned into a ten-digit number.

Then an epiphany, a vision, filled his mind with its effulgence. He remembered the sunlit scene of the first day he had sailed with Reim, the coarse feel of the mainsheet in his palm, the smell of rotting kelp in his nostrils—and Reim's finger pinned to a brooch inscribed with a single Greek letter: the letter Pi.

Pi was a number.

"Pi!" he yelled in excitement.

He entered the number as fast as precision would allow: 3141592653.

Nothing happened for a moment. Then a speaker above the keypad bleeped denial.

He put a fist to his head and began pacing.

"Too easy," he said. "They probably wouldn't even let him use it."

"Another number, then? Something less famous?"

"No. It has to be something to do with Pi. It was close to an obsession with him, a career never followed. The number, its history, the people surrounding it. Pi was his special treasure, and a link with one of his sons. He knew it to the thousandth decimal place."

He punched his forehead.

"I'm an idiot. I know the first three digits of the pass-code. I saw Cain key them in: 101."

"Somewhere after the decimal place in Pi, then?"

"Yeah—Pi's irrational: it goes on forever behind the decimal point. Maybe it's a sequence in Pi's tail that starts with 101."

"That's your key."

He closed his eyes and began again to calm his mind. As he strove to empty it of competing thoughts, fear of the clock's progress kept disturbing him in little adrenaline loaded jabs. Each tick was a pebble tossed into a pool of water he desperately wanted still so he might see his reflection. Memories disturbed him too, from the farm, following hibernation, when he had first placed weight on his leg, and felt the familiar juddering run up it; the wild look in Reim-Cain's eyes that night in the darkened bowl of the front yard; Dee, slumped and trussed in the chair, emptied of vitality. These memories and countless others fluttered through his mind like night insects, leaving trails of disturbance on the surface of his mind.

What eventually drove him to inner stillness was the thought of the virus Cain had escaped with. Compared to that, his own life seemed ... small. The strength of that revelation liberated him from besetting distractions. His mind calmed.

The image of a solitary door formed.

He knew at once there was no impediment to opening it. It had no keyhole. He had but to open it and enter, and find what he needed.

He stretched out a hand, then hesitated.

He hunted for the source of the uneasiness that crept over him. Clues to it were impressed on the image of the door. The door had been impacted from behind. Red paint had flaked off its surface under the blows.

It was not a real door of course, merely a concrete-looking representation for an abstract idea, a tangible model for an intangible reality. Something had set a guard here. A queer smell wafted upon the air, as of something run amok, of rotting food. He toed ground that was slick, water mixed with oil, and tasted cordite at the back of his throat. Above all, he sensed dissolution.

In a flash of insight, he realised that he himself had set this guard.

Intuitively he had known that what he was attempting held danger, had known it within moments of waking from hibernation.

Cain's story had bolstered this caution. Those who returned to the dweoming well exposed themselves to risk. Those who habitually drank again of the water that had succoured the fertile ground of their mind to the gifting's harvest did not escape unscathed. In the final state, they became unhinged. They began to rave.

Rasputin's saw how right his sense of being de-centred from a vast machine had been. And now he was attempting to put himself back in the centre of things. Back into the machine.

He braced himself, a hand poised before the door's handle, fearing it to be live with a thousand volts. He gripped it, turned and entered.

The view that confronted him was both familiar and new. He was once again within the eye—the realisation thrilled him. But all was not well.

The eye appeared diseased. Its once clear lens was dimpled, glaucomal, and marred down one side by an arching vein of opacity. Its walls still fluxed, transmuted and became fluid, but the spiralling, liquescent arms it sent searching inward broke apart, shedding drops of great pulsing globules, black as basalt and glossy. They hung like so many rogue planets, obscuring his view.

Beyond the eye still floated his memories and every kind of mental particulate, a riot of colour cavorting undimmed, but it was a riot indeed. The stars had let go their constellations and roamed freely. The skeins of memory stuff linking one to another were intact, but snarled and tangled. It was as if a tornado had landed in the Smithsonian.

He watched the depths of his inner world and felt the sickness of impotency. He swore.

"Rasputin?" It was Dee's voice. It was pushed to a lower register, and wavered, as though travelling through churning water. "We only have five and half minutes."

"Make it five, to be safe," he replied, his voice sounding unfamiliar, as though he held books ajut his ears.

He ignored the chaos surrounding him, and focussed his will upon the eye itself.

He spoke, one split personality to another: "Find me Pi."

The eye began to turn, and soon lost any affinity with the ocular. The sphere contorted as the membrane lost even a vague semblance of coherence. The space within flattened as the top and bottom began to twist in different directions—he felt as if someone were grinding a boot in the bowl of his skull.

The pain became overwhelming. He withdrew his will.

The eye moved a moment longer, then bobbled and became still.

"Four and half minutes," said Dee.

"Shit."

He gritted his teeth and commanded: "Pi, now dammit."

The eye writhed again, and he writhed with it. Its motion sent shockwaves into the panoply of all he was, causing yet more turbulence among his mental detritus.

Gradually, the top of the eye lost its contrariness, slowed its counter-motion. It stopped, poised, and began to turn in the reverse direction. It caught up to the lower half, and the eye ballooned, regaining its spherical shape. He felt the pain slacken.

The eye began drinking the distance between it and an object. It sipped at it in fits and starts. The force of its passage drew other entities into its slipstream, to clash and juxtapose idiotically around him: a man in a shoe store pressed hard upon his big toe—"See, Mrs. Lowdermilk, one foot is longer than the other"; a wasp crawled over his arm stop-start, antennae twitching, mesmerising him until it unsheathed its sting; a snatch of his mother's voice, "Dear boy—"

These stray memories peppered his attention until the eye slammed into something vast. The impact split it open like an over-ripe water-melon, and its destruction spilled him into the void. He spun, floating, until by force of will he stilled himself, created a ground to stand on and a gravity to tie him to it.

Only then did he look for what he had collided with.

His mouth fell open. Towering over him was a creature of the menagerie tended by the man. It had the form of a dragon.

"Four minutes," said Dee.

Panic trilled on his nerves.

"I wanted a number not a dragon," he cried.

The dragon tilted its head, bringing a jewelled-eye the size of a Cadillac to bear on him.

"Might as well ask for space without time, little one," it said.

"It speaks!" he shrieked.

"Only the universal language."

Rasputin straightened up. He was done cowering in his own mind.

"I want a number, dragon. A ten-digit number. I think it is in your tail."

The beast glanced along its coiled form to its tail. The appendage sprouted, thick at its base, but did not taper. It wound away into the void's ink, diminishing only with distance.

"There are many numbers in my tail, and more besides; it still grows. Which ten digits in particular did you desire?"

"Reim's."

"I'm not familiar with that index."

"It's not an index. It's a name: Reim De Groot."

The creature blinked. The motion of its eyelids was like the raising and lowering of a mainsail.

"The first three digits of the number are 101," said Rasputin. "I just need the next seven. Does 101 occur in your tail?"

The dragon bared its teeth, in what Rasputin belatedly realised was a smile. Saliva dripped from a tooth like a stalactite, became vapour, and whorled chaotically out of existence before reaching the ground.

"That sequence of digits occurs three hundred and ninety million, six thousand, and twenty three—twenty four—times in my tail. Which occurrence would you like me to recite?"

Great, thought Rasputin: *Pi is a smartarse.*

He had a flash of inspiration.

"What is the ten digit sequence in your tail beginning at place 314?"

"1558817488" said the dragon, suddenly serious.

"No good. What about 3141?" Wrong. "31415?" Wrong.

Rasputin spoke to Dee. "It's no good. There are too many places in Pi's tail that start with 101. Any more ideas?"

She was silent a moment, while he listened to the vault of the dragon's lungs heave rhythmically, then: "Are you asking in decimal?"

"What?"

"Are you asking in base-10? 101 could be binary."

He turned again to the dragon.

"Try those places again, but with Pi represented in binary—only 1s and 0s."

The creature pondered.

A transformation rippled along its body, from snout to the base of its tail and onwards. Green scales shrank, became more numerous and red. Its eyes, colossal amethysts, became rubies. Its wings folded in on themselves, again and again, until they were mere stubs, and then disappeared. Its body now had the sinuous look of a snake.

"Yes, at position 3141: 1010010100," it said, in a voice perhaps an interval of a fifth higher than before.

Rasputin almost squealed with delight.

"Dee, try 1010010100."

He heard the strike of keys faintly, then the familiar bleep of denial.

"Damn." He said to the dragon, "Any more?"

Rasputin conveyed another four candidate numbers to Dee. All were incorrect.

"Two and half minutes," said Dee. In her panic, her voice sounded nearly normal pitch.

"Get ready to yank the timer," he said, heavy with foreboding.

"Alright dragon: check for 101 again in those positions, for Pi represented in base 3, 4, 5—keep going."

He reasoned that the occurrence of 101 at the special positions would diminish as the base got higher.

The dragon morphed from its red sinuous form to something more squat, and bright yellow. It began to recite numbers, and Rasputin dictated them to Dee. Before long it changed again. In that guise it had two numbers, before changing again. Thereafter it began to morph in silence, pausing only occasionally to utter a ten-digit number. Soon it was warping so fast it began to blur in a kaleidoscope of colour. Watching it made Rasputin nauseous.

Finally he held his palms up and yelled, "Stop!"

It did, and he could see it was pale purple with crystalline flanks. Crystal spires, stark as wintering trees, without membranes formed its wings. Each eye was a hollow lit with a wavering green flame.

"What base are you in?" said Rasputin, curiosity momentarily trumping panic.

"An imaginary number."

He wasn't sure what that meant, but it sounded impressive. No wonder he was developing a headache.

To himself he said, "Where are you Reim?"

The dragon startled him by morphing again into a comparatively orthodox form with multi-hued scales.

It said: "The sequence of letters r-e-i-m occurs in my tail at position 1011167941, if encoded with the minimal 5 bits."

Rasputin was dumbstruck. Of course, numbers could encode *letters*. Computers did it every day. He repeated the number to Dee. The denial bleep was a stab to his heart.

"We've got perhaps twenty seconds," she said.

The dragon surprised Rasputin by speaking unbidden. It told him the position of the sequence r-e-i-m-d-g.

Rasputin repeated it, blurring his pronunciation with haste.

Bleep.

"Ten seconds. I'm going to pull it."

"No. Wait!"

A thought was forming. Too slowly, but there was something ...

Within the lesser love, is set the greater.

He turned to the dragon.

"Myrtle De Groot. His wife, m-y-r-t-l-e. Does that exist?"

The dragon paused for an infuriating second.

"Yes. Position 1015689788."

"I'm going to pull it," said Dee.

"No. Please. Trust me Dee—1015689788. If I'm wrong, then pull it."

It had to be right, didn't it? Or had he doomed them both?

He heard key presses. 1, 2, 3 … 10. A pause.

A click.

A hiss.

The door was opening.

He heaved himself out of within by a disorienting lunge for the surface, and into the real world.

The door stood open. Dee still held the vial.

"Put it down, carefully. We have to shut the door."

Dee placed the vial on the bench with slowed haste, and beat a path through the doorway. In the corridor, Rasputin fumbled after the button that would secure the door.

It clicked, thought about closing, then slid shut and sealed with a hiss.

Through the pane of glass, they watched as the vial jumped almost imperceptibly, as though it had hiccupped. Cracks laced its side, and the liquid within leaked onto the desk in a tiny pool.

"That's one deadly puddle," said Rasputin, turned his back to the door, and slid down it, exhausted.

Dee followed. "Where did you get the number," she said, her expression somehow both vacant and harrowed.

"Reim loved Pi. But of course he wouldn't look for himself within it. He might look for the wife he loved—someone cherished set within something cherished."

"*Might?*"

The light returned to her eyes and she punched him in the arm.

They sat in silence, beneath the fluorescent green glow, content to be alive.

A minute passed, then he said, "We have to find him."

Dee put up no argument.

It was when they rose, and stood leaning against the door, that Rasputin's phone rang.

There was no caller id. Dee shrugged. Rasputin picked up the call. "Dee? Monk?"

"*Jordy?*" Rasputin said.

Dee ripped the phone from his grasp.

"Jordan?!"

Rasputin reached across her and put the call on speaker.

"Dee?—yes, yes, it's me. Dee: I love you."

Her voice choked on a great sob. "I love you, too."

Rasputin pretended to stick a finger down his throat and said, "Don't get the phone wet." He leaned near the phone. "Where are you? What happened?"

"Your phone has been out of reach. It only just got signal, and began to upload a bug payload. I'm at Reim's place," he said, causing Dee and Rasputin to glance at each other in alarm.

"Well get the hell out of there," said Rasputin. "He's probably on his way there right now."

"I can't. I'm trussed like a Christmas turkey, and anyway—he's not coming. I know where he is."

"How?" they said in unison.

"I'm sitting at Hitler's laptop. It's the base station for his bugs."

"Bugs?"

"Yes, the one you're carrying, and another—for listening to yours. The laptop receives your payload and retransmits it to his mobile listening device, only ..." Jordy fell silent, and the pause was filled with the sound of key presses. "Data comes downstream from his phone too. There is a third channel spliced into all of this mess."

Rasputin shook his head, unable to follow it. The thought of Cain free was pressing on him.

310

"But you know where he is," he said.

"Yes. He's been parked in Winthrop Hall for a quarter of an hour."

"Okay. Call the cops. Tell them about the lab here. Tell them there's something very nasty locked inside, and they must not open it. Got it?"

"I already have. They took some convincing I wasn't some New Year's drunk. What are you going to do?"

"Go after Cain."

"Not with Dee, you're not."

Dee attempted to interject, "You don't know—"

"Don't know what, Dee?" said Jordy. "I know enough. I was listening." He broke off, and Rasputin heard an unfamiliar sound. His best friend sobbed.

Rasputin was puzzled a moment, then: "Cain's phone was transmitting?"

"Yes," Jordy managed, sounding as though it were a struggle to speak.

The scene in the lab had been bad enough as a participant; being audience to it must have been a peculiar kind of torture.

"If his phone had signal, why didn't mine?"

"I don't know. It'd be weak down where you are. Are your pockets lined with metal?" It wasn't a serious question, but Rasputin touched his pocket and felt the solid form of the gun through his jeans pocket. Being on the outside of the lab door must have pushed the signal strength across the threshold.

"Forget it. I'll go after him," said Rasputin.

"Wait for the police, Monk," said Jordy.

"No. If he gets even a whiff of them—blue lights and noise—who knows what he'll do. Best case he'll slip out of here easy as oil off grease. Worst case he'll get apocalyptic and crack open one of his vials for them."

Rasputin paused to gather his courage. "The last thing he'll expect is me."

"Rasputin," said Dee. "He still has his phone. He'll know we're out."

"No, he wont," said Jordy, his voice laced with regret. "The entire payload from within the lab—your escape—began uploading when you got out. But I killed the upload. As far as Hitler's concerned, you still don't have signal, you're stuck in the lab."

"That's it then," said Rasputin, and strode down the corridor.

Dee followed, speaking to Jordy. "Is Reim there with you?"

Rasputin winced. It was a long shot. When it fell short, it was going to hurt.

"Yes," said Jordy. "He's dead. I saw him die."

Rasputin halted at the door to the outer lab.

"Monk," said Jordy. Rasputin took the phone, brought it near. "He went with unbroken spirit. I only knew him for a few days, really, but he was made of something special. He didn't just roll over. When he saw what Hitler was, what he could do, what he was *doing*, he tried everything to undermine his disguise."

Rasputin thought back to the gaff that had given Cain away. Had Reim authored that ...?

"I think you're right," said Rasputin. "I never met someone so full of life, and so ready to die."

"How did you end up at Reim's?" said Dee.

"I told you I was going to unpick that phone. It was the only lead in this bizarre mess. I succeeded. Pity it turned out to be the tripwire on a trapdoor spider's nest. It led to Reim's place, where Hitler met me at the door and straight-out clubbed me."

"We're wasting time," said Rasputin. "He might leave any time. Where is he, *exactly*."

"An alcove behind the pipe organ, best I can tell. The hall's big stained glass windows would be letting in enough satellite signal to fix a location. And it's live signal, not dead-reckoned."

Dee broke into their conversation. "And if you find him? What then? Rasputin, he's a strong man—we know that. You're a cripple."

For the thousandth time, Rasputin cursed his ineffectual hibernation.

To Dee he said, "But I have this." He withdrew Cain's gun and mimed taking a pot shot at her.

"It's empty," she said.

"He doesn't know that."

"But—"

"Enough talk," he said, stuffed the gun beneath his belt, and exited the corridor.

Escape from the outer lab required only that a button be pressed. They soon emerged onto the darkened front steps of the biology faculty. The night air was balmy, and full of the scent of exotic flowers.

"What am I supposed to do?" said Dee. "Sit here, wave a handkerchief? Wring my hands?" Her hands were planted on her hips, elbows ajut, normally a sure sign he had kicked the hornet's nest. But tonight he would not yield.

"No. Go make sure of Jordy. Call a taxi. Break a window, if you have to, and get him out. With luck the cops might be waiting when you get there."

Her rigidity evaporated, and she suddenly looked small in the gloom.

"Promise me you won't do anything stupid," she said. "If you find him, stay out of sight until help comes."

"Sure. I'm an Arts student. If I find him, I'll hang back and ponder the paradox of the paralysis of violent emotion." He flashed her a grin.

He left her, a prayer on his lips for her safety, and struck out toward Winthrop Hall. Even for one unfamiliar with the campus, even at night, the hall was an easy mark. Its square tower loomed above the buildings and trees.

He tested the gun, making sure it sat snug, and hurried as best he could over a lawn slick with moisture from sprinklers.

His heart thumped louder than he recalled it ever having done. He strained for touch with his identity—the night, his flight through it, his destination, felt surreal. All conspired to render him a stranger to himself, a watcher of someone else's plight.

When he reached the tropical grove just south of the hall, he sunk onto his haunches in the deep dark beneath its boughs, amidst perfumed blooms like ragged paper, and cast a searching eye over the grounds. The hall lay no more than fifty yards away. Between it and the garden lay a bare lawn. It took little effort to imagine the hall an old keep, the garden, where he crouched, an encircling forest, and the lawn a *glacis*, a buffer to thwart besieging armies.

But tonight there were no armies, just one man versus another, and the order of the day was stealth not force—at least, that was his hope.

It was only when his leg began to complain, and he hauled himself upright on his cane, that he saw the movement. Beneath the hall was an undercroft, a long low room. Light spilled from its windows, and people were milling near an entrance. Peals of laughter like thunder filtered out, and the unmistakable ring of glass on glass.

"A party?" he whispered. The festive mood, so near yet as untouchable as a parallel universe, threatened him with that overwhelming sense of surreality. He fought it and focused his gaze on the people milling at the far fringe of the lawn.

He interpreted their groupings: one huddle of men and a woman were workmates; one, two couples in farther orbits were yearning for the seclusion of darkness; one man alone, warming himself with his arms, had a melancholic stance—another New Year's and what have I done with my life, perhaps?

The coast looked clear. He straightened up to his full height and forced himself to walk as casually as he could on his cane up a gentle slope toward the hall's entrance. He padded along a colonnade of carved limestone to where the hall's double-doors stood open. He paused in the deep darkness of its anteroom and considered the best course. Cain could be anywhere in there—and what on earth was he doing?

On instinct, he ducked across the threshold and snuck up a flight of steps that accessed the gallery level. It afforded a view of the whole hall and, he hoped, the alcove behind the organ.

The going was hard. He was hunched below the rim of the balcony wall at the front of the gallery level, straining to be quiet, and all the while dredging his mind for remembrance of the hall's exits.

An urge took him suddenly, to throw himself into the eye—surely it held schematics of the hall by which he might examine any conceivable breakdown. Resisting the temptation took such an effort he was forced to halt until it had passed.

It was when he moved again that a vague memory—a memory of the old-fashioned sort—of having passed into the hall from the undercroft came to him. The occasion had been a book sale held down there. He had discovered the passage that communicated with the hall while carrying a box of books too heavy to be exploring with.

He held the thought of that passage to a room lit and peopled, like a child grasping a torch beneath the covers—help was near.

He reached a point on the gallery level overlooking the stage. On one side of it sat a keyboard, and reaching up behind it, standing in diminishing ranks, were the pipes that gave voice to the keys. The deepest notes would come from tubes thicker than a man. (Perhaps Cain would stuff his dead body in one, to be discovered when someone next attempted The Ride of the Valkyries.) Rasputin knew from having attended Dee's graduation that the instrument possessed an overwhelming power of soul-sapping lugubriousness—a reality-check for bright-eyed graduates.

He realised then that the end of the gallery on his side terminated not in a dead-end, but a flight of stairs. He guessed they landed somewhere behind the keyboard and its alcove.

He went down on all fours, slowing almost to a halt. His cane rapped lightly on the wooden floor.

May as well sound the organ, he thought, grimacing. He laid it aside and went on without it.

He reached the lip of the stairs.

I just need a glimpse. Just to lay eyes on him and that'll be enough. Then hunker down, surveil. Make sure he doesn't scarper before help comes.

It was as he inched himself down the first stair, hands planted and lowering his rump from one to the next, that he heard the faintest *click*.

He froze.

Silence stretched out. He lowered himself down another step, stopped, straining to listen, and soon heard another clicking, scratching sound.

He had reached the stair's only right angle. Once he rounded it, he would have a direct path into the alcove. He drew a steadying breath and lifted himself, head tilted, till he could see over the balustrade and into the alcove.

Starlight came warped through a massive wheel of stained glass above the pipes. White keys gleamed in the dark, lying in terraces, and broken by half-tone blacks. Rasputin was still, poised, feeling his arms begin to tremble with the strain, willing his eyes to see into the pool of darkness.

He could not be sure, but he thought it was empty.

He lowered himself down the remaining steps carefully, and froze in the process of peering round the stair's foot. The scritching, scratching sound had to be coming from within the alcove.

Was Cain holed up under the keyboard? Was he injured? Perhaps he had run into the police?

Rasputin poked his head round the corner, and this time saw a small bundle sitting beneath the keyboard, on the foot pedals.

He let a guilty sigh leach through his teeth. Cain wasn't here.

He rose, crossed the few feet to the keyboard, stooped and grasped the bundle. He drew it out and held it close to see it in the poor light. As he did so, the bundle emitted a scratching sound. It startled him and he almost dropped it.

He paused.

It became silent.

He took a step backward. Three seconds later, the bundle emitted another sound.

He dug his hand into its soft folds and found something hard. He drew it out, and light began to dawn—and on its heels fear.

He held in his hand the phone that was partner to his. Through it, he had been hearing echoes of the motion of the phone in his own pocket, sent through the cell network to the laptop at Reim's house, then bounced back to this phone. It had been wrapped in a woollen cardigan. Reim's woollen cardigan.

He turned in time to see someone approach, their silhouette disappearing as the door to the undercroft swung closed behind. It had not looked like Reim's.

"You've changed," said Rasputin.

Cain shivered despite the warm evening. It stuttered his speech. "No point being a dead professor, wanted for the theft of a biological weapon."

"What are you talking about?" said Rasputin, and, to his surprise, felt a flush of anger heat his face. He ripped the gun from his belt and brandished it.

"Talk. I've got a gun."

Cain raised his hands, but Rasputin saw his smile glint.

"Shot with my own gun. How embarrassing."

Rasputin flicked the gun with a theatrical gesture.

"Okay," said Cain. "When the police raid your professor's home tonight they will find him not-long dead, the victim of someone else's greed. He was, after all, playing a high-stakes game. The virus will be missing, and the police will not know if he hid it before he died, or if it has been stolen for the second time this evening."

The point of the gun dropped as Rasputin struggled to process what Cain was saying. He didn't like the way he spoke of the thing as accomplished. Coming to himself, he jerked the barrel upright again.

His eyes were finally adjusting to the darkness. He began to make out Cain's new face.

"Who are you?" said Rasputin.

"I've already told you, at great length I might add."

"What mask is this?"

"You are looking at the form of a man once known as Gottfried Schürmann."

"Why that face?"

"Because it is the easiest for me to find when in a hurry. Your little stunt in the lab caused that hurry."

Fear jabbed Rasputin's guts.

"Adapt or die," said Cain. "Your professor had a lab within a lab. I have a bug within a bug. The one who invented it is the best, or so he brags."

The smile on Cain's Teutonic features touched his entire face.

He went on. "The police have been informed of Jordan's hoax call. I convinced them not to press charges. I suppose they will scour the recording of my call in weeks to come for clues to the thief and murderer at-large. You and I know it won't help a great deal, will it."

"Where will you be?"

"Mourning my best friend and my girlfriend."

Rasputin took a moment to comprehend, and then shouted, "I'll do it. I'll shoot."

"Hush! If you must threaten idly, do it quietly."

Rasputin jabbed the gun forward.

"You think I won't?"

"I think you can't."

Cain reached and inserted his index finger into the gun's barrel.

"I dare say you could give me a nasty bruise if you threw it at me, but it would be much more effective if loaded."

Cain withdrew his finger from the gun. The movement made a faint sound, like a bubble disappearing down a drain.

He said, "Wouldn't you expect the ultimate chameleon to be able to play dead? I heard you dispose of the bullets."

Cain's genial tone was beginning to wear thin. Beneath it, Rasputin could hear naked spite.

"Do you hate me that much you'd kill so many people just to spite me? Why not finish the job now. Then run, hide, lay low. You don't need to go on murdering."

"I don't hate you any more than the next. And I do intend to hide, lay low. Running would be disastrous. I'm no idiot. This"—he patted his pockets—"will jangle bells right at the top of the tree. Perth, Australia, might be the rear-end of the world, but when the shit hits the fan, your little city won't know itself. There will be a frenzy. They trusted to obfuscation to hide Pandora's Box, and will now see how foolish that was."

He chuckled. "To think, all I wanted in the beginning was a dweomer to kill. Do you know how many reports of savant-like behaviour I sifted through before I found you? Thousands. The gift inexorably manifests—your name appeared on an application for a medical procedure for research, submitted by a Professor Thorpe, if I remember correctly. I dispatched over a hundred phones, and surveilled them for the telltale signs of an imago."

"And here I am," said Cain. "Such are the twisted skeins of Fate."

"No. Tomorrow there will rise a storm, but I will be sitting in the last place they will think to look: right in the middle. I will adapt. As Jordan I will mourn. I'll try to piece together how and when the people dearest to me became entangled in a plot so dark. Folks will mark the deadness of my gaze, and gossip about it over café lunches. I will travel. And when I disappear, they will suspect suicide, and the gossip will shift to Jordan's parents."

Rasputin's blank exterior masked a frenzy of thought. He hunted for something to stall Cain, some spanner to throw into the cogs that threatened to grind him to nothing. But every alley turned blind. His own mind was becoming Cain's advocate. Why bother, it whispered, he is omniscient. He will have thought of it, covered it. You are smothered in web. You just don't know it. Be still and preserve the dignity of the dying.

Cain swept the alcove with his gaze, the vaulted ceiling of the hall, and lastly the wheel of stained glass, and the stars aflame beyond it.

"It is an evocative scene, a good place to die." He spoke as connoisseur savouring a vintage, an artist judging a composition.

The tone of his voice, its tremulous ecstasy, sparked Rasputin's memory. He had heard that same tone, those inflections, at moments during Cain's telling of his story in the lab—when panic had ebbed enough for him to attend to it. It had been woven through his monologue, dipping in and out of the mundanity and brutality, to glint like a golden thread through a pauper's mat.

This fervour—this *mysterion*—had surfaced most clearly in Cain's brief account of his visit to the bank in Zurich, to a safety deposit box. He had taken a man's life as a pretence just to fondle a painting—he had admitted as much.

Cain came a step closer. Rasputin smelled his sweat in the dusty air.

Rasputin could not reconcile this man-thing, blood fresh on his hands, with the aesthete his voice betrayed.

"You sniff at the Imago and their games," said Rasputin, "but what will you be doing on that Sunday afternoon a decade from now?"

Cain halted. He straightened his back and hooked his lips in a half-smile. His right hand reached to grasp his chin in the fork of thumb and fingers. The hand bore a dark stain, and he winced as he stroked his cheek.

"Good. Good," he said, and Rasputin felt the burn of that gaze now appraising him. "That's the real question isn't it: What is worth one's time? Not just today or tomorrow, but for Eternity. What is worth one's sustained scrutiny? One's intellect? Loyalty? Labour? Love? What will bear the flame of their focus, and, under it, neither diminish nor be consumed?"

"Yes, what?" The words burst from Rasputin in a geyser. He could not stifle them, nor hide their iron-hard sincerity. Tears stung his eyes—*not now! Not here!*

"See," said Cain. "I knew you were a kindred spirit. Fit brother for me." He said it with unfeigned kindness.

He glanced again at the window, as if reading the time there.

"I must go. Your friend won't find it so easy to free Jordan from his bonds. They were intended to last. But I will not leave too much to chance. His escape would be a tiresome mess to remedy."

Rasputin tensed.

"But, to your question, my provisional answer: during the war, many artworks passed under my nose in my role with the KunstSchutz. It was a heaven for an art historian, for one concerned to trace the expression of man's most sublime thoughts, and struggles to express the inexpressible: to capture eternity in time. One piece gripped me

320

like no other: Bacchiacca's interpretation of the myth of Leda and the Swan. The story goes that Zeus, in the guise of a swan, seduced Leda and raped her. By him she bore five eggs. The painting depicts her five sons amidst a wreck of eggshell, and behind them, Zeus-as-swan taking succour from Leda's breast. ... and Leda."

Cain's breath caught. He was gazing again into the heavens.

"I stole it, had it diverted before reaching Goering, who had ear-marked it."

Cain returned his gaze to Rasputin.

"Imagine my surprise then to find that painting hanging in the galleries of the Metropolitan Museum, sixty-odd years after having first laid eyes on it. No, I did not quite tell you all that has transpired in my life these past months. I awoke a kid in a candy store."

Cain reached across his body into his pocket with his left hand, and from it pulled a handkerchief. He dabbed his eyes.

"Leda was captured by the Americans where she lay in storage in a subterranean salt mine at the end of the war. The museum knows of the painting's shadowed provenance. When I found it, I sat beneath it for hours. I sat beneath her like one of her sons." He chuckled in reminiscence. "I have often put myself in the picture, as the son who sits at his mother's feet. But that son is blind. Half of his shell sits upon his head like an over-sized hat. He sits in the presence of profound beauty, but all he can see is what he has ever seen: the inside of his shell."

"Is that your answer?" said Rasputin: "A woman?"

"A woman?" Cain scowled. "No, not *a woman:* every woman." He shook his head violently, as though arguing with himself. "No, not every woman: whatever it is that shines but rarely, imperfectly, in the face of a woman—and even there, dies, vanishes in a moment. The most sublime art captures but its trace, this presence that obtrudes into our rude existence with its—" His shoulders hitched, his hands became claws "—*beauty?* I lack even a word for what would be worthy of worship for all eternity."

His shoulders slumped as the tension left him. "If only I could find it ... and hold it."

"That flame of yearning," said Rasputin, "burns in every man. Not just you. Someone I knew called it *Par Inust*: the Burning Within."

"That is incorrect," said Cain. "Your friend failed to construe his Latin, but perhaps he spoke better than he knew. It should be in the past tense. *Par Inust* is Burnt Within. And no, not everyone is burnt within. A precious few, in fact. But we are."

Cain appeared to return to the moment. "You see now that my quest for immortality, predicated on ultimate adaptability, is but a necessary condition to the real search. The search for unquenchable meaning."

"I do see," said Rasputin. "But I cannot let you continue to pursue it at the cost of others."

Cain tilted his head and squinted. Rasputin saw again in his face the cruelty that wonder had momentarily eclipsed.

"Who will stop me? Certainly not you—you, a boy, and a cripple." Cain tensed and coiled to strike. "Come. Let's have done with it. I want to know if your neck is a *pop* or a *snap*."

Rasputin flung the gun at Cain's face, and while Cain raised an arm to ward it off, grasped his pocketknife and flicked it open. He brought it up before him.

The gun had struck Cain a glancing blow. It deflected from his forearm and clattered down the stairs leading to the undercroft, and was lost in the gloom.

When Cain's eyes fixed on him again, he saw the knife in Rasputin's hand. He barked laughter.

"You going to stick me with that pin?" he snarled.

"No."

An idea had been for some time forming. It had begun earlier that same day, when he had awoken from hibernation to find nothing had changed. Then it had been merely the precursor to thought, an *inkling*—some part of his mind worrying out of view like a dog at a bone.

That bone was the realisation that his portal back into the world had been his sister, or, more precisely, that he believed his sister to have forgiven him.

This fact had been let loose into the currents of his subconscious, to be joined by another: Cain's speculation about what fuelled an imago's transformation—their heart's deepest desire.

Finally, upon seeing Cain's marred hand—a stain that persisted after his *changing*—the idea had been birthed into his conscious mind. And he had seen its truth. All his life he had been looking for an altar on which to lie.

Cain lunged at Rasputin.

Rasputin hooked his free hand around the man's back and hugged him with all his strength. Cain's hands found his neck and began to throttle his airway.

With his free hand, the one holding the blade, Rasputin found his own ribs. He slid the knife across them, like one swiping a glockenspiel, found a space, and drove it home.

The pain was like nothing he had ever felt or imagined—it was so *deep*. It threatened to drive the purpose from his mind.

He pitched forward, pushing Cain, and together they fell to the floor, limbs tangled, Rasputin atop Cain.

A warm, wetness spread rapidly across his chest. His heart was pumping the lifeblood from his body.

Cain went still, like a night-creature tasting the first hint of danger on the air. Then he began to scream, and Rasputin knew his blood was flowing out and over the man.

Cain's hands left Rasputin's neck, and he began to writhe, attempting to dislodge him. But Rasputin spread his weight and bore down with every ounce of strength he had.

The screams rose and the sound swallowed his senses.

Cain's struggles reached a peak, teetered there for what seemed an eternity, and began to ebb. His cries became wet, gurgling and guttural.

Rasputin's strength began to ebb too. The pain had diminished until it was simply the reminder of something awry.

Cain became still.

Rasputin's vision began to fail. He felt warm. He rolled off Cain's body, onto his back on the smooth floor. He arched his head in search of the window. He thought he would like to see stars one more time, even if stained green and red by the glass.

15.

RASPUTIN

Rasputin had let the current take him.

It had swept Reim's little craft near the Narrows Bridge. But now he needed somewhere calm and out of the way of river traffic. He raised the sail, drew the mainsheet taught and nudged the rudder. The bow spun until it pointed at the shallow water near the freeway.

There was little wind, and few craft plying it. He sailed to where the smell of dead seaweed filled his nostrils and dropped the small drag anchor. An intense nostalgia assaulted him. He remembered Reim.

He drew the sail in again, then sat square to the bow, hands hanging limp over his knees.

It was five weeks since Reim had died. Five weeks since he had nearly died.

He tallied how the world had changed in that time.

Dee and Jordy were engaged. It had been a long time coming, but events had served as catalyst. Only one thing marred Rasputin's joy at the prospect of his two best friends tying the knot—the thought of giving the speech. Beyond making fun of Jordy, which was almost a hobby in any case, Rasputin feared hitting the serious note. He'd witnessed the moment that had clinched it for Dee and Jordy on the safe side of a lab doorway—it recurred all too vividly in troubled dreams that were always lit a pale green.

Every day, it seemed, prodded him with some memory of that night.

That morning it had been Sam, now a full-fledged ASIO agent. He had first called to talk about the virus a week after it had been stolen—not so sluggish for ASIO—having been assigned to the task force investigating its theft because of his previous association with Rasputin. He called most days, crosschecking a detail or testing a theory.

Rasputin raised his eyes to squint at the distant shore, and, jutting above the tree line, the silhouette of Winthrop Hall's tower. Unlike the scene of his accident, he had no desire to ever set foot again in the hall.

The virus had not been found, because Cain's lifeless body had not been found. Rasputin had awoken in intensive care following their struggle to be told by Dee that he had been found alone in the alcove, lying in a pool of blood.

Dee had reached Reim's house quickly, but, as predicted, had made slow headway freeing Jordy from steel bonds. They had waited in vain for the police to arrive. What had arrived instead was a telephone call from the security agency charged with care of the C2 facility. The agency had been alerted by notification of repeated failed attempts to exit the lab—albeit with a mysterious delay. They had called Reim as point of course, and then investigated. Fortunately, the broken vial had been seen before anyone had entered the lab.

In an aside, Sam had informed him that Thorpe's indictment was stalled. The surgeon had left Australia for the States. Sam thought he intended to attach himself to a university there.

Rasputin's tangle with Thorpe seemed so long ago it lacked the power to frighten him anymore. He wondered what the surgeon's leaving meant for his brother, Joachim Thorpe, who still lay flesh-bound in Shenton Park. He felt a stab of pity for both men.

He let his gaze wander along the shores of the Swan. Cars sped, as always, along the road beneath King Park's frowning bluff. No one could reach him out on the water. He no longer carried a mobile phone.

The device had stopped working after delivering its final communiqué. It had died following a brief period of decay, as though it had reached its programmed shelf-life. When Jordy pried it open to look for the cause of the problem, he found pink stains etched into its circuits, as if some corrosive agent had burst within it.

Its last message had filled some gaps:

"I know what you are now, possessor of a most peculiar gift. But not one I need fear, unless I am foolish enough to open one of your veins.

I have let the Imago believe that you and Cain perished, each at the hand of the other. Do not draw attention to yourself and they will remain unaware of their error.

It was necessary for me to remove Cain's body. I'm sure you will evolve a story for your authorities that is compelling, or at least confusing, enough to satisfy them.

For the record (although there will be none) I am glad you were the victor. Cain aimed at a title that is mine: the ultimate chameleon. What he attempted to do in flesh, I achieve in an intangible medium. In truth, he deserved to lose. He used the tools of espionage, but did not stop to think—like the true spy—that if a bug can be conveniently hidden within a bug, why not a bug within a bug within a bug? (Even your friend, Jordy, noticed my splice-in.) It all made for a great show.

With heartfelt thanks and best wishes, C. "

True enough, their story, though filled with inexplicable holes, had finally been accepted. Or rather, it had been accepted that they—Rasputin, Dee and Jordy—believed it. They had agreed to state that a man disguised as their friend Reim De Groot had duped them. This was supported by the lab's security camera. The Reim-look-alike had escaped, leaving the real Reim dead. Thus they had salvaged Reim's reputation and come as close as they could to the truth. Anything more would have seemed ludicrous.

But in the long hours of recovery Rasputin endured while his body mended, his thoughts kept spiralling into one pit: what did it mean?

Yes, he had gained the abiding ability to access the inner eye. But in the intervening weeks, he had begun to feel its poison, that which sent weaker Imago ravening in their minds.

He had entered the eye on a handful of occasions for mere peccadilloes. And each time, its atmosphere had felt a little more rarefied, like supercharged air. It had begun positively to *hurt* just to be within, as though his nerves were aflame from lack of oxygen.

This danger was trebled when combined with how intoxicating it was to be within. The eye, despite being damaged, chaotic, no longer driven by the purpose of calculating and effecting the change, was still a marvel. The knowledge it had knit and would sell for snippets of one's sanity. Rasputin imagined the strain akin to waking one morning with an addiction to alcohol and the taps running with beer.

He had steeled himself to leave the door to the basement of his mind closed.

And sealed himself to his pledge by divulging it to Dee and Jordy. And yet ...

He now felt the need for one final dip, one more dive into the magic waters. Hence this trip in Reim's yacht, to where he could be alone and unmolested.

What did it all mean?

As he had lain in intensive care, and later in a normal ward, he had listened to the machines hooked up to him. The bleep-bleep of the pulse monitor, the occasional whoosh and hiss of the automatic blood pressure machine. Each read his body for its life signs.

Lying there, trapped within circling thoughts, he had formed an idea: why not read himself? Take the plunge, go deeper than ever before, perhaps all the way to the beginning—and there read himself?

No doubt the eye had continued reaching its fingers into all there was of him. Its web would have drifted wider and wider, and *deeper* into his past, in the complete archaeology of Rasputin. Perhaps it had reached back to his inception.

It was worth a try. A final time in the eye, he swore to himself.

He closed his eyes and quieted his mind. He felt the sun warm his skin, and heard the lap of water on the boat's hull. The faintest of breezes feathered his hair.

The door to the basement of his mind stood vivid in his imagination. He turned the handle. The door had been easier to open each time he tried it. Perhaps if he kept at it, it would begin to open of its own accord and suck him thither against his will, to rave …

He stepped over its threshold and entered the eye.

Its atmosphere immediately crackled in his ears and fizzed against his skin. A curiously delicious pain.

Staring up into the vault of his mind, he saw nothing was as he had left it. It never was anymore. Celestial warfare was waged while he slept, ate, and, he guessed, shat. Knowledge grew, ate old, imperfect knowledge, and gave birth to new. But lacking a guiding hand, as before the changing, the result could not be called ordered.

The dweoming tree had grown, dropped its precious fruit, and now grew wild.

Rasputin set himself, and formed a command never before given to the eye. He spoke: "Go back." The command desired no particular memory, no information, no feeling, but the past, as far back as it existed for the one called Rasputin.

He staggered beneath the weight of the drain on his strength. It was an energy-hungry load dropped on a fragile grid, dimming the lights in blocks across his mind.

But grudgingly the flotsam began to flow. Near memories—of today, and yesterday—the fastest, older memories more slowly, layered in banks of parallax.

He realised with a jolt that it was not the eye that spun. It was the entire heavens.

The whorling mental detritus began to part over him and bend downward in a roar that made Niagara a whisper. The farther from the eye, the faster the memory-stuff fell, until all had dropped below the horizon, leaving only the most recent memories circling before him, spinning at such a speed they began to blur into a ribbon of shifting colour.

The transformation continued, and the colossal energy drain of extruding his entire memory into a kind of internal geological column peaked. Pain lanced his head, and, casting a glance at the real-world, he saw that his higher consciousness had blacked-out. His body must be sprawled in the bottom of the boat.

All the while his mind continued to spin, pressing down on him. He was a pilot banking at Mach-1, being flattened by jet-powered G-forces.

"Go back," he said again, the commanding tone replaced by pleading. It did.

Memory by memory, link by link, he clawed his way down the chain of experience that dangled into his past, perhaps to the inception of his being.

Wetness brushed his cheek, and he saw twisting black feelers like waterspouts intrude from the eye's walls, thick at the wall and tapering in to a point. Each was a miniature of the vast spout down which he travelled, and each licked his face with its point and travelled chaotically over his body, tracing lines that left his skin burning in their passage.

From outside the eye, through a hash of unintelligible sight and sound, came snatches of voice and images he recognised. So much he had forgotten. A boy's face appeared and tumbled at cross-speed with the vortex wall. To Rasputin he was a stranger, and in the same instant, recognised: a friend from school whom he had forgotten ever existed. Rasputin had played many times at the boy's house. Its backyard had a cage for Newfoundland dogs.

The burning sensation on his skin intensified the further he fell, as though the friction of falling, a meteorite in his own atmosphere, were goading his flesh to fire. He was a flame travelling a fuse. Where he burnt was somehow changed, used.

He continued to slide down the mouth of his memories. The wall began to change colour subtly. It drifted from its broad palette, tied-dyed from every colour, into primary colours.

He felt in his stomach the speed of his plummet slow, and then abruptly, as though a blind were pulled over the only window on the sun, darkness.

He continued to fall still more slowly, until he was drifting down in the dark, alone in a diving bell approaching the sun-starved floor of the Pacific.

All was silent, save for a deep throbbing sound. It beat rhythmically on the eye's membrane. With every blow of the sound front, his chest cavity resonated.

He smiled, oblivious to the fire licking his flesh, wreathing his face. He realised where he was.

"More than I hoped possible."

The rhythmic sound grew to a roar, as at last he felt the eye touch down, and begin to settle. His body again had weight.

He peered through streamers of light coiling from his flesh. They were the only source of illumination but served only to deepen the darkness without. Elation at how far he had come ebbed and gave way to a poignant sense of loss. There was, after all, nothing there. No answer. No meaning.

For the second time since the accident he faced the temptation to make of his body a grave.

Then a glimmer appeared.

It was so slight, he could not at first be sure it wasn't some trick of the eye. It was as the first paling of dawn, far off, bringing the subtlest waning of the deep of night rather than the intrusion of light.

Then, in an instant, he fell through the floor of the eye and was immersed in a well of light so intense it pried open his shut lids, and bored into every particle of his being. It pervaded and suffused him. Destroyed Shadow. Laid bare.

In that moment, he feared the horror of annihilation—not of the vacuum of space, the nothing, but of the crushing glory of *everything*. He yearned to cower, to fold himself into a ball, but could not.

He could not later recall how the words came to him. Whether he heard them whispered in his ear, or carried them there himself as he came dangling into the darkness in a cage wrought of his own consciousness. Perhaps they had followed him down of their own accord, a tatter of memory fluttering in the life-vortex's tumult like a banner let loose on the breeze—or the sole scrap to fly free of the burning house.

They formed a single sentence, and he clung to it as though it were the point about which his being might coagulate and be. He hid behind it as if it might shield him from the light he felt threatened to rape him to nothingness like a wind-scoured dandelion.

It said: *I desire mercy not sacrifice.*

A message of power and content.

Then darkness wrapped him again, and he felt himself rising.

He heard the memory of his heart beat again on the eye.

The vortex had ceased to spiral. The entirety of his memory was fixed in a vertical gallery, past which he drifted as he rose.

Only once in his journey did he pause. He wanted only to be awake again, and in the real world, to forsake this too-rare air.

What made him pause were more words, which came like the first—which is to say he knew not how: "You no longer need this; but here, a gift."

He spun on the gentlest eddy to see a memory collage drifting past him. Parts of it were familiar, but even those were rendered new by their context—an unbroken tissue, clear and bright, no longer disjoint, unordered, and unparsed as they had been for so long. Sun, sand, waves. And a girl. His sister.

On instinct he tore his gaze away from the memories, but not before seeing their crispness and beauty. They baited him. He looked.

He saw and knew the mouth of the Blackwood River flowing past the town of Augusta at the southwest tip of the state. The river disgorged into the Southern Ocean, and in the shallows of its mouth he saw his family collecting bait, large, bivalve molluscs—cockles.

Cockles: he smiled again at the recognition. It was the word spoken by Temptation's host on the day of his accident, which had stirred deep waters that lapped against his conscious mind. He had not known then that what moved in the deep was the memory of a sibling he had chosen to forget.

And there she was, running along a fringe of grass bordering the beach. Behind her, he saw caravans and tents cozened by the drooping canopies of peppermint trees.

Again he saw her race past, tap his shoulder, turn and laugh. He looked into her face, and detected the first dulling of the pain that always lanced him.

Then she dashed behind the car, and he gave chase, tottering after her on legs that barely fell quick enough to prop up his tubby midriff.

The entire episode was there, connected and whole. He watched, felt, smelt, and tasted the salt on the air over the Blackwood, for the second time in his life.

As the time drew near, he steeled himself. *This is a kind of penance.*

His young self rounded the rear corner of the car for the third time, feeling the slap of thongs on his bare feet, and lost sight of his sister. The next memory to come from the bundle would be his shortcut across the front seats, then that sense of shuddering, of the heavens turning. The scream. The sight of his sister's tangled body pinned beneath a tyre.

He gritted his teeth to endure.

But here the memories ceased to fall as they had so many times before.

Instead, shocked by this departure from the script, he went on around the front of the car, trailing a sandy hand over its silver grill. Not until the return lap, his hand now brushing the white paint of the car's flank, did it happen. With a faint groan, as of a strut taking weight, the rear of the car dipped.

His young mind registered no panic. He continued on to the back of the car, which now sloped at twenty degrees.

He saw her then. She was pressed beneath a wheel. Perhaps she had hidden behind it. The sand bank that rose to meet the grass had subsided. The car had plunged with it.

Alarm registered in his young mind. Even at three, he knew something was desperately wrong.

Rasputin watched, tears streaming unheeded down his face, as little legs pumped through sand and up the collapsed bank. His thongs caught in the dry hummocks and came flying off in turn. He scrambled onto the passenger seat and looked at the hand-brake. Hadn't he been warned not to touch it?—danger, danger, his dad had said. But he hadn't touched it, and danger had attacked his sister anyway. Maybe now was the time for it.

He clutched the brake, tried to force it down like he had seen his dad do so many times, longing for the *thock* of the brake's release. He leant his weight on it. The release tripped and the shaft fell flat to the floor.

But nothing happened. The car did not move. It stayed stuck, at an angle.

His young self sat slumped in the passenger seat and began to cry angry tears. The vision of his bare, sand-encrusted, feet blurred. Through the windscreen he saw two people, adults, running toward the car, growing bigger.

At last Rasputin tore his gaze away. This grief, rediscovered in adulthood, had begun to scab over. He didn't need to pick at it.

He let it go, and rose again toward the present.

His passage to the surface felt as thought it took days. He didn't linger, even when he passed forgotten joys. For much of the time he did not observe, being lost in thoughts that ran to consolation: it was an old memory. She was forever beyond pain's tyranny. He was sure of that.

Slowly, he began to see he had not needed exoneration. That was the gift. He had already seen through to the truth: his sister would have forgiven him. What a valuable insight to have lost, had he already known there was nothing to forgive.

He blinked his eyes open. Water sloshed inches below his face in the hull of the yacht. He rose gingerly and sat. He stretched his neck, feeling it sting in the creases and knowing he would be sunburnt.

He recalled the words that had come to him at the bottom of the well of his being—beneath it: *I desire mercy not sacrifice.*

If he had carried them there with him, he could not remember where he had read them. He determined to search for them, but not in the basement—that door was shut now. He would bar it over. This search would be of the old-fashioned sort.

As he stretched stiff muscles, he felt the bulk of an object in his pocket. He drew it out. It was a block of wood, engraved with the symbol of Infinity: Cain's chop.

Clotho's message had carried a postscript to the effect that the chop and the wealth it represented were now Rasputin's. *To the victor go the spoils.*

He tilted the wooden block, watching one face catch the sun. True to its symbol, Infinity, it represented an unknown. Who knew how much money it stood for? He already had plans for it. He had a ticket booked that took in Hong Kong, and Burma—where a certain orphanage would receive an unlooked for and anonymous injection of funds—then Prague, and a long overdue talk with his parents. From there it was open-ended, as he did not yet know how cold the trail would be when he found it, or where it would lead.

He gazed up into the azure dome that encased the river and its city, and had a flash of recall of the first time he had sailed with Reim. The stars in their constellations pulsed through the blue.

But unlike then, he no longer felt at the centre of things. He smiled, and drew up the anchor. A current began to work the nose of the craft round to home.

"... the sprinkled blood that speaks a better word than the blood of Abel." Hebrews 12:24 NIV

EPILOGUE

No one smiles like a redeemed orphan.

Rasputin screwed his nose up at the thought. Too abstract. He tried again.

No one smiles like *Mary*.

Better.

Mary, found on a rubbish tip, thrown away like all the other rubbish by a stepfather who had no time for a girl.

She had sat atop the stinking pile for two days. Fixed to the spot as though it were Fate that had put her there, and there she must remain, until Reim's daughter Ineke had found her.

No one smiled like Mary.

But today it was the absence of her smile that had prompted the thought.

She sat in the dirt next to Rasputin, her eyes wet with tears, her arm in his lap. Along the baby-smooth skin of her forearm was opened a deep gouge. Blood was seeping from it in every direction.

Ineke De Groot's husband, Andrew, had bought a basketball ring from downtown Yangon. The older kids had rushed to gather wood, nails, and hammers with which to build a support frame. An hour later the kids were shooting hoops. No one had noticed the nail that had not been folded over until Mary had fallen on it.

Rasputin sat nursing the bloody arm while Andrew hunted for the first-aid kit. Before Andrew had left he had warned Rasputin with a gesture and a word, "Blood."

Blood. He meant HIV. Mary was HIV positive.

But sitting there, watching Mary's tears drip and mingle with the blood, Rasputin couldn't help himself.

He gave his hand a quick inspection. No broken skin. He took his handkerchief and mopped up what blood he could—it was a deep gash—then folded his hand over the wound.

Mary leant her head into his chest, and they waited like that, amid the laughter and whoops of the boys who were still playing, until Andrew returned.

When Andrew saw Rasputin's hand he shot him a look but said nothing. He donned latex gloves, peeled the hand away from the wound, and began swabbing it with sterile gauze.

Rasputin was watching Mary's reaction when Andrew said, "I thought you said it was deep?"

Rasputin looked at him and then down at the cut. He saw not the deep gash he knew had been there, but a shallow scratch, nothing worse than one would get from a broken twig.

Rasputin looked at Mary, astonished, but seeking her support. She simply smiled, as if it were the most natural thing in the world, and leapt up to join in the game.

Three days later Rasputin lay on his bed in the dark. Three nights and still sleep eluded him. He was exhausted and wired. He listened to mosquitos buzzing against the net that was suspended over his prone body, while two thoughts baited his mind and kept him from sleep. He chased them like a dog its tail, but could not latch on, bed them down, file them away.

The first was how Mary's wound had healed. The second had risen out of it: he should be dead. When he had stabbed himself to tap his blood and kill Cain, he'd known it was a mortal wound. Known and been happy.

But here he was, lying awake in a dorm with ten sleeping children in an orphanage on the outskirts of Yangon, the capital of Myanmar, thousands of miles from Perth.

At last he could bear it no more. He threw his sheet back and rose. He sent his hand under the net and rummaged by feel in his backpack for mosquito repellent, and when he found it, slicked every inch of bare skin he could find with its oily liquid. When he had first used it over a month ago, the children had told him without English that he smelled, and offered him the paste ground from the bark of the thanaka tree that they daubed on their cheeks. He had replied, without English, that he preferred to smell.

He let himself out on tiptoes, and crept to a gate that let onto the street running past the orphanage. It was padlocked. He unlocked it with a key, closed the gate behind him, and re-locked it. Sometimes relatives of the children came when they reached a *useful* age and stole them away.

This far from downtown Yangon there were no streetlights. Though the sky was dark, he could feel the weight of monsoon cloud pressing down. It was late. When the rain came, the streets would turn to rivers.

He had stayed longer than he intended. The kids had gotten under his skin.

He passed a group of men standing around a small fire, out late and biding their time till who-knew-what. The whites of their eyes reflected the fire's light as they watched him pass. Rasputin was too intent on avoiding potholes to acknowledge them.

A quarter of an hour later he reached his destination. Sheltering beneath the dark bulk of a banyan tree, snug in its cage of aerial roots, was a little shack of corrugated iron. A doorway gave onto a room lit by a twenty-watt bulb. A wide window was cut into the street-ward wall. Standing on the other side of it was an old Burmese man.

"Mr. Rasputin," the man said, smiling. "Troubled dreams?"

Rasputin summoned a smile, ordered coffee, and paid in kyats. He ducked his head and entered the shack. Two men were drinking tea over a makeshift table of wooden cartons. Rasputin sank onto a chair in the corner opposite, where the light was weakest.

His coffee came and he drank the strong, bitter liquid.

And steeled himself.

Was this how it started?

Were these fluttering temptations the first steps on the road to madness? To raving?

He thought of opium dens, jails without bars. But he was already enduring torture.

He paused. One last chance to change his mind. He could finish the coffee, return to the orphanage. Tomorrow, or the next day, he would be on a plane to Prague.

But he couldn't leave his head behind. It would taunt him. Tease him about the thoughts that had run through it the last three nights. Tempt him with the possibility that the miracle machine, his hibernation, had aimed higher than the death of one man.

The machine worked from the imago's deepest desire. But hadn't he, after all, had an even *deeper* desire than to atone for the death he thought he had caused all those years ago? A desire that dwarfed his guilt like the sun the earth?

When he had seen his sister crumpled beneath the wheel, and remembered her in the years after, he had wanted something more than to demonstrate his love unto death.

He had wanted her to live.

That couldn't be. No power of man could work that miracle.

But ...

He closed his eyes, and for the first time in months, went *within*.

He descended to the basement in his mind, to the door that he had closed and barred and sworn never to reopen.

And found it gone.

The shock prickled his skin.

In its place stood a wardrobe. (*Perhaps madness begins with a wardrobe?*) It sat exactly where the door had stood, the door that had been ravaged by the atmosphere of the wounded eye sealed behind it. The wardrobe was huge, oaken, and old. Carved into the face of one of its doors was a wintering tree, and into the other a rampant lion.

He grasped a handle and yanked open one of the doors. Inside were coats, and dust, and the smell of mothballs. He took one step forward, and peered into the darkness, hearing only the blood pulsing in his ears. Nothing moved but the sifting dust.

He sneezed, and sheepishly backed out. He had begun to close the door, when he noticed something flutter in the corner of his vision. He turned to find that a piece of paper had been stuck to the inside of the wardrobe door with a drawing pin. There was writing on the paper.

He pulled it free and held it near to read it.

It said:

"Greetings and salutations my little lamb.

My work is done; yours begins. If you are of good heart, we will meet again. You've known me as judge, inventor, and husbandman. Now know me as,

Your Friend.

PS: Shame on you for thinking the greatest construction ever made worked only death."

Rasputin thrust the note into his pocket and looked up. Driven now, he delved into the wardrobe.

Soon he felt the first touch of chill air upon his cheek, just as he knew he would. His hands, outstretched in the darkness, finding a way between coats, felt the prickle of branches. Before long his shoes bit into snow, and above emerged a brittle, star-speckled sky. Night in a wintering forest.

Ahead, a stone's throw away, stood a solitary lamp post. It shed a circle of yellow light on the snow, the only light beside the stars.

He approached it, and knelt near its base to look at a sapling bent over with snow. He poked at the clumps of snow bowing it down. It was barely a foot high and naked of leaves.

He looked up and peered around, but there was nothing to see but tree trunks and shadows and then nothing.

"Hello?" he said. The forest answered with silence.

He returned his gaze to the forlorn sapling. He rubbed his hands together, feeling the friction warm them. Then, casting a final glance into the forest, placed his hands around the sapling's finger-thin trunk.

He left them there like that until he could feel the wet seeping through his pants, then stood.

It could have been a minute or a day he waited to see a solitary leaf wriggle out of the tip of a branch, uncurl, and grow. The sight of it split his face in a grin.

When he opened his eyes, he was looking into the bottom of his empty coffee cup.

The old man came to clear it away, and asked if he wanted another.

"Beer, please," said Rasputin. "*Dagon.*"

The old man leaned back at the waist, and with smiling eyes said, "Oh ho! A celebration for Mr. Rasputin?"

"Yes, I think—" Rasputin's gaze searched the table, then returned to the old man. "I think, after all, I might be growing wings."

The old man shook his head good-naturedly and kept his thoughts to himself.

# # #

STRAWMAN MADE STEEL

Janus McIlwraith knows New York City. From the grimy basement bars where the underclass mutter and curse to the gleaming penthouse apartments where the elite plot and control, he's seen it all, and he's never been happy about it. He's a private investigator who works the city the old fashioned way. No internet. No databases. No smartphones.

Not that he has a choice in the matter.

Because Janus knows two New York Cities. There's the one with Facebook, The Tonight Show and iPods. And there's the one he enters through the mirror, the one with genetic supermen, skyscraper canons, and a certain subatomic particle that's misbehaving ...

And when McIlwraith takes on the case of the rich boy whose brutalized corpse is found in a dumpster, he little realizes how deep the case will cut—right to his very core, to the place where, like this city, his own soul is split in two.

BLOOD & INK

US exchange student Hieronymous Beck is Professor Jack Griffen's biggest fan. Why else would he inveigle himself into the English Literature course that Jack is running, and why else would he devote so much time to chatting with Jack after hours about the anatomy of crime fiction, the roles of heroes and villains, and his favourite true crime book of all time, In Cold Blood?

But everything changes when Jack Griffen picks up a list of five templates to murder that has been written by Beck.

The mild-mannered professor who has never incurred anything more than a parking fine suddenly finds himself in a deadly race to protect those he loves, as he is plunged into Hiero's crime writer's fantasy and the darkness of his student's heart.

CONNECT WITH THE AUTHOR

For updates on what's stirring the waters of the Dweoming Well:

Instagram: https://www.instagram.com/Brett.Adams.Author
Twitter: https://twitter.com/BrettAuthor
Facebook: https://facebook.com/DweomingWell
Goodreads: https://goodreads.com/author/show/6860949.Brett_Adams

www.ingramcontent.com/pod-product-compliance
Lightning Source LLC
Chambersburg PA
CBHW061926170626
46813CB00006B/2311